PRAISE FOR CAROLYN BROWN

Small Town Rumors

"Carolyn Brown is a master at writing warm, complex characters who find their way into your heart."

—*Harlequin Junkie*

"Carolyn Brown's *Small Town Rumors* takes that hotbed and with it, spins a delightful tale of starting over, coming into your own, and living your life, out loud and unafraid."

—*Words We Love By*

"*Small Town Rumors* by Carolyn Brown is a contemporary romance perfect for a summer read in the shade of a big old tree with a glass of lemonade or sweet tea. It is a sweet romance with wonderful characters and a small town setting."

—*Avonna Loves Genres*

The Sometimes Sisters

"Carolyn Brown continues her streak of winning, heartfelt novels with *The Sometimes Sisters*, a story of estranged sisters and frustrated romance."

—*All About Romance*

"This is an amazing feel-good story that will make you wish you were a part of this amazing family."

—*Harlequin Junkie* (top pick)

"*The Sometimes Sisters* is [a] delightful and touching story that explores the bonds of family. I loved the characters, the story lines, and the focus on the importance of familial bonds, whether they be blood relations or those you choose with your heart."

—*Rainy Day Ramblings*

The Strawberry Hearts Diner

"[A] sweet and satisfying romance from the queen of Texas romance."

—*Fresh Fiction*

"A heartwarming cast of characters brings laughter and tears to the mix, and readers will find themselves rooting for more than one romance on the menu. From the first page to the last, Brown perfectly captures the mood as well as the atmosphere and creates a charming story that appeals to a wide range of readers."

—*RT Book Reviews*

"A sweet romance surrounded by wonderful, caring characters."

—*TBQ's Book Palace*

"[A] deeply satisfying contemporary small-town western story . . ."

—*Delighted Reader*

The Barefoot Summer

"Prolific romance author Brown shows she can also write women's fiction in this charming story, which uses humor and vivid characters to show the value of building an unconventional chosen family."

—*Publishers Weekly*

"This story takes you and carries you along for a wonderful ride full of laughter, tears, and three amazing HEAs. I feel like these characters are not just people in a book, but they are truly family, and I feel so invested in their journey. Another amazing HIT for Carolyn Brown."

—*Harlequin Junkie* (top pick)

The Lullaby Sky

"I really loved and enjoyed this story. Definitely a good comfort read when you're in a reading funk or just don't know what to read. The secondary characters bring much love and laughter into this book— your cheeks will definitely hurt from smiling so hard while reading. Carolyn is one of my most favorite authors. I know without a doubt that no matter what book of hers I read, I can just get lost in it and know it will be a good story. Better than the last. Can't wait to read more from her."

—*The Bookworm's Obsession*

The Lilac Bouquet

"Brown pulls readers along for an enjoyable ride. It's impossible not to be touched by Brown's protagonists, particularly Seth, and a cast of strong supporting characters underpins the charming tale."

—*Publishers Weekly*

"If a reader is looking for a book more geared toward family and long-held secrets, this would be a good fit."

—*RT Book Reviews*

"Carolyn Brown absolutely blew me away with this epically beautiful story. I cried, I giggled, I sobbed, and I guffawed; this book had it all. I've come to expect great things from this author, and she more than lived up to anything I could have hoped for. Emmy Jo Massey and her great-granny Tandy are absolute masterpieces, not because they are perfect but because they are perfectly painted. They are so alive, so full of flaws and spunk and determination. I cannot recommend this book highly enough."

—Night Owl Reviews (five stars and top pick)

The Wedding Pearls

"*The Wedding Pearls* by Carolyn Brown is an amazing story about family, life, love, and finding out who you are and where you came from. This book is a lot like *The Golden Girls* meet *Thelma and Louise*."

—Harlequin Junkie

"*The Wedding Pearls* is an absolute must-read. I cannot recommend this one enough. Grab a copy for yourself, and one for a best friend or even your mother or both. This is a book that you need to read. It will make you laugh and cry. It is so sweet and wonderful and packed full of humor. I hope that when I grow up, I can be just like Ivy and Frankie."

—Rainy Day Ramblings

The Yellow Rose Beauty Shop

"*The Yellow Rose Beauty Shop* was hilarious, and so much fun to read. But sweet romances, strong female friendships, and family bonds make this more than just a humorous read."

—The Readers Den

"If you like books about small towns and how the people's lives intertwine, you will love this book. I think it's probably my favorite book this year. The relationships of the three main characters, girls who have grown up together, will make you feel like you just pulled up a chair in their beauty shop with a bunch of old friends. As you meet the other people in the town, you'll wish you could move there. There are some genuine laugh-out-loud moments and then more that will just make you smile. These are real people, not the oh-so-thin-and-so-very-rich that are often the main characters in novels. This book will warm your heart, and you'll remember it after you finish the last page. That's the highest praise I can give a book."

—Reader quote for *The Yellow Rose Beauty Shop*

Long, Hot Texas Summer

"This is one of those light-hearted, feel-good, make-me-happy kinds of stories. But, at the same time, the essence of this story is family and love with a big ole dose of laughter and country living thrown in the mix. This is the first installment in what promises to be another fascinating series from Brown. Find a comfortable chair, sit back, and relax because once you start reading *Long, Hot Texas Summer*, you won't be able to put it down. This is a super fun and sassy romance."

—*Thoughts in Progress*

Daisies in the Canyon

"I just loved the symbolism in *Daisies in the Canyon*. As I mentioned before, Carolyn Brown has a way with character development with few, if any, contemporaries. I am sure there are more stories to tell in this series. Brown just touched the surface first with *Long, Hot Texas Summer* and now continuing on with *Daisies in the Canyon*."

—*Fresh Fiction*

the Perfect Dress

ALSO BY CAROLYN BROWN

CONTEMPORARY ROMANCES

The Magnolia Inn
Small Town Rumors
The Sometimes Sisters
The Strawberry Hearts Diner
The Lilac Bouquet
The Barefoot Summer
The Lullaby Sky
The Wedding Pearls
The Yellow Rose Beauty Shop
The Ladies' Room
Hidden Secrets
Long, Hot Texas Summer
Daisies in the Canyon
Trouble in Paradise

CONTEMPORARY SERIES

THE BROKEN ROAD SERIES

To Trust
To Commit
To Believe
To Dream
To Hope

THREE MAGIC WORDS TRILOGY

A Forever Thing
In Shining Whatever
Life After Wife

HISTORICAL ROMANCE

THE BLACK SWAN TRILOGY

Pushin' Up Daisies
From Thin Air
Come High Water

THE DRIFTERS & DREAMERS TRILOGY

Morning Glory
Sweet Tilly
Evening Star

THE LOVE'S VALLEY SERIES

Choices
Absolution
Chances
Redemption
Promises

the Perfect Dress

CAROLYN BROWN

Montlake
Romance

Published by Montlake Romance, Seattle

www.apub.com

Amazon, the Amazon logo, and Montlake Romance are trademarks of Amazon.com, Inc., or its affiliates.

ISBN-13: 9781503905276
ISBN-10: 1503905276

Cover design by Laura Klynstra

Printed in the United States of America

*This book is for
my granddaughters,
Graycyn Rose Rucker and Madacyn Rayne Rucker,
who helped me write this story without even realizing
that their beauty and love are an inspiration to me
every day.*

$\mathcal{M}$ en! Can't live with 'em, and if we shot 'em all, we'd be out of business," Mitzi grumbled as she entered through the back door of the custom wedding-dress shop that she owned with her friends Jody and Paula.

"Ain't it the truth." Jody adjusted her beaded headband and filled three cups with herbal tea. She threw her long blonde braids over her shoulder. "Some days I could poison Lyle."

"And yet if anyone else even mentioned that, you'd burn them at the stake." Paula picked up a cup of tea and carried it to the table. She'd gotten her dark hair and dark eyes from her Texan mother, but all the superstition came straight from her Louisianan father. She waved a hand over the cup three times before she tasted it. At thirty-five, she'd never been married—but then technically, neither had any one of them. Jody had lived with Lyle since they'd graduated from high school, but they rejected the tradition of a marriage license.

Jody's brown eyes flashed. "Oh, honey, I wouldn't waste gasoline or wood to burn anyone. I grow my own food, remember? I'd poison the tomatoes, and it would look like whoever bad-mouthed my boyfriend had had a heart attack. And you don't have to do that with your tea. I wouldn't dream of poisoning you."

At almost six feet tall and fitting into size-eighteen jeans, Mitzi had learned to be comfortable in her skin but not until she was an adult. Before that she'd endured lots of bullying about her size. Of course today it came rushing back, all over a wisecrack a man had made in the tiny little pastry shop on Main Street in Celeste, Texas.

"Dammit!" she swore. "I forgot to bring in the doughnuts. I'll be right back."

Someone must've forgotten to inform the people who made calendars that in East Texas, hot weather didn't wait until the last days of June. The official first day of summer was still three weeks away, but this day—in May—the weatherman said it would reach three digits. Mitzi's dad had joked that he'd already seen a few lizards carrying canteens.

Sweat beads had formed on Mitzi's upper lip by the time she returned. She set the box on the table and grabbed a paper towel to dab at her face. But before she could get the job done, her maternal grandmother, Fanny Lou, slipped in through the back door. Mitzi's dad had bought the house for them to put their business in, but Fanny Lou had given them the seed money for fabrics, new sewing machines, and the separate air-conditioning unit for the dressing room. She refused to be called a partner, but she loved to drop in at any old time. Not that Mitzi minded. After being away for so many years, she loved to have her grandmother around, no matter what time of day it was.

Fanny Lou wasn't quite as tall as Mitzi, unless she was wearing her cowboy boots. Her bright-red hair sat on top of her head in a messy bun that looked somewhat like she'd stuck her finger in a light socket. Set in a bed of wrinkles, her bright-blue eyes always twinkled behind wire-rimmed glasses. On this day she was dressed in bib overalls, a faded red T-shirt, and her signature boots. She set a paper bag filled with tomatoes and cucumbers on the table.

"Hotter'n the devil's pitchfork out there. I brought y'all some stuff from my neighbor's garden. Lord knows I can't eat all that and if I could, I wouldn't. Old women like me don't have to eat their vegetables.

They can eat doughnuts when they want." She sniffed the air. "I smell something wonderful."

"Orange spice tea or coffee. We've got both made. Which one?" Mitzi asked.

"Thanks, darlin'. I'm not much for tea, but coffee sounds wonderful." Fanny Lou picked up a doughnut and bit into it. "God, this is good. Now what's put a frown on your face, Mitzi?"

"Yeah, somebody's got her panties in a twist this morning." Jody had always been a bit chubby and short, barely coming up to Mitzi's shoulder, but after high school she'd lost weight. Now her faded jeans hung on her frame.

"It was some stupid guy who was in line at the pastry shop. He was talking to his buddy over in the next aisle about some woman he'd taken out over the weekend. He said there were advantages to dating a fat girl. They provided shade in the summer and warmth in the winter." Mitzi carried two cups of tea to the table and went back to pour her grandmother's coffee.

"What did you do?" Paula asked.

"I hope you snatched him baldheaded and then slapped the thunder out of him for not having any hair," Fanny Lou said.

"I glared at them until they looked up at me. As cocky as they were, I'm pretty sure they were infected with short-man's disease, because it didn't take them long to get their order and get out of there. They didn't look familiar," Mitzi said, "but they'll be telling tales tomorrow about the big red-haired Amazon who threatened to whip them with one arm tied around her back."

"And with egos like they've got, they'll say that they left you bleeding on the floor right beside the cinnamon bun display," Paula laughed. "You should've at least put a curse on them. I've given you enough through all the years that you could've picked out one that was appropriate."

Mitzi pushed her tea to one side and poured herself a cup of coffee. She dipped a doughnut into the mug, not caring that crumbs fell back into it. "Oh, come on, Paula. Last time I got mad at someone, you said to never put a bad gris-gris on anyone, because what goes around comes around."

"You got one of them curses I can have?" Fanny Lou asked. "I'm mad at Jody's mama. She whispered in my ear after church last week that I should be dressing to live up to my image. I might be the richest old gal in Celeste, but that don't mean I have to get all gussied up. My knit pantsuits were good enough fifty years ago, and they do just fine today. Besides, I knocked the mud off my boots on the way in the doors, and God ain't told me that I have to do anything more. Until He does, Wanda can keep her mouth shut."

Jody's chuckle oozed sarcasm. "You're lucky that's all she had to say. She's always bitchin' to me about something. I'm livin' in sin or else God is punishing me by making me barren until I marry Lyle properly."

"Well, if Paula wasn't so stingy with her curses, we could take care of two birds with one stone," Fanny Lou said.

"You could throw salt over your shoulder next time you see Wanda. In the Cajun world that means you don't want her to step foot in your house again," Paula said.

"I wouldn't let her in my front door if she knocked, which she won't because I took up for Jody when she and Lyle moved in together." Fanny Lou reached for another doughnut. "'What goes around comes around' will apply to those men and to Wanda for saying such ugly things. But enough about that. It's nine o'clock and time to open the front door for business."

"You're right, Granny. We've got a wedding dress to get ready for a final fitting this afternoon," Mitzi said.

"And you've got an appointment with Ellie Mae to help her design one this morning. So get rid of all that anger." Fanny Lou sipped her coffee.

"I'll need an apple fritter to get that done." Mitzi grabbed the last one in the box.

"Poor Preacher Frank will probably breathe a sigh of relief when he gets her married off." Fanny Lou lowered her voice. "You know what they say about preachers' daughters? Well, she flat out passed the test on that one."

"For real?" Jody asked. "You mean she don't have a halo up under all that blonde hair?"

Fanny Lou snorted. "Honey, that girl might be an angel, but if she is, it's because she's done had the hell screwed out of her."

Mitzi almost choked on the pastry. "Granny!"

"Truth is truth. You can sugarcoat it or roll it in cow crap, and it don't change a thing." Fanny Lou shrugged. "I got to go to the beauty shop and get this mop of hair washed. I ought to get it cut off, but my darlin' Oscar liked it long. God rest his soul and love his heart." She rolled her eyes toward the ceiling. "And if you're up there flirting with Henrietta Cooper, I'll wring your neck when I get there." She focused on Mitzi. "Y'all got any other news I can take to the beauty shop?"

"Nothing I can think of," Mitzi said.

Fanny Lou finished off her coffee and carried the cup to the sink. "See y'all later."

They all three waved as she breezed back out the door. Jody picked up another doughnut and pushed through the swinging doors into the sewing room with Mitzi right behind her. Beyond the kitchen was a huge dining room that now had three sewing machines and a long cutting table taking up the space. The foyer was a sitting room with two plush, pink sofas and lots of pattern and wedding books on the coffee table between them. To the left was the curved staircase. A plus-size mannequin wearing a wedding dress, with the train stretched out to the top step, showed off the partners' first attempt at designing and making a wedding dress for Paula's sister, Selena, a couple of years earlier. Before it was over, they'd also made a bridesmaid dress for Paula and an outfit for their mother, Gladys, to wear for the wedding.

What used to be the living room was now lined with shelves holding bolts of lace, satin, silks, and even cotton eyelet. That's where Mitzi took clients after they'd given her an idea of what kind of dress they wanted for their special day, to do measurements and put together a schedule of fittings. The master bedroom served as their fitting room, with extra air-conditioning power added. Jody and Paula had agreed with Mitzi when she suggested that the dressing room was a top priority. There was nothing worse than a tiny room with no air-conditioning vents for a curvy woman trying to get into and out of clothing.

Mitzi unlocked the front door, straightened the bridal books on the coffee table, and opened a pattern book to the first page of the wedding dresses. At nine fifteen the door swung open, and Ellie Mae Weston hurried inside. "I'm so sorry I'm late. My mother insisted on coming with me, and I had to talk her out of it. I can't even imagine what kind of dress she'd try to get me into."

"Have a seat and let's talk about what you want." Mitzi pointed to the sofa on the other side of the coffee table. "You said you'd bring pictures."

Ellie Mae pulled out a folder and laid it on her lap. "I've narrowed it down to ten, but I'm tellin' you up front, I do not want a white dress. I'm a size twenty-two, and I don't want to look like one of those oversized marshmallows."

"It's your day," Mitzi said in agreement.

"That's what I told Mama, but she's afraid of the gossip," Ellie Mae laughed. "She thinks I'm still a virgin at twenty-five and should wear white and a veil over my face. Good Lord! It's going to be hot in July. What if a mosquito flew up under there? I'd be battin' at it instead of sayin' my vows."

"How big is the wedding list?" Mitzi asked.

"We invited everyone in church and all the relatives. We're having the whole thing out at Darrin's folks' place in their big barn. Mama's not happy about that, either, but good Lord, there's a thousand people in Celeste. If even a third of them came, the church wouldn't work." Ellie Mae opened her folder and started going through the pages.

Mitzi's mind wandered as she waited. Ellie Mae was right about the population of Celeste, Texas, but Fanny Lou had said that to get that many folks, the census takers counted the dogs and cats. Folks had thought Mitzi and her friends were crazy to put a specialized bridal shop in a town that small, but it wasn't far from the bigger town of Greenville, Texas.

Besides, there wasn't another shop like it for miles and miles around. So from the time they'd opened the shop a year ago, they'd been swamped with business. And maybe next year they'd even get invited to attend the Dallas Bridal Fair. They hadn't opened the shop in time to nab a place this year, but they were on the waiting list.

Mitzi had thought about renting one of the empty downtown places in those two small city blocks when she first got the idea of a custom specialty shop, but none of them had the ambience that the old house did. It seemed like one of Paula's omens that it occupied the corner of the last block zoned for commercial business.

After a couple of minutes, Ellie Mae laid a picture out on the table. "I like the neckline and sleeves on this one, but I don't want that empire waistline. Everyone would think I was pregnant for sure."

Like all small Texas towns, Celeste was a place where everyone knew everyone else, and usually what they were doing. All it would take was a few phone calls for a pregnancy rumor to float around.

Then Ellie Mae pulled out a second picture of a formfitting dress. "This is the style I like, but I want it fuller in the back so I can dance at the reception without feeling all cramped up." She laid another picture on the top of those. "I want a train like this with our initials done up in beaded, interlocking hearts on it. I've been looking at wedding dresses for ideas for a year."

"Sounds like you've done my work for me." Mitzi gathered the pictures back into the folder. "Let's go into the fabric room. What color do you have in mind?"

"Black lace over pale-pink satin."

Mitzi thought she should really warn the cell phone company. Those towers between Celeste and Greenville were going to sizzle when folks learned that Ellie Mae was wearing black to her wedding. Her father, Frank, was the preacher in the biggest church in town, and her mother, Nancy, played the piano on Sunday morning. If Mitzi had been an author instead of a seamstress, she could fill a whole book with nothing but the gossip over a black wedding dress.

"That right there." Ellie Mae reached for a bolt of black Chantilly lace as they walked into the room, but she was too short to get a hold on it.

Mitzi pulled it down and then removed a bolt of white bridal satin and one of pale pink. She rolled out several yards on a long table and overlaid the black lace on both.

"Not the pink," Ellie Mae said. "Mama's going to flip out over the black anyway, but over the pink it looks like I'm naked under the lace. That white does look pretty. What would it look like with white beading?"

Mitzi took out a drawer full of medium-size beads and laid some out in a double heart. "What do you think?"

"I love it." Ellie Mae's blue eyes glittered. "I'll use a circlet of white roses in my hair with just a touch of black lace."

"Maybe since your mama wants a veil, we could do something like this." Mitzi picked up a beautiful black-lace hat with a wide brim and set it on Ellie Mae's head. "This might be an option instead, and it looks lovely with your blonde hair."

Ellie Mae turned toward a mirror and gasped. "Look at me! It's so different, and I can wear my hair down in big waves. How about a pouf of black illusion at the back with a little bit trailing down my back?"

Mitzi took a roll of illusion from the shelf, cut off two yards, and using straight pins, fixed it to the back of the hat.

"Yes! That's it. I love it. When can you get started?" Ellie Mae asked. "And can we keep it all under wraps? I'm not even sure I want Mama to see it before the wedding day."

"The Perfect Dress has the same confidentiality laws as a therapist," Mitzi told her. "I'll get the dress drawn up, and you can come in on Friday to approve it."

"Fantastic. Darrin will be wearing a white tux with a black-and-red paisley cummerbund, and I'm carrying red roses," Ellie Mae said. "It's all going to be beautiful."

"Yes, it is, and very unusual. I may have to stock up on black lace after this. You could start a brand-new trend." Mitzi had trouble keeping her mind off what Fanny Lou had said about Ellie Mae being an angel.

"That would be something, wouldn't it? What time do I come by on Friday?"

Mitzi opened her appointment book. "How does eleven thirty work for you? You'll approve the dress. I'll take some measurements. We'll be done in less than half an hour unless you want some adjustments. We'll make your appointments for several fittings and get started on Monday morning."

"Great. I'll take an early lunch from my job. Thank you for everything." Ellie Mae hugged her.

After sending Ellie Mae on her way, Mitzi carried her notes to the sewing room and slumped down in a wingback chair. "You're never going to believe this. Ellie Mae Weston is getting married in black lace."

"Does her mama know?" Jody asked.

"No, and we are sworn to secrecy," Mitzi answered.

Paula pulled a silver angel charm from her pocket and kissed it. Neither Jody nor Mitzi had to ask what she was doing. They knew she was putting a protection aura around Ellie Mae's mama so she wouldn't have a heart attack.

෧

After a week, Graham Harrison still hadn't gotten everything unpacked in the new house in Celeste. He didn't regret moving there, not after that last bout of bullying his girls had experienced at their bigger school. From what Alice, his sister, said about the smaller Celeste schools, they didn't tolerate such things, and as the high school English teacher, she'd be on the watch. He poured a cup of coffee and carried it to the kitchen table. The girls were up that morning and rattling around in their bedrooms, so he only had a few more minutes of peace.

Dixie breezed into the kitchen, poured a glass of orange juice, and grabbed a box of cereal. "Mornin', Dad."

"Mornin', sweetheart." Graham wondered what kind of life his girls would have if their mother had stuck around. But that was water under the bridge, and even though she was living in Dallas now and had said she wanted to be a part of their lives, it was about fourteen years too late.

Tabby stopped long enough to give him a kiss on the forehead. "Did you talk to that place about our dresses for Mother's friend's wedding yet?"

"It's on my to-do list today. Did y'all decide what color or style?"

"Lizzy said bubblegum pink and whatever style we like. I hate that color," Dixie said with a groan. "I'm going to look like a big mound of cotton candy."

"The senior bridesmaids are wearing burgundy, so Lizzy thought we'd be cute in pink. She hasn't seen us since we were babies and only asked us because Mama put a guilt trip on her," Tabby said. "I still don't want to go."

"Well, Lizzy better get ready for a big surprise when we show up as junior bridesmaids in our bubblegum-pink dresses." Dixie poured a bowl of cereal and added milk. "We're not little girls anymore."

Tabby giggled. "You got that right about us not bein' *little* girls anymore."

Graham could put his amen on that, but he kept his mouth shut. He was six foot five, and his twin daughters had taken after him instead of their petite blonde mother. Last time he'd measured the girls, they were both five feet, ten inches, and like him, they certainly weren't beanpoles.

He'd taken them to every dress shop in Greenville, Dallas, and even Austin trying to find a dress for their mother's best friend's wedding in July, but they'd found nothing suitable in their size. Then they'd moved to Celeste, and Dixie had seen the sign for The Perfect Dress just down the street from the house Graham had bought. When she looked it up on the internet, they'd found the place made customized wedding, bridesmaid, and prom dresses—but only for plus-size women.

"Daddy, will you run by there on your way to work? It might be too late for us to get anything special made, so get ready to beg or bribe," Dixie said.

He'd gotten used to doing all things a mother should do from the time the girls were born. His ex-wife, Rita, just flat out didn't have a drop of mothering instinct, and once she'd found out that his folks controlled the family money and weren't happy with his eloping right out of high school, she wasn't interested in being married. She'd left him when the girls were barely two years old.

Yet last winter she'd called and wanted to see the twins. He'd let them make the choice. They agreed to meet her for ice cream but only for an hour. From what little they'd said about it, it had been like meeting a stranger. He could tell they were relieved when she didn't call again for two months. That time it was to ask if they would be in her best friend's wedding as junior bridesmaids. They agreed to spend the day with Rita, but they wouldn't say yes to staying overnight. That meant Graham would drive them to Dallas early that morning and pick them up after the wedding reception.

"We should have big ball gowns so we really would look like cotton candy," Tabby said. "With one of them big southern flounce collars and a wide satin sash. That'll teach Mother to just tell us a color and to pick out our own style. I still think she was ashamed of us. She's so short and tiny, and she wanted daughters that looked like her. She said that she recognized us that day because we reminded her of Aunt Alice."

Little bits of their opinions on that day kept filtering down with time. Graham glanced up at both of them and realized that they did look a little like his sister. Maybe not in the face as much as their build—tall, big-boned girls. But their eyes came from Rita—clear light blue, a striking combination with all that thick black hair.

"Now that sounds like a great idea. We could have the lady at the dress shop make us look like Scarlett O'Hara," Dixie said.

"Girls, this might not be the time for revenge." Graham wouldn't blame them, but he couldn't let them go through with that kind of thing.

"I think we should wear a big old southern hat, too," Tabby said.

"No, Mother says Lizzy is having fresh rosebud circlets made for our hair, with burgundy ribbons down the back," Dixie reminded her. "Maybe we should go barefoot, paint our toenails black, and wear toe rings. Daddy, can we get henna tattoos on our shoulders that say *wild girls*?"

"You can*not*," Graham said, raising his voice a notch.

"Well, rats," Dixie said. "Then how about we get two-piece dresses and pierce our belly buttons? We could get one of those . . ."

"No!" Graham's voice went up another octave.

"Then let's do formfitting pink-satin dresses with a side slit up to our . . ."

Graham's palms went up in a flash. "That's enough, ladies. I don't want to hear about slits up to wherever. I'm going to work, and your job today is to finish unpacking, get your bedrooms organized, and do your laundry. I'll call as soon as I talk to the lady at the dress shop, but it might be this afternoon. I don't know what time she opens, and I'd like to talk to her in person. I can't imagine why she'd put a place like that in Celeste."

"Me, either, but I'm sure glad she did," Dixie said.

"Especially if she says yes." Tabby nodded. "Text us when you know something? That way if they can see us anytime today, we can walk down there."

"Will do." Graham picked up his briefcase and headed out the back door.

He drove down Main Street to the dress shop, saw that it wouldn't be open for another thirty minutes, and called his secretary, Vivien, who told him that he had meetings starting at nine that morning with each of the departments of his family's Cadillac dealership. That meant he'd have to take care of the dress business during his lunchtime. Maybe if the shop owners could set up an appointment, he'd have time to run by his new house and tell the girls.

He made it to work with five minutes to spare before his first meeting and greeted Vivien with a wave as he walked inside the dealership.

"The Service Department is in the conference room." She handed him a folder. "I'll buzz in with a reminder in forty-five minutes. That way you can wrap this one up and have a short break before the Finance Department arrives."

"Couldn't run this place without you." Graham meant what he said. His dad had died last year and left him the dealership, lock, stock, and barrel. Vivien—a forty-year company veteran—helped make a smooth transition.

"Your daddy used to say the same crazy thing. Everyone is replaceable." When Vivien grinned, her wrinkles deepened and her brown eyes became slits. Graham remembered a time when her hair had been black, but now it was streaked with gray. She hadn't talked about retiring, but she was pushing seventy.

He patted her on the shoulder. "You aren't everyone, darlin'."

Without even a reminder from Vivien, the last meeting finished fifteen minutes early. She'd already gone to lunch when he headed out the door to make the drive from Greenville to Celeste. Not knowing if the dress shop closed for an hour at noon, he drove faster than the speed limit and arrived with fifteen minutes to spare.

Since the business was in a house, he wasn't sure whether to ring the doorbell, knock, or just walk in. He chose the latter and found no one sitting behind a desk. Instead, a tall red-haired woman with the most piercing blue eyes he'd ever seen poked her head out around a doorjamb.

"Can I help you?" she asked.

"I hope so," he said. "I just moved here, and my twin daughters need bridesmaid dresses in July. Would you have time to make something for them by then?"

Those eyes looked vaguely familiar, but he couldn't remember having ever met her. Maybe they just reminded him of Rita's, since they'd been talking about her that morning.

She came out into the room and motioned for him to have a seat. The plush, pink sofa enveloped him—fairly comfortable for a man his size, but he was sure glad his girls weren't there with their cameras.

"I'm Graham Harrison." He focused on a place over her left shoulder to keep from looking right at her eyes. "My daughters aren't petite little things. The bride said anything would work as long as the dresses matched and they were cotton candy . . . no, that's not right." He stumbled over the words. "Bubblegum pink."

The lady sat down across from him. "I'm Mitzi Taylor, and yes, we make bridesmaids dresses in sizes fourteen and up. How old are these girls?"

"Fifteen—size sixteen in jeans. Like I said, they're not little girls. They're almost six feet tall and what folks call 'big girls.'" He almost blushed. A dad shouldn't have to know those things or their shoe size or their favorite deodorant, but when he'd had to be both mother and father, there was no choice.

"And I can see why." Mitzi's blue eyes seemed to size him up for height.

"So can we make an appointment with you? And will you have time to do that kind of thing before July?" he asked.

"Budget?" She fidgeted with a notepad.

"Whatever they want is fine," he answered.

"Okay then, let me check the calendar. I don't think we've got any appointments after three today. Do they go to school here in Celeste?"

"They will in the fall. We only moved here a week ago. My sister is a teacher at the school here. Alice Harrison. Maybe you know her?" he said.

"Yes, I do," Mitzi said. "You probably don't remember me. I was a freshman when you graduated right here in Celeste."

"I thought you looked familiar." He nodded. "But I couldn't place you."

"I'll take a peek at my calendar. You wait right here." For a tall, big woman, she moved gracefully to the next room and returned in only a few seconds. "I'm free at three thirty. Will you be bringing them?"

"Thank you!" He let out a whoosh of air he hadn't even known he was holding inside and stood. "We only live a couple of houses down, so they'll walk here on their own. Do I give you a down payment today?"

"No, we'll see how things go, and then I'll work up a total price for the materials and labor. If you agree and sign a contract, then we'll get busy sewing up the dresses," she answered.

15

"Sounds fantastic to me." He handed her a business card. "You can reach me there or leave a message, and I'll get right back to you. You wouldn't believe how many places we've been trying to find what they need, and all the time you were right here."

"That's the way it goes." She put the business card in her hip pocket.

Graham couldn't wait to get home.

When he did, the girls were already sitting at the table, eating leftover lasagna from supper the night before. Dixie looked up with a quizzical expression as he walked in.

"You have a three-thirty appointment at The Perfect Dress. Turns out I went to school with the owner. She'll be nice to you. Got any of that lasagna left?"

Tabby beamed. "That's great, Daddy. There's one more helping. And I made brownies this morning, so we have dessert."

Graham's mind wasn't really on food—it was on Mitzi's blue eyes and that gorgeous red hair. Why hadn't he ever noticed her when they were in school?

Chapter Two

itzi rushed back to the sewing room, where the hum of two sewing machines filled the air. "Graham Harrison just came in the shop to set up an appointment for his two daughters. He said they only live a few houses up the street from us. He looked like a bull in a china shop sitting on that pink sofa. And of course he didn't even recognize me, but I sure knew him the minute I laid eyes on him."

At the mention of that name from the past, work jolted to a halt.

"Yoo-hoo!" Fanny Lou yelled from the kitchen into the sudden silence. "Y'all in the sewing room?"

"Yes, ma'am," Mitzi leaned out the door and hollered.

"I've got homemade cookies. Y'all already had dinner?"

Jody stopped her machine and headed toward the kitchen with Mitzi and Paula right behind her. "Where did the morning go? I'm starving."

"No wonder," Paula said. "All you ever eat is salad and vegetables."

"And you'd be healthier if you did the same," Jody told her.

"But we all eat cookies, so that unites us, right?" Mitzi said.

"I bought 'em at the church bake sale, but Edna Green made them, and she makes the best in town." Fanny Lou removed plastic wrap from a paper plate of peanut butter cookies. "Guess what I heard today. Graham Harrison moved down the street from y'all."

The phone rang and Mitzi picked it up, grateful to have a moment to collect her thoughts about Graham living so close. "The Perfect Dress. How can I help you?"

"This is Rayford Thompson from the Dallas Bridal Fair. We'd like to notify you that you've moved up on the alternative list. So if someone drops out, you will be contacted to fill that place. We like to keep our top two applicants informed in case travel is an issue."

"Thank you so much." Mitzi felt like her feet came a foot off the floor as she hung up and spun around. "We've got a shot at the bridal fair this year. Only one person has to drop out for us to get to go."

"That's fantastic." Fanny Lou stuck her hand in the air for a high five. "You should take Selena's dress and the mannequin and maybe even one of the pink sofas for the display. Of course, you'll need an archway that you can decorate with flowers to stand her under, and you should rent either some big ferns to go on each side or maybe a couple of those tall candleholders. You should be thinking about putting a bouquet in the mannequin's hands, and oh—you definitely have to have some kind of little treats. I've got a tiered crystal stand for those. People will stick around your area longer if you have food."

Mitzi threw an arm around her grandmother as Fanny Lou rambled on. "Someone has to drop out before we get to go and it might not happen."

"You should be ready anyway. I'll talk to the ladies at the doughnut shop and see if they'll do a special order of tiny cakes or maybe even little bitty bite-sized doughnuts." Fanny Lou picked up a cookie and took a bite. "Now, about Graham Harrison."

"All the girls in high school swooned over him, including Mitzi, but she hasn't told us if he's still as sexy as he was back then." Jody took a bowl of salad from the fridge along with a plate of vegetables that she stuck into the microwave to heat.

"He's aged very, very well, and I'm having cookies," Mitzi said.

"Smart girl," Fanny Lou said. "Life is short. Eat dessert first. So you had a little crush on Graham?"

"Everyone did," Mitzi answered.

"Not me. I was always in love with Lyle," Jody said.

"Well, according to what I heard at the church bake sale today, Graham moved his daughters here to Celeste because they were being fat shamed down in Greenville. One of them knocked a girl on her ass, blacked both eyes, and bloodied her nose with one punch. It was the last day of school and they said they were going to suspend her for the first two weeks of next year for fighting," Fanny Lou said.

"She should get a medal, not suspended," Mitzi fumed.

Fanny Lou took a gallon jug of sweet tea from the fridge. "Who all wants a glass?"

Three hands went up.

She filled four glasses with ice and then tea and carried them to the table. "I remember when he went to work for his dad at the Cadillac dealership—right after he and Rita got married. His dad gave him a job on the lowest level, and he had to work his way up. Rita was furious because she thought they'd get a big house and a new Caddy every year. Stupid woman figured since his folks had money that he had an open bank account."

Paula took the ham and cheese containers from the fridge while Mitzi pulled a loaf of bread from the cabinet. "You eating with us, Granny?"

"I'll eat with you and Paula, but I don't want any of that salad stuff Jody is having. I'll eat what I want and die when I'm supposed to. Slice some of them tomatoes I brought in here earlier. And I'd rather have bologna instead of ham and mustard instead of mayo," Fanny Lou answered.

"Me, too," Paula said. "I want one like hers."

"I was thinking the same thing." Mitzi set about making three sandwiches.

So Graham was divorced and raising girls on his own. Bless his heart for getting them away from a school that bullied them because of their size. Mitzi could relate to the girls. But then, so could Jody and Paula. She'd always figured that Jody adopted her own modern-day hippie style to combat those feelings of insecurity. Paula had retreated into superstition. Mitzi had just plowed her way through emotions and other kids, spending a lot of time in the principal's office for fighting.

She pushed all that to the back of her mind, put the sandwiches on plates, and carried them to the table. "Y'all know that this job for Ellie Mae could turn into a big thing. I bet her older sister will be the maid of honor and her mother will want a fancy dress."

"That's what you're in business for, isn't it?" Fanny Lou said. "Man, this brings back memories. Friday night was bologna sandwich night when I was a kid."

"Why?" Jody asked.

"Because Mama always cleaned house on Friday, and she didn't have time to make a big meal," Fanny Lou answered.

"Funny how an hour of beading takes forever and our noon hour goes so fast." Jody pointed to the clock.

"Good Lord!" Fanny Lou finished off her sandwich and grabbed a cookie. "I've got an appointment with my CPA at one and it's a fifteen-minute drive to Greenville. See you girls later. You have my permission to flirt with Graham, Mitzi."

Mitzi's cheeks began to burn. "I had a *teenage* crush on him. I've grown up since then."

Fanny Lou winked as she headed for the door. "Paula, since you live with Mitzi, I'm putting you in charge of being sure she takes her birth control pills every morning."

Mitzi felt even more heat in her cheeks. "Granny!"

"When you get old you get to say whatever the hell you want to." Fanny Lou closed the door behind her.

They'd just finished eating when the door opened and their one o'clock appointment arrived. It took Jody, Paula, and Mitzi to get her into the dress, a creation of white tulle over bridal satin. It certainly wasn't what Mitzi would have chosen for the short lady, but with the help of Spanx and high heels, she was stunning. They added a sparkling tiara with a fingertip veil and turned her around on the stage to a huge three-way mirror.

Tears began to flow as both her hands went to her cheeks. "Oh, my! I'm beautiful. For the first time in my life, I feel like a princess."

Jody grabbed a box of tissues and wiped her tears away. "Of course you are, darlin'. With those big old brown eyes and your gorgeous face, you've always been beautiful. Don't cry, because I never let anyone cry alone."

"It's perfect. Look, I even have a waist. I can't wait to wear this next week." She pulled out another tissue and dabbed her face. "You've got the right name for this place. I'll be telling all my friends about The Perfect Dress."

Paula held a small trash can toward her so she could toss the tissue. "Word-of-mouth advertising is the best in the world. Want to take it off now?"

She turned every which way to catch her reflection from all angles. "I don't want my bridesmaids or anyone to see me in this until Saturday. I want to wear it forever, but please let me enjoy it for just five more minutes, and then I'll take it off."

"Want me to take a picture with your phone?" Jody asked.

"Nope." She shook her head. "I'd be tempted to show it off. This way it'll just hang in my apartment until Saturday when I take it to the church. Hey, I heard that Ellie Mae is having y'all make her dress, too. I can't wait to see what it looks like. Is she going with lace or satin?"

"That, darlin', is confidential, just like your dress is," Paula reminded her.

"Thank God for that," the woman said. "Okay, my five minutes of beautiful are over. Help me out of it. I'm glad I've got five bridesmaids to help me get dressed on my special day. I could never do this alone."

Jody and Paula took care of that, and then Mitzi gently put the gown in the zippered white bag with The Perfect Dress logo done up in gold lettering. She tucked the veil in one outside pocket and the shoes in another.

"There you go. All ready for your big day."

"Thank you all." She blew kisses as she headed behind the trifold screen to put on her jeans and shirt. "This is just the best dressing room ever. Us chubby ladies need room and lots of cool air when we try on clothes."

Mitzi whispered for Jody's ears only, "So when are you going to let us design a hippie wedding dress for you?"

"Lyle and I don't believe in having to buy a marriage license. We may have a ceremony someday, but we won't ever . . ." Jody started.

"You could always jump the broom," Paula suggested. "In some cultures that's as binding as a paper from the courthouse."

"We might do that," Jody laughed. "But for now, we've got sewing to do, and the Harrison girls will be here in an hour or so, so get down the pink, Mitzi."

"I'm fairly well caught up," Paula said. "I'm going to prop up my feet in the kitchen with a big cold soda right out of the bottle."

"Open one for each of us," Mitzi told her. "I'll be there soon as I get the final payment and papers signed on this dress."

֍

The girls came into the shop right on time that afternoon, their eyes huge as they tried to take in the totally feminine foyer and the wedding dress on the staircase.

Mitzi was waiting.

"I understand you girls need bubblegum-pink dresses. I'm Mitzi, and I own this shop with my two friends, Jody and Paula. I'll introduce them to you in a few minutes," she said.

"I'm Tabby, and I look horrid in that color, but oh well." The girl rolled her eyes toward the ceiling.

"And I'm Dixie. I'm the oldest by five minutes. I hate pink, too. I mean like really hate it."

"Are y'all twins?" Mitzi asked.

They nodded.

"Only we're not identical. My hair is darker," Dixie said.

"And my feet are a size bigger." Tabby's eyes kept darting around the room, as if she were a chocoholic turned loose in a candy store.

With their clear blue eyes and translucent skin, makeup companies would fall all over themselves to sign a contract with these girls. High cheekbones and a full mouth would have plus-size catalog companies begging for the same. Thank goodness their hair was different, or it would have been difficult to tell them apart. Dixie's black hair lay in curls down to her shoulders. Tabby's hair was straight as a board and fell to her waist.

"What style have you got in mind?" Mitzi asked.

They both giggled.

"I thought we should teach Mother a lesson and go all southern belle with a hoop skirt and a big flouncing collar," Tabby answered.

"And I thought we should show up lookin' like we just came from the street corner in pink satin cut down to our belly button and up to our butts on the side," Dixie giggled. "But I guess we should be nice."

"Why? We haven't seen Lizzy since we were too young to even remember her, and we've only seen Mother once since we were toddlers. 'Nice' isn't really an option," Tabby said. "I vote we do something they'll never expect and not tell them until the wedding day."

Mitzi thought of Ellie Mae and her black dress and of the client who had left just minutes ago with her dress. If Mitzi ever did fall in love, she could never keep her dress and the big day from Jody and Paula. But then, they'd probably be the very ones who made it for her.

"You know we're like just blowin' off steam, Tabby," Dixie said. "Let's just do something simple and get it over with. I don't want to be uncomfortable all day just to make a statement to Mother."

"Well, I can tell you one thing for sure: I'm tellin' her exactly how I feel after this wedding is over, and you can't stop me. I don't care if it makes her mad at me," Tabby said. "Now let's talk about these nasty pink dresses."

After Mitzi's mama died, she and her dad still kept up the Sunday-morning-breakfast tradition. In her opinion, parents who abandoned their children should be punished severely—and a hooker dress on a teenager just wasn't going to cut it.

"I've brought down some pink lace, satin, and other fabrics for you to look at. With your skin tones, you'll be beautiful in that color. If I were doing your makeup, I'd use just a hint of pink lipstick and a thin line of blue eye shadow to accent your gorgeous eyes. Has she chosen hats or . . ."

"A circlet of roses with burgundy ribbons." Tabby's eyes rolled toward the ceiling again. "She must think we're still little girls."

"What if you had the hairdresser pull up the sides of your hair into a crown braid so the flowers would sit right in the middle and then loosely curl the rest of your hair?" Mitzi picked up a sketch pad and quickly drew what she had in mind.

"Wow!" Dixie exclaimed. "That's beautiful. Can we take that with us to the hair place?"

Mitzi ripped the page off the pad and handed it to her. "Now, let's talk style. Swing dresses are all the rage. What if we did something like this?" In a few minutes she'd whipped up a picture. "You won't want to use heavy satin or it won't flow right, and what do you think of cutting it off right here and doing the top in pink lace?"

Dixie frowned and finally shook her head. "No, make it all the same material, but give us wide straps instead of a high neckline."

Tabby pulled the neck of her T-shirt to the side. "Wide enough to cover our normal bra like this so we don't have to wear a strapless. I hate those things."

Mitzi picked up a thick eraser and redid the top of the dress. "How about some burgundy trim somewhere to tie in those ribbons?"

Tabby pointed at the hem. "Just a hint around there. No, wait! I saw a dress last week at the mall that had a little ruffle of tulle around the bottom."

If Mitzi had daughters, she'd want them to be just like these two girls—all up in fashion and color. She picked up a burgundy pencil, and with a few flicks of the wrist, she put in a ruffle of soft illusion. "What do you think?"

"Neither," Dixie said. "Draw what the back will look like. I've got an idea."

Mitzi tore that sheet out and quickly redrew the dress from the back. It didn't look all that different from the front, except the back had a hidden zipper to give them dressing ease.

"Okay, now draw a burgundy bow right there with streamers that hang to the bottom of the dress," Dixie said. "And take away that stuff on the bottom. It will draw attention to our legs and we'd rather folks looked at our faces."

"And besides, the people will see our backs as much as our fronts," Tabby said. "Oh! And we can have burgundy high heels. I hope we're at least a foot taller than all the bridesmaids."

Mitzi drew in the bow and scribbled some color on it and the dress. "Why would you want to be taller?"

Tabby tipped her chin up. "Because Mother won't like it. She's this little petite thing that barely comes to our shoulders. I think she left us when we were babies because she was ashamed of us. She knew we'd be bigger than her by the time we were in the third grade."

Dixie looked a little sheepish, as if maybe she shouldn't reveal that about her mother, but it was the truth. "Daddy kind of wanted us to play basketball, but neither of us like sports so well."

"So what do you like?" Mitzi blinked away the tears in her eyes. Even if Rita had other reasons for leaving Graham, the girls had grown up thinking that she was ashamed of them. And then to disappoint their father, too—bless their hearts.

"Clothes, makeup, and making flower arrangements. We got to take a class in that at the vo-tech school last summer and we loved it." Tabby pointed to the mannequin on the stairs. "You should put a bouquet in her hands. You could even change it out with the seasons. Like red roses at Valentine's and yellow or pale pink for the summer."

Dixie's head bobbed up and down. "And orange daisies for fall and maybe poinsettias for Christmas."

"If I get some silk flowers tomorrow, could you come in the afternoon and make a bouquet for her?" Mitzi asked.

"Yes!" they both said at the same time.

"Ask your dad if it's all right, and let me know. Right now let's go look at fabric." Mitzi picked up her sketches and carried them into the huge old living room.

"Oh. My. God!" Tabby's hands went to her cheeks. "Have I died and gone to heaven? Look at all this beautiful stuff."

Dixie wiped her hands on her jeans before she touched the bolts of lace and satin. "I could live in this room."

"This one." Tabby immediately pointed at a bolt of soft-pink silk.

Mitzi took down a bolt of the same material in a dark burgundy and laid it beside the pink one. "With the bow out of this? We have satin shoes here that we can dye to match either color. So what do you think?"

"Yes, yes, yes." Tabby clapped her hands. "Can we try on the shoes and see what heel height we want?"

"Of course." Mitzi pointed. "Shoes are right there. Just find your size and start trying on. There are footies in the basket right there. So we're agreed on the fabric and the style for the dress?"

Jody came into the room and went straight to a container with dozens of tiny drawers full of beads. "Hello, ladies, I'm Jody. You must be the Harrison girls. Looks like you've chosen some pretty colors."

Paula came in right behind her and laid the bodice of a dress on the table. "And I'm Paula." She smiled.

"I'm Dixie. Pleased to meet y'all." The girl's eyes darted around the room, trying to take everything in.

"That's beautiful. What kind of skirt goes on it?" Tabby asked.

"Mermaid," Paula answered. "How're you liking Celeste?"

"We've only been here a week. I guess we'll make friends when we start school." Dixie pulled out a pair of three-inch spike heels in a size nine.

"Or maybe we'll get to know some of them when we go to church with Aunt Alice." Tabby put on a pair of shoes identical to the ones that Dixie had and walked across the floor in them. "You can wear high heels if you want. But not me. I'm not wearing something that makes me feel like I'm walking on stilts all day."

Jody cocked her head to one side. "Must be a long wedding."

"Don't know how long it is exactly, but Mother said we'll be there from eight in the morning to midafternoon. The wedding is at ten. I don't know why we can't just show up at nine thirty." Tabby opened a box and slipped her feet into a pair of shoes with kitten heels no more than an inch high. "I might be able to stand these. If not, I'll embarrass everyone and kick them off. We can still do our toenails in a horrid color, Dixie."

"I vote we do every one of them in a different color," Dixie laughed.

"Yaaas," Tabby said. "Bright neon colors with polka dots on them."

"Y'all sound like you'd make real good little hippies," Jody said.

"Yep, we would, only we ain't little. We'd make real good big hippies," Tabby agreed.

"I could stay here all day and visit with you kids, but I need to get back to work." Jody pulled a small drawer full of beads out from a container and carried it out of the room with her.

Paula glanced down at the sketch Mitzi had drawn. "You're going to love this design for your dresses. It'll be so comfortable you'll feel like you're wearing a nightgown. And the color will be beautiful on you both with your skin."

"You really think so?" Dixie asked.

"I never lie, especially not to kids. They can smell a lie a mile away," Paula declared.

"You're a smart lady." Tabby set the shoebox on the table. "I want this pair—in pink, not burgundy. That way if I want to take the bow off the back and wear the dress to church later, they'll match."

"I'd say you're pretty smart." Paula pulled out a drawer and removed a zipper, measured it against the bodice, and then exchanged it for a longer one. "Maybe I'll see you in church. I go to the same one your aunt Alice does. She's a friend of mine."

"Then I'll tell her I met you. Paula, right?"

"That's right. Paula Walker. See you Sunday, if not before." Paula carried the top of the dress and the zipper out of the room.

Dixie chose the same shoes in a size smaller. "And pink for me, too. I've got a floral pashmina scarf that would be pretty with this dress for church."

"Well, ladies, that just about does it," Mitzi said. "We'll let y'all think about this style overnight. I'll figure up an invoice to give to your dad, and we'll do measurements and make any adjustments tomorrow if that works for you."

"Yes, ma'am," Dixie said. "And you'll have some flowers for us to work on, right?"

"If it's okay with your dad," Mitzi reminded them.

"He won't care. He don't get home until at least six, and you close at five. We can throw a roast in the slow cooker and be home in time to put supper on the table," Dixie said. "This has been so much fun. I'm glad we get to come back tomorrow."

When they'd gone, Mitzi went back to the sewing room and slumped down in a chair. "Paula, can you put a spell on something so that I can have those girls? They've stolen my heart in only an hour."

"All kids steal your heart. You've always been drawn to them, from babies to teenagers," Jody said. "If you'd been smart, you'd have three or four by now."

"I haven't met the right guy," Mitzi said.

"Honey, you don't have to be married to get babies. Do I need to tell you about the birds and bees?" Jody teased. "Me and Lyle's been livin' together for fourteen years, and we ain't married."

"And you don't have kids," Paula said.

"That's by choice," Jody declared. "Mine, lately, not his. He says that we're getting to the age where we'd better be making a final decision on that. I told him we got five more years."

"How'd you come up with that number?" Paula asked.

Jody pushed her chair back from the sewing machine and headed toward the kitchen. "I need something to drink. Y'all want a glass of tea?"

Paula followed her. "Just water. You didn't answer me."

"We'll all be thirty-seven in five years. Now add in a year to get pregnant and deliver, and that'll make us thirty-eight. That's pretty close to forty, so we'd have to hustle to have a second one. Forty might be the new thirty, but after that age, having babies can get kind of tricky," Jody said.

Mitzi had been too busy to think about a final date for having children, but now she could almost hear the proverbial clock ticking in her ears. She loved Jody and had always supported her decision to live with Lyle without a marriage license, but that wasn't the lifestyle Mitzi wanted. She wanted the whole thing—the romance, the engagement, the big wedding, and, most of all, a husband who'd love her just the way she was. She'd thought maybe the last relationship she'd had could develop into something lasting, but he had wanted to change her.

"Think about it," Paula said. "Even then, we'd be almost sixty by the time our child gets through college."

Mitzi opened the fridge and got out a root beer. "Don't you know sixty is the new thirty? I'll still be designing and making wedding dresses when I'm eighty."

"Me, too," Paula said.

"What's that got to do with having babies?" Jody asked.

"A lot," Mitzi answered. "I plan on staying young until the day they lay me out in a coffin, so if I want to have babies after forty I'll do it."

Paula shivered. "Don't talk about funerals."

"We all got to die someday," Mitzi said. "So my child loses me when she or he is only forty. I wasn't even that old when I lost my mama. Or you, Paula, when your dad died."

"Or me, when my daddy left and my mama said it was because I was livin' in sin with Lyle. Don't know how that could be since he left her for a younger woman," Jody said through clenched teeth. "But the precious golden child of the church, Miss Ellie Mae, is getting married in black, so maybe they'll pray for her instead of me every Sunday."

Mitzi patted Jody on the shoulder. "I've told you for years, it's their loss. Let's call it a day and go home."

"I'd rather stay here," Paula muttered.

"What was that?" Jody asked.

"She said she'd rather stay here," Mitzi answered. "And I don't blame her. The minute we get home, her mama calls."

"She has two daughters, but I'm the one she calls every day to do something. Last night it was to change a light bulb and water the plants. Then she pouts if I go home before eight and gets mad if I stay two minutes past eight." Paula downed the last of her water and carried the glass to the sink.

"I'm glad my dad has a life and that Granny is so independent," Mitzi said.

"Count your blessings. I think I'll just run by Mama's for thirty minutes and get it over with. I'll see you at the house," Paula said.

"Tell her that we have plans and you have to get home. I'll get everything here locked up and shut down for the night and be there by the time you make it home," Mitzi yelled over her shoulder as she left the kitchen.

Paula had moved in with Mitzi when they started the shop. They'd thought about living in the upstairs part of the shop but wanted to keep work and home separate. When Mitzi stepped out into the blistering hot heat, she wished all she had to do was walk up the stairs to get home—not drive a couple of miles out of town and mow the overgrown lawn that afternoon.

Moving to Celeste last winter had seemed like the right thing to do. They'd really wanted and needed Jody to join them in the new business, and there was no way she'd move to another location. So Paula had given up her job as a librarian in Tulia. Mitzi gave notice at the exclusive bridal shop in Amarillo where she'd worked in the back room altering wedding dresses. And Jody quit her job as a waitress at the Celeste Café.

Mitzi's dad, Harry, had insisted on giving her the money that had been saved for her college education—that she'd only dipped into for one semester—to set up shop. At the time, Mitzi had thought it would be fun to have a roommate, but she hadn't figured on Paula's mother issue. Gladys Walker was only seventy years old, but with all her imagined problems, she acted more like ninety.

The small two-bedroom house they had rented was a short drive, but it was long enough that the van had just cooled down when Mitzi pulled into the driveway. She hated to turn off the engine and step out into the heat again, so she just sat there a few minutes. The place fit them perfectly, with a great room serving as living room, dining room, and kitchen separating bedrooms on either end of the house.

Mitzi would far rather be inside cooking than mowing the lawn, but she had no choice. It was her turn. Paula had taken care of it last week. She inhaled one last breath of cold air before she opened the car door and headed across the yard. Once inside, and before she could talk herself into putting it off for another day, she changed into shorts and a tank top. She'd just finished mowing the lawn when Paula drove her pickup truck into the driveway. She carried a milkshake in each hand and handed one off to Mitzi as she slumped down on the porch step.

"What's this plan you had for this evening?" Paula asked.

"It was an excuse, but we could say we were planning to cook supper together." Mitzi shrugged. "But I'm not hungry after drinking this."

"Me, either," Paula said. "Why in the hell didn't we put our shop in Tulia or even up in Greenville instead of Celeste? Then Mama would be hollerin' at my sister, Selena, instead of me, but since she lives twenty miles away and is married—" Paula stopped. "End of rant, because we're here and we can't undo what's done."

"Seemed like the right thing to do at the time. We should get your mother involved in something," Mitzi said.

Paula finished off her milkshake with a slurp. "You mean other than sit in her recliner, watch television, and think up things for me to do? And don't even start in on letting her come to the shop. She'll drive us all crazy. I'm going to drive down to Selena's place to talk to her about helping out more." Paula looked downright glum, making Mitzi wonder if maybe she was going to talk to her sister about more than just helping out with Gladys.

"Threaten to move Gladys in with her," Mitzi suggested.

"I want her to help, not give her a heart attack. Don't wait up for me. I'll probably be late." Paula set her empty cup on the porch and stood up. "See you in the morning, if not before."

Mitzi picked up both cups and carried them inside. Her thoughts went back to Dixie and Tabby and how excited they'd been about the whole business of creating bouquets for the mannequin. Maybe if they were really good at floral arrangements, she could turn one of the upstairs rooms into a little flower shop. They could earn a little money making up the corsages and boutonnieres for weddings.

She groaned when it finally dawned on her that she'd promised the girls that she'd have flowers there the very next day. That meant taking a shower and going to Greenville to buy them that night. While she was letting the cool water wash away all the sweat, she made a mental list of all the places that would be open after five.

After she'd finally cooled down, she stepped out of the shower. Pulling her wet hair up into a ponytail, she decided against makeup and dressed for comfort. Starting on one end of Greenville and hitting every store that might have silk flowers, she bought more than she needed in each place. By the time she reached the Walmart, the back of her van was already loaded. She grabbed a cart and headed straight for the artificial-flower aisle. Rounding the end of an aisle, she crashed into another cart.

"I'm so sorry," she muttered.

"No problem. I wasn't watching where I was going. I think they'd call it a no-fault accident."

She looked up and into Graham Harrison's eyes. There she was in a faded T-shirt, jeans that had seen better days, hair all messy, and no makeup. There was no place to hide, and it would've been rude to ignore him.

"Well, hello, again. I don't think we've done too much damage to the carts," she said, hoping he'd think her red cheeks were the result of sunburn.

"They still roll and hold a lot of merchandise. Actually, it's the store's fault. They should install traffic lights." His eyes bored into hers. "I understand you and my girls have designed the perfect dress for the wedding. I'm almost afraid to go home after what they told me they might do."

"It's really a sweet little dress that they can wear to church afterwards, so don't worry. I loved working with them. They're amazing girls. I may have a little business proposition for them, but maybe they should talk to you about it before I say anything."

"They've already called me twice." He grinned. "But wait until you get to know them better before you think they're too wonderful, especially Tabby. She's the mouthy, ornery one. Dixie has a quieter, gentler nature. But they're both good kids."

"How are you settling in?" Mitzi asked.

"We're almost unpacked. Moving from a small house to a big one isn't as difficult as if it'd been the other way around," he answered. "And the change will be good for the girls. They had a rough year."

"Oh?" She feigned ignorance and glanced at his cart. Hair products, Stetson aftershave, a package of three red oven mitts, and three rib-eye steaks.

"Bullying problems over their size. My sister, Alice, talked me into bringing them to Celeste. She says the school here has a motto about bully reporting called 'Stand Tall. Tell All.' I hope she's right."

"Must be something they decided to do after we were in school," Mitzi said.

"Did you have problems?" Graham asked.

Immediately, Mitzi wished she hadn't said that out loud. Now he'd look at her as a fat girl for sure. "Sometimes." She blushed again.

"I'm sorry. Guys get bullied when they're undersized, but girls are right the opposite. None of it makes a bit of sense to me." His phone pinged, and he fished it out of the pocket of his dress slacks. He read the text, typed in a return note, and then pushed his cart around hers. "Supper is going to be cold if I don't hurry. Thanks again for everything. And hold those wings and halos in reserve until you get to know the girls better."

Oh, I would love to get to know them better, and you, too, Graham, she thought as she watched him disappear around the corner. *They are a mirror of myself at that age.*

Chapter Three

Mitzi noticed Paula's note on the table as she passed by it that morning. She flipped on the light and read that Paula would be a few minutes late to work. "Probably Gladys again," she muttered as she headed to the refrigerator.

At seven in the morning sunrays were usually streaming through the window, but not that day. A loud clap of thunder followed a flash of lightning, and then hard rain sounded like bullets hitting the metal roof. The light above the table flickered and then went out.

"Well, there goes the electricity," Mitzi groaned. "I guess I'll pick up pastries for breakfast. Paula was the smart one, leaving before all this hit."

She made her way to her bedroom in the semidarkness, got dressed, and picked up an umbrella on the way outside. She'd barely made it off the porch when a solid gust of wind blew it out of her hands. She watched it flip a couple of times before it hung up in the lower limbs of the huge pecan tree at the corner of her house. There was no way to run between the raindrops as she dashed to the van, so she was soaked when she slid into the seat.

"Thank God I've got extra clothes at the shop," she muttered as she started the engine and headed to town.

She used the drive-through window to order a dozen assorted doughnuts, but even with the small awning over the window, the sack was water-splotched by the time she pulled it into the vehicle. She hadn't expected to see Paula's car in the parking lot when she parked behind the house, but Jody's old truck wasn't there, either. Grabbing up her purse in one hand and the brown bag in the other, she hurried through the rain to the porch.

"I shouldn't have dropped my keys in here somewhere," she scolded herself as she fished around in her purse. When she finally located them and got inside, she held her breath and flipped on the lights.

"Hallelujah!" she shouted. "We've got power. The whole town isn't without electricity like usual when it storms."

It didn't take her long to change clothing, dry her hair, and apply makeup. Then she made a pot of coffee and removed the doughnuts from the soggy bag.

"Hey, where's everyone at?" Fanny Lou rushed in the door and set a dripping umbrella in the basket. "From heat to pouring-down rain. It's true if you don't like the weather in Texas, you can stick around for twenty minutes and watch it change."

"Good morning to you, Granny." Mitzi poured two cups of coffee and set them on the table.

"I see you bought doughnuts again. Bless your heart. I swear, if the pastry shop ever closes its doors, I'm selling the Taylor estate and moving to Greenville," Fanny Lou declared. "So what did you think of Graham's daughters? I heard that you ran into him in Walmart last night, too. Did you flirt?"

"Good Lord, Granny!"

"I'm sure Jesus *is* very good, but answer my questions." Fanny Lou laid all the pastries out on a plate.

"It was love at first sight with his girls, and no, I didn't flirt. How did you find out that I'd seen him at Walmart?"

Fanny Lou shrugged. "Honey, how often does someone as powerful as Graham Harrison move back to town? He's divorced. He owns a Cadillac dealership. And he's good-lookin'. So where's Paula and Jody?" She sipped at the coffee.

"They haven't made it in yet, which is unusual."

"Good," Fanny Lou said. "I've got news about Lyle, but it might just be gossip, so I don't want to tell it in front of Jody."

Every hair on Mitzi's arms prickled. "Is it bad news? Is he sick and dying?"

"Nope, but he was seen with a young woman in a jewelry shop down in Greenville last week. I heard they were looking at rings," Fanny Lou said.

"Maybe he was getting her take on a ring so that he could propose to Jody. I bet he wanted to keep it a surprise. That would be so romantic. He's been in love with Jody since they were teenagers." Mitzi hoped she was right and that Lyle wasn't doing something stupid.

"It would be nice if that's what it was," Fanny Lou said. "But the person who saw them said he had his arm around the woman's shoulders. Are you going to tell Jody?"

Mitzi shook her head. "Nope. It's gossip for sure. She and Lyle are the same as married and have been for years."

"'Same as' isn't really married," Fanny Lou said. "Maybe you should call those girls and see about them. If the rumors about Lyle are true, Jody might be killing him right now. Paula could be helping her dispose of the body." She picked up a doughnut with maple icing.

Mitzi dug around in her purse for her phone and called Jody, but it went right to voice mail. Then she called Paula.

"Hello." Paula sounded as if she'd been crying.

"Are you okay? I'm worried about you and Jody," Mitzi said.

"I've got a stomach bug. I've taken some medicine. I'll be in by noon," Paula told her.

"I'm sorry. Rest all you need to. Are you home?" Mitzi asked.

"I am now. I got up feelin' bad and went to get something to make me better. We must've missed each other. See you later," Paula said.

"Let me know if you need anything. I hear Jody coming in now. If you need to stay home all day, that's okay. Just get some rest, and maybe you'll feel better by Monday." Mitzi sure hoped that whatever Paula had caught wasn't contagious.

Jody arrived looking like she could chew up tenpenny nails and spit out thumbtacks. She stood a huge umbrella beside the door on the rug and stomped across the floor to pour a cup of coffee.

"What's got you in a mood?" Mitzi pointed toward the plate of doughnuts.

"Lyle, and I don't want to talk about it," Jody answered as she picked up an apple and plopped down in a chair. "Y'all ever heard of Quincy Roberts?"

"Who hasn't? He's buying up land out there by y'all's trailer, but rumor has it he won't buy without the mineral rights. He's this big oil tycoon," Fanny Lou said.

"He wanted to buy our property, and I said no. Ever since, Lyle's been actin' weird," Jody said. "If he sells without my okay, I may leave his sorry ass or poison him for real."

"Can he do that? Sell without you signing?" Mitzi asked.

"Oh, yeah, he can. His aunt sold us the trailer and property. She'd only do it if we put it in his name only because she said someday he'd leave me. I didn't care at the time because she was a mean old b— witch," Jody said.

Fanny Lou shot a knowing look at Mitzi.

Mitzi didn't want to admit it, but her grandmother might be right. "Maybe he's going to surprise you with something and he's afraid to say anything. Or maybe he wants to sell the trailer and land and use the money for a down payment on a house."

"I don't like surprises," Jody said. "And I don't want a house in town. I like where I live. Maybe I'll get over this horrid mood if I start sewing. It's past time to open up for business." Jody took a sip of the coffee and set it back down.

"No one is going to come out in this weather and we don't have anything until Ellie Mae at eleven thirty. We can talk as long as you want," Mitzi said.

"That's right, darlin' girl." Fanny Lou laid a hand on Jody's arm. "Men are hard critters to understand. They seldom ever open up about their feelings because they think it'll make them look like a sissy. Maybe Lyle is just going through a tough time at work, or perhaps he's worried about whether the tomatoes are going to produce. They think about heavy stuff and things that don't amount to a hill of beans all in the same second."

"Was Oscar like that?" Jody asked.

"Of course he was. He was a man," Fanny Lou answered.

Mitzi decided to change the subject. "Well, I hope it stops raining by this afternoon so the Harrison girls can come in for a couple of hours. Having them around might help all our moods."

Jody looked around the room. "Where's Paula?"

"She's got a stomach bug. I told her to rest as long as she needs to," Mitzi said.

"Lord, I hope I don't get it. Men are worthless when the woman of the house is sick," Jody said. "They turn into old, grouchy bears, and Lyle's been hard enough to live with. Okay, enough bitchin'. I need to get back to work." But she tarried awhile longer to have another half a cup of coffee.

"Now that business about menfolk is sure the truth," Fanny Lou giggled. "We might need rain, but I sure wish it would stop. I've got a doctor's appointment at nine thirty, and I really don't like drivin' in it. Well, would you look at that?"

As if on cue, the rain stopped, the clouds parted, and the sun shone brightly through the kitchen window. "If I'd known my wish was going to be granted, I would've wished that Paula would get well or maybe that my hair didn't kink up when it rains." Fanny Lou started for the door.

Folks say that the wife knows when something isn't right, and Jody was proving it. But Mitzi sure hoped that the rumors were wrong. If they were true, Jody would be crushed.

"I'm probably worried for nothing anyway."

"Yep," Mitzi agreed.

Jody rinsed her cup and then headed out of the kitchen. Mitzi followed behind her, arguing with herself about whether to say anything at all to her friend.

Sleep on it. The voice in Mitzi's head sounded just like her mother. *Don't rush into anything before you have all the facts and evidence.*

Jody went right to the sewing machine and started working on a dress. Mitzi got out her sketch pad, erased a couple of lines, and then held it out at arm's length to study it.

"Is this about the right size for Ellie Mae? If I make her too small, she'll be disappointed with the finished product, but I don't want to make her any bigger than she is." Mitzi turned it around so Jody could see.

"Looks about right to me, but you're the one who can look at someone and guess their measurements within two inches. I betcha we get a run on black dresses after this wedding," she answered. "You goin' to get married in black?"

"Nope, not me." Mitzi shook her head. "What about you? If you and Lyle ever go to the courthouse, what color are you going to wear?"

Jody shrugged. "Don't know, but it won't be black lace."

Mitzi laid the drawing down and removed a pattern from an envelope. Cutting the pieces out, she let her thoughts wander back to Graham. He hadn't changed so much since high school. There was a little gray in his temples, and he wore his dark hair styled shorter than he had in high school. But that made him even sexier. The new glasses only added to his good looks.

At the sound of a long sigh from Jody, all Mitzi's thoughts of Graham were replaced with worry.

"Are you all right?" she asked.

Jody shook her head. "What are those bad years in a marriage?"

"I've read that it's the seventh, thirteenth, and twenty-fifth," Mitzi answered.

"Makes sense. Daddy left Mama for a younger woman just before their twenty-fifth anniversary. Of course, it wasn't her fault. Nothing has ever been or will ever be." Jody's tone held a lot of sarcasm. "It was all my doing. They didn't even want kids, so I was a big surprise. She should drop down on her knees and give thanks that she had me. That way she had someone to blame for everything that went wrong."

Mitzi wasn't sure how to answer that.

"Me and Lyle had a rough patch about our seventh year. We're into the fourteenth. Maybe he's just slow and this is really like our thirteenth."

Mitzi laid her scissors down and asked, "What exactly makes you think something is wrong?"

"Sex only twice in the last six months. Once at Christmas and then a couple of weeks ago but the second time was when I insisted," she said.

"He's pretty young to need Viagra," Mitzi said.

"Oh, he didn't need that. Before Thanksgiving it was two, three, or more times a week, then boom." She snapped her fingers. "He was too tired, or he fell asleep on the sofa."

"Maybe he was working overtime and really was too tired," Mitzi suggested.

"Oh, he was doing that a lot." Jody nodded. "So maybe you're right. I'm probably worried for nothing."

"Yoo-hoo, where is everyone?" Ellie Mae's shrill voice floated down the hall.

Mitzi glanced up at the clock. "Good grief, where did the morning go?"

"I slept away part of it." Paula appeared in the doorway. "Sounds like Ellie Mae is here."

"Are you feelin' better?" Jody asked.

Paula sat down at her machine. "Little bit. I figured I can feel sick here or at home. Here I can at least take my mind off it with work. I don't have a fever, so I'm not contagious. Probably just something I ate."

"Jody, get her opinion on what's happening while I go take care of this," Mitzi said as she headed out of the room.

"Sorry I wasn't right here. The time got away from me," Mitzi apologized as she showed Ellie Mae the sketch pad with front, back, and side drawings of her in the dress.

Ellie Mae clapped her hands and squealed, "It's perfect. I don't want to change a single thing. It's just what I dreamed it would be. I'm so glad that you're making it for me in such a short time. You know we really planned on a fall wedding, but then we got this great deal on a honeymoon cruise for July, so we pushed it up. When do I start fittings?"

"A week from today," Mitzi said. "We'll do one a week until the dress is finished and then one final one with the hat and shoes. That way we can be absolutely sure that you don't want to add a bead or change your mind about shoes."

Ellie Mae sucked in a lungful of air and let it out slowly. "I'll feel like a princess. Oh, and would you please make Darcy's dress? I'm only having one maid of honor, and I want her to wear red satin. I'm not real picky about what style, though. I'll leave that up to y'all."

Mitzi bit back a giggle. "Have you told your sister your colors?"

"Nope, but red is her favorite color. But at least talk her into leaving off long sleeves and a collar if you can. She's conservative," Ellie Mae laughed.

"So we'll slit up the sides to her hip, then?" Mitzi teased.

"I'd love that, but she'd just faint dead away if we even mentioned it. Now let's go get me measured." Ellie Mae headed toward the fitting room.

Mitzi wrote down all her measurements in a notebook as she worked. "So is eleven thirty good for you each Friday? We can stay late if you need to come after work instead, and I'll need Darcy to come in the first of the week to get things going for her."

"No, this time is great. I'll tell Darcy to call you and set up an appointment for Monday morning. I wish you did flowers. I want a special kind of bouquet," Ellie Mae said.

"Bring me a picture, and we'll see what we can come up with," Mitzi said.

"I don't know that I can find a picture, but I can kind of describe it. I want one of those draping bouquets like was popular twenty years ago. In my opinion big girls shouldn't carry a little tiny nosegay that gets lost in the pictures. No, ma'am. We need something bold that says, 'Look at me,' and it should be red roses."

"I've got a couple of girls who are going to play around with making a bouquet for the mannequin. If you like what you see next week, we'll see what they can do for you." Mitzi hoped that she wasn't putting the cart before the horse. Maybe Graham wouldn't want the girls to spend time at the shop, or maybe their work would look like crap.

Ellie Mae touched the sketch with more reverence than she probably did her Bible. "This is going to be the wedding of the year here in Celeste. Thank you so much. And tell those girls to do up one in red roses with some of the black lace from my dress for accents. See you next Friday." She hurried out the door.

Mitzi went by the kitchen and picked up three bottles of cold water. She carried them into the sewing room, setting one at each of the stations. "So did Jody tell you about Lyle?"

Paula opened her bottle and took a long drink. "Yes, she did. It's too early for him to be having a midlife crisis, so I figure he's just tired or else maybe he's got a big surprise up his sleeve for her."

"And he's been working overtime, too." Mitzi nodded. "It's close to noon. Let's make a sandwich."

"Not for me," Jody said. "I'll just cut up some of those cucumbers and onions that Fanny Lou brought us into a salad. I had green beans and new potatoes in the fridge at home, but I forgot them."

"No wonder you're as skinny as a rail," Paula said.

"I'm not a dyed-in-the-wool vegan. I'm just a vegetarian. That's not so bad," Jody said. "There's all kinds of fake meat at the market."

"It would be horrible for me. I love steak, fried eggs, and oh, my gosh, fried catfish." Mitzi led the way to the kitchen.

"Haven't had any of that in more than a decade," Jody reminded them.

"Miss it?" Paula asked.

"Sometimes, but Lyle and I agreed to live like this, so . . ." She shrugged.

The rest of the day went by like a snail headed for his own funeral. Jody was still in a snit because of Lyle. Paula worked on finding existing patterns that could be adapted to sew what Ellie Mae and the twins wanted. Mitzi watched the clock and could have shouted when the girls arrived fifteen minutes early.

"Hey, we're here!" Tabby called out.

"In the sewing room," Jody yelled.

In seconds they were at the door, each of them holding up a tote bag. "Did you get flowers? Where can we work? We brought our scissors and tape and all that stuff we had for class so you don't have to buy any of that." Tabby bubbled with excitement.

"The flowers are still in the van because it was raining this morning, but I didn't realize you needed more than that, so I'm glad you brought supplies." She wasn't about to admit that she was so rattled after she talked to Graham that she'd filled up the cart and barely had room to fit them into the back of her van with all the other flowers.

"We'll bring them in," Tabby said. "Just tell us where to put them."

"How about for now you work out of the kitchen? But we really should discuss what I'm going to pay you to do this," Mitzi said.

"Pay?" Tabby gasped. "We don't need money. This is for fun."

"But what if later, someone sees the mannequin display and wants the store to do their flowers? You can't do that for free. Follow me, and I'll unlock the van." Mitzi led the way across the foyer to the kitchen, opened the back door, and pressed a button on her key fob to open the hatch on the van.

The girls put their heads together and whispered, then Dixie said, "If that happens, we'll talk about it then. Right now we're just glad to get out of the house and get to play around in this place."

"This is like amazing," Tabby said when she brought in the first armload of flowers. "We weren't expecting to have so much to work with."

"I guess I got carried away." Mitzi smiled at their enthusiasm.

"Heaven must be just like this." Dixie hugged herself when the countertops were filled with flowers.

"I'll leave you girls to it. Could you make the first bouquet in red roses and use some of the black lace on the table in the fabric room for an accent? Then maybe come back the first of the week and do up one in fall colors that we'll use in October?"

"We'd come back every day and sweep up the scraps from the floors to get to spend time here," Dixie said.

"Could we use some black ribbon, too?" Tabby asked. "We'll be careful and not be wasteful."

Mitzi nodded. "Use whatever you want out of the fabric room. Just keep track of what you use, yardage and price, just in case someone comes in and wants to buy it right off the mannequin. Notebooks are kept in the cabinet to the right of the sink."

"Wow!" Dixie's blue eyes popped. "You really think that could happen?"

"You never know. Better to be prepared with a price than to stammer and stutter around. Y'all have fun. If you have any questions, I'll be over in the sewing room."

She was proud of the girls for their excitement and willingness to work. If only her last boyfriend had loved Mitzi just the way she was, she could have had a couple of kids by now. She hadn't realized just how much she did want babies until the girls came into her life. More than just want. Right then it was an aching need.

The giggling and arguing could be heard across the foyer the rest of the afternoon, and more than once, Jody or Paula stopped sewing and talked about how nice it was to have the girls in the shop. She'd been right—the twins did bring sunshine and happiness into the place. But it also brought home the fact that Mitzi might never have a family if all men were like her last boyfriend.

Just before closing time, the bell on the front door sounded, and Mitzi pushed back from her sewing machine. She was surprised to see Graham standing in the foyer when she peeked out around the corner of the room. Her heart skipped a beat and then took off with a full head of steam. Her pulse raced and her hands got sweaty. Dammit! Granny should have never teased her about flirting with him.

"I got off work a little early and thought I'd pick the girls up. Thank you for letting them hang out here. That's kind of you," he said.

"They're not hanging out. They're working," Mitzi said. "I'd be glad to pay them."

"For real?" He cocked his head to one side.

"Sure. They can help out a couple of hours a day and make a little extra money, if you don't mind." Just looking at him brought back all those feelings she had when she was fifteen. Even though she wasn't a teenager anymore, she couldn't control that giddy feeling.

"I don't mind at all," he agreed. "Who'd have ever thought I'd have feminine girls who don't give a hoot about sports? But instead of money, why don't you offer to make them a few items of clothing? Finding things that they like is a real problem sometimes."

"That sounds like a great idea. I'll talk to them about it. I've asked them to come back on Monday. And I want them to make another bouquet, if that's all right with you." She moved a little closer.

Dixie stuck her head out of the kitchen. "I thought I heard your voice, Daddy. How'd you get away from work so early?"

"Had a nice slow day, so I left before five. Thought maybe we'd have supper in the café downtown," he said.

"Ta-da!" Tabby came out into the foyer with a huge red-rose bouquet in her hands. "We made it pretty big since the mannequin is a big girl like us. When we get married we don't want to walk down the aisle with a little old single calla lily in our hands."

Fate!

That's exactly what it was. The bouquet was almost exactly what Ellie Mae had described, and Mitzi beamed with pride at the magnificent work they'd done. "I'd like to keep this one back for a week. Could you make another one for the mannequin on Monday, maybe in pink so it would be different than this one?"

"Why?" Dixie asked.

"Because one of my customers may want to buy this one, and if she does she may also want you girls to do the corsages and the rest of the flowers," Mitzi answered.

"You're serious? It's that good? It looks a little oversized and gaudy to me," Graham whispered.

"I'm dead serious. See you girls on Monday. We'll get you measured then. Paula is looking for a pattern that we can adapt for your dresses," Mitzi said.

"Can Daddy see the sketches you made?" Dixie asked.

"And are you tellin' us that we might get a job doin' this?" Tabby asked.

"I'd sure like it if you girls could work for me from three to five each day this summer. We can talk more about it when you get here Monday. Your dad is waiting to take you to supper right now." She picked up a pad. "The sketches are right here." She flipped it open so Graham could see.

His hand brushed hers as he took it from her, sending waves of tingles through her body. She had to get a firm grip on this silly schoolgirl crush. She'd be seeing him often if the twins were at the shop every day. Besides, if he was still attracted to the same kind of woman as Rita, he'd never see Mitzi as anything but an overweight woman who was good to his kids.

"Those are very nice, girls. I'm glad you didn't get crazy," he said.

"We wanted to," Tabby said.

"But we decided to be classy." Dixie took the bouquet from her sister and tinkered with a few of the flowers before laying it on the coffee table. "When I get married, I want one just like this."

"On that note, I'm getting both of you out of here," Graham laughed. "I don't want to walk you down the aisle for at least ten years. Fifteen would be better."

Mitzi locked up after them and plopped down on the pink sofa. A thirty-two-year-old woman should be over a crush she'd had when she was fifteen, so why was there a picture in her mind of herself in a white dress walking down the aisle toward Graham? She blinked several times to get the visual from her head. She'd have a better chance of waking up a short, skinny blonde tomorrow morning than of Graham ever being attracted to her.

Chapter Four

"Lyle, I'm home, and we need to talk," Jody called out as she entered the trailer that Friday night. "Whatever is making you act like a jackass is going to stop, and we're not selling this trailer to Quincy. It's our home. It's paid for. And I've worked my butt off to make us a nice garden spot."

No answer.

She knocked on the bathroom door and it swung open. She flipped back the shower curtain and he wasn't there. She checked the bedroom and looked out the kitchen window to see if he was in the garden, then went back to the front door and opened it. His motorcycle wasn't there, so that meant he wasn't home from work.

"Dammit!" she fumed as she threw herself down on the sofa and shut her eyes. At midnight she awoke to find him still not there, so she took a quick shower and got into bed.

In her dreams she stood on the front porch of the trailer, looking southwest across the tops of the trees at the dark clouds. As the eerie quietness surrounded her, she had the feeling that the coming storm was going to be the one that ripped her mobile home apart. Then the tornado alert sirens began to sound. The sky took on a strange greenish color, and suddenly the wind started grabbing everything that it could pick up. She tried to get back into the trailer but froze.

She opened her eyes to find sweat covering her body and the alarm ringing right beside her ear. She quickly turned it off and reached over to shake Lyle awake. But he wasn't there. She sat up so quick that it made her dizzy. Pictures of him lying in a ditch with his motorcycle on top of him flashed through her mind. She threw the covers to the side and ran to the living room, expecting to find him on the sofa, but no. She quickly dug through her purse for her phone—no calls or messages, which only meant if he was hurt, he wasn't in the hospital. He had to be unconscious.

She hit the speed dial for his number, and it went straight to voice mail. She jerked on a pair of jeans, didn't even bother with a beaded headband or braiding her long hair, and pulled a T-shirt over her head as she went out the door. She was inside the truck when she realized she hadn't gotten her purse, so she raced back inside, grabbed it, and ran back to the vehicle. She tried calling Lyle again every three minutes, but it went to voice mail each time.

Driving slowly and stopping every time she saw a black skid mark veering off the road, she just knew that she'd find him dead somewhere between Celeste and Greenville. When she reached the outskirts of town, she drove straight to the ranch where he'd worked as a hired hand for the past eighteen months. The only time she'd been there was for the Christmas party last year, but it wasn't hard to find. A few times he'd worked very late and then stayed in the bunkhouse with the guys. She hoped that was the case this time, but his motorcycle wasn't there, either. Still, she parked in front of a long, low building where three guys were sitting on the porch, having their morning coffee. They all waved when she rolled down the window.

"You done passed the ranch house, darlin'," one of them yelled.

"I'm looking for Lyle Jones," she said, raising her voice.

"He ain't comin' in today, honey. He left at noon yesterday. He's got a big weekend planned. He'll be back on Monday if you want to come back," the guy said.

"What kind of weekend?" she asked.

"A huge one. If you're his sister, you were supposed to meet him at the courthouse yesterday. Guess you're too late."

"I'm not his sister," Jody said.

One guy chuckled. "Then, honey, you're too late for anything."

"What's that mean?" she asked.

"Ask Lyle," another one laughed.

"Thank you." Jody rolled the window up and turned the truck around. Sister, huh?

His older sister lived in Houston and never had liked Jody. She seldom came around and when she did, she stayed in a hotel. She was trouble on wheels, and pretty often, after Lyle spent time with her, he was hard to live with. However, he did always tell Jody when Brenda was coming to visit. Why would he withhold that information now?

She was still fuming when she got back to the trailer. Thank goodness it was Saturday and the shop was closed or she'd be late getting to work. She tried calling him again but didn't get an answer, so she went inside and brewed a pot of coffee. She poured a cup and carried it to the sofa. She'd only taken one sip when her phone rang. She grabbed it so fast that she fumbled the cup and spilled it on the carpet. She forgot all about the stain it would leave when she saw Lyle's number come up on the caller ID.

"Where in the hell are you? Did you and Brenda hit the bars last night? If you're in jail, I'll be damned if I come bail y'all out. You can just rot in there, and why did you take off work yesterday? What's so big that you can't even tell me why you aren't coming home?" She stopped long enough for a breath. "Did you go and sell our place to Quincy? Is that why you didn't come home?"

"Jody, slow down," he said. "We need to talk."

"What do you think we've been doing?" She finally got control of her shaking hands. Even if he sold the property, he was alive and not lying in the morgue. They could deal with anything if he was alive, right? "I've been out looking for you and was about to start calling hospitals. Why didn't you come home last night?"

"Because I got married," he blurted out.

"You did what?" Jody shook her head. Surely she'd either heard him wrong, or else he was trying to make her laugh so she wouldn't be angry.

"We haven't been doin' so good the past six months. You know that, Jody. I want kids. You don't know what the hell you want. I kind of had an affair," he said.

"You did what? How do you *kind of* have an affair? Either you cheated on me or you didn't. Which one is it?" Her voice shot up an octave with every word.

"The ranch foreman's daughter and I—"

"You mean that teenager, the one I met at the Christmas party? Katy, or was it Kristin?"

"Her name is Kennedy," Lyle answered. "She's almost *twenty*, Jody."

"You're serious, aren't you? This is not a joke?" Her hands trembled and her stomach twisted into a tight little knot.

"Yes, Jody, I'm serious. We're on a weekend honeymoon right now," he said. "She told me a couple of days ago that she's pregnant, so I'm doing the right thing. We're moving the trailer to the ranch. It'd be real good if you could get your things out by tomorrow evening. The movers are coming Monday evening to take it away. You can have the travel trailer. I can't pull it with my motorcycle anyway."

Her whole world was crumbling beneath her feet. She was going to drop into a deep sinkhole any minute, but he sounded like he was discussing whether they should put in ten or twenty tomato plants that year. "I didn't mean for this to happen, but it happened, and I'm not letting my child grow up without a father like I did."

Her coffee cup crashed to the floor from her hands and broke into dozens of pieces. She opened her mouth to give him a stinging tirade of cuss words, but nothing would come out. She was every bit as frozen as she'd been in the dream.

"Are you there?" he finally asked.

"Yes," she whispered.

"I didn't mean to hurt you, Jody. In some ways I'll always love you, but . . ." He paused.

She could imagine him raising a shoulder in a shrug. A picture flashed in her mind from the Christmas party the year before. Kennedy, the daughter of the foreman on the ranch, had worn a tight red dress that barely covered her underpants. She was curvy, like Jody had been back when she and Lyle first started dating.

Jody hadn't had a honeymoon, but then Lyle had declared that a marriage license was just a piece of worthless paper that the government used to make money. When she moved in with him, he was living in a one-room garage apartment. They'd lived there for four years while they saved enough money to buy a used trailer house and a couple of acres of ground from his aunt.

"How long has this been going on?" Jody's knees buckled and she fell backward onto the sofa. This couldn't be true. She would have known if he was having an affair. She was his wife, even if it wasn't on paper.

"Since Christmas," he answered. "We kind of got together out in the barn the night of the Christmas party."

That's when she hung up, and tears began to stream down her face like a raging river. She curled up in a fetal position on the sofa and cried until her sides ached, her head pounded, and there were no more tears. Her phone pinged, and she opened it to find two messages. The first one was from Mitzi, asking her if she wanted to join her and Paula for a girls' night out that evening. The other was from Lyle.

She opened the latter and read that he was sorry, but he was happy and he hoped that someday she would forgive him. Evidently, tears could be replenished at the drop of a hat—or maybe in this case, the opening of a message.

Jody got a fistful of plastic grocery bags from a cabinet drawer and headed back down the narrow hallway. Like a bolt of lightning, it hit her—Lyle had to have taken money from their savings to pay for their little *weekend honeymoon.*

Strewing bags the whole way back to the living room, she started to cuss instead of cry. Her hands shook as she typed in the right codes for her online banking account. Yesterday, there had been more than three thousand dollars in the joint checking account. Now there was only a thousand. And the savings account was gone, all but for one hundred dollars.

She sank down to the floor and leaned her head on the sofa, hoping to stop the room from spinning. There wasn't a thing she could do about it. She and Lyle weren't married, and they'd opened the joint accounts years ago. But come Monday morning, she'd be at the bank when it opened, and the meager amount still there would be transferred to one in her name only.

Her phone rang and she almost didn't answer it. No way was she talking to him again—not right then or maybe ever. But then she saw Mitzi's picture.

"I need you and Paula. It's an emergency," her voice quavered.

"Are you sick? Did someone die?" Mitzi asked.

Jody started to sob uncontrollably again. "Just come out here, please."

"We'll be there in five minutes. Don't do anything stupid until we get there," Mitzi said.

"Okay," Jody blubbered.

She was still sitting on the floor, staring at her phone, when Mitzi and Paula burst through the front door. "Look." She held it up. "He didn't sell the property to Quincy. He was having an affair with a younger woman. And he took all our money to take her on a honeymoon and God knows what else, and all I've got is a travel trailer. It leaks and it doesn't even have a bathroom. I gave up everything for him! His sister even came from Houston for the wedding. I gave up steaks and fried chicken so I'd be thin like he wanted, and he married a chubby woman who dresses like a hooker. I became a vegetarian!"

Mitzi sat on the floor with her and took the phone from her hands. "Who is this a picture of?"

"Remember I showed it to y'all after the Christmas party at the ranch last year? Lyle married her yesterday," Jody screamed. "He's on his honeymoon with our money right now. Married her. Because she's pregnant, she gets a honeymoon and a damn marriage license." Her voice came back down to a whisper. "What am I going to do? And look at this." Jody tapped the phone a few times and handed it to Mitzi.

Paula eased down on the other side and slung an arm around Jody's shoulders. "What am I lookin' at?"

"Our bank account. It's almost all gone." She covered her eyes with her hands.

"Okay, start at the beginning." Mitzi turned the phone off.

Between bouts of hiccups, sobs, and anger, Jody started with when she'd gotten home the night before and told them what all had happened right up until that moment and then asked again, "What am I going to do?"

"You're going to move in with us." Mitzi handed her a box of tissues from the end table.

"And if you want us to, we'll buy three shovels and bury his body in a place where he'll never be found." Paula hugged her even tighter.

"Y'all only have two bedrooms. I can't move in with you."

"We have a living room with a sofa that makes out into a bed. The mattress is thin, so we'll take the one from your guest room to go on top of it," Mitzi said.

"And we'll take whatever else that you want. We'll load up your truck and be out of here in an hour," Paula said.

"I can't do that," Jody argued.

"Yes, you can, and you will," Paula said.

"I could just take a room upstairs in the business." Jody wiped her cheeks and tossed the tissues toward the trash can, glad to have the support of her friends.

"No, you don't need to be alone." Mitzi got to her feet. "First thing is the mattress. You don't want the one you've slept on with that cheating sumbitch, do you?"

Jody shook her head. "I can't believe this is happening."

"You'll get past the denial and the numb feeling, and then you'll get mad," Paula said. "We'll get your personal stuff, and then we'll trash this place if you want us to."

"No, I want his new little pregnant wife to see me everywhere in this place." Jody rolled up on her toes. "The picture box is in my closet." Like a woman on a mission, she stomped down the hallway and brought down a cardboard box. While Mitzi and Paula folded and put her clothing in garbage bags, she picked out several photos of her and Lyle through the years. She was tempted to tuck them in the cabinets, stick them on the bathroom mirror, and maybe even slip them under the pillows on the bed. But she couldn't do it.

"God, why didn't I see this? I knew something was wrong, but I never thought he was cheating on me," she groaned. "I had my head stuck in the sand so far that my scrawny butt was sticking up in the air."

"Enough of that. That hussy might be younger, but she needs to remember that he was cheating on you the whole time. Once a two-timin' sumbitch, always one, so she just might lose him the same way she got him someday," Paula said as she and Mitzi maneuvered the mattress down the hallway.

Jody's chin quivered. "Y'all pinch me and wake me up. This is all a nightmare like the one I was having this morning, isn't it?"

Paula set her end of the mattress down and asked, "What nightmare?"

Jody told her about the tornado and then clamped a hand over her mouth. "Evidently somewhere in my subconscious, I must've felt that a storm was brewing."

"Of course you did. It was a sign that there was a mental storm brewing in your life, but you are strong. We're here for you just like we've always been. We've stuck together through everything since before we started school. We'll get you through this," Paula said.

"You got a gris-gris you can put on this place when we're done?" Jody asked.

"Honey, karma will bite Lyle on the butt better than any spell I could cast on this old trailer," Paula said. "Think about it. He's used to having you make his meals from food you grow. He never has to lift a finger to help with anything around here other than a little garden work. She's young, and from that Christmas picture, she's a handful, and she's pregnant. He's going to pay dearly." Paula picked up the mattress again.

Jody understood that they were trying to make her feel better, but it wasn't working. Her stomach was in knots, her hands were clammy, and tears streamed down her face.

They came back inside and began to carry out black plastic bags of her clothing. She didn't want any of her clothes—her hippie days were over. She'd been the other half of a couple who stood for something, and now she was nothing but a woman who'd thrown away years of her life. This all had to be a terrible nightmare. She and Lyle would laugh about it when she woke up. He'd tell her that she was the only one he'd ever loved, and everything would go back to normal. She shook that idea from her head. This was the cold hard truth—reality in a two-minute phone call.

"The bastard didn't even have the nerve to tell me to my face." Anger washed over her as she rolled up on her feet, got a box of matches, and stormed outside. She emptied several bags of clothing into a pile in the firepit that she and Lyle had built last year and lit them up. As she stood there watching the outfits burn, Mitzi came outside and slung an arm around her shoulders.

"Do you want the chest of drawers in the guest room? You'll need something to put the rest of your clothes in. The closet in the living room is pretty small," she said.

"Mama might forgive me and let me—"

"No!" Mitzi shook her head. "She'd make you miserable if you moved in with her, and besides, we'd be worried sick about you."

Paula tossed another bag of clothing into the truck. "You don't want to live with her. You know what I'm enduring with my mother, even though I've moved out."

"Yes, I'll take the chest." Jody nodded. "I'll go through my things later and throw away a lot of those clothes because I'm not going to be that woman anymore. And I want to go to Greenville this evening for fried chicken."

"You got it," Mitzi said. "And we'll have bacon for breakfast in the morning."

Chapter Five

I didn't sleep very well. Maybe it was eating fried chicken after all these years of not having meat, or the fact that I couldn't turn off my mind. One minute I wanted to take one of Lyle's guns out to that ranch and shoot him dead, and the next I blamed myself for the whole thing. If I'd been prettier or younger or would have had children, maybe he wouldn't have left," Jody said as she entered the kitchen that Sunday morning.

Mitzi had been standing at the back door, staring out into the yard, and Jody's voice startled her so badly that her heart had to slow down before she could speak. "Good mornin'," she finally said.

"Truth is I went off birth control six months ago. On the day of the Christmas party, and now I find out that's the very day his little fling started." Jody went to the refrigerator and looked inside. "Irony at its best. Only thing better will be if I'm pregnant after all this time."

"Jesus!" Mitzi gasped.

"I'm going to church. Lyle didn't believe in religion any more than he did eating anything that has a face. I might as well just burn all the bridges this weekend," Jody said.

"Good for you." Mitzi didn't know whether to wish that Jody was pregnant or to hope like hell that she wasn't. "You can go eat with us at the café after services. Daddy and Granny will be glad for you to join us."

"Join us for what?" Paula yawned as she entered. "I'm going to have hot tea this morning. Anyone want in?"

"No, I've already got a pot of coffee brewing," Mitzi answered.

"Have you lost your taste for coffee?" Jody asked.

"That dark roast kind gives me heartburn," Paula said. "Now who's joinin' who for what?"

"I'm going to church," Jody announced. "How about you?"

"If you're going, then I am. I wouldn't miss that show for the world."

"What show?" asked Mitzi.

"Her mama is going to be there," Paula said.

"So's yours," Jody reminded her.

"Which is the very reason I usually don't go," Paula said. "But today we need to be there together."

"Exactly. I got your back." Jody grinned for the first time since Mitzi and Paula had arrived at the trailer the day before.

Covering her yawn with a hand, Mitzi tried to focus on what the preacher was saying, but her mind kept jumping around from one thing to another. She thought about the possibility of Jody being pregnant. In some ways she envied her friend for even having the chance, but how would Jody ever move on if every day she saw a reminder of Lyle right there before her? Then she wondered about Paula's decision to quit drinking anything with caffeine and all liquor. Maybe she should have a physical to be sure her heartburn wasn't something serious, like a malfunctioning gallbladder. Graham Harrison and his girls crept into the circle of worry, too. Should she keep the relationship with the twins on a professional level, or was it all right to get into a deeper friend-type relationship with all three of them?

Jody poked her in the ribs.

"What?" she whispered.

"I think you're supposed to listen to the preacher," she said out of the side of her mouth.

"I was!" Mitzi frowned.

"You were thinking about Graham. Your whole body language changes when you think about him," Jody said.

"Shhh." Jody's mama, Wanda, tapped her on the back.

Mitzi sat up straighter and did her best to pay attention, but it was impossible. Wanda had disowned Jody when she and Lyle moved in together right after they'd graduated from high school. How was she going to take the news of him cheating on Jody? It was bound to get out real soon, if it hadn't already.

The preacher finally ended his sermon and asked one of the deacons to give the benediction. The minute the last amen was said, Mitzi's father was on his feet, shaking hands with those around him.

"These old pews get harder on my backside every Sunday." Fanny Lou stood up and groaned, then nodded toward Wanda.

"Mama." Jody nodded as well.

"I told you this would happen, that no man will buy the cow when he's getting the milk free," Wanda hissed at her.

"Are you braggin' that you're right or callin' me a cow?" Jody asked.

"You've disgraced yourself again. Where are you stayin' since he's married someone else?" Wanda's mouth was set so tight that it was a wonder the words could escape.

"She's stayin' with me and Paula," Mitzi answered.

"That's where she should've been all along or else livin' with me." Wanda's high-pitched voice grated on the nerves. Poor Jody didn't need that when she was trying to sort out everything.

"We'll take good care of her," Mitzi promised.

"Why do you care anyway? You haven't even spoken to your daughter in years," Fanny Lou asked.

"She could have been a help to me, but oh, no, she had to cause so much trouble that she drove her father away and then embarrass me in front of all my friends by living in sin," Wanda said through clenched teeth. "And now she's gettin' her comeuppance."

"I'm standin' right here, Mama," Jody said.

"Maybe so, but I'm choosing not to see you. God says we should hate what He hates and love what He loves. He doesn't love the way you've lived," Wanda told her.

"Well, I'm sure glad God loves *you* even when you're self-righteous," Jody replied.

"You're sure showin' a lot of Christian love, Wanda. You should be supporting your daughter in this tough time," Fanny Lou snapped.

From the expression on Wanda's face, Mitzi expected her to plumb stroke out. But she whipped around and stormed out of the church by a side door.

"Reckon she'll get into heaven if she dies this week since she didn't shake the preacher's hand?" Fanny Lou giggled.

"Granny!" Mitzi scolded, but she couldn't keep the twinkle from her eyes.

"I might have voiced it, but you were thinkin' it. Lyle wasn't much of a man to tell Jody about his affair and marriage on the phone. If you ever have a feller like that, I'll kill him and drag his body down Main Street behind my old pickup truck," Fanny Lou whispered. "I'm tempted to go out there and do it to Lyle."

"And I'll help you." Mitzi's father, Harry, motioned toward the side door. "Let's take our chances on not dying this week and skip shaking the preacher's hand. Whoever gets to the café first should save a table for the five of us."

"Granny, you want to ride with me? Jody came with Paula this morning," Mitzi said.

"I was just about to suggest that. Then afterwards you can bring me back here to get my truck," Fanny Lou answered.

As soon as the van doors were closed, Fanny Lou started firing questions. "So how long do you think this affair was going on? Was he sleeping with both women? Is there a chance that Jody is pregnant, too? Now wouldn't that be horrible."

"He's been cheatin' on her for about six months," Mitzi answered. "I don't know if she's pregnant, but Jody confided in us years ago when we were still young that she has a fear that she'll be a bad mother like Wanda. So that's probably why they didn't have children." Mitzi sent up a silent prayer for Jody to not be pregnant, even though she hadn't been on birth control. That would be too much of a burden for anyone, even her strong-willed friend, to carry.

"Jody is nothing like her mother," Fanny Lou argued. "She'd make a great mama if and when she ever decides to have children, but I hope she's not expecting a baby now. That wouldn't be a bit fair to her, to have to raise up a child to a man who broke her heart."

Mitzi drove from the church straight downtown and groaned when she saw how many cars were parked on Main Street. "We're going to have at least a thirty-minute wait," she fussed as she parked a block away from the Celeste Café.

"I should've slipped out before the benediction and saved us a table," Fanny Lou said. "But I wasn't about to leave you to deal with Wanda alone. I could see she was fuming all through church."

"How? She sat behind us." Mitzi unbuckled her seat belt.

"I kept a watch on her out of the corner of my eye," Fanny Lou said. "She came loaded for bear and someone was going to get it."

"Well, we've got time." Mitzi flipped the rearview mirror around and applied fresh bright-red lipstick to match the dress she'd chosen to wear that morning. "No need in getting in a hurry since we'll have a long wait anyway."

"But we might as well go on in and get our name on the list. There's your dad parking right beside us," Fanny Lou said. "When he and your mama married, I didn't think I was going to like him, but he was so good to my daughter that I came to love him like a son. I hope you find a man as good as he is someday."

"Me, too, Granny." Graham's image flashed through her mind.

Harry was out of his truck and tapping on the window before Mitzi put her lipstick away. She opened the door, and he said, "Let's go on inside."

He ran his fingers through his thin gray hair and cleaned his glasses on a snowy white handkerchief. "Danged things fog up when I get out of the truck in the heat. Boy, Wanda was on a rampage, wasn't she? I thought I might have to step between her and Fanny Lou."

"One more hateful word out of her mouth and they'd have had to bring out the mop and cleaners, because I was ready to knock the shit out of her," Fanny Lou said as she got out of the van.

Mitzi slid out of the driver's seat and looped her arm in her father's. "I never thought I'd be taller than you. When I was a little girl, you were ten feet tall."

"You can thank me for that." Fanny Lou wore a bright-red pantsuit that morning and her white cowboy boots with gold tips on the toes. Her red hair was twisted up and held with a big clip that sported stones of every color.

Mitzi pulled her grandmother close with her other arm, and the three of them walked down the wide sidewalk together. "We match today, Granny."

"If I'd gotten the memo, I would have worn a red tie instead of this bolo," Harry chuckled.

"We'll have to remember to keep you in the loop," Fanny Lou teased.

Harry's face went from happy to serious in the blink of an eye. "I was sorry to hear about Jody and Lyle, but I might've helped Fanny Lou if she'd tied into that woman. I might not agree with Lyle and Jody's lifestyle, but they seemed happy. I'm right glad she's stayin' with you and Paula, though. That'll be good for her."

They entered the café together, and Harry raised his voice above the noise of a full house to tell the waitress they needed a table for five.

"Be at least half an hour," she said.

"Mitzi!" someone yelled from the middle of the room.

When she located the voice, Mitzi saw Dixie waving in their direction. Mitzi waved back, but Dixie motioned to empty chairs at their table. In a few long strides, Tabby had crossed the floor and said, "Y'all come join us. We've got a real big table and we haven't even ordered yet."

"This is my dad, Harry Taylor, and my grandmother, Fanny Lou Labelle. This is Tabby Harrison. She and her sister are helping me out at the store. Oh, and here's Paula and Jody." Mitzi waved. "These folks want us to join them for dinner."

"Sure." Harry nodded. "I bought your mama's last Cadillac from Graham, so it's not like we're sitting with strangers."

"I wouldn't care if we were," Fanny Lou declared. "I'm hungry."

"Great!" Tabby said. "Follow me. I'll get all y'all through the maze."

Graham was on his feet when they got to the table. He pulled out Mitzi's chair before he shook hands with Harry. "Y'all have met my sister, Alice. She teaches school here in Celeste. Alice, this is Mitzi Taylor and her father, Harry."

"And you know me from church, Alice," Fanny Lou said. "Thank y'all for inviting us to sit with you."

Even seated, there was no doubt that Alice was a tall woman. Dark hair framed a round face, and her eyes matched Graham's shade of mossy green. "It's great to see all y'all again."

Mitzi was seated between her father and Graham, with everyone else circling the table. Sitting that close to Graham caused that old crush to rise up and flush her face with heat. She should say something, but her tongue was tied—unusual for her. Everyone had a menu, so she picked hers up and hid behind it.

"Dixie and Tabby said they had a great time at the store, and that you've designed a dress for them to wear to their mama's friend's wedding," Alice said.

"I think we've settled on a style that they can use more than one time," Mitzi answered. "And they're really good with bouquets. We might be able to hire them for a few hours every week once the news gets out that we can offer flowers as well as dresses."

"Daddy said that we can work, but we talked about it and we decided we don't want money for our jobs. We want you to teach us to make our own clothes. Daddy says he'll buy us a sewing machine if y'all don't have an extra one for us to use," Dixie said all in a rush. She sucked in more air. "I've already been designing some shirts I want to make."

"They're real simple for our first-time project," Tabby added.

"That sounds like a great idea to me," Harry said. "That's like getting back to old-time bartering. They make flowers. You give them sewing pointers. Why don't you take the sewing machines from the house? You and your mama sure made a lot of clothing on them when you were these kids' age and they're still set up in the sewin' room. They could use one at the store and take the other one home with them."

Mitzi laid a hand on his shoulder and gave a gentle squeeze. "That would be great, Dad."

Graham leaned toward her and whispered, "I'd be glad to pay for the lessons."

"If you do, then I'll have to put them on the payroll for the work they'll do with flowers," she answered.

"Then I guess we'll call it an even swap." He stuck out his hand to shake on the deal.

Mitzi shook with him and wasn't a bit surprised at the warmth his touch created. "It's a deal."

"So we can come work every day at three?" Dixie asked.

"Why don't you make it right after lunch? Say twelve thirty," Mitzi said.

The girls high-fived and then pulled a couple of pens from their purses and began to draw on their napkins.

"This is great," Alice said. "I was trying to figure out something for them to do this summer. I coach a summer-league softball team, but as you probably already know, they're not into that at all."

"I'm glad to have the help." Mitzi was excited to have the girls in the shop every afternoon, but that wasn't what made her heart throw in extra beats that day. Every time she inhaled, she got a whiff of Graham's shaving lotion; when he leaned over to whisper, the warmth of his breath caressed the soft spot under her ear.

The waitress finally made her way to their table and removed an order pad from her pocket. "Okay, folks, y'all ready to order? The Sunday special is turkey and dressin', hot rolls, mashed potatoes and gravy, cranberry sauce, and green beans. Sweet tea comes with the meal and so does dessert—pecan pie, chocolate pie, peach cobbler or blackberry."

"That's what I want," Dixie said. "And I'll have chocolate pie for dessert."

"Same here," Tabby said, and the two of them handed their menus to the waitress.

Harry's order included the pecan pie and Fanny Lou's the chocolate.

"Peach cobbler," Graham and Mitzi said at the same time.

"I'll have the special with blackberry cobbler." Alice handed her menu across to the waitress and then focused on Graham and Mitzi. "Looks like you two are in sync when it comes to dessert."

Mitzi wouldn't mind being in sync with him on where to eat that peach cobbler, like in the middle of a big king-size bed after a rousing bout of hot sex. At that thought, she could feel heat crawling from her neck to her cheeks. She picked up a paper napkin and fanned her face. "It's sure warm in here, isn't it?"

"Kind of cool to me," Paula said.

"It's probably hot flashes startin' in on you," Fanny Lou whispered.

Mitzi wanted to crawl under the table. "I don't think so."

"Can you believe these tall nieces of mine aren't interested in softball or basketball?" Alice asked from across the big, round table.

"We're going to take fashion design in college and grow up to be like Mitzi," Dixie said. "We'll have our own shop for bigger teenage girls. Only we want to design things that girls wear all the time, not just for formal affairs."

Alice giggled. "Graham, who would have thought a Harrison would say something like that?"

"I know. They must be a throwback to our ancestors from the Civil War," he chuckled.

"Yep, I know exactly what you're talkin' about," Harry said. "All Mitzi ever wanted to do was sew. When Paula's sister got married a couple of years ago, these three"—he nodded toward Jody, Paula, and Mitzi—"designed and made the dress. And that's when they all really got the fever to put in their own shop."

"Some of us don't like to sweat." Mitzi winked at the girls.

Unless it would be during a hot little makeout session with Graham. Paula's voice rang in her head.

Go away. You're makin' me blush, she argued.

The waitress brought their sweet tea, and Paula flashed Mitzi a look and a nod of the head that Mitzi interpreted to say, *You're right beside him. You would have given up your sweet little Mustang in high school for an opportunity like this and you haven't said a dozen words to him.*

"So where is Selena these days?" Alice asked.

"She still lives down around Greenville," Paula answered.

Paula set her mouth in a firm line and gave Mitzi one of those looks. Mitzi took a deep breath, turned to face Graham, and changed the subject. "Daddy says that you sold him Mama's last Caddy."

"That's right," Graham said. "Had to order it special because she wanted a baby-blue one. What was that, thirteen years ago? I'll always remember the sale because it was my first one. I'd finally worked my way up to salesman."

"Yep," Harry said. "It's still parked in the garage. I take it for a spin every now and then and once a year get it tuned up. Delores loved that car. I just can't get rid of it."

Mitzi wondered if Graham had trouble getting rid of Rita's things. He must have really loved her to give up his future for her. He'd gotten an offer to play basketball for the Longhorns, and of course, his father owned the dealership, so money wasn't an issue. She stole a sideways glance at him. Did he still have feelings for Rita?

Graham sipped his tea and then set it down. "I understand about holding on to things. Mama's car and Daddy's truck are parked out at their place. I should go through the house and get rid of things, since we're going to live here in Celeste. But I haven't been able to do it yet."

Mitzi laid a hand on his arm. "Don't rush or you'll regret it. Mama's been gone two years. Daddy and I'll give away her things when he's ready."

No one else seemed to notice, but Mitzi could feel sparks flitting around the room like fireflies on a summer night. If just touching Graham in sincere sympathy could cause that, what would happen if he kissed her?

Stop it, she scolded herself.

Harry shook his head slowly. "Time ain't been right for me to get rid of anything. I knew your daddy very well. Never knew your mama. When did she pass?"

"When I was sixteen," Graham answered. "Alice was already out of college and teaching, but it was tough on both of us."

"Still is some days," Alice said. "And someday, when the time is right, like Mitzi says, we'll go through the house and put it on the market. Neither of us wants to live there, and it's not good for a place to set empty."

Mitzi glanced over at Graham and caught his gaze, but then he quickly blinked when Dixie shoved a napkin his way.

"Look at what we've drawn for our first project," Tabby said.

Mitzi glanced down at the napkin. "This one would be a better starter project than the last one you showed me."

"Very nice," Graham said. "Does this mean that we won't need to go school-clothes shopping at the end of summer?"

"Of course not," Dixie answered. "We'll still need jeans and shoes."

Mitzi could have sworn that someone was staring right at her, so she scanned the room, and sure enough Wanda was shooting evil looks her way. No doubt about it, Fanny Lou, Harry, and all the girls from the shop sitting with Graham and his family would fuel the rumor mill for the rest of the day.

Chapter Six

itzi parked the van and crossed the grassy lawn in her bare feet. She dropped her shoes on the porch step and sat down beside Jody, who looked like she'd been crying again. "Where's Paula?"

"Her mother called. She said she'd be back by suppertime. Mothers!" Jody threw up her hands.

"Don't let Wanda rattle you," Mitzi said.

"She called about fifteen minutes ago," Jody said. "She gave me the third degree again and said that if I'd made Lyle marry me, this wouldn't happen. She used the old 'why buy the cow when you're getting the milk for free' adage three more times during the conversation."

"Ignore her. You did the right thing by going to church and standing up to her," Mitzi said.

"She also told me that you were definitely on a date today, because Graham picked up the bill, and evidently y'all have been seeing each other on the sly for a while, because you were introducing each other to family. And that she hopes y'all don't sin in front of those girls." Jody rolled the kinks out of her neck. "According to the sermon she gave me, I've wasted my life, but there might be hope for me if I admit she was right and repent of my sins. But I don't feel like I need to repent for anything other than trusting Lyle."

"I'm so sorry. You just keep going with us to church. That'll show the whole lot of them that Lyle isn't putting you in a corner—that you are a strong woman who can take control of her own life," Mitzi said.

"You think in one week that will be true?" Jody asked.

"Maybe not, but we can put up a brave front and make them believe it's the truth," Mitzi answered.

"We'll see how the week goes. I could use a cold beer. How about you?" Jody asked.

"Let's go inside where it's cool. I'd like to change into something more comfortable than this dress," Mitzi answered. "But what if you're pregnant? Should you be drinking beer?"

"I'm not jumping through hoops and giving up beer until I know for sure. Now, I need to know something—why have you been keeping Graham's proposal a big secret, especially since I've told you everything?" Jody teased as she followed Mitzi into the house.

"You're in a better mood." Mitzi stopped under the AC vent in the living room and enjoyed a moment of cold air flowing down on her.

"It comes and goes. One minute I'm crying. The next is a whole 'nother story. I've been up and down so much today that I'm not sure who I am. Talk to me about Graham to take my mind off Lyle and his new child bride." Jody went to the refrigerator and returned with two icy cold cans of beer. She opened one and took a long drink from it, then set the other one on an end table beside a recliner.

Mitzi headed down the short hall to her bedroom, left the door open, and raised her voice as she changed into a pair of loose-fitting pajama pants and a T-shirt. "I think he's just grateful that I told the girls they could come to the shop for half a day through the summer."

Paula was sitting in a rocking chair with a glass of iced sweet tea in her hands when Mitzi made it back to the living room. "My mama called, too, mainly to fuss at me because I didn't sit with her in church. But I got the news about us having dinner with Graham, too. Wanda called her as soon as she could. What is it with old women and gossip? We're not going to be like that, are we?"

"Hell, no!" Jody sat down in the middle of the floor. "We should make a pact to never get old or trust a man."

"You've got a bed right there," Mitzi asked. "Why are you sitting on the floor?"

"I'm all sweaty and dirty. Don't want to mess up the sheets." Jody handed her the beer from the end table and patted the floor. "I'm glad we had dinner with Graham. It took the heat off me for a little while."

Mitzi sat down and leaned back against a recliner. She took a long drink from the can and then set it on an end table. "Lyle marries someone else. I've been seeing Graham on the sly. What kind of drama can you add to that, Paula?"

⌒∽

Paula pushed her dark hair behind her ears. She'd wanted to tell them that she was pregnant for weeks, but the timing was never right. At first she didn't want them to think she couldn't hold up her part of the business, and then this past week, when she decided she absolutely had to say something, thinking about it had upset her stomach. Then Jody called with the news that Lyle had married his pregnant girlfriend, and she sure couldn't say anything then. She and Mitzi needed to be there for Jody during that time, and that still wasn't over. But was now the right time?

"She's taking a long time to answer. Makes me wonder if she's dreaming up some fake news to make us laugh," Jody said.

"Like she's going to try to convince us that she's got a secret boyfriend, and she really isn't going to book club once a month or taking off work an hour early to help her mother but she's sneaking out to see him," Mitzi giggled.

Jody joined her in what started off as a giggle but turned into infectious laughter, and then she got the hiccups. "Paula can't keep a secret. She's always told us everything. If she had a boyfriend, she would be smiling all the time."

And now they were teasing her about not being able to keep secrets. She almost blurted it out just to show them, but when she opened her mouth, nothing came out. Then she figured that she'd get back at them, since they thought they were so funny.

"That's it. I've got a secret boyfriend. Graham and I've been seeing each other for a month. That's why he moved here," she finally said.

Mitzi looked like she was about to cry.

Jody stared at her like she had an extra eye right in the middle of her forehead.

"Are you telling the truth?" Mitzi's eyes swam in unshed tears.

"I don't believe you," Jody whispered.

"I'm so sorry. I was trying to be funny, but that was mean," Paula hurriedly apologized. "But after that shock, what I do have to say won't be near as dramatic. Here's the truth." Paula took a deep breath and laid her hand on her stomach, which she concentrated hard on settling with a few sips of sweet tea.

"You're turning a little green around the mouth," Jody said. "Do you, are you . . . I can't even say the words."

"Do you have something incurable?" Mitzi whispered.

"No, it'll be cured in about three months," Paula whispered.

Fresh tears flowed down Jody's face. "I've been selfish thinking only about me and my heartache. How long have you had this?"

"Six months, but I only found out about it three months ago. I'm not dying—I'm pregnant," Paula spit it out.

The whole house went silent. Not a single tree limb brushed against a window. The refrigerator motor wasn't running, and the ceiling fan didn't even squeak like normal. Paula wished she had a tigereye stone tucked away in her bra. Those brought courage.

"You're kiddin' again, right?" Jody finally whispered. "We'd have known if . . ."

"This is huge. When? Where? Who's the father? Are you getting married and leaving us?" Questions poured from Mitzi.

Paula shook her head. "Slow down and listen to me. At first I was in denial. You know I've never been regular. I didn't even know until three months ago. Then the doctor said that there was a possibility I'd have a miscarriage, so . . ." Paula hesitated a minute before she continued. "But when I went for my checkup this week, I'd passed the second trimester and she says she thinks the baby is going to be fine now. I didn't want to worry y'all."

"B-but you don't look . . ." Jody stammered.

"Us big girls don't always get the popular baby bump." Paula laid a hand on her stomach.

"Or people think we're pregnant when we aren't," Mitzi said. "Who, what, when?"

"Long version or short?"

"Every single word," Jody said.

"Okay, here goes. I was seeing a man in Tulia," Paula said.

"Clinton?" Jody said. "The sumbitch who went back to his wife, right?"

Paula nodded.

"You stayed in bed for a whole weekend after he left. We ate half a gallon of ice cream and used more than two boxes of tissues," Mitzi said.

Another nod.

"And I drove out there to be with y'all," Jody said. "That's part of the reason we decided we should put the business here in Celeste to get you out of that area."

"I couldn't have gotten through it without y'all. I really loved him." Paula's chin quivered.

"Does he know about the baby?" Mitzi asked.

Paula shook her head. "No, and he's not going to, so that can't leave this room."

"Why can't he know?" Jody asked.

Heat traveled from Paula's neck to her cheeks. "His wife is pregnant. He's a bastard, but I won't ruin her life or the baby they're going to have. She went through in vitro twice just to have a child. It's complicated, but they were only separated, not legally divorced. Y'all know the story. It's not her fault that I loved him, but he didn't really love me."

"Remind you of anyone?" Jody asked.

"Of course it does," Paula said. "That's what came to my mind immediately when you told me about Lyle. I wondered if you might be pregnant, too."

"We'll know in a few days. I'm regular as clockwork," Jody said.

"Well, we won't worry about that right now." Mitzi took control. "What we're going to plan for now is a new baby, which means we need a bigger place."

"I vote that we move into the upstairs of the shop," Jody said.

"But we decided that we needed a house so that we'd have a life and not work every day until bedtime," Paula said.

"But," Jody argued, "there are five good-sized bedrooms, a bathroom, and a small room that the previous owners used for an office. One for each of us and one to make a nursery, and we can put a sofa and television in the other and call it a living room."

"It might work." Mitzi stood up and began to pace the floor. "But the only way would be if we vowed to separate work and our personal lives."

"The smaller room could be the nursery," Paula offered.

"I think we should use a bigger one and give the little one to the girls to do their flower business," Jody said.

"Sounds good to me," Mitzi said.

"Rent's up on the fifth, so we'd have to do it in a hurry, like in two days," Paula said. "Maybe we should think about it for a few weeks and give a notice. We'll lose your deposit if we don't."

"Yes, but we won't have to pay the extra rent or utility bills, so we'll actually be ahead of the game." Mitzi sat down at the table. "We can move tomorrow evening after work."

"I can't believe we're even thinking of this," Paula said. "But we'll have to promise that we don't bring work upstairs."

"Exactly, and we each have a life to live, so we don't have to tell each other where we're going or what time we'll be home," Jody said.

"What are we going to do with that mannequin?" Mitzi moved from the kitchen chair to the middle of Jody's couch-bed. "Whoa!" She held up a hand. "We're freaking out about moving and we're forgetting the big picture here. Paula is going to be a single mother and she needs our support."

Paula went to sit on the edge of the bed. "Thank you. I'm okay now that I've told y'all."

"No, you're not." Jody sat on the floor beside the bed. "I won't even know for a few more days, and I'm still totally freaking out about being a single mother. So fess up, Paula. We're here for you."

"Okay." Paula held out her trembling hands. "I go to bed wondering if I'll be a good mother. Look at our moms, Jody. Are we going to be like them? Demanding, judgmental? It scares the crap out of me. Then I wake up worried that my child will feel cheated since she won't have a father. So, yes, I'm freaking out, but knowing y'all are here for me helps."

"Have you told your mama?" Jody asked.

"Not yet. I tried to tell Selena when I went down to see her the last time, but I just couldn't do it. You're the first ones I've told," Paula admitted. "You want to break it to Mama for me?"

"Hell, no!" Jody shook her head emphatically. "If I happen to be pregnant, I'm going to tell my mama I found the baby in a cabbage patch."

Paula glanced over toward Mitzi and raised an eyebrow.

Mitzi threw a hand over her forehead in a dramatic gesture. "I love you, girl, but not that much. Gladys will breathe fire, and I'm real fond of my eyelashes and hair."

Chapter Seven

*n*ever again," Jody said as she threw back the covers and sat up on the sofa bed.

"'Never again,' what?" Mitzi yawned.

"Never again will I fall in love." She had had a sleepless night, worrying about her own pregnancy possibility. Like Paula, she was terrified of being a bad mother. And if the poor baby only had her, and not a decent father to balance things out, then it would be twice as bad.

"Don't say that. You're a good person. You deserve to be happy." Paula got bacon and eggs from the refrigerator and began cracking the eggs into a bowl.

"So do you," Mitzi said. "So do all of us."

"Maybe, but trust is tough after this kind of thing." Jody kicked herself for not seeing the signs. Paula hadn't had a beer in months, and she loved beer. She did drink a little sweet tea, but she didn't go around with a glass in her hands from midmorning until suppertime. If Jody hadn't been so wrapped up in her own problems with Lyle, she would have recognized all the signs. "Let's make a decision about moving and then go forward without looking back."

"You always say that," Mitzi said. "Are we ever able to not look back?"

"I'm going to give it my best shot." Paula set the eggs aside and started frying bacon.

"Me, too," Jody said. "That's not saying I'll always get the job done, but when I fall on my face, I have these two amazing friends who'll help me get back up."

"Yes, we will." Mitzi popped open a tube of biscuits and arranged them in a pan. "So I'm in for the move. It'll save money and we'll have more room. Jody can even have a private bedroom for when she gets a boyfriend."

Both of Jody's palms went up defensively. "That's not happening. Paula, I need one of your stones to carry around in my pocket to ward off all feelings of love."

"That would be a jasper stone. It helps control emotions. I'll give you one before we leave for work this morning. I've carried a moonstone with me for weeks. It helps with pregnancy," Paula said. "And by the way, I checked the signs last night. This week is a good time to move, but next week isn't. It seems like an omen to me."

"I've always thought your superstitions and stones were a little wonky," Mitzi said. "But I might be willing to sleep with a love one under my pillow."

"Under your pillow won't work," Paula scolded her seriously. "It's got to be next to your skin. You need a rose quartz. Put it next to your heart."

"If y'all are going to try this, then I'm game, too," Mitzi said. "But it'll have to show some power to turn me into a believer."

"Will your jasper stone keep me from wanting to strangle Lyle?" Jody asked.

"Maybe I'd better give you a sodalite stone. It's a little stronger than the jasper. So we're really going to move into the shop?" Paula asked.

Jody cocked her head to one side. "I'm all for it, but what about all those stairs? You going to be able to get up and down them?"

"I'm pregnant, not crippled. Women have lived in two-story houses with babies for centuries," Paula answered.

Mitzi shook her finger at Paula. "But you got to promise that you won't lift anything heavy. I'll call that moving company from—"

Paula grabbed her finger. "I will not be treated like an invalid. I'll concede to not carrying my dresser and mattress up the steps. But I won't be mollycoddled. Understood?"

"So we're in agreement about the move and not babying you?" Jody asked.

"Looks like it." Paula nodded. "But right now we've got to get to work. Wedding dresses don't wait, and we've got to get Ellie Mae's bodice done this week for her first fitting."

"You're awfully quiet, Mitzi," Jody said. "Are you having second thoughts?"

"I'm sorry. I was thinking about whether it would be wise to get a mover to just come take care of it for us or to use your truck and make a dozen trips," Mitzi answered.

From the slight blush on Mitzi's face, Jody didn't believe that was the entire truth and nothing but the truth, but she didn't argue. "We should use my truck and save the money. No more than y'all've got, we can do it in probably five trips," Jody said. "Get it all out tonight, and then put things away a little at a time."

Mitzi nodded in agreement. "I'll call Granny and Daddy. They both have trucks and they'll be glad to help. Lord have mercy! Our lives have sure changed since we left work on Friday."

"Thank God I've got y'all to help me through it," Jody whispered. "It seems like Saturday was a hundred years ago."

"Amen." Paula laid a hand on Jody's arm.

⌒⍵

As Jody worked that morning, she really tried to keep her mind off the fact that the trailer where she'd lived for more than a decade was being taken to a ranch near Greenville that day. But it was impossible. One minute she tried to figure out what she could have done different—was this partly her fault for not giving him more attention, more sex, less nagging? The very next thought was that the damn stone in her bra was doing nothing to keep her from wanting to tie him to a chair and use him for target practice.

Paula nudged her ankle with a toe. "Penny for your thoughts."

"You can have them for free," Jody said. "This is all surreal. I gave Lyle my heart, my soul, and my life for more than fourteen years. How can he just walk away like that without even telling me to my face? And what do I do now? I feel like an empty shell. We've got so much on our plates right now that y'all don't need to be taking care of me. We're moving. You're pregnant. The world is spinning too fast."

Mitzi tucked a strand of red hair back into her ponytail. "Look at it like this: You're like an empty gallon-sized pickle jar. You're cleaned out and you're ready to be filled up with whatever you want. You can put one thing in it a day or a dozen. It's your choice because Lyle doesn't control your choices anymore."

"I'll try to steer my thoughts that way, but today I want revenge, not new beginnings," Jody answered.

"Hey, where is everyone? We're here." Dixie's and Tabby's voices blended together as they entered the back door of the shop.

"In the sewing room," Jody called out to them. "I'll put their names in my jar. Their positive attitude is like sunshine after the storm."

"Isn't it great that the girls are comfortable in their skin?" Paula whispered.

"I wish I'd had more of that kind of confidence," Jody said. "Then I'd still be a size sixteen instead of a four."

Mitzi stifled a giggle. "Never heard that before. Most of us want to be petite little trophy women."

"Look what it got me," Jody said. "Some trophy."

"What do you want us to do—oh, my goodness, that black lace is pretty." Tabby entered the sewing room ahead of Dixie.

"Raise your right hand." Just seeing Tabby's exuberance over a bolt of black lace erased part of Jody's horrible mood.

Both of their hands shot up.

"Now repeat after me," she said. "I do hereby swear to never tell anyone about anything that happens or is created at The Perfect Dress."

The girls said the words so seriously that Jody almost laughed. "Okay, you are sworn in as legitimate employees. This is Ellie Mae's wedding dress."

"Oh. My. Gosh!" Dixie gasped. "I didn't know you could get married in black."

"That's the same lace that we used in the bouquet we made," Tabby said.

"And I'm going to show that to Ellie Mae," Mitzi said. "If she likes it, then she might want you to do the rest of the flowers for the wedding party. But right now I want you to work on that pink bouquet we talked about for the mannequin and then help me get it down from the steps to the foyer. There's a slim possibility that we'll get to go to the Dallas Bridal Fair and if we do, I'd like to show off some of your work."

"For real?" Dixie's eyes widened out as big as saucers. "Our bouquets might get to be on display?"

"Yes, but it's still a long shot, and we may need to build an arch and decorate it, too. Be thinking of what color bouquet you think our bride should carry, and we'll make the arch flowers match. It can't hurt to be ready."

Jody blinked several times to keep the tears at bay. As a teenager, she'd dreamed of a wedding where she'd stand under a decorated arch with her groom. She'd wear a white dress and flowers in her hair. When she got a little older, she'd envisioned an outdoor wedding with mountains in the background. She'd loved Lyle enough to throw her dreams away, and now they were shattered.

"We can be ready, but the mannequin looks so good on the stairs," Tabby said.

"The three of us are moving into the upstairs part of the shop, starting after work today," Paula explained. "So we've got to clear that off."

"Holy crap on a cracker!" Tabby threw a hand over her mouth. "That wasn't very nice."

"Aunt Alice says it all the time," Dixie giggled. "Can we help? Daddy is real strong and he can lift a lot. Why are y'all moving in here so fast? Are you packed? Why didn't you live here all the time?"

"Because Paula and I have been living in a small house and now Jody is moving in with us and we need more room. And we haven't packed a thing," Mitzi said. "But there's a lot of room upstairs, so we're going to utilize it."

"Well, I know how to pack," Dixie said.

"Me, too. We're good at it, and we want to help," Tabby said.

"And we're grateful to you," Paula said. "But maybe you girls better ask your dad before you volunteer him."

Tabby yanked her phone from her hip pocket. "Daddy, we need help moving Mitzi, Paula, and Jody to the shop. They're goin' to live upstairs. You and Aunt Alice can meet us here at five thirty, right?"

She only listened a second before putting it back. "He says he'll have to go home and change clothes, but he'll be here soon as he can. Now come on, Dixie. We got a mannequin to move and a bouquet to make. God, I love this job."

"Me, too," Dixie said as she headed toward the kitchen.

"You going to let them move it all by themselves?" Jody whispered.

Mitzi pushed back her chair. "Not only that, but I'm going to turn them loose on redoing the foyer."

"I'm likin' this idea of having helpers a lot," Paula said.

Jody frowned. "But what if they don't do it to suit us? Will you let them down easy when we have to redo it ourselves? I couldn't bear to hurt their feelings."

Memories flooded back of all the times when she'd tried to do something nice for her mother only to have it backfire. No wonder it had been so easy to move in with Lyle and to want to please him so much after living with her mother. Jody remembered one time when she thought it would make Wanda happy if she cleaned house for her while she was at the beauty shop.

Without even realizing it, Jody put her hands over her ears as she replayed the sound of her mother screaming that day: "You've washed all the glitter off my precious angel. Now it's worthless. Why can't you ever do anything right?"

Wanda had picked up the tiny angel knickknack, thrown it in the trash can, and for years, if she thought about it, she still got angry.

So that's why I tried so hard to please Lyle, Jody thought.

"Of course," Mitzi said as she left the room.

It took Jody a while to remember why Mitzi would even say that, but then she remembered the conversation about the foyer.

"She's still crushing on Graham, isn't she?" Paula whispered.

"Probably always will." Jody toyed with one of her long braids. "Is that the reason she wants his daughters around?"

"I don't think so. She loves kids and they remind her of us when we were in school." Paula pulled her dark hair out of her ponytail and shook it loose. "I'm getting a headache, so I'm going to the kitchen for an aspirin."

"Are you all right? Do we need to call the doctor?"

Paula held up a palm. "I'm fine. It's just a headache."

"I'll go with you. I want a soda and one of those candy bars in the drawer," Jody answered. She had to push back the guilty feelings about eating candy and drinking soda. First her mother had fat shamed her and then Lyle had, too.

The girls had a notebook and a tape measure out when Jody and Paula passed through the foyer. They were deep in conversation about how to arrange things so folks could get around the furniture to go to the fitting room and the kitchen, and yet to show off the mannequin at the same time.

"Guess I misjudged them," Jody admitted when Mitzi handed her a can of root beer in the kitchen. "I swear they could be your kids."

"No, mine would never be that beautiful," Mitzi said.

"So how're you feelin' about Graham coming to help move?" Paula swallowed two aspirin and opened the drawer where they kept the candy bars.

"It was just a high school crush," Mitzi answered. "With all this help, we should be out of there before dark."

Paula ripped the paper from the candy bar and took a bite. "I've been craving chocolate like you wouldn't believe."

"I never met Clinton. What does he look like? Are you hoping the baby doesn't look like him?" Jody grabbed a candy bar and told the niggling voice in her head to shut up.

"He's about six feet tall, blond hair, blue eyes, and just slightly overweight," Paula answered. "If the baby has blue eyes, I'm going to say that they were inherited from Aunt Mitzi. If the baby has blonde hair, we'll declare that it came from Aunt Jody."

"And if it turns out to be a big person, it's from all of us," Mitzi told them.

Jody bit off a chunk of candy bar and chewed slowly. If by some crazy reason she was pregnant, then what would her baby look like? She was blonde and had brown eyes. Lyle had brown hair and green eyes. Would it be a girl or a boy? Suddenly, having a baby didn't scare her like it used to do. If Paula could do this alone, then so could she.

∽

Mitzi was busy tidying up her work space at five o'clock when Dixie and Tabby bounced into the sewing room, both smiling as if they'd just won the lottery.

"Come and see what we've done. If you don't like it, then we'll change it but . . ." Tabby paused.

"But we just know you are going to love it. The bouquet in the mannequin's hand matches the sofas, and we did a pretty floral arrangement in shades of pink for the coffee table, and we had so much fun." Dixie finally stopped for a breath.

Mitzi pushed the material back and stood to her feet. "Okay, ladies, it's quittin' time. Let's go see what these interior decorators have done."

Dixie and Tabby went ahead of them and stood on the bottom step of the staircase as they filed into the foyer. Mitzi almost didn't even want to look out of fear that she wouldn't like it, and it would break her heart to tell them to put it back the way it was. She inhaled deeply and kept her eyes on the floor until she could see the mannequin in her peripheral vision.

"It's beautiful," Jody said.

Mitzi could hardly believe the sight. If she'd hired a professional decorator, it couldn't have looked a bit better. "It looks like it came right out of a bridal magazine," she whispered.

Tabby clapped her hands. Dixie pumped her arm. "Yes!"

Graham poked his head in the door. "I got off a few minutes early with a used pickup from the lot. I understand there's some moving to go on around here?"

Tabby made a motion with her hand. "Daddy, look at what we just did. We rearranged the foyer and brought the bride down from the stairs."

"And we made the bouquet in her hands and the arrangement on the table," Dixie said.

"Very nice, girls." Graham beamed with pride.

Every time Mitzi had seen Graham lately, he'd been dressed in slacks, loafers, a white shirt, and a tie. She'd thought he'd been downright sexy then, but now he was even more so in denim shorts, a knit shirt, and sneakers.

"You're staring," Jody whispered.

"They did this all on their own," Mitzi said. "And thank you for offering to help us out. Jody has a truck, too, and my dad and Granny are bringing theirs. With all that, it shouldn't take long."

His eyes locked with hers and held for a moment before Dixie grabbed his hand. "Okay, Daddy, me and Tabby will ride with you. Mitzi, you can lead the way since we don't know how to get to your place. Do we have boxes?"

"I'll stop by the grocery store and pick up whatever I can get," Jody said. "Y'all must've been really organized when you moved."

"Oh, yeah, they were," Graham chuckled. "We had lists and more lists."

Mitzi remembered then that their house was a mess. Jody's things were still sitting in plastic bags in the living room. Dirty coffee cups filled the sink, and the laundry bin in her bathroom overflowed.

Why are you worried? Her mother's voice popped into her head. *He's not your boyfriend. He's only a neighbor who's offering to help you move.*

Jody elbowed her. "Say something. It's getting awkward."

Mitzi took a step forward. "We're glad for the help, and we might wish we'd made lists before we get done. We only decided to do this last night on the spur of the moment when we realized we need more space. We haven't gotten a thing packed or done."

"I hear there's some moving goin' on around here," Alice said as she pushed the front door open. "What a lovely little area."

"Thank you." Dixie curtsied. "Tabby and I did it this afternoon."

"We had to get the bride off the staircase," Tabby explained.

"Thank you for offering to help," Mitzi said.

"I understand y'all've only been in the house a few months. Graham and the girls had been in their place since they were born. Makes a big difference. I brought Daddy's old truck. Where do we start?" Alice asked.

"Fantastic!" Paula said. "If we can get the big furniture out tonight, we can go finish up the small stuff in Mitzi's van tomorrow. And I'll add my thanks to Mitzi's."

"Me, too," Jody chimed in.

"That's what neighbors are for. Now if you ladies will lead the way, we'll get this job done before dark." Graham started for the door.

"We're all parked out back. The house is located just east of town." Mitzi wished he'd at least have said *friends* instead of *neighbors*.

"Out in the old Flynn place, right?" Alice asked.

"That's right," Paula answered.

"Then we'll meet you out there. Opal Flynn was a good friend of my mama's. We used to go out there on Sunday afternoons when Graham and I were kids." Alice followed her brother and the girls out the front door.

By the time Mitzi locked up behind them and reached her van, both Jody's truck and Paula's car were already gone. She was about to open the door when her father pulled in beside her and rolled down the window.

"I'm ready to help. I stopped by the store and got us some boxes," he said.

Mitzi leaned her forearms on the open window. "The house is pretty crowded with Jody moving in with us."

"I figured it would be," Harry said. "There's a lot of room upstairs in this old place. Seems like a smart idea for y'all to live up there. Be right handy in the winter if it gets icy."

Mitzi hadn't even thought of that, but it made good sense. Getting a baby out in bad weather would be asking for trouble. "Guess we'd better be going. The rest of the moving crew is probably already out there."

"Rest?" Harry raised a gray eyebrow.

"Graham and his girls and his sister are all helping," she answered.

"Right neighborly of them. See you there." The window started up as soon as she took a step back.

Neighborly.

There was that word again. Paula would say that it was an omen to help her realize exactly where she stood with Graham, but how could she control that crazy feeling in her heart every time he was around? So much for the rose quartz stone in Mitzi's bra.

She arrived at the house and held the door open for Graham as he and Alice carried Paula's mattress outside. His arm brushed against Mitzi's on the way through the door, and her pulse jacked up a few notches.

Neighbor, my ass! she thought. *I feel more than that, but I'll just have to get over it.*

Harry and Fanny Lou arrived right behind her. Two hours later there wasn't so much as a dust bunny left in the house. Mitzi had stayed behind to vacuum after everyone else had left. She finished the job and then sat down on the living room floor to catch her breath.

It had been a total whirlwind of a weekend. Last Friday everything had been pretty normal; then Saturday, Jody's world came crashing down around her; and now here it was Monday, and they'd moved to the shop. Mitzi had never been real good with change, and so much was happening so fast. In another three months, they'd have a baby in the shop, too.

"God, grant me the serenity . . ." She couldn't remember the rest of the prayer, so she stood up and said, "And all that other stuff." She carried the vacuum out to the van and headed back into Celeste just as the sun sank over the far horizon and dusk settled on East Texas.

"I can't believe we got this done in one evening." Jody was carrying in boxes from her truck when Mitzi arrived at the shop. "We've only got a couple more left, and we've decided to go to the café for some supper. We should treat all these good folks."

"You're right," Mitzi agreed. "If we'd only had one truck, we'd have been there past midnight tonight and we'd have to go back again tomorrow."

"I'm starving," Tabby said as she and Dixie jogged from the back porch. "We'll be glad to help unpack tomorrow. We're real good at setting up a kitchen. Aunt Alice taught us how when we moved into our house. Coffee mugs above the pot. Glasses to the right of the sink."

"See y'all in the house. I'm not going to stand here and talk while I'm holding boxes," Jody said.

"I'll open the door for you." Dixie ran on ahead.

"Thank you girls for offering, and yes, we'd love to have you help with unpacking." Mitzi stacked one box on top of the other and headed toward the house.

"I'll go tell everyone that we're done for today. Mr. Harry and Daddy are setting up the last of the beds right now. Why doesn't Jody have one?" Tabby followed behind her with the vacuum in her hands.

"Because we haven't bought one for her, but we will. Tonight will be the last time she has to sleep on the sofa," Mitzi answered. "She only moved in with us over the weekend."

"We heard y'all talkin' about it, but we weren't eavesdropping, we promise. That man should be tortured."

"Oh, he will be," Mitzi chuckled. "Fate will bite him right on the butt."

"I hope so. Jody is too sweet to be treated like trash."

Jody was on the phone when they put their load down in the kitchen. "I'm calling the café and telling them to get a table ready for nine."

"Great. I'm going to run up and see what they've got done." Mitzi was halfway up the stairs when she met Graham coming down. Two big people passing in a narrow space left no room to do it without touching. She could almost count his thick eyelashes through the lenses of his glasses that had slid down slightly on his nose. His hand grazed her bare arm as he reached to push them up. Her shiver had nothing to do with the cool air flowing from the air conditioner vent right above her.

"I understand we're all going to the café for supper?"

He was close enough that his breath reached to that soft spot on her neck, creating even more moisture on her palms. She caught a reflection of herself in his glasses and bit back a gasp. She'd sweated off every drop of makeup. Stray red hair had escaped her ponytail. Good Lord! Had her deodorant failed her, too?

She forced a smile. "My treat for all the help."

"You might regret that. We're not a bit bashful when it comes to food." He grinned.

"Neither are any of us. We'll just hope that the café doesn't run out," she teased.

He laid a hand on her shoulder. "Thank you again for taking my girls under your wing. I've never seen them this happy."

"Thank you for letting them take *me* under their wing," she said. "They're proving to be great help, but I wish you'd let me pay them."

"Let's keep it simple. You teach them to sew, and they can do whatever you need done to help out around here." He moved his hand and headed on down the stairs.

She didn't touch the warm spot on her shoulder, but she sure wanted to. She took the rest of the stairs two at a time and peeked into each room. Dressers and chests of drawers were in place, and beds were put together and ready for making up. Even the spare mattress was on the sofa in the living room.

Paula came into the room behind her and said, "Never would have guessed that only yesterday we got this idea. Wish that wedding dresses went together so fast. And"—she wiped a tear away—"I'm getting excited about the baby now. This was the right decision. I can't wait for us to start decorating the nursery."

"Me, either, but I've got a confession—I'm jealous," Mitzi said.

"Well, I got to admit that your dad would be a helluva lot better with you being a single mother than my mama is going to be. I might be shunned like Jody has been all these years," Paula said.

"It's really not so bad when you consider the alternative of having to put up with her." Jody joined them. "The café will have our table ready when we get there."

Mitzi draped an arm around Paula's shoulders. "Jody is right. Just think of all the extra little things like changing light bulbs and watering plants that you've been doing for Gladys. She's going to miss that, but it'll give you more time and less stress."

Jody nodded and headed back down the stairs. "Amen to all that, but I call first dibs on getting to rock the baby to sleep. Have you thought of names?"

"No, but we can do that later." Paula lowered her voice. "Has the rose quartz worked any magic for you, Mitzi?"

"No. Maybe. I don't know." Mitzi laid a hand on her chest.

"Don't give up. Sometimes it takes a while," Paula said. "Right now, we need to pay our helpers by buying them supper." Paula turned around and started down the stairs with Mitzi right behind her. "I go for another ultrasound on Thursday. If the baby is cooperative, we could have a gender-reveal party on Friday night. And I know what you're thinkin' without even looking at you. I'll tell my mother right after my visit for the ultrasound, when I know whether the baby is a girl or boy. I've put it off long enough."

"Want me to go with you when you do?" Mitzi felt both sorry and happy for Paula: sorry that she had an unsupportive mother and happy that she was going to bring a baby into their family circle. The three of them had been friends for so long they were family whether DNA agreed with them or not.

Paula turned at the bottom of the staircase. "Yes, and Jody, too. I'll need all the help I can get."

The table was ready when they arrived at the café. When everyone sat down, Mitzi found herself between Graham and Alice. Jody, right across from her, raised an eyebrow. Mitzi didn't need a book to know what was on her mind.

The waitress hurried right over to them with her pad in hand. "What can I get y'all to drink? I hate to tell you, but we only do the grill after eight."

"That's fine," Harry said. "We've kind of got our hearts set on your bacon cheeseburger baskets, or at least I have. And a cup of coffee."

"Yes," the rest of the group chimed in.

"Only sweet tea for me," Paula said.

The others raised their hands to indicate the same.

"Daddy, when did you start drinking coffee this late?" Mitzi asked.

"When I figured out that it doesn't keep me awake like your mama thought it did," he answered. "How about you, Graham? You a late-night coffee drinker?"

"No, sir," Graham said. "Anything after five keeps me up all night. Crazy thing is that sweet tea doesn't and it's got caffeine, too, so go figure."

Mitzi filed that bit of information away in her head. Someday she might need to remember that he liked sweet tea but didn't drink coffee after five.

Chapter Eight

We could sure use that bridal fair to come through," Mitzi said as she worked on Ellie Mae's dress. "I bet we'd be the only plus-sized display there. Word-of-mouth advertising is great, but this would really give us a boost."

"We might have to burn a little midnight oil or hire an extra person if we get much more work," Jody said.

"Wouldn't that be amazing?" Paula said.

Dixie poked her head in and asked, "Where do y'all want us to take the flowers now that the kitchen is going to be used for real?"

"There's a couple of empty rooms upstairs. We've got plans for the larger of the two, but you girls can move the flower business into the smaller one. I'll get bins this weekend so you can keep them sorted by color. Daddy said he'd bring the sewing machines and a folding table on Friday. That way you'll have a place to work with whatever project you've got going," Mitzi answered.

Dixie's hand went to her cheek. "We get our own room in your house! That's like totally awesome."

Tabby crossed the room and wrapped her arms around Mitzi's neck. "Thank you. Thank you."

"You are very welcome." Mitzi hugged her back. "For now you can just sort the flowers in the empty boxes from unpacking."

Jody chuckled when they'd left. "They're worth their weight in gold. All of us should've gotten pregnant in high school so we'd have kids about that age."

"And mothers in the insane asylum," Paula laughed.

"Not a bad idea some days." Jody laughed with her, but her expression changed when her phone rang. "Speak of the devil." She put it on speaker and kept sewing beads on a veil. "Hello, Mama."

"I heard that you and Paula moved into the upstairs of that house y'all bought for a shop, and that Mitzi is living with Graham Harrison. I'm glad her mama has done passed and don't know that her daughter ain't no better than mine," Wanda said.

"You are on speakerphone," Jody said.

"Good. I ain't sayin' nothing I wouldn't say in church. It's a cryin' shame the way young people today just live together without a marriage license. Society might accept such things, but I don't." Wanda's voice got higher with each word.

"I assure you, ma'am, I'm not living with Graham," Mitzi said in a tight voice. "Paula and I talked about moving in here when we bought the place, but we wanted to keep work and our private lives separate."

"What changed your mind? Graham Harrison living just down the road?" Wanda asked.

"Space changed our minds," Jody said. "And finances. We don't have to pay rent here, and besides, after the way you've treated me, I don't owe you an explanation."

"I treated *you*?" Wanda screamed. "You disgraced me by living with Lyle. Now look where that got you. I called to invite you to supper Friday night, but after that comment I'm not going to. Goodbye!"

Jody tapped the phone screen and left it lying on the table. "Well, ain't that nice."

Paula frowned.

Mitzi reminded her that was the punch line from an old joke where a country girl told her rich city cousin that her husband had sent her to finishing school to say "Ain't that nice" rather than "Screw you!"

Paula remembered the joke and giggled. It soon turned into laughter and a guffaw that had her snorting. Then Mitzi and Jody joined in, and the twins came in from the kitchen.

"What's so funny?" Dixie asked.

"Mothers," Paula said.

Tabby raised a hand. "Testify, ladies."

That set everyone off on another bout of laughter. When Paula snorted again, Dixie got tickled, and soon all five of them were wiping tears.

"Our mother ain't funny," Dixie finally said.

"No, she's downright crazy." Tabby nodded.

"Join the crowd." Jody took another tissue from the box and then tossed the whole box toward Tabby.

"Oh, yeah," Paula said.

"What about you, Mitzi?"

"Her mama was a saint," Paula said. "She loved Mitzi just the way she is, took up for her when anyone said a word about her size, and told her every day that she was beautiful. Me and Jody weren't so lucky."

Dixie pulled out a chair and sat down. "Or us. We figure our mama knew when we were only a year old that we weren't going to be petite little blondes like her, so she left."

Tabby leaned on the back of her sister's chair. "Of course, there was the old boyfriend who came back into the picture. Daddy doesn't know that we know about him, but we figured it all out. She left us before our second birthday and was remarried within three months to the guy she dated before Daddy. It don't take a genius to do that math."

"Three months?" Jody gasped. "The divorce wouldn't have been final."

Dixie frowned. "They got married in Arkansas. We didn't even see her again until last year."

"And then we felt like she was ashamed of us," Tabby said.

Mitzi could have strangled Rita and enjoyed watching her turn blue. Gladys and Wanda were both a piece of work, but to leave your children and let them think it was because they were big girls—that should be a cardinal, go-to-hell sin.

"Well, darlin's, we love you just the way you are," Jody said. "Don't ever change to suit someone else's vision of what they want you to be. I tried that and it don't work. I was just about your size when I started living with Lyle. I'd just gotten out of high school, and I'd been a big girl my whole life. But he wanted me to be slim, and he insisted that we be vegetarians and grow our own food like hippies. So I did and look what it got me."

"We heard that he told you on the phone he'd done married someone else. What kind of man does that and why?" Dixie asked.

"Because his girlfriend is pregnant." Jody's tone was icy cold.

Dixie moved over to Jody's chair and hugged her. "My daddy knows just how that feels, except Mother wasn't pregnant. She didn't ever have any more kids, thank goodness."

"So you never want any little half brothers or sisters?" Mitzi asked.

"Not from Mother. She'd probably want us to come live with her so she'd have live-in babysitters. We used to wish Daddy would remarry so we could have a brother or sister because we love babies, but not from our mother. That would be a nightmare," Dixie said.

Tabby barely gave her sister time to finish the sentence. "But he works all the time anyway, and never has time for dating."

"Whoa!" Dixie said. "He dated that one woman for a year."

"And we hated her," Tabby reminded her. "We had to really work at making him see how mean she was when he wasn't around."

"Mean?" Mitzi knew she was fishing for information, but she couldn't help herself. If someone had hurt the girls physically, she might still go after them.

"We were only thirteen then," Dixie said. "She tried to boss us around and one time she even slapped Tabby."

"No!" Paula's hand went over her mouth.

"Yep, she did and said if we told Daddy that we'd get worse. We told him anyway, and we never saw her again," Tabby said. "But now we've got to get back to work. We want to get our room all organized before quittin' time today."

The business phone rang about the time they cleared the room, and Mitzi grabbed it, saying, "The Perfect Dress."

"Miz Taylor, please," a masculine voice said.

Mitzi crossed her fingers. "Speaking."

"This is Rayford Thompson. We spoke earlier about the Dallas Bridal Fair. Are you still interested?"

"Yes, sir, we are," she said.

"We have an opening if you want to join us on June fifteenth. It's an all-day affair. If you're having someone model for our red-carpet show that evening, it costs a little more, but the prices will all be on the form I can send you."

"We'd love to take that spot and yes on modeling the dress." Mitzi was already picturing one of the twins in Paula's sister's wedding dress.

"I'll send you the link to the form. You fill it out and pay at that time," Rayford said. "It will have all the information about setting up and the day's schedule included, along with the dimensions of your space. Thank you, Miz Taylor. We're glad you can join us."

"Thank you." Mitzi tried to keep her cool, but she wanted to jump up and down like a little kid at Christmas. As soon as she hung up, she whipped around and practically yelled, "We're going to the Dallas summer bridal fair. And we've been invited to put a model on the runway."

"Holy smokin' hell." Jody's eyes grew bigger and bigger. "I can't model it for sure, not now. Give me a year to get my weight back up, and if we get to go next year, I'll do it."

"Well, I dang sure can't. I'm pregnant, and besides, that dress is a sixteen. I haven't seen that size since I was in junior high," Paula said.

"Me, either, but one of the twins would fit into it perfectly," Mitzi said.

"Fit into what?" Dixie asked.

"That wedding dress out there. We got our invitation to the Dallas Bridal Fair." Mitzi thought about pinching herself to see if she was dreaming, then she thought of the rose quartz in her bra. Did it bring good luck as well as love? If so, she might keep it next to her skin forever.

"Tabby can do it. I'm too clumsy. But I want to go and help. Maybe even make a few corsages to take along?"

"I can do what?" Tabby wandered into the room. "Y'all got so loud. What's going on in here?"

Dixie gave her a short version of the story.

"Oh. My. Gosh! Am I dreaming? I really get to walk on a runway. I've got to practice my pivot."

"You'll have to ask your dad before we set anything in stone," Mitzi said.

"He'll say yes. I know he will," Dixie said. "And he'll probably even come so he can see us."

"He's a pretty good father, isn't he?" Mitzi said.

"The best," Dixie said.

Chapter Nine

Jody put the final pin in the lace around the edge of a chapel-length veil and laid it to the side. "I wish I'd been more like Dixie and Tabby when I was fifteen. When I was that age, I'd just entered the rebellious stage. Lyle and I'd started having sex, and we thought we knew everything. I wish I'd known then what I know now. To see them this excited about the bridal show is . . ." She searched for the right words. "It's the way I wish I would have been, but then no one ever took much interest in me, other than when I was allowed to come visit at your house, Mitzi. I used to wish your mama and daddy belonged to me."

"I wasn't as focused as they are when I was twenty-five." Paula finished basting two long pieces of skirt together and stuck the needle into a pincushion. "It is something else to see two fifteen-year-old girls so excited about everything, including the bridal show."

"Don't put them up too high on a pedestal." Mitzi gathered elastic through a blue-satin wedding garter.

"Why? They've kind of earned their position on it." Jody's thoughts slipped back more than half a lifetime before. The summer she was fifteen and, according to her mother's standards, too young to date, she'd snuck out the bedroom window and met Lyle at the park every chance she got. They were young and stupid, and no one, not even adults, could tell them how to live their lives.

"Because it will be painful when one of them does something stupid and falls off their pedestal," Mitzi said.

Jody was so far into her own thoughts that she didn't hear what Mitzi had said.

"Earth to Jody," Mitzi teased. "You looked like you were a million miles away."

"I was," Jody admitted. "Do you think it was because we weren't skinny that our self-esteem was low when we were Dixie and Tabby's age?"

"No, it was because two of us had dysfunctional families," Paula answered. "We weren't the only big girls in Celeste schools."

"Yes, but we were the only ones in our class," Mitzi reminded them. "Twelve boys. Ten girls. The biggest of the other seven girls was a size six. And every family is dysfunctional. It just matters to what degree."

"Not yours," Paula said. "Your dad is a sweetheart."

"Yes, he is." Mitzi stood up and rolled the kinks from her neck. "And my mama would've fought an army for me using only a kitchen butter knife, but she could manipulate the devil into letting her set up a snow-cone stand in hell. And Lord, don't even get me started on the guilt trips she could lay on a person."

"You didn't have to live with an ultrareligious mama who made you pray twice a day on your knees for thirty minutes," Jody said.

"Or parents who argued constantly over Mama's hypochondria and Daddy's superstitions," Paula added.

"Like I said, there's no such thing as a perfect family. But don't get me wrong, I wouldn't take a million bucks for my family." Mitzi started out of the room. "It's break time, and since I didn't take time for breakfast, I'm warming up a sausage biscuit. Y'all want one?"

Jody was on her feet in a second. "Yes, and thank you. I'd forgotten how good meat tasted. I may have two. Do we have grape jelly? And we are going to have to lay aside that vow we made about closing shop at five o'clock. Some folks take a whole year to get ready for a bridal fair, and we've only got a little while. We need to make a really good impression, and get our name on the list for next year."

"Grape jelly is in the fridge." Paula pushed back her chair. "Living in the house does have benefits. Like sleeping a little longer and real food in the office fridge. And you are right about burning a little late-night oil. This bridal fair is huge, and for us to get to show off our plus-sized idea? Well, darlin's, that's out of this world."

"On another note, thinking of cooking in here, we should put one of those wax-burning candle things in the foyer. Maybe one that smells like roses or vanilla. Some food smells just don't say that you're in a bridal shop," Jody suggested.

"Great idea," Mitzi said. "Ellie Mae sells those. When she comes in for her next fitting, I'll order a couple. Maybe one for the fitting room, too. Wonder if they have a cute one that looks like a wedding cake?"

Jody took five sausage biscuits from the freezer and popped them into the microwave. "Wedding cakes make me think of the bridal fair. I wonder if Graham is going to let Tabby model for us, and are we buying, renting, or talking Harry into building an arch for us?" Her thoughts went back to the idea of a wedding and children. When she found closure, would she ever trust a man again?

"I hope so. That dress should fit her perfectly. She's even the same height as Selena, so we won't have to shorten it." The oven dinged and Mitzi removed the food. "Now that we're moved in and settling down, how are you, Jody? We've been so busy that it seems like months instead of days since Lyle left."

"I got up real early this morning and drove out to the place. That sumbitch dragged the trailer out right over my garden, so there'll be no fresh vegetables. All that's left out there is a couple of beat-up old lawn chairs. I sat down in one and cried like a baby." Jody choked up but refused to shed another tear. "Lyle was my life. I gave him my heart, my soul, and my virginity when I was fifteen. Not even steaks and sausage can heal the pain."

Paula hugged her tightly. "You should've woken us. We would have gone with you."

"I needed to do it all alone," Jody said and then jumped back a few inches at a sharp nudge from Paula's stomach. "The baby just kicked me."

Paula laid a hand on the spot. "It's been really active lately. I just hope it's willing to let me know today if it's a boy or girl so our little party can be a gender reveal. In some ways I envy those girls who have a baby bump. I just feel fatter than usual."

"How much weight have you gained?" Mitzi asked.

"Fifteen pounds. The doctor says that twenty should be my limit," Paula answered.

"Getting to feel the baby kick like that made it real," Jody said. "Are you sure you're not going to tell the father? He's missing so much."

How quick would you tell Lyle if you find out you're pregnant? the pesky voice in her head asked.

Jody shook her head to push the voice away. *I might even tell him that it didn't belong to him.*

Paula picked up one of the biscuits. "I'm positive. He's experiencing it with his wife, and I don't want to share other than with y'all. It might be selfish, but he lied to me about his marriage. Mama's right about at least one thing that she preaches all the time. Every choice has consequences. Mine is this baby for having sex with a guy without checking out his story. His is that he'll never know he has this child because he lied to me."

"I'd feel the same way—my mama said that same thing so often that I felt like it was branded on my brain." Mitzi opened her biscuit, added grape jelly to it, and then passed the spoon and jar over to Jody.

"Mine, too, only she had it cross-stitched on a pillow she insisted on keeping in my bedroom," Jody said. "Maybe I should've paid more attention to that pillow, but I never thought Lyle could do something like this."

"We were both pretty gullible," Paula said. "It just took you years to figure it out. I didn't get but a few months."

"Count it as a blessing." Jody finished off her first biscuit and unwrapped the second one. "I didn't know how much I missed having meat in my diet. I wonder if the new wife is vegetarian."

"I hope that she eats meat six times a day and she makes him cook it," Mitzi said. "Whatever made y'all decide to go vegetarian anyway?"

"Lyle wanted us to live off the land," Jody explained. "We didn't abuse our bodies with liquor or with tobacco, and we didn't eat anything that had a face. I loved him enough that I went along with it. Truth is, I was so tickled to have a boyfriend in high school and to move in with him that I would have stood on my head in hot ashes to please him."

"Well, I supported you and the way you wanted to live, but if I had to give up my double-bacon cheeseburgers, I could get real bitchy real fast," Paula said.

"Are we tellin' your mama tonight?" Mitzi asked. "And when are you tellin' Selena?"

"Might as well get it over with," Paula said. "My appointment is at four thirty and it's only for the ultrasound, so it won't take long. Why don't y'all close up shop and then meet me at her place? I think I'll call Selena and have her meet us there. That way I can kill two birds with one stone. Then we'll celebrate."

"Celebrate what? That we know if it's a boy or girl or that we were there when you told your mama?" Jody asked.

"Both," Paula replied. "Will y'all please be my birthing coaches? Classes start in a few weeks."

"Of course," Jody and Mitzi answered at the same time.

"What do you really want this baby to be? A boy or a girl?" Jody asked.

"I'm not saying because I'm afraid I'll jinx it," Paula said. "I know nothing about boys and very little about raising a child at all, so I suppose I should say the old thing about 'as long as it's healthy,' but in my heart I really want . . ." She hesitated. "I can't say it out loud. What if I say a boy and it's a girl, and somehow she hears that I said that when she's about fifteen and thinks I didn't want her at all? Or if I say I want a girl, and it's a boy and he does the same?"

"Whatever it is, we'll learn as we go," Mitzi said.

"Yes, we will," Jody agreed.

$$\sim$$

Paula was the only one in the ultrasound waiting room that afternoon until Ellie Mae came in. Heat started on Paula's neck and crept around to her cheeks. She tried not to look at Ellie Mae, but there were only so many ceiling and floor tiles that she could study.

Ellie Mae finally broke the awkward silence. "Guess we've both got a little secret, unless you're here with Jody."

"What makes you think that Jody is pregnant?" Paula asked.

"That's the gossip around town. That Lyle left her because she's been cheating on him and got herself pregnant," Ellie Mae answered.

Paula lowered her chin, inhaled deeply, and let it out slowly. "Lyle left her because *he* was cheating and his baby mama is also practically a baby. He's probably the one spreading that rumor to cover his own guilt."

"Sorry bastard," Ellie Mae muttered. "Then it must be you. When are you getting married?"

"I'm not. Is this your first ultrasound?"

Ellie Mae nodded. "Yes, and no one knows about the baby except me and Darrin. So please, please keep my secret. My mama is going to stroke out over the wedding dress. If she knew I was pregnant, she'd lay down and die from the embarrassment. So why aren't you getting married?"

"I don't want to marry the guy. I found out that he's as big a bastard as Lyle," Paula answered. "When are you due?"

"The end of October. Being a big girl does have its advantages, doesn't it? We don't look like we've swallowed a watermelon," Ellie Mae said. "How about you?"

"First of September. I'll keep your secret if you keep mine," Paula said.

"You got a deal. When are you tellin' your mama?" Ellie Mae asked.

"Tonight," Paula answered.

Ellie Mae chuckled. "Looks like I get the best end of the deal. We're not tellin' anyone until we get home from the honeymoon. Honeymoon babies cook fast!"

A lady in green scrubs opened a door and said, "Paula, are you ready?"

"Yes, ma'am." She got up and patted Ellie Mae on the shoulder. "Hope you find out that it's what you want it to be."

"Me, too. And thanks for keeping my secret." Ellie Mae ducked her head as if she were embarrassed to even say that. "If you want to tell Jody and Mitzi, it's okay. I trust them. And I'll need the dress to expand."

"Thank you." Paula picked up her purse and waved over her shoulder.

"Right in here. You've already had this done once, so you know the drill," the lady said. "Do you still want to know the gender?"

"Yes, I do." Paula was so nervous that she didn't recognize the woman until she was on the table and saw her name tag. "Hey, you did this last time, didn't you?"

"Yes, ma'am, I did," Rachel said. "And he or she was not very cooperative."

Paula got onto the examination table and pulled her pants down below her belly and her shirt up to her breasts. Rachel tucked blue paper into the band of Paula's pants and then squirted gel across her tummy. "Got a good strong heartbeat. Would you look at that?"

Paula turned her head to the monitor to find her baby lying in a position that left no doubt about the gender. Tears flooded her eyes. Finally, she was getting what she'd prayed for and wanted so badly.

"Well, there's no doubt now, is there?" Rachel handed her a tissue. "Why are you crying? Are you disappointed? Looks like you're going to have a healthy baby."

"They're tears of pure joy," Paula said.

She was glad that Ellie Mae was gone from the waiting room when she left. As nosy as she was, Ellie Mae would have wanted to know the gender, and Paula wanted to hold that secret awhile longer. She craved a big waffle cone of soft ice cream, but butterflies were having a party in her stomach. Once she'd told her mother the news, she'd have something to eat.

She drove from Greenville to Celeste slowly. She'd gotten finished earlier than she'd thought she would, so the girls wouldn't have had time to drive to her mother's place just yet. To keep her mind off the fit Gladys was going to throw, she thought about the dilemma that Jody was in. Paula had never had to go through that time of wondering if she was pregnant or not. She'd never had regular periods and had taken the pill to regulate her cycle. Even that didn't work most of the time, and she'd gotten the news sprung on her when she went in for her yearly physical.

Thinking that she should buy Jody a pregnancy test, she almost stopped at Walmart but decided against it. Maybe Jody wouldn't even need it. After all, she and Lyle had had sex only once in the past month. That sorry bastard Lyle should be shot.

Chapter Ten

With trembling hands, Jody pulled the pregnancy test out of its box. She'd bought one of the most expensive—one that promised a true reading as early as two weeks after conception. Tomorrow was the actual day for her period and she was usually regular, but she'd been under a lot of stress. Following the directions to the letter, she did what it said and then laid the stick on the counter.

Her chest tightened, making it hard to breathe. She watched the time tick away on her phone. She couldn't look at the results. If she was pregnant, she'd rather let everyone believe that she really was having an affair like Lyle had said. The shame would be on her, and her baby wouldn't have to grow up in the shadow of Kennedy's.

Finally, she inhaled and looked at the test. Exhaling loudly, she looked up at the ceiling. "Thank you, God."

When she returned to the sewing room, she found Mitzi putting the last touches on Ellie Mae's hat. "I just took a pregnancy test," Jody whispered. "It was negative."

Mitzi laid the hat aside. "Don't you have to wait ten days after a missed period?"

"I got one of those fast ones. It's been close to a month since Lyle and I had sex, so I figured it would show, and it's negative."

"How do you feel about that? Are you a little disappointed?"

"Not one bit." Jody shook her head. "The way Lyle's gone all paternal, he would insist on visitation rights. Can you see little miss Kennedy having to care for two babies? Who do you think would get the better care? And as they got older, who would be shoved into the shadows?"

"I think I understand Paula not wanting to share with Clinton a little better. Her baby would be the same as what you said," Mitzi said.

"Besides"—Jody shivered—"I'd hate to tell my mama. Gladys is going to throw one big hissy fit."

"That's why we're going with Paula. Growing up, I had no idea that y'all's mamas treated you the way they did. I didn't even think about the fact that we always spent time at my house and never at one of y'all's." Mitzi's eyes rolled up toward the twelve-foot ceiling. "You ever wonder what kind of stories the walls of a house would tell if they could talk?"

"My mama's house would shock most people in town." Jody picked up her needle and started basting a bodice together. "Everyone thinks she's so godly, but . . ." She glanced over to find Mitzi staring off into space without blinking.

"Are you sleeping with your eyes open?" Jody giggled.

"What? I'm sorry. I was thinking about this house. Remember when we were kids and Miz Ellen entertained us in this room? What were you saying?" Mitzi asked.

"I always loved coming here for that Sunday School Christmas party she hosted." Jody remembered that sweet old lady's floral perfume and the sugar cookies that she served them about once a month.

"Ever wonder what really went on in this house before she died and we bought it?" Mitzi asked.

"The hallway would probably recite Bible verses to us. And I'd be willing to bet that the pregnancy test in the bathroom trash can is the first one these old walls have ever seen," Jody giggled. "Paula should be getting her ultrasound about right now. Want to make a bet on whether it's a boy or girl?" Jody finished the basting job. She picked up a bead with a pair of tweezers, dipped it into a small cup of fabric glue, and laid it on a veil that she'd started working on.

"Which would you want if you were pregnant?" Mitzi asked.

"A girl," Jody said without hesitation. "I wouldn't want to be a boy's mama if he treated a woman like Lyle has treated me. I'd think I'd failed at teaching him how to behave. If I had either one, no matter what the circumstances, I'd never make the child feel unwanted."

"We'll all make sure Paula's baby doesn't feel like that," Mitzi said.

"What was that about a baby?" Fanny Lou breezed into the sewing room and sat down in Paula's chair. She removed a straw hat with a wide brim and laid it on the table. That day she wore a T-shirt with Minnie Mouse on the front, faded jean shorts that barely reached her bony knees, and cowboy boots. "Thank God for air-conditioning. Lord, it's hot out there. If it feels like this in June, it'll only be three degrees cooler than hell when July and August get here."

"We're tellin' Gladys and Selena tonight, so you can't tell anyone until after that, but Paula is pregnant. She's getting an ultrasound today and hopefully we'll know if it's a boy or girl," Mitzi said.

"Who's the father and when's the wedding?" her granny asked.

"The relationship was over before she found out she was pregnant. So there's not going to be a wedding," Jody answered. "Smart girl if you ask me. Want a glass of iced tea?"

"Gladys is going to have a pure old southern hissy fit, and Selena won't be far behind her. Thank you for the offer, but I'd rather have an icy cold beer." Fanny Lou picked up her hat and fanned herself with it.

Jody pushed back her chair and headed for the kitchen. "Don't say anything until I get back."

Full silence tracked Jody to and from the kitchen until she returned with a long-neck bottle of Fanny Lou's favorite brand and handed it to her.

"Thank you, darlin'. Maybe this will keep me from dyin' of a heatstroke. Old women like me shouldn't get out when it's pushin' a hundred degrees, but I get bored. Besides, I just love to come visit with y'all. It makes up for all the time when y'all weren't here in town." Fanny Lou laid her hat back down and took a long draw from the bottle. "Now back to Gladys. She's always been a hypochondriac. It got worse when she got pregnant with Paula. Selena was about four years old, and Gladys didn't want another child."

"So we were both unwanted?" Jody asked.

"Wish I could tell you different, but I can't," Fanny Lou answered.

"I'm shocked that you aren't even surprised about Paula being pregnant," Mitzi said.

"Nothing surprises me anymore." Fanny Lou turned up the bottle again. "So what else is new around here?"

"We're having a little dessert party tomorrow night that can also be a gender-reveal party if Paula finds out the sex of the baby. You'll come, won't you?" Mitzi said.

"I'll have the bakery make a cake. Maybe pink on one side and blue on the other," Fanny Lou said.

"If I told you I was pregnant, too, would it knock your socks off?" Mitzi joked.

"Nope, but I would tell you not to name the baby Francine and call her Fanny. I never have liked my name," she answered. "Are you expecting? And if you are, who's the father?"

"No, I'm not." Mitzi grinned. "But I am jealous of Paula because I've always wanted a house full of children."

"Well, I can tell you right now, I'm not a bit jealous of Paula. I wouldn't mind having kids, but at this point, I damn sure don't want Lyle to be the father," Jody said with conviction. She felt like she'd dodged a bullet when that test turned up negative.

"I agree with you," Fanny Lou said. "If you want kids, Mitzi, you might be thinking about a serious relationship. You'll be thirty-two in less than a month, so you're getting a late start."

"Not in today's world," Mitzi said. "Thirty is the new twenty."

"Bull crap," Fanny Lou said. "Society changes, but women's bodies don't. After thirty that little nest of eggs you got inside you begins to shrivel up. So if you want a lot of kids, you'd better marry a man who's already got a few to give you a head start, and then have one every two years until there ain't no more eggs."

Jody could practically hear her biological clock ticking. "Lots of women don't have babies until they're in their thirties, nowadays."

"Ah, Granny, us big girls provide more warmth for that little nest of eggs than skinny girls," Mitzi laughed.

"Hey, now," Jody scolded.

"Honey, you're a plus-sized girl trapped in a skinny girl's body. You'll break free of that cage in a year or so," Mitzi told her.

Jody giggled. "I hope so. I liked me better when I was a little bigger."

"I should be going," Fanny Lou said. "I'm meeting my book club at the café at five. I'll see y'all when it's over." Fanny Lou's knees popped when she stood up. "Gettin' old ain't for sissies, girls. Only the strong get to do it."

"We're not planning to start until seven, so that works great, and you are not old." Mitzi gave her grandmother a hug. "You'll still be drivin' that old truck out there and helping run this town when you're a hundred."

"I hope so, darlin'." Fanny Lou picked up her hat and shoved it down on her head.

When they heard the back door shut, Jody whispered, "Is she really going to her book club dressed like that? Where does she shop anyway?"

"Garage sales. Goodwill. Thrift stores. Last time she was in a real dress shop was at my dad's cousin's wedding. She fussed about the price of the outfit for a full year. But then she redid her will to say that she would be buried in it," Mitzi laughed.

"Good Lord!" Jody gasped as she got up and moved toward the foyer. "She's a hoot. You're so lucky to have her in your life, Mitzi."

"I know it," Mitzi said. "When my mother died, I couldn't have gotten through it without her. It was tough on her, losing her only child, and at the time I thought I was helping her. She stepped into the mother role without me even realizing that she was the one doing the heavy lifting when it came to grief."

"That's the way it should be." Jody nodded. "I've decided that I can choose not to be like my mother. Someday I do want a baby, just not right now. I was so glad to see that negative sign I almost squealed. Does that make a lick of sense?"

"It does to me," Mitzi said.

Jody followed Mitzi's eyes to the clock. "It's quittin' time. I'm getting nervous about dealing with Gladys and Selena, aren't you?"

"Yeah, but Paula needs us," Mitzi answered.

Before Jody could agree, the twins popped into the room. "Guess what, we got our room all fixed and the table is ready for our sewing machines. Do you think maybe we could get them tomorrow? We can't wait to get started."

Dixie went straight to the veil Jody had been working on. "That's gorgeous. Whoever is wearing it should keep it for their daughters and granddaughters. When I get married, I'm going to wear my Granny Harrison's veil. Grandpa said I could before he died last year."

Tabby laid a hand on her sister's shoulder. "Grandpa was our hero. I can't remember when he wasn't there for us. That house where he lived—this might sound crazy, but sometimes we can still feel him when we go there. He was the one who told us if anyone bullied us, we should take a step forward and knock the hell out of them. I'm glad I did because it brought us here."

"We're glad you're here, too," Jody said.

"Hey, I've got an idea about the bridal fair. We could bring Granny's veil. Y'all didn't make it, but it could be a prop," Dixie said.

"If your dad doesn't mind, you could sure let us look at it," Mitzi said. "It might give us an idea for a veil if someone asked for a vintage wedding dress. And I wanted to ask you—"

"Hey, do I have some pretty girls hidin' in this place?" Graham's deep drawl floated down the foyer.

Mitzi and Jody both followed the girls to the foyer. Jody stood back just a little and watched the expressions on all of them.

"Mitzi's got something to ask us." Dixie beamed as if the idea of Mitzi having something special up her sleeve truly tickled her.

"Oh?" Graham winked slyly at Mitzi, but it didn't escape Jody's watchful eyes.

"I hope it's not that the bridal fair has been canceled." Tabby's eyes filled with tears. "I really want to wear that pretty dress and walk on the runway."

"Nothing like that. And thank you for letting the girls join us and letting Tabby model for us." Mitzi fidgeted with her hands, like she did when she was nervous.

"Couldn't say no to an opportunity like that. What's the news you've got for us?" Graham asked.

"We're having cake and ice cream tomorrow evening. Would you and the girls like to come?" Mitzi tucked her hands in the pockets of her capri pants.

"Love to. Can we bring anything?" Graham asked.

His eyes went all soft and dreamy when he looked at Mitzi. Her cheeks probably looked like she had too much blush. Could it be possible that there really was chemistry on both sides? Had this gone beyond a one-sided crush?

"Not a thing," Jody answered for Mitzi. "We've got it all covered."

"Well, then, let's go home, ladies. You can tell me all about your day while we have supper," Graham said. "Thanks for the invitation and we'll look forward to being here."

They'd barely made it out the door when Jody elbowed Mitzi. "You still like him, don't you?"

"Yes, I do, but a lot of good it'll do me. If he ever does get into a relationship, it'll be with a cute little thing like Rita," Mitzi said.

"Never say never," Jody warned. "Let's lock up and go over to Gladys's house. It might be the last time we ever see it standing, because after today, it might explode into flames."

"You got that right." Mitzi nodded.

⚬

When Paula turned the corner, Mitzi's van was already parked next to the curb, and there was Selena's little VW bug right behind it. Paula pulled in, ate a couple of antacids to calm her nervous stomach, and got out of the car. Maybe she should put this off until tomorrow or the next day, or after she'd had the baby.

Mitzi and Jody met her at the sidewalk leading up to the small-frame house with red roses climbing up the porch posts. Paula usually loved the sweet scent of the flowers, but on this day they almost gagged her.

Jody looped her arm in Paula's. "I'm not pregnant. I took a test today and it's negative."

"I almost stopped and bought a test for you. Glad I didn't." Paula dreaded going into the house. The outside always looked like something out of a gardening magazine, and there wouldn't be a spot of dust on the inside. But if it was true that the heart of a home was the mother, then the core of that place was rotten.

"You okay?" Mitzi asked.

"No, but I will be in a little while." Paula sat down on the porch swing. "I need just a minute. I used to sit here for five minutes when I came home from school to get settled before I went in the house, and I still do every time I come over here. That's Selena's new car out there.

115

Y'all know that she's always driven a small car, liked tiny jewelry rather than the big clunky stuff like I wear, and now she's all taken up with little dogs. She has a Chihuahua that she carries in her purse, so get ready for it."

"Maybe it makes her feel smaller than she is," Mitzi said.

"Probably," Paula agreed.

"Can't they hear us?" Jody whispered.

"No, they're watching television." Paula pulled a tissue from her purse and wiped sweat from her brow. She'd dreaded this moment for months, but it would all be over in the next few minutes. No doubt, she'd take a mental beatdown, but at least it would be done and finished.

"Do we know if the baby is a boy or girl?" Mitzi asked.

Paula nodded. "Not saying yet. Okay, I'm ready. Let's get it over with. Dammit! I turned thirty-two two months ago. Why do I feel like I'm a teenager coming in five minutes later than curfew?"

"Because you and I would give anything for our mothers to love us unconditionally. But, honey, it ain't goin' to happen." Jody opened the old screen door and knocked.

Paula pushed past her, turned the knob, and went right inside without waiting for her mother to yell at them to come in. "She doesn't get out of her chair except for meals and to go to the bathroom. It's us, Mama," she called out as all three of them made their way to the den at the back of the house.

"Selena is here, too." Gladys's voice sounded happy.

"I brought Mitzi and Jody, and we can only stay a little while." Paula didn't know what to do with her hands. She wanted to hold them over her stomach to protect her child from what was about to happen, but instead she dropped them to her sides.

"Oh." Gladys's tone changed instantly. "Well, y'all have a seat. I was hoping that you'd go to the drugstore for me before they close. Selena can't stay long. She has to get home and cook supper for her husband."

Gladys shot Paula a dirty look. "I don't guess you're ever going to need to go home and cook, are you?"

"Probably not," Paula said. "Hello, Selena."

"What's this big occasion?" Selena smiled. "Are you dating—better yet, are you engaged? We've been planning your wedding for the past half hour. I'd offer to let you wear my dress since that would get some use out of it other than dressing up a mannequin." Her brown eyes started at Paula's toes and traveled to her neck. "But then again, I'm so much smaller than you, it wouldn't be possible."

"I told Selena talking about you ever finding someone was just a pipe dream." Gladys's cold stare made Paula feel like a piece of trash.

Paula took a long look at her mother. One side of her chin-length gray hair was pulled back with a bobby pin. She wasn't a big woman, but then she wasn't a thin person, either. If someone put her in a crowd, there wasn't one feature that would make them take a second look. Too bad she'd been a churchgoing woman all her life, because she would have made an excellent bank robber.

She smiled at that idea, and Gladys shot a dirty look her way. Paula was never going to make her child feel guilty for having a good time or even for smiling. She'd grown up with negativity her whole life, but things were going to be different for her baby. It was going to come into the world with so much love, it would never feel like she did right then.

"What's so funny?" Gladys asked. "I'm an old woman who lives alone and has to beg her children to come see her a few minutes every so often."

"I was thinking about your pretty red roses." Paula knew better than to sit on the embroidered pillow in the rocking chair, so she laid it on the sofa before she sat down. The coffee table, the side tables beside every chair, and even the back of the sofa were covered in crocheted doilies of one size or another. And knickknacks ranging from clowns to angels were scattered everywhere. When she was a child, she could feel their little black beady eyes staring at her, and even now they seemed to be condemning her for not being a better daughter.

"If it weren't for Selena, they'd die. She's the one with the green thumb and knows when to spray and when to fertilize. You would kill a silk flower arrangement. And I don't see what's funny about red roses, so wipe that grin off your face." Gladys's very tone was demanding.

"Mama, let Paula tell us what she's got to say so I can go home." Selena tucked a strand of brown hair behind her ear.

"Paula might not know much about roses, but she makes beautiful wedding dresses," Mitzi defended her.

"Glad she's good at something." Gladys glared at Mitzi.

"And she was a damn fine librarian before that. You should be proud of her for getting her degree," Jody said.

Gladys waggled a finger at Jody. "Don't you cuss in my house."

"Mother, I need to tell you—" Paula said.

"Are you dying?" Gladys turned the finger to point at her. "If so, Selena will need to buy me a new black dress. My old one is so worn from going to funerals that it's faded something terrible."

Jody gasped. "Mrs. Walker! Paula is your daughter. You're talking about her like she's a stranger, or worse yet, a dead stranger."

"Thank you." Paula shot a dirty look toward her sister. "It's nice someone will stand up for me."

"Hey, don't go shootin' daggers at me. I've stood up for you lots of times," Selena said.

"Name one, please." Paula could hear the coldness in her own voice.

Gladys tipped up her chin and looked down her nose at Jody. "Young lady, don't you use that tone with me or Paula's sister, who was good enough to drive up here. So watch your smart mouth."

"I'm pregnant," Paula spit out.

Gladys turned her focus to Paula. "You are what? And you didn't even invite me to the wedding or tell me that you got married? What kind of daughter are you anyway?"

"I'm not married. I'm not getting married. I will be a single parent. And now that I've told you, I'll be leaving." Paula's hands knotted into fists as she glared at her sister.

"I knew it was terrible news." Selena hopped up and went nose to nose with Paula. "You're ruining the family name. We'll never be able to hold our heads up in Celeste again. God almighty, Paula, don't you even know how to use birth control?"

"Well, I expected it years ago, with the friends you ran with. Do you even know who it belongs to?" Gladys screeched.

"I do, but I'm not marrying him," Paula said.

"If you're going to raise up a bastard child, I'd just as soon you didn't bring it around here," Gladys snapped. "Matter of fact, why don't you just stay away from now on. Selena, I'll need you to sit with me to be sure I don't have a heart attack over this. Oh, sweet Jesus," Gladys moaned. "They might even throw me out of my church. Girl, get me an extra nerve pill right now."

"Look what you've done," Selena spat.

Gladys pointed at the door. "You can go now. And don't come back. You are dead to me."

Paula had expected her mother to yell at her, but to disown her completely cut to the center of her heart. "But Mama—"

Gladys sighed dramatically as if it were her last breath. "Just go. Selena will take care of me."

"If you change your mind, you've got my number." With tears in her eyes, she started outside.

"Just get out," Selena yelled. "You've done enough damage for one day. If Mama dies, this is on you."

Paula could hear her riffling through the multiple pill bottles on the cabinet. She could have told her what the "nerve pills" were called, but instead she kept walking.

"I won't change my mind this time. You've gone too far. I hope it's a girl and she deals you nothing but misery," Gladys screamed after her.

"Now I know how poor Wanda has felt all these years. You and Jody are both horrible, mean daughters."

By the time they were close to the van, tears were flowing down Paula's cheeks and dripping onto her shirt, leaving big, round wet spots. "Well, that went horrible, but I'm not really surprised at any of it except that"—she broke down into sobs—"that she said I'm dead to her."

Both Mitzi and Jody drew her into a three-way hug.

Jody wiped the tears away from Paula's cheeks with her own shirtsleeve. "We love you, and we'll love this baby so much it'll never know that its grandmother was so hateful."

Paula hugged them back. "At least it's over—now I can move forward."

Jody was the first one to step back. "And now Selena gets to jump at her every beck and call. I thought my mother was bad, but good Lord, that was brutal," Jody said.

"A mother should never say things like that to her daughter." Mitzi crawled into the driver's seat of her van.

"The way she feels about me, I don't know why she didn't drown me at birth." Paula's chin quivered. "But at least I don't have to come over here every evening for a while."

"Or ever," Mitzi said. "You never told us that things were that bad at your house."

"I was too ashamed, and I blamed myself. It wasn't until I went to college and got some therapy that I came to terms with it," Paula said. "Jody, will you drive my car? My hands are shaking so bad, I'm . . ."

"Of course." Jody followed Paula to her vehicle and slid in under the wheel.

Paula handed her the keys and then leaned her head back on the seat. "It's over. Tell me that I've told her and that I'm not having one of my recurring nightmares about it."

"It's over," Jody assured her as she started the engine. Mitzi pulled out onto the street in her van and Jody fell in behind her. "Gladys is downright batshit crazy. If she hated both of you, it would be one thing, but to despise one just means she's got problems that go beyond sleeping pills. Why did you even agree to move back here?"

Paula grabbed a tissue from the console and blew her nose loudly. "I'm so damned emotional right now. Thank God I've got you and Mitzi to help me get through it."

"This shouldn't be happening to you." Jody drove the rest of the way to the shop and parked behind Mitzi's van. Paula couldn't make herself get out of the car—not yet.

"Give me a minute. Just one all by myself. You and Mitzi can go on inside. I'll be there in a little bit." Paula needed a little time to settle her nerves. A fast-beating heart, a racing pulse, and a brain that was about to explode couldn't be good for the baby.

"You got it," Jody said. "Holy shit!"

Paula looked up to see a new white double-cab truck pulling in behind her car and Lyle getting out of the driver's seat. She slung open her door, anger replacing hurt, and went to Jody's side.

Jody exploded out of the car, meeting Lyle halfway from his truck. "How dare you even show your face on this property."

"Hey!" He held up both palms.

He was dressed in a fancy western shirt with pearl snaps, creased jeans, and if his boots didn't cost five hundred dollars, Paula would eat that big silver belt buckle. "I just came to get your signature on the title to the motorcycle. It's in both our names, and I'm selling it."

"Why?" Jody asked.

He handed her a piece of paper. "I've got this truck and don't need it. Besides, I'm going to be a father and my image has changed."

Jody ripped it in half and handed it back to him. "You can wipe your sorry butt on that. I'm not helping you with anything."

All of the emotions that Paula had felt at her mother's house were suddenly transferred to Lyle. How dare he show up looking like a fancy rancher in his new truck and ask her friend to sign any damn thing?

"You best get your sorry ass out of here," Paula growled.

Mitzi joined them. "Or else you could get blood on your fancy new truck seats."

"So you have to have your fat friends take up for you these days, do you?" Lyle sneered.

Jody took several steps forward. "I can fight my own battles. I'm not signing any papers, so leave."

"Come on, Jody. You know things weren't good with us for a while, and I can't sell the cycle without both our names on the title. Thank God your name isn't on the property," he said.

"And what does that mean?" she fired back at him.

Lyle crossed his arms over his chest and glared at her. "It means that I'm working on a deal with Quincy Roberts. When he buys the land, I'm going to use the money for a down payment to have a house built on the ranch. Kennedy deserves something better than a trailer house. Her dad gave us an acre of land for a wedding present."

"And whose name is that in?" Jody asked. "Is your new bimbo going to work her ass off to pay for it like I did ours?"

"Don't call her names. She's my wife." If looks could kill, Jody would have been nothing but a greasy spot on the grass.

You never were the wife, her mother's voice taunted her.

"I'll always have a special place for you in my heart." He held out his arms as if he would hug her.

She glared at him. "You can light a match, stick it up your rear end, and burn that special place and that damned motorcycle at the same time."

Paula and Mitzi both giggled.

Lyle shot them a dirty look and stepped closer to Jody.

Paula took a step forward, her hands clenched into fists. "I think it's time you left."

"Me, too," Jody said.

"You always did like your friends more than you loved me," he growled. "That's what was the matter with our relationship."

"Bullshit!" Jody said. "You not being able to keep your jeans zipped was what destroyed us and you know it. Get out of here and don't come back."

She turned around and stormed into the house, leaving him standing there. He jumped into his truck, slung gravel against the house, and disappeared in a cloud of gray dust.

"Are you okay?" Paula and Mitzi asked at the same time when they made it inside.

"I'll be fine when I cool off," Jody said. "The bastard had no right comin' up here in his fancy clothes and new truck to ask me to sign so he could sell his motorcycle. Who does he think he is?" Jody said in a rush before she took a deep breath. "Special place in his heart, my ass—he was just butterin' me up so I'd sign the title."

"You keep that attitude," Mitzi said. "If you ever have a doubt about any of that shit being your fault, just remember the way you feel right now."

"I promise I will." Jody took a beer from the refrigerator, twisted the cap off, and took a long gulp. "Too bad you can't have one of these, Paula."

"Honey, I'd rather have a double shot of Jack Daniel's on the rocks," Paula laughed. "But you deserve that after the way you stood up to him."

"And you deserve a whole bottle of whiskey after what you endured tonight." Mitzi pulled the tabs on two cans of root beer and handed one to Paula. Then she raised her can in a toast. "To friendship."

"Amen." Jody touched her bottle to Mitzi's can.

"Halle-damn-lujah!" Paula raised hers to join them.

Chapter Eleven

*M*itzi sat up straight in bed that Friday morning when the alarm went off. Until she slapped the alarm clock, she wasn't sure if she was awake or still in that horrible dream. She'd dreamed that Paula's baby was stillborn and they were planning the baby's funeral.

She blinked several times and then caught the aroma of bacon and coffee finding its way under her bedroom door. She was awake, thank God, but she hoped that was one dream that never came true.

Throwing back the covers, she got up and dressed in a sundress. She even applied a little makeup. When she reached the end of the stairs, she called out, "Hey, I'm following my nose."

"Me, too," Jody said from right behind her.

"Bacon, biscuits, and western omelets." Paula pointed to the counter. "I woke up hungry, so I made enough for all of us."

"Thank you." Mitzi picked up a plate and heaped it up with food.

"I didn't even realize how much I missed this kind of breakfast," Jody said as she filled her plate and carried it to the table. "I love pastry, but it takes second place to this."

Mitzi carried her plate to the table and sat down. "So how are y'all this morning?"

"Much better," Paula answered. "I wasn't surprised at the way Mama reacted, but I wasn't ready for the pain that it caused. Selena called last night to rake me over the coals, again. I let her go on for a few minutes, then reminded her that I'd been disowned, so that leaves her to jump every time Mama said frog."

"What'd she say about that?" Jody asked.

"She hung up on me," Paula answered. "She and I've been down this path before. She's so much like Mama that they can't get along for long."

"That ought to be a circus," Jody said.

Paula shrugged. "Mama's disowned me many other times before."

"Why didn't you ever tell us all this?" Jody asked.

"It was too embarrassing to tell anyone, even y'all," Paula said. "But I'm fine this morning. Now that telling them is over, I feel like a weight has been lifted from my shoulders."

"Remember me tellin' y'all that my mama made me pray on my knees twice a day for thirty minutes?" Jody asked.

Mitzi's eyes widened so big that they hurt. "I remember, but I still can't figure out why she'd do that."

"Evidently she thought I was going to be a bad child and was hoping that would help me be good." Jody set about eating breakfast.

"How old were you?" Mitzi asked.

"I can't remember when I didn't do it. I thought everyone did it. Mama said you didn't talk about what you did in secret because that was a sin," she said between bites.

"That's just downright mean," Paula said.

"Holy crap! I said 'Now I lay me down to sleep' when I was a little girl, but thirty minutes would be an eternity to a kid," Mitzi said.

"It was." Jody nodded and turned her attention toward Paula. "When did Gladys disown you the first time?"

"When I accepted the scholarship to West Texas A&M in Amarillo. She wanted me to commute the fifteen miles to Commerce and go to Texas A&M there. She said I owed it to her and Daddy to live close by and take care of them," Paula answered. "She didn't speak to me the whole first semester. At Christmas I'd planned to stay on campus, but Selena guilted me into coming home."

"That's when you stayed with me the last few days of the break, and we told my parents that I was quitting school and going to work full time at the bridal shop in Amarillo, wasn't it? I was sure glad you were there when I told them," Mitzi remembered.

Paula finished her breakfast and carried her plate to the sink. "Best holiday I'd ever spent. Made me kind of glad that Mama kicked me out."

"Speaking of the holidays, are we going to your dad's this Christmas?" Paula asked. "Or will we invite all of them to join us here?"

"I vote we have it at Graham and Mitzi's down the street," Jody teased. "And before we get into that, I want to apologize for that hateful remark Lyle made yesterday. Him calling y'all fat made me madder than him telling me that his precious Kennedy deserved something better than a trailer house. I fumed about it all night, even dreamed that I burned the trailer to the ground before he could move it."

"Forgiven," Paula said. "And I like your idea. That gives Mitzi and Graham six months to get over their shyness and for one of them to ask the other one out."

"Forgiven, and I'm not shy," Mitzi protested. But Paula was right. When it came to Graham, she acted like an awkward teenager.

"I was there yesterday when he showed up to get the girls. There's definitely vibes between y'all. You may have to be the bigger person and ask him out if he doesn't get up some nerve," Jody said.

"Maybe the time is right for something to happen between y'all now," Paula said.

"I'll wish in one hand and spit in the other and take bets on which one fills up the fastest," Mitzi said.

Ellie Mae arrived right on time at eleven thirty that morning, and Mitzi ushered her back to the fitting room. Ellie Mae quickly removed her shirt and stood in front of the mirror. Mitzi slipped on the bodice of her dress, and Ellie Mae squealed like a little girl.

"It's going to be exactly what I wanted, only prettier than I could have ever imagined," she said.

"Okay, now be very still while I mark the back seam, and then I'll pin it so you can feel the fit and see if we need to tighten or loosen anything." Mitzi laid the pincushion on a small table in front of the mirrors.

"Did Paula tell you my news?" Ellie Mae asked.

"About what?" Mitzi asked.

"I'm pregnant, but only Darrin and I know—and, well, Paula because we ran into each other at the ultrasound place. We'll spring the news on my family after they get over the shock of this gorgeous dress," Ellie Mae said.

"Congratulations." Mitzi's thoughts were on what her grandmother had said about Ellie Mae being the typical preacher's daughter.

"Thank you. We're really excited. We'd wanted to start a family right away, but imagine my surprise when I went to see my doctor and found out I was already five months pregnant," Ellie Mae gushed. "That's when we moved up the wedding date by three months. Didn't want to go into labor walking down the aisle."

"I guess not." Mitzi finished pinning the bodice. "How does that feel?"

"Make it just a little tighter. I'll be wearing Spanx," Ellie Mae said. "Wait. Don't. I might gain a few more pounds. Can you just leave a big seam allowance in case we need to adjust right at the end?"

"Of course. So do you know what you're having?" Mitzi asked.

"A boy and we're so happy about it. What about Paula?"

Mitzi unpinned the dress and stuck the pins back into the cushion. "She hasn't told us yet. I've also got something I want you to look at after you get dressed."

"Did you finish the hat?" Ellie Mae's voice quivered with excitement as she slipped her shirt down over her head. "I'm going to love it as much as I do the dress."

Mitzi carefully put the bodice on a satin hanger and hung it on a rack. Then she disappeared into the fabric room and brought back the bouquet the girls had made. Ellie Mae reached out to touch it.

"I'm so damned emotional, but this is beyond beautiful. It's exactly what I told you I wanted. I don't care how much it costs. Who made it? And will they do the rest of my flowers?" She held it close to her body, as if she were walking down the aisle with it.

"The Harrison girls," Mitzi answered. "And yes, they'd love to make the rest of your flowers. Just make a list and email it to me. They could get started on your sister's bouquet this afternoon. Got a rough idea of what you want?"

"White roses—about half this big, but do some red touch-up with whatever satin or silk she picks out for her dress. She said she could come in right after lunch today if that's okay?"

"That would be a perfect time," Mitzi said.

"Can I take it with me today?" Ellie Mae ran the fingers of her right hand over it as if the bouquet were made of precious metals.

"Yes, ma'am, you can. We might possibly have the rest of the flowers done next week when you come in for the skirt fitting, if you'll send me a list of what all you need."

"Thank you." Ellie Mae nodded.

"I can put that in a plastic bag for you," Mitzi offered.

Reluctantly, Ellie Mae handed it back to her. "I can tell you right now that I want a red-rose boutonniere for Darrin and a white one for the best man. And I don't want little bitty things, either. Do them up fancy with three rosebuds in Darrin's and some black lace like my bouquet. And the others should have two with some red in it from Darcy's dress. I'll send you a list this afternoon of the mothers, grandmothers, aunts, and special friends that will need corsages. Thank you, thank you from the bottom of my heart for helping me to have the most beautiful wedding in the whole state." Ellie Mae waited until her bouquet was in plastic before she wrapped Mitzi up in a tight hug.

"That's what we're here for," Mitzi assured her.

༄

Fanny Lou arrived for the party that evening with a decorated cake from the bakery. One side had blue icing; the other, pink. A big question mark had been piped in the middle.

"That is too cute," Mitzi said.

"I came early to help. How are we going to do this since we only have four places at the table?" Fanny Lou asked.

"We've got a long table set up in the fitting room. Jody is setting out pink bowls and blue paper plates." Mitzi eyed the cake.

Fanny Lou shook a long, bony finger toward Mitzi. "You touch that and I'll ban you from getting a single bite. I heard that Ellie Mae had a fitting and took her bouquet home. Her mama loved it."

"That's why we do what we do," Mitzi said. "Come on, Granny—I love buttercream frosting. No one would notice if I just got a taste from the back corner."

"Don't even think of it!" Fanny Lou scolded as she carried the cake out of the kitchen.

Dixie and Tabby came through the front door and stopped when they saw the cake. "What's the question mark for?" Dixie asked.

"You'll find out later," Fanny Lou answered.

Mitzi heard the girls in the foyer and joined them as they followed behind Fanny Lou.

"We thought this was just a cake and ice cream get-together, maybe to talk about the bridal fair," Dixie answered.

"There's a surprise tonight, but we will probably talk about the bridal fair afterwards." Mitzi had worried all day about how Graham and Alice would take the news. She'd wondered, if she had teenage girls, how she'd handle the issue they would be facing. In Amarillo or even Tulia, things would be different, but Celeste was old school with a double dose of morality. Even in modern times, folks still looked down on single mothers.

"I brought homemade ice cream." Harry carried an oak bucket into the room and set it on the end of the table.

Mitzi crossed the room to give him a hug. "Is it banana nut?"

"Is there any other kind? Is that cake what I think it is?"

Mitzi pulled him over to a corner.

"Do I need to get my shotgun down from above the mantel?" he whispered.

She shook her head. "It's Paula, not me."

He clamped a hand over his mouth. "Holy crap! Does Gladys know?"

"She does now, and so does Selena," Mitzi answered.

"No wonder the temperature in town has risen so high. I bet she's breathing fire," Harry said.

Mitzi nodded. "You are so right about that. I feel so sorry for Paula." She lowered her voice to a whisper. "Gladys told her that she was dead to her."

Harry just shook his head. "Gladys has always had problems, but that's harsh even for her. When's the wedding?"

"Not going to be one. The father was separated from his wife but went back to her before Paula even knew she was pregnant," Mitzi said.

"When is the baby due?" Harry asked.

"September."

"Well, I got to say, I'm glad it's not you, but if Paula needs anything, I'll be here for her. Gladys shouldn't treat her like that." Harry shook his head.

"Thank you, Daddy."

"Anything for you, Paula, or Jody," Harry said. "I'd still like to wring Lyle's neck for what he did."

"You'd have to stand in line." Mitzi looped her arm in his, and together they rejoined the group.

Chapter Twelve

*G*raham rushed into the house, taking his shirt off as he climbed the stairs to the second floor. He threw it at the dirty clothes hamper and kicked his shoes off in the hallway leading to the bathroom. He took a quick shower, shaved for the second time that day, and hurriedly dressed in casual khaki shorts and a pullover shirt.

He'd been looking forward to seeing Mitzi all day. There was something building between them, like the embers of a slow-burning fire. It might fizzle or it could break into a full blaze, but whatever happened, he was ready for it.

Walking down the street from his house to hers, he laid it all out like a credit report. On this side were the deficits; on the other were the assets. The asset side was winning when he rang the doorbell.

Tabby's eyes glittered when she answered the door. "Guess what, Daddy? Harry brought homemade banana-nut ice cream. Remember when Grandpa used to make that for us on our birthdays?"

"I sure do, and it's been a long time since we had it." Graham looked over the top of his daughter's head to catch a glimpse of Mitzi, but she wasn't there.

"And guess what else," Harry said before he could answer. "I've got two sewing machines out in my truck that we can bring in later."

"That's all pretty great news," Graham said. "Y'all lead the way."

"Y'all come on in and we'll get into this ice cream and cake." Jody motioned from the fitting room doorway.

"I might embarrass you girls tonight. I haven't had supper, and y'all know how much I like homemade ice cream," Graham said.

Mitzi came out of the kitchen with a stack of napkins in her hands. "My dad is here and he'll give you a run for your money when it comes to cake and ice cream. He's got a sweet tooth."

"Oh, honey, I can lay claim to the sweet tooth title of the whole county." Graham winked at her.

Mitzi's face was slightly flushed from getting the tables set up, and her hair had been piled up on top of her head. She wore a pair of flowing yellow pants and a multicolored shirt, but what appealed to him most was that she wasn't wearing shoes.

"Who goes first?" Dixie asked.

"The one who asks that question," Mitzi said.

"Yay!" Dixie pumped her fist in the air and picked up a plate. "I can't wait to taste it."

"I'll do the dippin' if we can get Paula to cut the cake," Harry announced.

"As you can see," Graham whispered in Mitzi's ear, "none of us is bashful when it comes to food."

"Neither are we," Mitzi said.

Paula brought in a pitcher of sweet tea, and Jody carried in one of lemonade. They were discussing last-minute details of the bridal fair.

"We really need an arch. Just standing the mannequin up there without a backdrop seems kind of tacky," Jody said.

"Those things are expensive. We'll only use it once or twice a year, and that's assuming that we get invited to do more shows," Paula said.

"I could build you one," Graham offered. "I've got the tools, and it wouldn't be that big of a job. I'd be glad to do it Sunday. I'll even pick up the lumber and things we need to build it on my way home tomorrow. It's the least I can do for all you've done for my girls."

"That's so sweet, but—" Mitzi started.

Graham shook his head. "No buts. Is two o'clock good for you? Alice is taking the girls to the movies, and they're leaving right after we get lunch at the café. Want to help me, Mitzi?"

∽

"Sounds great." Mitzi was amazed at his offer, not only to do the job but also to let her help. Granny had always told her that the best way to get to really know someone was to work alongside them for a few hours. She visualized Graham all hot and sweaty, and got so engrossed in the pictures flashing through her mind that she forgot all about the reason they were having the party that evening.

"Paula, are you going to cut this cake or not?" Harry asked.

Mitzi loved cake, but she would have gladly given it up to keep the pictures in her head from disappearing.

Paula picked up a knife and held it above the cake for a minute. "I have something to say. First of all, thank you all for being here this evening and thank you for helping us move earlier in the week. Good friends are priceless, and I'm glad for the privilege of calling y'all my friends. This is a gender-reveal party, so let's see if we're having a baby girl or boy."

Fanny Lou rubbed her hands together. "We can't wait to see if you cut into the pink or blue side of the cake."

Tabby crossed her fingers. "We'll take either one—"

Dixie butted in before her sister could finish the sentence. "But we want a girl real bad."

"This is so exciting, but what I really want is a chunk of that cake to go with this ice cream," Harry chuckled.

Paula cut a piece of the pink cake.

"A girl!" Dixie high-fived with her sister. "Can we babysit when she's born?"

"What's her name going to be?" Tabby slapped Dixie's hand. "Our first project on our new sewing machines needs to be a pretty quilt for her."

"Congratulations, Paula," Graham said.

Alice held up her bowl of ice cream. "A toast with ice cream, since we don't have any Irish whiskey. 'Wee little baby, fresh from God's arms. You light up the world with your sweet baby charms.' Congratulations, Paula. I can think of nothing more exciting than being a mother."

"Amen!" Fanny Lou said.

Pure happiness shone in Paula's face as she cut portions of cake and put them on paper plates. "Y'all are the best. Thank you so much. Just so you know, I'm not marrying the father. I found out about the baby after we'd been broken up for a while and he's no longer in the picture."

"Good Lord!" Fanny Lou scolded. "If you were the first woman who got pregnant and didn't marry the father of the baby, we could drown you in the river. But you're not the first and you damn sure won't be the last. We haven't had a baby in the family since Mitzi was born. This is a blessing, and I, for one, am calling dibs on rocking her to sleep the first time you need a few minutes."

Harry raised a hand. "Couldn't have said it better myself."

Everyone got a piece of cake and went to sit around the table, leaving Mitzi and Graham by themselves.

A dark shadow passed over Graham's face, prompting Mitzi to ask, "Are you okay?"

"I'm fine, but . . ." He paused. "I don't want to be a naysayer, but it's a tough row, raising a child on your own. It's even harder when they get old enough to realize that they only have one parent and think it's their fault that the other one isn't there. Paula's going to need lots of support."

"Did you have support?" she asked.

"Yes, I did. Alice was and is amazing. My folks were wonderful, always ready to help out with whatever we needed. Dad adored the girls and they did him, but no matter how much I reassure them, they have the feeling that Rita left because they were big girls. They think she was ashamed of them," he said. "I don't know what to do. Got any ideas?"

"Can I think about it until Sunday?" she asked.

"Of course." He crossed the room to sit with his girls.

She watched him out of the corner of her eye, and went to sit down at the other end of the table.

Jody nudged her with an elbow. "So what were y'all talkin' about over there? It looked pretty serious."

"He's going to help me build an archway for the bridal fair on Sunday," Mitzi answered.

"That doesn't sound much like flirting," Jody said as she headed over to the table for a second piece of cake.

Depends, Mitzi thought. *I felt more talking about hammers and nails with him than I have in the past when guys tried to sweet-talk me into bed with them.*

Chapter Thirteen

Saturday morning was for catching up on paperwork, but Graham couldn't keep his mind on work. He finally leaned back in his chair, propped his feet on his desk, and laced his hands behind his head. Closing his eyes, he watched everything that had happened the night before play through his head like a movie, repeating the scenes involving Mitzi. He was already looking forward to the next day, when they could have more time together—when no one would drag one or both of them off.

He picked up his phone and sent a text to Mitzi saying that he was looking forward to the next day and got one back saying that she was, too, and then his cell phone rang. Hoping that it was her, he answered it on the first ring.

"Daddy, guess what." Dixie's voice always shot up a few notches when she was excited. "Mitzi and Paula and Jody are coming down to Greenville to buy stuff for the bridal fair next week. Mitzi asked if we wanted to go with them. Is that okay? We really, really want to go. We're going to have lunch with them, too. Please say yes. And some of the stuff might be heavy, so could you meet us somewhere and help? And could you bring a truck in case it all won't fit in the van?"

"Just text me where you are about"—he checked his schedule—"one o'clock. And it looks like I can take off the rest of the afternoon, so I'll be glad to also help you unload at the shop when you're done."

"Yay! This is going to be a great day," Dixie said.

He laid the phone on his desk and pumped his fist in the air. Things were looking up if he got to see Mitzi three days in a row.

"Good mornin'." Vivien's voice crackled through the intercom in his office. "Your ex-wife is here. Shall I send her in?"

Talk about bursting a bubble. He backed up and sat down in his chair, not knowing what to say. "That's not funny, Vivien."

"Funny or not, I'm here." Rita's voice, gravelly from years of smoking, came through the machine on his desk.

"I'm busy. Make an appointment," he said coldly.

"I'm coming in there whether you like it or not."

Graham hadn't seen her since the day she walked out on him. He'd talked to her, making arrangements that one time for the girls to see her, but had managed not to actually come face-to-face with her. And now he only had a matter of seconds to prepare himself.

"Hello, Graham," she said as she waltzed into his office like she owned it. "So you're finally sitting in the big office. This is where I imagined we'd be when I married you. I'd take over Vivien's desk and you'd be right here, but your parents didn't like me."

"My parents were disappointed that I wasn't going to college, and Vivien wasn't ready to retire. What are you doing in Celeste?" he asked.

Rita's makeup did what it could, but it didn't cover all the crow's-feet or wrinkles around her mouth. She still wore her trademark bright-red lipstick. And he wasn't surprised to see that her skirt was way too short and tight for a woman her age. When she crossed her legs, he could see all the way to the crotch of her lace panties.

"My grandmother—do you remember her?" She pulled a silver cigarette container from her purse. "Mind if I smoke?"

"This is a smoke-free place, so you'll have to wait. And yes, I remember your grandmother very well. She lived up around Whitewright and was in a nursing home, right?"

"She died. I stayed in Sherman last night and attended her funeral this morning—just a graveside. I thought about asking if the girls might want to go, but they wouldn't remember her." She dropped the cigarette case back into her purse. "You're lookin' good, Graham."

"Thank you." He'd thought about the moment that they'd see each other again at least a thousand times over the past years. Right after she left, the idea of ever seeing her again was both painful and brought on anger. Now the pain had subsided, but there was still more anger than he wanted to admit.

"That's all you've got to say. Just thank you? You could tell me that I look good, too."

"You look good, too, Rita," he quipped.

"I go to the gym every day, and I'm determined not to ever dress like an old woman. I'm glad you noticed that I'm not giving in to age, but I didn't come here to fight with you. I just thought I'd drop in and break the ice. That way when you and the girls come to the wedding, it won't be awkward between us." She uncrossed her legs and bent forward, giving him a good look at the edges of a black-lace bra and lots of cleavage.

"I'm not going to the wedding. I've reserved a room in a nearby hotel. I'll drop them off and pick them up. And things will always be awkward between us, Rita. How could they not be? You left me with two little girls to raise by myself and didn't even call them for years and years."

She reached for the cigarettes again and giggled. "I smoke too much when I'm nervous. I was young and didn't want to be tied down. I've grown up now and made a few changes in my life."

"Why would you be nervous?" he asked.

"God, Graham . . ." she fumed.

"No, just plain old Graham Harrison. I might have Daddy's office now, but I don't claim being a god," he said.

"You might as well be one the way you're sittin' there all pompous, looking down on me." She got up and paced from one end of the room to the other. She looked a little taller than he remembered in those high-heeled shoes.

"That's you and your guilt, not me," he shot back.

"What do you want? For me to apologize, cry, and say that leaving was a big mistake?" Rita rounded the end of the desk and kicked off her shoes.

"No, I just want you to do what you've been doing. Choices have consequences, Rita. You chose to leave and not look back. Now you have to live with that decision. Like my grandpa used to say, 'Sometimes it's too late to do what you should've been doin' all along.' Anything else you want to talk about?" Graham asked.

"I hated being a wife and a mother, but most of all I hated being a daughter-in-law, but now we don't have to worry about that, do we, darlin'?" Using her foot, she pushed his chair back enough so that she could hop up on the desk right in front of him. She leaned forward, cupped his face in her hands, and kissed him.

He didn't feel anything except the need to brush his teeth. It was like licking the bottom of an ashtray, and was that whiskey he tasted on her breath?

"Your old daddy looked at me like I was trash, but honey, we can start all over now and be a family. The girls are at an age when they need a mother," she whispered seductively.

He pushed the chair back and stood up. "The girls have always needed a mother."

"Then let's put the past behind us and concentrate on the future. After the girls come with me to the wedding, I'll file for divorce," she said.

"Whoa!" He held up both palms. "There is no future for us, Rita. I don't make the same mistakes twice. And I won't ever hear you put down my folks again. They were there when you weren't."

She flipped her long blonde hair over her shoulder, slipped her small feet back into her shoes, and picked up her purse. Instantly the cigarette case was back in her hands. "I've always gotten what I want. You know that, Graham." Her mouth turned up in a smile but it didn't reach her eyes. "I want a baby. I'm not too old to have one." She fumbled with the cigarette case, turning it over and over in her hands, as if it were her security blanket. "I even planned on giving up smoking for a baby, but when we went to a fertility clinic, we found out that my husband, Derrick, is sterile."

Karma is a bitch on steroids, Graham thought.

"Aren't you going to say it serves me right?" Rita asked.

"No, I'm truly sorry. Have you thought of adoption?"

"I don't want to adopt. I want the pregnancy, the birthing, and the whole nine yards again." She nodded. "How are the girls going to feel about having a brother or sister that they only get to see once a year?"

He thought of how excited they were the previous night about Paula's new baby. "You'll have to ask them about that, not me. I can't imagine why you're even telling me this. It's none of my business."

"I would like to . . . hell, Graham, you never make anything easy. I want to build a relationship with them and with you, and like I said, I'm not giving up. We can rekindle what we had," Rita said.

"It's a little late to build something now. Besides, they think you're ashamed of them, Rita. They told me that the way you looked at them made them feel like they were fat and ugly. Their words, not mine."

She jumped up so fast that she dropped the cigarette case on the floor. "It was just a surprise, that's all. With your size, I wasn't expecting them to be able to wear my jeans, but God almighty, Graham, they're huge."

"Not huge." Graham glared at her. "They're big, but they're not fat, and they're beautiful. Why would you even want to be around them when you feel like that?"

"They should know their siblings even if I have to adopt, don't you think?" She bent to pick up the case and shoved it in her purse.

"Like I said before, that's up to them, but in my opinion, building even a friendship with them will take a long time, and a baby won't be the glue that binds them to you as a family." He crossed the floor and opened the door. "Don't pop by my office again. What we had died years ago."

She looked up into his eyes as she passed by. "I guess you wouldn't be willing to donate a little sperm so my child would be their full brother or sister? We can go to a clinic or we can do it the old-fashioned way."

"Jesus, Mary, and Joseph," Graham gasped. "Are you crazy? Does Derrick know you asked such an insane thing? And think about it, the next child would most likely be a larger person, too."

"If you don't want to help me, I've got a short list of guys who've been flirting with me for a year or more. If you are willing, like I said, it can be through the clinic or through the bedroom. We were pretty good in that area until I got pregnant."

Graham was speechless.

Rita went on. "Derrick and I've been . . . well, let's just say that I've fallen out of love with him. Or maybe I never did love him. Maybe he was just an escape from bawling babies and a husband who didn't make enough money to get me what I wanted." Her tone was as flat as if she'd just said that it was raining outside.

Graham shook his head emphatically. "You didn't like bawling babies and not having money when we first met. What's changed?"

"I've changed a lot, Graham. Now I want to be married for the right reasons. I'll make someone a good wife, and I'll be a good mother this time," she answered. "Give that some thought when you get into a cold bed alone tonight."

He motioned toward the door. "Goodbye, Rita."

"Never hurts to ask and test the waters, does it?" She tiptoed and kissed him on the cheek. "My biological clock is ticking. Bye, Graham."

He shut the door behind her and slumped down into the nearest chair. She'd been there less than fifteen minutes but it had seemed like hours. He knuckled his eyes to ease the pain in his head, but it didn't work. Maybe it was the smoke on her breath when she kissed him that caused his headache. He went to the cabinet, took out some air freshener, and gave the room a thorough spraying.

Had she changed? Could they be a family at this point? Should he give her one more chance? Questions floated through his mind, but there didn't seem to be any answers. Pulling out a drawer, he took out a bottle of Advil and checked the date. They'd expired two years ago, but he swallowed two with a sip of cold coffee anyway.

"No!" he said. "Never."

"Never say never," he thought he heard Vivien's voice say in his head.

"This time I can say it because I'd rather be dead than go back to Rita," he swore out loud.

"Good for you. I'm leaving now. You're on your own for the rest of the day," Vivien said.

"I'm sorry. I didn't know I'd left the line open. Did you hear that whole thing?"

"I did, and Rita doesn't seem to have changed a bit. She's always been a bulldog when she wants something, so be careful, and if there's anything I can do, let me know," Vivien said.

"Just keep her out of my office," Graham told her.

"With extreme prejudice," Vivien laughed.

"If necessary," Graham chuckled.

Mitzi glanced at herself in the foyer mirror as she passed by on Saturday morning—red hair wild enough to scare little children, no makeup, and eyes swollen with sleep.

"Is it too early for a shot of bourbon?" she muttered as she headed across the kitchen floor.

"Yes, it is, and you look like the last rose of summer a hound dog hiked his leg on," Jody said.

"I feel like she looks," Paula said. "If we weren't pressed for time, I'd suggest we all go back to bed and forget that we need to go Greenville today to get everything we'll need for the bridal fair next Saturday. We have to get napkins imprinted with our logo, a couple of cases of champagne, and those little plastic flutes. If we're not too late to get it done, let's get the flutes stamped with the logo, too."

"And maybe we should buy one of those tall banners that you pull up from the bottom and hook at the top. We could put pictures of several of the dresses we've designed on it, and set it up at the end of our table," Jody said.

"All good ideas. Give me an hour to wake up and throw on some clothes." Mitzi slumped down in a chair at the table. "What are y'all's plans for tomorrow afternoon?"

"Well, I'm going to church in the morning with y'all," Jody said. "I thought about what you said about showing my mama and everyone in Celeste that I'm a strong woman. Besides, we both need to be there to support Paula, since it's all over town by now that she's pregnant. But after we get some lunch, I don't have any plans. What'd you have in mind?"

Paula brought the leftover cake and a stack of paper plates to the table. "I'll have to set an example for the twins later, but today I want cake for breakfast. After church, I'm going to measure the nursery and probably spend a million hours on Pinterest."

"Graham and I are going to build the arch for the bridal fair. He offered to buy the materials for it, and I started to protest, but then he said to let him do it as a thank-you for what we've done for his girls." Mitzi tucked a strand of hair behind her ear and cut herself a big chunk of blue cake. "I couldn't say no."

"Then it's not a date?" Jody squealed.

Mitzi groaned. "I don't think so. Do y'all remember Rita?"

"Skinny, short, and blonde hair." Jody nodded.

"A gold digger," Paula answered.

"Exactly." Mitzi picked up a fork and started on her breakfast cake.

"So?" Jody asked.

"Short and small is what he's attracted to, and he probably has trust issues, so it can't be a date," Mitzi answered.

"If he kisses you before you leave, it's a date," Paula said.

"I agree." Jody headed to the refrigerator and removed a takeout box. "Y'all can have dessert for breakfast. I'm heating up a bowlful of leftover spaghetti and meatballs."

Mitzi polished off the last of her cake and carried the plate to the trash can. "I'm going upstairs to make myself decent. Maybe I shouldn't even bother. God knows I won't be able to shrink myself down to a size six by any means. I'll be down in half an hour."

"The girls will probably show up in a few minutes," Jody reminded her.

"I'll hurry, then." Mitzi zipped into the bathroom, took a quick shower, and returned to find another message, this time from Dixie, saying that her dad would meet them at the party store with a truck to help carry heavy stuff.

"Well, that changes whether or not to use a curling iron on my hair," Mitzi said as she rushed through applying makeup, threw outfits on her bed as she discarded one after another, and finally changed twice—all in half an hour.

Chapter Fourteen

Paula stood back a few feet and looked at the four plus-size mannequins lined up before them. Did she really look like the size-eighteen one when she was naked? She avoided mirrors when she wasn't dressed, so maybe she did. She cocked her head to one side and decided that her breasts were smaller than the mannequin's and her butt a good deal bigger.

Mitzi put in her two cents. "I vote that we get a bald one so we can change her hair color with wigs. The one with the preformed hair looks a little weird."

Paula stepped back and studied them. "I like the idea of changing out her hair color, too."

"Agreed. That way it looks more real," Jody added. "What do you think, girls?"

"Why do you need a second one?" Dixie asked. "The one at the shop is fine."

"We'll use that one for the wedding dress until a few minutes before you model it. We'll use the new one to display a bridesmaid dress. Paula still has the one that she wore to her sister's wedding," Mitzi explained. "We might be the only exclusively plus-sized custom wedding-dress shop there, and we really want to show off what we can do."

"Like if the bride is skinny but her bridesmaids are all big girls?" Tabby asked.

"That's right," Paula said.

"So it's decided on that one?" Jody pointed to the mannequin in the middle of the lineup.

All the others nodded.

"Now we need to give her some hair." Paula led the group to the back of the store, where the wigs were on display.

"I think she needs to have red hair like Mitzi's." Tabby walked down the length of the shelf lined with all shades of auburn hair. "Like this one."

Dixie cocked her head to one side. "That one has too much red."

"Third one from the end," Graham said.

At the sound of his voice, they all whipped around.

"Daddy! Where'd you come from?" Dixie asked.

"You snuck up on us." Tabby grinned.

"Y'all were pretty intent on wigs. What are they for?" Graham asked, his eyes never leaving Mitzi.

"Our new mannequin," Tabby answered. "And it's going to wear the bridesmaid dress that Paula wore in her sister's wedding. The dress is emerald green, so we thought it should have red hair." She finally stopped for a breath. "Oh, my gosh, you're right. This one is perfect."

"We have both blonde and brunette wigs, so it makes sense to buy an auburn one," Jody said.

"Sure does," Paula agreed and then whispered to Mitzi, "Better get one last long look at him before we go to the next store. After he loads our mannequin, he might go on home and you won't see him again today."

Mitzi ignored her. "Thank you so much for helping us today, Graham. We'd have had trouble getting our new mannequin in the van with all the seats up. I believe we've gotten everything we need in this store." She picked up the Styrofoam head with the wig pinned to it and started for the front of the store.

"Okay, then lead the way to whatever I need to help get in the truck. I'll get it loaded and meet y'all at the next one. Just tell me where it is." Graham fell in right beside her. "Want me to carry that?"

"Thanks, but I've got it," she said.

"This bridal fair is a really big thing for you, isn't it? The girls are more excited over this than Christmas, but why are y'all working so hard at it?" Graham asked.

"We might be the only place in Texas that deals in custom-made plus-sized wedding dresses. This fair is a really huge deal. Folks come to it from all over the United States. Getting to go will increase our visibility even more than full-page ads in a bridal magazine," she explained.

"Well, then, what can I do to make it the biggest and best display in the whole shindig?" Graham asked. "You want to borrow the '59 Caddy that's on display at the dealership? You could put a bride and groom in the back seat, but you'll have to have a male mannequin and a tux. Why don't you start carrying a line of rental tuxes for the guys, too?"

"If this brings in the business that I think it will, we won't have time to make tuxes." Mitzi set the wig on the counter and told the lady which mannequin they wanted.

The cashier rang up the total. "Take the sales slip and pull around back to the service doors. The guys will load it for you there."

When they finished the transaction, Mitzi handed Graham the papers. "See you at the party store on Main."

"I know where that is. You girls want to ride with me?" he asked.

Dixie only hesitated for a minute. "Sure we do. You might get lost and need us to show you the way."

When they left the store, Graham and the girls went right. Paula, Mitzi, and Jody went left toward the front parking lot. Paula could hardly contain the giggles until they got in the van.

"Y'all were flirting," she sing-songed.

"Mitzi and Graham sittin' in a tree," Jody started the grade-school chant.

"Go ahead." Mitzi backed out and headed toward the party store. "Get it all out of your systems. And yes, I was imagining him in a custom-made tuxedo. Matter of fact, I was picturing him all sweaty with a hammer in his hand, too. I like a man who's not afraid to work and show his muscles."

"Good for you," Paula said.

Mitzi caught every red light from the place they'd bought the mannequin to the party store. When they arrived, Graham was waiting, but the girls were nowhere in sight. He opened the door and stood to one side.

"Well, thank you, sir." Paula smiled.

"My pleasure," Graham said, but again his eyes were on Mitzi as she brought up the rear.

Dixie and Tabby rounded the end of a display. Their eyes were lit up like they'd just found the pot of gold at the end of a rainbow. Then suddenly Dixie's expression changed dramatically.

"What's the matter?" Mitzi asked.

"Gloria just came through the door," Dixie whispered.

"Who's Gloria?" Paula asked.

"The girl I put on the ground for her smart mouth," Dixie said.

"Ignore her," Mitzi said. "If you say or do anything, she'll have power over you. Pretend like she's an ugly old mangy dog."

Dixie's giggle turned into a guffaw. "That's the funniest picture I've had in my head in years. Now I'm going to laugh every time I see Gloria, and 'dog' is right because she is a bi-atch."

"Dixie!" Graham said.

"Well, she is," Tabby agreed with her sister. "She better keep away from me. I didn't get to hit her, and we're not on the Greenville school property. I might take her down," Tabby said, and then frowned. "A woman is waving at y'all."

Graham glanced in that direction and held up a hand. "That's your mother's cousin, Kayla. She came and spent some time with us right before you girls were born. Haven't seen her since then."

There was no doubt the woman was pregnant and due to deliver any day from the size of her baby bump, but it was the man walking behind her who caused the room to start spinning. Paula steadied herself on a cart that had been left empty in the aisle and hoped that she didn't faint. With her luck she'd cause that cute little unicorn display to tumble, too, as she went down.

Jody nudged her with an elbow. "Are you okay? You look like you just saw a ghost."

"I'm fine," she answered. Right there, not six feet from her, was the father of her child, and he was acting like he'd never seen her. And his wife looked like she was a hell of a lot further along than six months.

Kayla laid a hand on Graham's arm. "I haven't seen you in years. I'd like you to meet my husband, Clinton, and this"—she laid her hand on her stomach—"is our second son. Maybe we'll get a daughter next time."

"Pleased to meet you, Clinton." Graham stuck out a hand.

"No!" Jody whispered. "Is that . . ."

Paula nodded. "It is."

Clinton shook hands with him. "Likewise. How do you know my wife?"

"I'm a cousin to his ex-wife, Rita," Kayla answered. "She and I have been in this area to plan our grandmother's funeral, and we've been going through her house, getting it all ready to sell. Congratulations on y'all going to give it another try when she gets a divorce. I always thought you made a cute couple."

Clinton was careful not to make eye contact with Paula, but she glared at him the whole time. She'd bet he was never separated from Kayla, and now that bi-atch, as Tabby had called Gloria, had ruined everything for Mitzi as well. It was a good thing that a stuffed unicorn's horn couldn't kill a man, because even with a touch of dizziness, Paula couldn't miss his black heart at that distance.

Her eyes wandered to Kayla's big belly. Was that twins? When was the baby even due?

"Rita told me at the funeral that you'd moved back to Celeste but you still run the dealership here." Kayla flipped her long blonde hair over her shoulder and shifted her focus to the girls. "She said the girls were all grown up, but good Lord! Last time I saw y'all, you were just babies. Which one is Dixie and which one is Tabby? Mercy, but y'all are big . . . I mean, t-tall . . . girls," she stammered.

Dixie waved a hand. "This is Tabby. I'm Dixie."

"I'll see you at Lizzy's wedding, I'm sure, but right now I'm starving for pizza, so we're off to a late lunch. Been craving it ever since I got pregnant. Who are all y'all?" She looked from one person to another in the group.

"I'm sorry. I should've already introduced all y'all. This is Mitzi, Paula, and Jody," Graham said. "And Kayla, Rita was wrong. We're never getting back together."

"Never say never," Kayla said.

"Nice to meet all y'all." Clinton finally made eye contact with Paula.

The tension was so thick it would take a machete to cut through it. Dixie and Tabby looked like they could chew up two-by-fours and spit out Tinkertoys. Mitzi had one of those forced smiles on her face.

Jody bumped Paula on the arm and whispered, "Are you okay?"

"Later," Paula answered, but she gripped the handle of the cart so tight that her hands ached.

The awkward silence deafened them until Clinton finally pulled Kayla close to his side and spoke up. "Darlin', we'd better get you fed and headed toward home. I didn't even want her to come down here this close to her due date but"—he kissed her on the cheek—"women have a mind of their own."

"When are you due?" The words slipped out of Paula's mouth so fast that she wasn't sure she'd said them out loud.

"Next week. We left our three-year-old home with Clinton's mama. She adores him and Timmy thinks he's on vacation when he gets to stay with his nana. It's good to see you, Graham. I was always sorry that things didn't work out between you and Rita, and I'll be praying that y'all can forget the past and move on to a wonderful future together. There's nothing like a close-knit family."

"Not going to happen. Have a nice day." Graham turned his back on them.

Clinton escorted Kayla away with his hand on the small of her back, and Paula turned to watch them. "She looks like she could go into labor any minute."

"Yes, she does," Mitzi said. "Do you feel okay? You are really pale."

Paula sucked in a lungful of air and let it out slowly. "It's a small world. I never thought I'd see Clinton again."

"You did good," Jody whispered.

"That was . . . oh, my, God," Mitzi said.

Dixie had already pulled Graham a few feet away. Her hands were on her hips and Tabby shook a finger under his nose. Evidently they didn't want Kayla's prayers to reach God's ears.

"We'll talk about it when we get home," Paula said. "I don't want to say anything in front of Graham. He's got his hands full. So let's go finish up our shopping."

"That's not so easy right now," Mitzi said.

"If you let Kayla or Rita get under your skin, then they'll have power over you, and God might even hear those prayers." Paula pushed the cart forward. "Girls, are y'all ready to help us design some cute napkins for the bridal fair?"

"This ain't over," Dixie told her dad.

"We'll finish talkin' when we get home," Tabby said.

Graham reached out and laid a hand on Mitzi's shoulder. "We should talk about this tomorrow."

"I agree." His touch sent all kinds of tingling vibes throughout her body, but if there was even the remotest chance that he still had a thing for Rita, then she should be fighting the attraction. "But for now we've got work to do, and I don't want to ruin the day for the girls."

"You're amazing," he whispered.

"Why would you say that?"

"You're putting my girls first." He dropped his hand and followed the others.

An hour later everything had been designed and ordered and they'd bought a new folding table. Graham carried it out to his truck and they parted ways—again the girls riding with him so there would be more space in the van.

"I wonder if there'll be anything left of the inside of that truck when they get to Celeste." Jody pulled the seat belt across her body.

Mitzi backed out of the parking space and headed out of town. "Why would you say that?"

"They put their anger on a back burner in all the excitement of picking out things, but it'll come forward pretty quick when we're not around," Paula answered for her. "I got the impression that they damn sure don't want Rita back in their lives."

"Not even if Graham still loves her?" Mitzi asked.

"Not even if she sprouts wings and dons a halo," Paula answered.

"She's bad," Jody piped up from the back seat. "But what about that sumbitch, Clinton?"

"We'll talk about that later. I need some time alone." Paula laid her head back and closed her eyes.

Graham's truck was parked in the driveway, but the girls weren't there. Mitzi pulled in behind him and got out of the van. She raised an eyebrow and asked, "You still in trouble?"

"Not anymore. I reassured them that their mother and I weren't getting back together. Then Alice called and invited them to go swimming with her at the lake. They said for me to tell y'all that they had the best time today, and that they'd see you in church tomorrow," Graham said.

Paula stomped past them and onto the porch. She unlocked the door and disappeared inside. Jody nodded toward them as she carried the wig into the house.

"I'll hold the door for you to bring in the mannequin and the table," Mitzi said.

"Thanks," Graham said. "Lookin' forward to seein' you tomorrow."

"Me, too. I don't mean to be rude, but I need to go in and . . . it's a long story, but we need to support Paula right now," she said.

"Something happened with Kayla back there, didn't it?" Graham lowered the tailgate and picked up the mannequin.

Mitzi nodded as she grabbed the handle on the edge of the folding table. "It did, but I'm not free to talk about it right now."

"Didn't mean to pry," he said.

"You aren't. We were all right there in the awkward situation," Mitzi assured him.

"I'll be ready to put together that arch tomorrow. You need to tell me how wide and tall you want it and then we'll go to work," he said as they made their way to her porch.

"I'll be there by two o'clock," she told him. "And thank you again for helping us today."

He set the mannequin in the middle of the kitchen floor. She leaned the table against the wall and walked him to the door. She felt like she was in a vacuum with no sound or emotions. Everything had been sucked right out of her when Kayla made those comments, and yet at the same time, there was still chemistry between her and Graham when he turned and gave her a sly wink.

"That really is your gorgeous hair color." He nodded toward the Styrofoam head sitting on the coffee table.

"You really think I have pretty hair?"

"I think you are a beautiful woman, Mitzi. See you tomorrow." He tipped an imaginary hat and walked outside.

Jody came out of the sewing room with two beers. "I hid until y'all got done in case you wanted to talk." She handed one bottle to Mitzi and tipped the other one up. "It's been a helluva day, hasn't it?" She rolled her eyes toward the stairs. "Do we leave her alone until she comes out or barge in and make her talk?"

"If she don't spit it out, she's goin' to explode," Mitzi said.

"I'll get the ice cream and meet you there in a couple of minutes," Jody said.

Mitzi nodded and took the stairs two at a time. By the time she reached the top, Jody had joined her with a quart of rocky road ice cream and three spoons.

"Do you think this will do the trick?" Jody asked. "Or do I need to run back down there and bring up a package of chocolate cookies?"

"I think that's enough," Mitzi whispered.

Jody knocked gently on Paula's door.

"Go away. I'm not through crying," Paula sobbed.

Mitzi turned the knob to find it locked. "Either let us in or I'll kick the damn door in."

They heard the click when Paula unlocked the door, but the door remained closed. Mitzi threw it open and marched right into the room. Paula was curled up in a fetal position in the middle of the bed, her hands over her eyes, tears still rolling down her cheeks.

"I'm pregnant and hormonal and in shock and I'm stupid," she said between sobs.

"I can agree with three, but that last one is up for debate." Mitzi crawled up into the center of the bed and laid a hand on Paula's shoulder. "Sit up, honey. Talk to us so we can help. And if you don't stop crying, then I'm going to start, and you know what that does to my face."

Jody followed Mitzi's lead, settled cross-legged to her left, opened the container of ice cream, and stuck three spoons in it. "And with all the drama in my life right now, I sure can't let you two cry without me sobbing, so let's eat ice cream and scream, bitch, yell, kick holes in the wall—whatever it takes to get over this. I can't believe that sumbitch acted like he didn't even know you." Jody dug deep into the ice cream and shoved the spoon toward Paula's mouth. "Open up or it's going to drip all over your shirt."

Paula sat up and took the spoon from Jody. She laid a hand on her stomach as if she was protecting her child. "She just kicked. I think she's tellin' me everything's gonna be all right."

"Of course she is. Just like that Kenny Chesney song—somewhere in the lyrics it says that the monkey on his back jumped off. If you'd have knocked the shit out of Clinton today, that monkey would sure be off."

"Tastes pretty good," Paula said. "I saw your face when Kayla said that about Rita, and I'm so sorry, Mitzi."

The lyrics to the Chesney song ran through Mitzi's mind. The chorus talked about a sign hanging on the wall that said everything's gonna be all right, and she wanted so badly to believe that.

Jody shoveled a spoonful into her own mouth and groaned. "This tastes so good."

"I'm so gullible. I believed all his lies. I bet he thinks a fat woman is so desperate for attention she'll believe anything," Paula said.

With so many tangled-up relationships going on around her, Mitzi began to think that maybe she was the lucky one of the three. Sure, she was attracted to Graham, but she'd have to think long and hard before she gave that bit of chemistry a chance. Not when Rita was evidently so determined to worm her way back into his life.

Paula went on. "Remember what I told you at the time about his wife just finding out that the in-vitro procedure had finally worked with their first child? And now I find out he's got a three-year-old son with her, too." Paula grabbed her head. "Brain freeze."

"Good!" Jody said. "It might help freeze the stupid feeling that you've got about yourself."

"You're not stupid. You are not fat," Mitzi said. "You trusted him. He lied. Now he has to pay for it."

"Do you realize his wife was already pregnant when he was sleeping with me? And he had a toddler at home? What a jerk!" Paula dug into the ice cream again. "The son of a bitch didn't even act like he knew me, but if he had, then his sweet little wife, who's probably a size six when she's not pregnant, would have had questions."

"Makes me wonder how many more kids he's got out there." Mitzi stuck her spoon in the ice cream and shifted her position to lean against the headboard.

"You might want to get our little girl tested so you can compare DNA with all her boyfriends when she starts to date," Jody suggested. "Wouldn't want her going out with her half brother."

"I may just move to Australia. I don't think he's ever been there, but then who knows, the way he lies." Paula stuck her spoon in the ice cream and rested her hand on her stomach. "I know for absolute sure now that I'm never telling him about this baby. And this is one time I'm glad I'm a large person and don't look all that pregnant."

"What are you going to tell the baby when she asks?" Jody asked.

"I'll cross that bridge when I have to. Maybe I'll tell her that he died."

Mitzi gave Paula a sideways hug. "Which might be the truth if he messes around with another woman with a temper hotter'n yours."

"We can always keep an eye on the obituaries from that part of the state," Jody said.

Paula leaned forward and hugged Jody. "Or I could make a voodoo doll and poke pins in all the appropriate places."

"Now that sounds like a good thing, only I'd rather take him out in the woods, nail one of those appropriate places to a tree stump, and give him a knife. When he's brave enough to cut it off, he can try to make it home before he bleeds to death," Jody said.

"*Whew!*" Paula wiped the back of her hand across her forehead. "And I thought I had evil thoughts today."

"Not as evil as I did," Mitzi said.

"I can only imagine." Paula turned to look at her. "Let's talk about all that shit about praying for Rita."

"Graham and I are going to talk about it tomorrow," Mitzi said.

Paula grabbed Mitzi's hand in her left one and Jody's in her right. "Let us pray."

Without hesitation, both of them bowed their heads. "Dear Lord, I know that You have said that vengeance is Yours, so I'm leaving Clinton in Your hands. I expect You to deliver Your method, whatever You see fit, quickly and with much pain. And while You're in a vengeful mood, please take Rita out of the picture. I'm not asking You to kill either of them, however, please don't ever let us have to look upon their faces again. And one more thing, if Kayla has sent up a prayer, go ahead and delete it. It's not a good one. Amen." Paula squeezed their hands and raised her head.

"Amen," Jody said.

"Amen," Mitzi added.

Chapter Fifteen

Graham grew more anxious as the time with Mitzi drew near. He leaned on the porch post and watched for her. After what had happened in the party store, he should be honest with her, but he damn sure didn't want to spend all their time together talking about his ex-wife. His heart kicked in an extra beat when he saw her coming down the street. Yesterday morning she'd worn her hair down, but now she'd piled it up on her head in what his girls called a "messy bun." He wanted to go meet her, take her hand in his, and walk beside her, but he stood still until she started up the steps.

"Hello," he said. "You ready to get to work? I've got all our stuff laid out in the backyard. There's plenty of room on my screened back porch to store the arch when we get it finished. Did you figure out what size you want it to be?" Dammit! That sounded like something he'd say to a guy, not to a gorgeous woman. He should have at least offered her a cold beer.

"Think we can get it done this evening?" she asked.

"I hope so." He closed his eyes and kicked himself for being so damned awkward. "That came out all wrong. I didn't mean that I don't want to spend time with you. I'm not very good at this. Would you like a cold beer or something to drink before we get started?"

"I'd love one," she said. "I didn't know what to bring in the way of tools."

"I've got everything we need." He opened the door for her. "I'm rambling to cover up being so awkward around you. Leave it to me to mess up in the first two minutes."

She laid a hand on his arm. "You didn't mess up anything. I'm every bit as nervous as you are."

Her touch stilled his nerves. "Thank you for that, Mitzi."

He led her through the foyer and into the kitchen, where he took two beers from the refrigerator and handed one to her, then realized that he should have opened it for her. He could run a dealership, buy and sell cars, organize and take care of all the departments without blinking an eye, but every day he knew Mitzi, the more tongue-tied and awkward he became.

"Bring your beer and follow me." He led her from the kitchen out onto the screened porch.

"My granny has a room like this, and I've always loved it."

"It was part of the reason I wanted this house. My grandparents had one like this, too, and I used to enjoy spending time there with my grandpa while he told me stories about his younger days." He opened the door out to the backyard, where he'd laid out the lumber, the four-by-eight sheet of lattice, and all of his tools.

"Looks to me like you're pretty organized." She pulled the tab from the top of her beer, took a long drink, and then set it down on the porch. "Let's get busy. I think it should be at least six feet wide to accommodate our bride mannequin. If we get to go next year, we may get us a male mannequin and dress him up in a suit or tux."

He didn't want to talk about bridal fairs or even wedding arches. He wanted to reinforce what he'd said to Kayla the day before about never getting back with his ex-wife. Mitzi needed to understand that for him to ever be able to ask her out on a date—and that's what he really wanted to do.

She laid out the plans on the porch. "So we build a frame, then cover it with lattice, right?"

"Yes," he said. "I did some research and found out that it should be about seven feet tall and five feet wide, but with your model being a big woman, I thought we'd make it bigger."

I want to ask you out on a real date, he thought.

"That sounds good. What can I do to help?"

"First we build a base for it to sit on," he said.

Maybe a movie or a play in Dallas after we have a romantic supper.

"It doesn't have to be really well finished. We'll be using a lot of flowers and greenery on it," she said.

I wonder if maybe it would be easier if we did something like a picnic with the girls at first.

"I've already sawed the boards for the base," he said. "I thought we'd make it in five pieces. The two bases, the sides, and then the arched top. That way after the bridal fair, we could take a few screws out and store it flat."

I'm going to ask her to go out on my pontoon boat before she leaves here today.

He picked up a board and carried it to the chop saw he'd set up on the porch. "If you'll hold that end and keep it steady, I'll take a foot off the other end."

In an hour they had the framework done and the plastic lattice cut to size and bent over the whole thing. She sat down on the back porch and leaned against the porch post. Sweat stuck her hair to her face and forehead, and her arms glistened with moisture.

Dammit again! He should have stopped working halfway through the job and offered her another beer or at least a bottle of water. He was failing miserably as a gentleman.

"I have a pontoon boat," he blurted out as he sat down beside her. "The girls have been begging me to take it out. Want to go with us next Sunday after church? You can invite Harry and Fanny Lou and

Paula and Jody if you want." He held his breath, waiting for her to say something.

"That would be fun," she said slowly.

"Want a drink of something?" Lord, nothing he said came out right. "I mean . . ."

She laid a moist hand on his sweaty knee. "Graham, I'm a little . . . what's the word . . . *discomfited* is what Granny would say . . . around you, too. I had a crush on you in high school, you know."

"Well, I've got one on you now." He wiped his face on the tail of his T-shirt and hoped that she thought all the sweat was from the weather.

"For real?" Her eyes widened.

"Yes, ma'am," he said. "It took all the courage I had to ask you to go on a boat ride next Sunday."

"Bullshit!" she said and then put a hand over her mouth. "You were so popular in high school, and so self-confident."

"That's just the way you saw me," he said. "I'm going to get another beer. Want one?"

"Yes, I do, and let's have it inside. It's damn hot out here." She wiped her face on her shirtsleeve.

"Okay." He stood up and offered her a hand.

See there, that wasn't so hard to admit, was it? His dad's voice was in his head.

She put her hand in his and let him pull her up to a standing position.

"I want you to know that I meant it when I told Kayla it's over between me and Rita. My ex-wife came by my office yesterday, and I told her the same thing." He kept her hand in his all the way to the kitchen, only letting go of it to get the cold beers.

She sat down on a barstool and sucked down several gulps before she came up for air. "That really tastes good, and you don't owe me any explanations about Rita."

"I like being with you, Mitzi, and I want to be honest with you. All I felt was relief that I wasn't still with her." Graham turned his head and their eyes locked. "I realized that I never really loved Rita, and that makes me feel guilty in a way."

"Why?" Mitzi asked.

"I married her, and you're supposed to love someone if you vow to be with them in sickness and health," he answered.

"You've grown since she left. You had the girls to take care of and a business to run. Now you see things clearer than you did back then," she said.

"Thank you for that."

They sat in silence for a few minutes, without the need for words to fill the vacuum. Then Mitzi finally asked, "Did you ever want to do something with your life other than stepping into your father's shoes at the dealership?"

Graham shook his head. "No, ma'am. I didn't even want to go to college, but Mama wanted me to have that experience. After Rita left, I got my business degree by taking online courses at night. Experience and what my dad taught me was far more helpful. How about you? Ever want to do something other than what you do?"

It was her turn to shake her head. "Mama wanted me to be a high school home economics teacher, only they don't call it that anymore. I think it's called FCCLA. Never can remember what all the letters stand for, but it's the same as the old home economics classes. I made it through one semester of college, wondering the whole time why in the hell I needed American History 101 to teach young girls and boys how to cook and sew."

"Or English Composition 101 to learn how to run a car dealership," Graham chuckled again. "So what did you do after that semester?"

"I got a job doing alterations in a fancy wedding-dress shop in Amarillo," she answered. "Paula, Jody, and I'd dreamed about putting in our own shop and catering to plus-sized women for years. Then"—she frowned, as if she wasn't sure if she should go on—"Paula was dating the father of her baby and it became a bad breakup. She needed a change, and after we'd made her sister's wedding dress, we really got serious about wanting to put in our own shop. Jody was more than ready for us to come home and put in a shop, so we finally said it was now or never and we did it last December. We figured we'd have to build up the business for two years before we'd start seeing enough profit to pay our salaries, but we were wrong. We've made dresses for women from four states already, and we never lack for something to keep us busy. I wouldn't want to do anything else."

"Well, y'all have been a godsend to my girls. I've never seen them this happy," Graham said.

"Daddy!" Dixie's voice blasted through the walls.

"In the kitchen," he called out.

"I should be going," Mitzi said.

"No need to rush off because the girls are home. They'll be excited to see you." Graham laid a hand on her arm.

"Hey, Daddy, guess what!" Dixie stopped in her tracks as she burst out onto the porch with Tabby and Alice right behind her. "Hi, Mitzi!"

Tabby pushed around Dixie and gave Mitzi a hug. "We didn't go to the movies. We went to the fabric store instead and got stuff to make us some shirts. We bought two patterns, and we want you to tell us which one is easiest."

"Can you come inside and look at the stuff right now?" Dixie asked. "You'll be the first one other than Aunt Alice to get the tour of the house, too."

"I'd love to see what you've bought." Mitzi set her empty can on the table and stood up.

Graham was a little jealous of his own daughters for being able to steal Mitzi from him right when they were getting into a more comfortable place with each other.

Alice reached out and grabbed Mitzi's wrist. "Next time *you* take them to the fabric store. I was bored to death."

"Be glad to," Mitzi agreed without hesitation. "It's like taking a trip to heaven for me."

"Baseball, basketball, or even football is my piece of heaven. Give me anything that bounces or can be thrown, and I'm good. Plaids, florals, patterns, and all that kind of thing—not so much," Alice said. "I can only stay a little while. There's a game on television I want to see."

Dixie grabbed Mitzi's hand and pulled her into the house, leaving Alice and Graham still on the porch with the rest of the cookies between them.

"So what's this all about?" Alice asked as soon as they were alone.

One of Graham's wide shoulders popped up in a shrug. "I'm not sure. Maybe friendship that could work into something more later. Right now, it's a nice pleasant afternoon with a beautiful woman."

"Well, good for you. It's about damn time you moved on with your life," Alice told him. "And I like Mitzi. She fits in with the family and she loves the girls. I've got to get home or I'll miss all the pregame stuff."

"When are you going to move on and settle down?" Graham asked. "You've still got time to have a couple of kids of your own."

"Probably never." She picked up his beer and downed what was left. "I heard Rita came to see you at the shop yesterday. Please tell me . . ." She looked genuinely worried.

He stood up and draped an arm around her shoulders. "You have nothing to worry about, sis. That ship sailed and probably sank in the middle of the ocean a long time ago."

"The girls told me you said that, but I had to hear it from you. See you later." She hugged him and left by way of the back door.

Graham followed the buzz of the conversation upstairs. He leaned on the doorjamb to Dixie's room for several minutes before anyone noticed him.

Mitzi was talking about patterns and what would be the easiest one for them to start with. She even gave them some advice on how important ironing was when they were sewing. Four pieces of fabric were stretched out on the bed along with a couple of packages that must be patterns. Mitzi picked up one long piece and gathered it in her hands, then held it up to Tabby's face.

"Beautiful color for you. Brings out the color in your eyes and the floral pattern is small, so it won't overpower you," she said.

Tabby took the fabric from Mitzi and draped it around her neck like a scarf. She crossed the room to look at herself in the mirror. "It does bring out my eyes. I love big flowers, but I feel like I'm a whole botanical garden when I try on a shirt with them. Why do companies make big girls things in horizontal stripes and huge roses, anyway?"

"I know, darlin'." Mitzi patted her on the shoulder. "And heaven forbid, buying a bathing suit. The designers think if we wear anything bigger than a size ten, it should have flowers the size of dinner plates on it."

"Or like you say, stripes that go around our bodies," Dixie said. "That's why we want to design and make our own things." She turned and flashed a bright smile at her father. "Oh, hi, Daddy. We didn't hear you coming up the stairs."

"I avoided that squeaky step," he said.

"Tabby and I'll have to remember that when we're old enough to date next year and break curfew," she teased.

"I don't intend to be late." Tabby elbowed her sister.

"And I'll be waiting in the living room with the lights on until you get home, so you don't need to worry about that step." Graham shifted his eyes over to Mitzi. "Did you get the house tour or were they so excited about all this that you came right up here?"

"I got the tour," she answered. "You have a lovely home."

"Thank you," he said. "We would have liked one more bathroom, but the girls are learning the art of sharing."

"Not gracefully." Tabby shot a look toward Dixie. "She takes like for . . . ever to do her hair. Even to come to work at the shop, it takes her hours to put it up in a ponytail. Every hair has to be just right."

"Well." Dixie popped her hands on her hips. "Miz OCD here takes even longer to make her bed. If there's a wrinkle it drives her crazy."

"You're going to waste your time with Mitzi by arguing?" Graham asked.

"Sorry about that," Dixie apologized. "So we thought we'd make a shirt for the Fourth of July out of red-and-white stripes." She held up a length of the fabric. "And then we'd put a ruffle around the bottom of the star material. We even thought we'd really be twins that night and dress alike. What do you think?"

Mitzi picked up a pattern. "Using this one?"

Tabby nodded. "It's only got a few seams."

◦⁀◦

Mitzi loved spending a little time with the girls and talking fabrics and patterns, but she would have rather stayed in the kitchen and visited with Graham longer. He'd said he had a crush on her. That was a big enough deal to tell Paula and Jody about, but she didn't want to jinx it. She wanted to hold it tightly in her heart and enjoy the thought for days, rather than hours.

"So what do you think?" Dixie asked.

Mitzi almost asked *About what?* before she remembered the pattern in her hand. "This one would be good to start with. If you have any questions, just holler at me. Right now, though, I should be going. Paula and Jody will be home soon, and I've got plans with them this evening," Mitzi said.

"I'll walk you out," Graham said. "And if you two start up that tiff after I'm gone, be sure there's not blood involved."

"Daddy!" Dixie and Tabby said at the same time.

"Okay, then, if there's blood, clean it up before bedtime," he said.

When they reached the bottom of the stairs, she said, "You're really good with them."

"So are you." He traced her jawline with his fingertip, his touch sending shivers down her backbone.

She reached up and touched his face in a similar way. Time stood still, and the only sound was the beating of her heart. His eyelids fluttered shut and she moistened her lips with the tip of her tongue. One of his hands gently traveled down her arm while the other one cradled the back of her head. His touch created a ball of heat in the pit of her stomach, and it grew even larger, warming her from the inside out when his lips met hers in a fiery kiss that rocked her world. Her arms snaked up around his neck, and he pulled her closer to his body.

When it ended, he gave her a quick kiss on the forehead. "I've wanted to do that for a long time. I'll walk you home."

"It's only a block. You don't have to do that," she said.

"A gentleman always walks his date to the door." He grinned as he laced his fingers in hers.

Date? Kiss? Jody and Paula had said that if he kissed her, it was a real date, but how could it be when they'd spent the afternoon with saws and hammers instead of candlelight and wine?

When they reached her door, he brushed another sweet kiss across her lips. "I'll see you before then, but I'm really looking forward to next Sunday."

She went inside to an empty house and headed straight to the kitchen for a bottle of water. Glad that neither Paula nor Jody was home right then, she wanted to bask in the idea that she was going out with Graham. Even if they'd be surrounded by friends and family on a pontoon boat, he'd said it was a real date.

"Hey, anybody home?" Harry startled her when he popped in the door.

"Just me," Mitzi said. "Want a bottle of water or a beer?"

"No, I'm good, and I'm glad you're here alone. I know you and Graham have been doing a little flirting dance. I need to talk to you about that." Harry pulled out a kitchen chair and sat down.

"Is it about Rita going to the dealership?" Mitzi asked.

Harry nodded. "I guess you already know what I'm about to say. If there's a chance of them making a family—"

"I just came from his house," Mitzi butted in. "He told me exactly that there's no chance of him and Rita ever trying to make another go of it."

"Tabby and Dixie don't want their mother in their lives?" Harry frowned.

"Do you remember Rita at all?" Mitzi finally sat down across from her father.

"Not well. Seems like she was pretty wild," Harry answered.

"She's blonde, blue eyed, and even smaller than Jody is right now. The girls told us that when they saw her again after more than ten years, they felt she still didn't want children who didn't look like her," Mitzi explained. "I've got a date with him next Sunday. We're taking the girls out on his pontoon boat. You and Granny are invited, too."

"Just be careful." Harry pushed back the chair. "I love you and sure don't want to see you hurt. And, honey, that don't sound like much of a date."

She stood up and hugged him. "I promise that I'll be careful. And, Daddy, I'm finding out that all dates don't involve roses and lookin' at the moon together."

"If you fall for him, darlin', make sure it's for him and not to get those two girls," Harry said as he wrapped his arms around her.

"Yes, sir." She stepped back.

"Just an old concerned daddy who can't stand for his baby girl's heart to get broken. Your mama and I loved each other so much. I want that for you," he said as he opened the door.

"Me, too, Daddy," she said. "Me, too."

Chapter Sixteen

Jody sat in one of two old lawn chairs in the middle of a bare spot where her trailer used to be parked. Less than two weeks ago she was in a committed relationship. In some ways it seemed more like ten years, but sitting there, the pain was still very raw. To her right, what was left of her garden had shriveled up and looked like a bed of weeds. Ruts were dug deep into the ground where the trailer had been taken out right over the top of all the plants that she'd cared for so lovingly.

"It's a testimony of my life right there," she said. "Smashed and dead."

"Excuse me?" A man's voice seemed to come from the white clouds above her.

It startled her so badly she almost fell backward in the chair. She glanced to her left to see a man with one foot braced against a big pecan tree, his arms crossed over his broad chest.

"Who are you, and what are you doing here?" she demanded.

"I might ask you the same thing." He removed his cowboy hat and wiped sweat from his brow with a snow-white handkerchief he took from the hip pocket of his Wranglers.

"I'm Jody Andrews and until ten days ago, I lived with Lyle Jones in the trailer that set right here." Her tone sounded cold even to her own ears.

"I see. Mind if I sit down?" He held his hat in his hand. "I'm Quincy Roberts."

She nodded toward the other chair. "I hear you're going to buy this property. Is that true?" Jody asked.

"I'm dealing with Lyle for it. It's the last little corner, and I'd like to have it, but we're haggling over mineral rights. Even though I'm not interested in drilling for oil, I don't buy anything that doesn't totally belong to me," Quincy said. "I heard about how Lyle left you high and dry. Why on earth would you come back out here?"

"Closure," she answered. "Seeing my garden like this with nothing left of a fifteen-year commitment but two old lawn chairs almost does it for me." She pushed up out of the lawn chair. "What are you going to do with this land, anyway?"

"Run cattle on it. Maybe even a few hogs," he said. "I'm an oil man, but I like to get my hands dirty. It makes me happy. What are you doing now that Lyle's married to another woman?"

Hogs! Stinky old pigs wallowing in a mud puddle in the hot summer. Now that could bring her to the acceptance stage pretty damn quick. She took a few steps toward her old truck. "What do I do? Well, Mr. Roberts, I'm not sitting at home, wasting away to nothing. I'm a strong woman, and I've got good friends. If you see Lyle you can tell him that. If you're asking what I do for a living, I make custom wedding dresses for plus-sized women."

"What are plus-sized women?" He got up and followed her to her truck.

She turned around. "Larger ladies. Everyone deserves a perfect dress."

"Everyone deserves a perfect life. Guess you didn't get it, did you?"

"Bit of a smart-ass, aren't you?" She leaned against the truck. "Do any of us ever get a perfect life? Is there even such a thing?"

"Not in my world," Quincy chuckled. "And I've been called worse. So where are you living now?"

"My partners in the business and I live above the shop. It's in an old two-story house on Main Street. Shop is on the ground floor," she told him.

His eyes went to the pitiful garden. "What happened to that little garden is a shame. I know what it takes to keep one weeded and watered."

According to what she'd heard, Quincy could buy the town of Celeste, have it bulldozed, and then turn the whole thing into a hog pen. Why would he even have a backyard garden?

"You looked surprised. I told you I like to get my hands dirty," he said.

"Me, too, and I'm sure I'll miss having a place for one next spring," she said. "It's nice to have met you, Mr. Roberts."

"My friends call me Quincy," he said.

"But we're not friends," she told him, but she wondered what it would be like to get to know him better.

"We could be, Jody." He settled his hat back onto his head. "Is it okay if I call you Jody?"

"Sure," she agreed. "Like I said . . . Quincy . . . it's a pleasure to meet you. And just a heads-up, Lyle is anxious to sell, so hold out for those mineral rights." She didn't care if Lyle even got fair market price for the place, because she'd never get anything out of it.

"Oh, I will. I don't give up easily." He tipped his hat toward her and turned around.

She could see a white pickup truck on the far side of the property. She'd probably been thinking so hard about how she'd like to strangle Lyle that she hadn't even heard it when Quincy drove up.

She stopped at the snow-cone stand on her way back through town and got three with lids—all rainbow with cherry, coconut, and grape— then drove straight home so she'd get there before they all turned to nothing but liquid.

"Hello! Y'all home?" she called out as she kicked the back door shut with the heel of her cowboy boot.

"Up here in the living room," Mitzi yelled.

Jody took the stairs two at a time. "I brought snow cones."

Paula reached out a hand as soon as Jody was in the room. "Bless your heart. I wanted one but the line was so long that I didn't stop on the way home. Where have you been?"

"You first," Jody said. "What'd you do? Shop for the baby?"

"I saw a movie today that made me feel much better about everything. Clinton is a first-class bastard. I feel sorry for his wife, but he's her husband, not mine." She dipped into the snow cone with the plastic spoon that came with it. "I'm glad you're here. Mitzi wouldn't tell me a blessed thing until you arrived."

"I didn't want to tell it twice. Graham asked me for a date next Sunday. We're taking his pontoon boat out on the lake, and y'all are invited," she said before she took the first bite of her snow cone.

"I believe you're old enough to go on a date without chaperones," Paula said.

"The girls are going and so is Alice. You might as well come with us," she said.

"It's not a real date until it's just the two of you, but I'd love to go out on the lake, so I'm in. Now your turn, Jody?" Paula said.

Jody curled up in the recliner across the room from the sofa where the other two sat. She needed a few minutes to talk without tears or cussing, so she turned to Mitzi. "I'll tell you in a minute, but I want to hear more about you and Graham. I know it was hot out there building the arch. How did it turn out?"

"It was a sweaty job but I'm pleased with it. He's storing it out on his screened porch until we need to load it, and he made it so that afterwards it can be dismantled and stored flat," she said.

"Did he kiss you and make you all hot and sweaty on the inside?" Jody asked.

"Yes, he did," Mitzi answered.

"Well, I'll be danged." Paula clapped her hands. "I told you it was a real date. Do you believe me now?"

"Maybe," Mitzi said. "But what do I do now? If we started dating and decided we didn't like each other, then would that ruin my friendship with the girls? And they like me as a friend, but what about as their dad's girlfriend? It's all so complicated. And then there's the thing with Rita." She told them about Rita showing up at the dealership.

"You sure you even want to deal with that?" Jody asked. "It could sure get sticky if she starts attending graduations and birthdays and all that."

"Are you blind-trusting him?" Paula asked.

Mitzi could understand both questions. Jody was probably giving thanks again that she wasn't pregnant and having to deal with those events with Lyle. Paula had gone into a relationship trusting Clinton, and look where it had got her.

"I'm going to take it slow. What could possibly happen on this next date with all y'all around us anyway?" Mitzi asked.

"Okay, then we want to know how the kiss made you feel," Jody demanded.

"If I were in the second grade, I'd say it was like Prince Charming kissed a princess and I was that girl. But as a grown-up, the fact that he walked me home and held my hand the whole way meant as much as the kiss," Mitzi answered.

"From the looks of your mouth, it's like we're back in elementary school." Paula took a bite from her snow cone.

"With all our lips turning cherry red, it does, doesn't it?" Jody finished off her snow cone and set the cup aside. "Now it's my turn. Lyle was serious about selling the property. Quincy Roberts was out there today looking at it."

Mitzi leaned forward on the sofa. "We need details."

"He's tall, maybe around six feet. Not as tall as Graham or as big. Broad shoulders and he was wearing starched jeans and boots, and an expensive cowboy hat. I only got a glimpse of his truck, but it was one of those four-door numbers and real shiny white. Is that enough details?"

"No, keep going," Mitzi said.

"He had brown eyes and a face that was all angles. I'd guess him to be in his late thirties, maybe even early forties," Jody said. "That's all I know. We exchanged a few words. He reminded me of a cowboy from a television commercial about expensive whiskey."

"With a name like that, we'd remember him if he went to school with us," Mitzi said. "I wonder what he wants with that piece of property."

"He said he wants to run some cattle out there or raise hogs," Jody said. "I think that's kind of poetic after the way Lyle has treated me. It sounds kind of crazy, don't it? Smelly hogs runnin' on that land kind of brings me closer to feelin' peace about this whole thing."

Mitzi laughed out loud. "That's too funny."

Paula giggled with her. "You should've told us you wanted to go back out there again. We would've gone with you."

"I needed to go alone." In one way Jody was glad that she had gone alone, but in another she wished that her friends had been with her so they could render an opinion of Quincy. "I should have at least had part of the money from the sale. Don't seem fair that I worked and made more than Lyle did most years, and yet, he gets everything but a leaky trailer and a couple of worn-out lawn chairs."

"I mean about Quincy. Did you feel an attraction to him? Sounds like he is a nice-lookin' guy," Mitzi asked.

"Who even cares? I'll never see him again," Jody said.

"Crap!" Mitzi said.

"What?" Jody cocked her head to one side.

"I wanted you to say that you were intrigued by this Quincy guy," Mitzi answered.

"It hasn't even been two weeks since Lyle left. I'm not a bit interested in any man right now, not even a rebound. Besides, we've got your love life to worry about and a new baby coming into the family. This is not the time for a romance for me," Jody declared.

⁓

Guilt poured down on Mitzi like hard rain. Even if they were putting up a good front, both her friends were still hurting. What right did she have to be happy that she'd shared a kiss with her old crush? Telling them about it was like rubbing their faces in her happiness.

"Why the sudden long face?" Jody asked.

Paula laid a hand on Mitzi's shoulder. "Don't let us rain on your day. We made our choices and we're living with the consequences. We're happy for you."

Jody's head bobbed up and down. "Of course we are. We want to hear about you and Graham. It puts a little ray of hope and sunshine in our lives."

"Here's to the future." Paula laid her hand on the table. "Y'all with me?"

"To the future." Mitzi put hers on top of Paula's.

"Amen." Jody added hers to the pile.

Then, like they did when they were little girls, they all jerked their hands free and high-fived each other.

"I know we said we weren't working on Sunday, but let's break the rules. I'm going downstairs to finish up the hem on Ellie Mae's dress," Paula said.

"I'll go with you." Jody stood up. "I can always bead a veil. That job takes a lot of time, and when I'm working, I'm not fretting."

"Well, I'm not sitting up here all alone all evening. I'll work on a pink-satin quilt for the new baby." Mitzi tossed her empty cup into a nearby trash can.

"That's so sweet," Paula said. "But what you should be doing is looking up a pattern for your own dress. Like I told you before, you're going to be the first one of us to get to the altar."

Jody started out of the room but stopped and looked over her shoulder. "Just make sure you get a marriage license. You've seen what can happen if you don't."

"I'm not sure I even want a perfect dress," Mitzi said. "I'd just as soon get married in shorts and bare feet on a beach somewhere."

They paraded down the stairs and were headed toward the sewing room when a hard rap turned them all around toward the front door. Since she was the last in line, Mitzi opened it, and Ellie Mae fell into her arms. Makeup ran down her face in black streaks as the tears flowed. Sobs wracked her body and soaked Mitzi's T-shirt.

Jody hurried over to pat her on the back. "Did someone die?"

Paula guided both her and Mitzi toward a pink sofa, grabbed a fistful of tissues, and put them in Ellie Mae's hand. "Stop cryin' and tell us what's happened."

"Darrin doesn't want . . ." Ellie Mae blew her nose on a tissue and tossed it in the small trash can. "He doesn't want . . ." The sobs started again, and then in a high-pitched squeal, she said, "Want to marry me anymore. I'm pregnant. My family's goin' to disown me, and that beautiful dress you're makin' . . . oh, my God, what am I going to do?" She bent over and gagged.

Paula quickly ran for the small bathroom trash can and put it in front of her. "Did your mama find out that you're pregnant?"

"No," Ellie Mae wailed.

"Do you need a glass of water?" Jody asked.

"I'd throw up anything I try to put in my stomach right now. I didn't know where to go. I couldn't go home. Mama doesn't know about the baby, and it's a boy." She dragged out the last word in another high-pitched wail. "I don't know anything about boy babies, and I'm going to be a single mother, and a boy needs a father," she sobbed.

"We're not living in the Stone Age, darlin'." Paula patted her on the shoulder. "It's not a sin to be a single mother."

"Your daddy isn't a preacher. I've never even been around little boys." Ellie Mae's voice went so high that it lost the last syllable.

The music from Blake Shelton's "Honey Bee" startled Mitzi for a couple of seconds when it filled the foyer. Then she realized the sound was a ringtone coming from Ellie Mae's purse, which she'd thrown on the floor just before collapsing in Mitzi's arms.

"That's Darrin's ringtone," Ellie Mae whispered. "I don't want to talk to him."

"Then turn off your phone," Jody suggested.

"No, I might change my mind. I want to think about it." Ellie Mae blew her nose on another fistful of tissues and tossed them into the trash can. "We were in bed. He said he was glad that he was my first, because that was important to a man."

Mitzi shut her eyes to keep from rolling them toward the ceiling. "And?"

"We're getting married so I thought it was best that I was honest. So I told him that he wasn't the first, but he'd be the last." Her chin quivered and the sniffles started again.

"How about you? Had he had other women before you?" Jody asked.

"Of course. He had the whole college experience. Frat parties. Women whose names he didn't even know, all that kind of thing," Ellie Mae answered.

"And he wanted a virgin? That's not fair," Paula said. "What's good for the goose is good for the gander."

"How did he not know that you've been in other relationships? Celeste is a small town," Mitzi said.

"He's from up in Oklahoma. He moved to Greenville last fall. I met him at a church social down there, and we hit it off from the first day." Her face turned crimson. "I kind of knew he was the one, so I played hard to get. We didn't have sex until Thanksgiving."

Ellie Mae jumped like she'd been shot when another hard knock turned everyone's attention toward the door again. "I don't want to see him, not yet. Tell him to go away."

Mitzi cracked the door to find a tall, muscular guy on the other side holding his hat in one hand and a lawn chair in the other. The hat looked new. The lawn chair's webbing was frayed and sagging.

"I'm Quincy Roberts. Is Jody Andrews here? She said she worked at a wedding dress shop, and I believe this is the only one in town," he said.

Mitzi stuck her head back inside and said, "Jody, there's someone here to see you."

"If it's Lyle, tell him to go to hell," Jody said.

Mitzi raised both eyebrows. "It's not Lyle."

With a puzzled expression, Jody left Ellie Mae's side, but when she saw who was at the door, she grabbed Mitzi by the arm and said, "Don't you dare leave me alone."

"Hello again, Jody. You forgot your chairs when you left. I'm returning them." When Quincy smiled, his blue eyes twinkled.

"Throw them in the trash. I don't want 'em," she said.

"They're still pretty good chairs, and could be rewebbed. How 'bout I just set them here on the porch? Would you be free to go for a cup of coffee with me?" Quincy asked her.

"We've got sweet tea in the refrigerator," Mitzi said before Jody could refuse. "And we've still got leftover cake. There's a situation going on in the house, but y'all are welcome to sit in those lawn chairs and have a visit. Just go on and sit down. I'll bring out tea and cake."

"That's nice. I have a terrible sweet tooth." Quincy unfolded the chairs and set them up a couple of feet apart.

It took Mitzi only a few minutes to put pieces of cake on a couple of plates, fill glasses with ice and sweet tea, and take it outside on a tray. She set it on the porch between the chairs and turned to go back inside. But before she'd taken a step, Quincy's phone rang.

"Excuse me. I really have to take this call." He stood up, left the porch, and took a few steps out into the yard.

"I'm not talking to you for a week. You could have told him I wasn't here," Jody whispered. "Is Ellie Mae any better? You do realize she hasn't paid her bill in full. We still need payment for all the flowers and her mother's and sister's dresses. I need to be in there calming her down."

"She's relating to Paula better than me," Mitzi whispered back to Jody. "And we both needed a break from her. Besides, I wanted to see what Quincy was like."

"You are a dead woman. I could have refused to go for coffee with him, and this could've been avoided," Jody hissed out the side of her mouth.

"Do I need to be careful what I eat or drink? Are you going to poison me?" Mitzi asked.

"I'd like to. Do you realize that only one person needs to drive down the street and see me out here with him?" Her phone rang before she could finish the sentence.

"Hello, Mama."

Jody shot a dirty look toward Mitzi and listened for a good thirty seconds before she said, "No, Mama, I have not been cheating on Lyle. I only met the man this afternoon. He's buying the property where our trailer used to be, and he brought my lawn chairs back to me."

Another few seconds passed and another dirty look or two, then Jody said, "I'm hanging up. I don't have to listen to this." She shoved the phone back in her purse and sent another sideways look toward Mitzi. "See what you caused."

"Hey, it's either have a nice, pleasant conversation with a handsome guy or listen to Ellie Mae whine until dark. Your choice, but if you're smart, you'll stay out here even after he's gone," Mitzi said.

Quincy ended his call and rejoined them on the porch. "Cake looks great, and I am thirsty. That was the Realtor that has the property. We were discussing my offer," he said. "I don't know that I caught your name."

"Mitzi Taylor," she said. "And I should go on back inside."

"Hey, are you kin to Harry Taylor?" Quincy asked.

Mitzi stopped at the door and turned around. "He's my father."

"Good man. I've had some dealings with him in the oil business. He's the one who used to inspect things until he retired." Quincy sat down in the chair and turned his attention to Jody.

"See y'all later." Mitzi escaped back into the house to find Ellie Mae sipping sweet tea and having an Oreo.

What a day, Mitzi thought as she sank down onto the sofa across from Paula and Ellie Mae. *Instead of floating on air because Graham kissed me, I'm wrung out from all this drama. I wonder if he thinks I'm still a virgin—that since I'm a larger woman, no man would've ever wanted to go to bed with me.*

"I've got to make a bathroom run," Paula said as she pushed up from the sofa. "Too much lemonade this afternoon."

"I understand, and I think Mama might be getting suspicious about me needing to go so often," Ellie Mae said. "This tastes even better than ice cream."

Mitzi suddenly felt guilty because she hadn't thought to get out a quart of ice cream and four spoons. That was the standard problem solver in her friendship with Paula and Jody. "Would you like a bowl of ice cream?"

Ellie Mae took another cookie from the package. "Not when I can have these. I'm a chocoholic."

Paula covered the short distance from the small half bath at the end of the foyer and sat down beside Ellie Mae. "Sometimes ice cream works. Sometimes it takes cookies. Feelin' better? Ready to talk to him now?"

"Not yet. He really hurt my feelings," Ellie Mae said.

Jody came inside at the same time someone knocked on the back door.

"I bet that's Granny." Mitzi headed that way, not ready to talk about the Rita-and-Graham situation with Fanny Lou but glad for an excuse to get away from the foyer drama again. She practiced her *we're taking it real slow* speech all the way through the kitchen. No way was she telling her granny about the kisses.

She unlocked the door and opened it to find Clinton Ballard. His face was set in stone, and his arms were crossed over his chest.

"May I help you?" Her tone dripped icicles, but she couldn't help it.

He opened the screen door. "I want to talk to Paula."

Mitzi blocked his way into the kitchen. "Too bad. She doesn't want to talk to you."

"So she told you about us, did she?" he growled.

"Yep, so we all know you're a son of a bitch," Mitzi answered.

"I'm going to talk to her." He started to push his way past her.

Mitzi put her hands on his chest and walked him right back outside. "You can wait right here. I'll see if she wants to even lay eyes on you. If not, then you'll have sixty seconds to get off our property."

"Or what?" He threw open the door again.

"Or I'll call the police. If they get here before I can load my shotgun, I'll let them take you to jail. If not, then they can call the coroner," Mitzi answered.

"Just go get her and stop making threats," he growled.

Mitzi reached for the gun hanging above the door on two hooks and racked in a shell.

He put up both hands and stammered, "Take it easy, lady. And for your information, I am a policeman."

"Not in Celeste, you're not. You stay right there while I ask Paula if she'd like to visit with you." Mitzi slammed the door in his face. She stopped at the cabinet, took down the tequila, had two big gulps right out of the bottle to steady her nerves, and laid the shotgun on the table. If Ellie Mae saw the gun, she might take it away from her and shoot Darrin. Then she made her way to the foyer and told Paula that someone was there to see her.

Paula raised an eyebrow. "Who?"

"Clinton Ballard is at the back door. The shotgun is loaded and right there if you need it. Want me to go with you?"

"Yes." Paula's chin quivered. "Why would he come here?"

"He wouldn't tell me."

"Ellie Mae, we've got some business to take care of but we'll be right back," Mitzi said.

"I'm okay," Ellie Mae whimpered. "But you won't be gone long, will you?"

"No, honey," Paula answered. "Just a few minutes. Can we bring you anything when we come back?"

"No, I've got cookies right here." She tried to smile.

"Okay, then." Mitzi patted her on the shoulder and then almost jogged to the kitchen. She picked up the gun as they passed the table.

"She says you might have a word or two, but you're to stay on the porch," Mitzi told him as she took a couple of steps to the side so he could see Paula.

"It took you long enough," he growled as he reached for the door.

"Oh, no!" Mitzi pointed the gun right at his crotch. "Don't even think about coming inside."

"Do we have to talk through a screen door? Can't I come inside the house?" he asked. "Paula, I need to talk to you privately."

"Whatever you've got to say to me can be said in front of Mitzi, and if she says we keep the screen between us, then that's what we do," Paula told him.

"Okay, then. I'm sorry that I led you on, but I was lonely. Kayla was sick all the time, and I was trying to take care of my father, and—"

Paula held up a palm. "Real apologies don't need buts, ifs, or ands. You should've been honest with me, Clinton."

"I know." He ducked his head, but it wasn't very convincing.

"Why are you even here?" Paula's hands knotted into fists.

"To ask you not to tell Graham because he might tell Kayla and it would ruin my marriage. I hate talking through this screen. Someone might see me out here," he said.

"You got a choice. You can stay out there or come inside and I'll help Mitzi clean up the blood," Paula said.

"That's pretty harsh." Clinton's head jerked back up and he glared at her.

Paula eyed him from toes to eyes, wondering all the time what in the world she'd ever seen in him to begin with. "Go home to your wife. Try being faithful to her. And stay away from me. I never want to see you again." She slammed the door and slid down the wall. She dropped her head to her knees and took a deep breath. "Do you think he could tell that I'm pregnant?"

Mitzi sat down cross-legged in front of her. "Nope. He's only interested in saving his own hide. The bastard doesn't care that he broke your heart or got you pregnant. Can I get you anything?"

"No, I'll be fine when my heart stops pounding. Been a helluva day, hasn't it? Don't let it ruin your perfect time with Graham. And please don't tell Graham, not to appease Clinton, because I don't give a damn about him, but for the baby's sake. If he said something to Kayla or Rita, it could eventually get back to Clinton that I'm pregnant."

Mitzi held up a pinkie finger. "Remember when we did this when we were little girls?"

Paula linked her finger with it. "We're big girls now, and it's still friendship before relationship."

"After today, I'm not so sure that I ever want a relationship," Mitzi said.

"Don't let what's going on with me and Jody spoil what you might have. Good Lord!" Paula eased her way to a standing position when someone knocked on the back door again. "If it's Clinton again, load that shotgun. This time I mean to do more than scare him. We can drag him inside, and then bury him in the cellar out back soon as it gets dark. The dirt floor won't be too hard to dig up. I'll even repair the hole in the screen myself."

Mitzi eased the door open a crack and shook her head. "It's Darrin. Do we let him in or not?"

"Sure, we do. Unless you want to offer to let Ellie Mae crash on our sofa upstairs," Paula answered.

Mitzi opened the door wide and unlatched the screen door. "I suppose you're here to see Ellie Mae?"

"I've been driving all over town, looking for her car. I finally spotted it out front but there wasn't a parking space." His eyes were swollen, as if he'd been crying, and his hands trembled when he motioned toward his truck. "Tell her that I made a huge mistake. I love her, and we're havin' a baby, and—"

"We're not the ones to tell all that." Paula pointed. "She's in the foyer, and you might lead with the line about loving her."

He rushed that way, and in a few seconds, Jody joined them in the kitchen. "Quincy is gone, and I refused to go for ice cream or coffee with him. Darrin is still here, but they don't need a referee since he dropped down on his knees, laid his head in her lap, and cried like a baby. We might as well sit out here until it's done. There ain't no way we can go to the sewing room or upstairs without interrupting them. I could barely get through the foyer."

Paula was the first one to pull out a chair and sit. "It's like we got a sign outside. Clinton was here."

"You're shittin' me," Jody gasped.

"Nope, not one bit. Mitzi even loaded the shotgun," Paula said.

"Is he dead? I didn't hear a shot. Please tell me that he's layin' on the back porch, bleedin' out," Jody said.

"No, he's not dead, but he might be if he gets tangled up with another woman and she finds out he's married," Mitzi answered.

"One can always hope." Paula went to the refrigerator and brought out what was left of a cheesecake. "If he was out there with a gutshot, I'd eat a piece of this, then go brush my teeth before I called the ambulance."

Mitzi got out three forks and laid them on the table. "It's probably going to take a while for the lovebirds to get things settled between them."

"If they can make up and be happy, it'll be worth it," Jody said. "But I'm disappointed y'all didn't hurt Clinton, the sorry bastard, a little bit. You could have at least used the butt of the gun to wreck his balls."

"I just want him to disappear so I can get on with my life. Things are getting quiet in there. Think it's safe to peek around the corner?" Paula said.

Jody pushed back her chair and leaned around the doorframe for a look. "They're kissing. We don't have to offer to let Ellie Mae move in with us."

"I would have vetoed that," Paula said. "She's way too dramatic for me to put up with her for more than an hour or two. When they get done making out and leave, let's forget about sewing. I want to go upstairs, bring up a movie on Netflix, and forget about all this crap."

"Amen to that." Jody had barely taken a seat again and picked up her fork when Ellie Mae and Darrin came into the room, holding hands and having trouble taking their eyes off each other.

"The wedding is back on," Ellie Mae said. "We've got it all worked out—Darrin has got a promotion and we're transferring to Dumas, Texas, right after the wedding. We don't know anyone there, so it'll be a brand-new start for both of us."

"That's great," Jody said. "See you Friday for a fitting?"

"I'll be here, and thanks to you all for the support today," she said.

"And for letting me come inside." Darrin grinned sheepishly. "I acted like a jerk, and I know it."

"Yes, you did," Mitzi said. "But we don't drown men or shoot them for one mistake. After that it gets kind of iffy."

He leaned down and kissed Ellie Mae on the forehead. "Yes, ma'am. It won't happen again. I almost ruined the best thing in my life because of my pride. I've learned my lesson."

"See y'all in a few days," Ellie Mae said as they left by the back door and passed Fanny Lou coming inside.

"Well, now if that wasn't downright weird," she said. "Ellie Mae looked like she'd been crying and yet was the happiest person alive. So what's happening?"

"Which story do you want first? The one about my baby daddy, or Jody's new boyfriend, or the one about Mitzi kissing Graham?" Paula asked.

"Or maybe you'd rather hear about Ellie Mae?" Mitzi kicked Paula under the table.

"Given all those choices, I think we need to go upstairs to some more comfortable chairs," Fanny Lou answered. "Mitzi, lock the doors. Jody, get us some chips and dip. Paula, you can bring up three beers and a glass of sweet tea for you. The rest of us deserve something stronger with stories like these to tell."

"I don't have a new boyfriend." Jody gathered two bags of chips from the cabinet and a jar of salsa from the refrigerator.

"Even if you don't, it'd be good for Lyle to think you do. Sorry bastard," Fanny Lou fumed on the way up the stairs. "I heard that two men had been knockin' on the back door this afternoon. I came to be sure y'all hadn't put in a brothel."

Mitzi had been following her upstairs but stopped and gasped, "Granny, that's not funny."

Fanny Lou looked down at her from the landing. "I didn't think so, either, especially when you didn't ask me to be the madam. That's why I came to see what was going on here. Let's get settled in y'all's livin' room, and each of you can tell me all about it. And we'll start with Jody, since I want to know why Quincy Roberts was sitting on the porch with you."

Jody rolled her eyes. "Do you know him?"

"'Course I do. He's just one of the richest oil men in North Texas. Ever heard of Wildcat Oil? You know the one on the billboards with a big mountain lion on the side of the trucks? He started the business from scratch and did very well for himself," Fanny Lou said.

"He was just returning the lawn chairs he thought I'd left behind," Jody explained.

Fanny Lou took a long drink of her beer and burped loudly. "Never did learn to do that like a lady. Now tell me the whole story."

Mitzi listened to Jody's and Paula's stories with half an ear and tried to figure out a way to downplay the kiss, but it simply wasn't possible. Every time she thought of it, heat filled her face in a blush.

Chapter Seventeen

We need a trailer with our logo on the side," Mitzi groaned that Monday morning when she was listing all the things that had to go to the bridal fair the next Saturday.

"We'll rent a U-Haul. It won't have our logo, but we can get everything in it," Paula said. "I'll be in charge of that. We can pull it behind your van."

"We'll look like the poor country cousins," Mitzi whined.

"But, honey, when we get in and get set up, The Perfect Dress will be the belle of the ball," Jody informed her. "How many of these things do you figure we went to when we were dreaming about having our own shop?"

"And the way we always voted on which one was the best of the whole show?" Paula cut out Chantilly lace to cover the satin bodice of a dress.

"Well, we're going to get that honor this year," Jody declared. "Even if we don't have our own personal van with our logo on the side."

"Maybe we'll get enough business that we can buy one for next year," Mitzi said.

"That can be our goal." Jody nodded.

"We're here," the twins called out from the foyer.

"And we're ready for you," Mitzi yelled. "Meet us in the fitting room."

"Yes!"

Mitzi caught sight of Dixie pumping her fist in the air as she led her twin across the foyer into the fitting room. "This is the bare bones of the dress," she explained as she took the dresses off the satin hangers. "Seams are still raw, but we want to make sure it lays pretty on your shoulders without any wrinkles and that the arm holes are the right size."

"Oh, Dixie, we've got to learn to make things like this. I feel pretty." Tabby squealed as she stepped up on the platform in front of the three-way mirror.

Mitzi pinned the shoulders up another half an inch. "Honey, you are beautiful. Don't ever let anyone tell you otherwise. This is a lovely color on you and the style is so becoming. I'm glad you chose it."

Paula helped Dixie into her dress and stood to the side while she made her way onto the platform with her sister. "I don't think you'll have to do anything to this one, Mitzi. It's a perfect fit."

After a quick rap, Fanny Lou stuck her head in the door. "Got room for one more in there?"

"Of course," Dixie said. "Come on in and tell us what you think. Be honest with us. Are these going to be fancy enough for junior bridesmaid dresses?"

"They'll have burgundy bows at the back," Tabby said.

"You're going to steal the whole show." Fanny Lou pulled up two chairs—one to sit in and the other to prop her feet on. "Maybe I should get y'all to make me a dress."

"You gettin' married?" Jody asked.

"Oh, hell no!" Fanny Lou answered. "Once was enough for me. I loved my husband, but I've been a free bird too long, and I'm too old to live with anyone at my age."

"Maybe you're too old for anyone to live with you," Mitzi teased.

Fanny Lou tucked her hands inside the bib of her overalls. "That, too, but Elijah Cunningham asked me out to dinner. Since he's made reservations at a fancy restaurant in Dallas, I probably shouldn't wear what I've got on right now, should I?"

"You are kiddin' me." Mitzi could hardly believe what she was hearing. "Elijah has to be eighty, is shorter than you, and as skinny as a broomstick. You've never dated, so why start now?"

"I wish my dad would date," Dixie said before Fanny Lou could answer. "All he does is work, sleep, and try to be a dad."

"He's good at all of it, except the sleepin' part," Tabby said seriously and then lowered her voice. "He snores when he's really tired."

"So you want your dad to date?" Paula asked.

"Oh, yes, we really do," Dixie answered. "If he'd find someone like Mitzi, then he'd never let Mother move back in with us."

"What do you mean 'like Mitzi'?" Jody asked.

If they'd been sitting, Mitzi would have gladly kicked her shins under the table.

"You know." Dixie continued to stare at her reflection in the mirror. "Not like a skinny Minnie, and nice to us because she understands."

Tears welled up in Mitzi's eyes. "Y'all are going to make me cry."

Tabby smoothed the front of her dress. "Well, we sure don't want to do that. And much as I hate to take this dress off, even if it's not finished, it's quittin' time. We're makin' meatloaf for supper, and it needs to be in the oven in fifteen minutes."

"You're sure good, girls," Fanny Lou said. "Most of today's generation don't care much about cookin' and sewin'."

Tabby gently pulled the dress over her head, careful not to get stuck by the pins. "That's the part of helping Daddy that we like best. According to what we hear, Mother wasn't much of a cook and couldn't sew on a button."

Is their attitude a direct result of Rita's leaving them at a young age? Mitzi wondered as she helped Dixie out of her dress. "Well, we all have our strong points and weak ones. Mine is cleaning the bathroom. I can do it, but it's not my favorite job."

Dixie threw up a hand. Mitzi high-fived her. She could just wring Rita's neck for not seeing what sweet, kind daughters she had.

"We take turns doing that job each week because we hate it so bad," Dixie said.

"Mitzi has a reason for that. When she was about fourteen, she found a big tarantula hiding behind the toilet," Fanny Lou said. "She's been afraid of spiders ever since."

Mitzi shivered. "That thing jumped onto my arm and crawled to my shoulder before I got up enough nerve to bat it off. It hit the wall, fell back on the floor, and started crawling toward me again. Those big old eyes were just plumb evil."

"I'd have died," Tabby said. "I like hate spiders. Even them little bitty ones. Dixie kills them for me."

"I hate mice. Tabby empties the trap if we catch one in the house." Dixie pulled her shirt over her head. "We'll see y'all tomorrow. We've got most of the corsages done, but if Ellie Mae sends another list for more like she did last week, we've still got lots of stuff to work with."

"We still have boutonnieres to get done, but they won't take very long." Tabby gave Mitzi a hug on the way out of the fitting room. "I know we keep saying this, but honest, this is the best summer."

"Did you hear that?" Fanny Lou asked. "You just got an open invitation to date their daddy."

"I love those girls, but I've got to admit that I'm a little scared. What if Graham and I got into a relationship and it went sour like all my others? Then it would be awkward for them. That's a conversation for another day, though, since relationships aren't built on one afternoon and a kiss."

"What's this about a kiss?" Fanny Lou's eyebrows shot up. "I didn't hear about that."

"He kissed me yesterday," Mitzi admitted.

"That's a pretty big deal," Fanny Lou said.

"And they're going out on Sunday after church to ride around on the lake in his pontoon boat," Jody said.

"With the twins, Alice, and these two tattletales if they want to go. That's hardly a date, now is it?" Mitzi said.

"Dates don't have to be dinner and a movie. Dates mean spending time with each other," Fanny Lou told her.

"You are so right, Granny." Mitzi thought about the time she and Graham had spent together. "But now, let's talk about your date with Elijah."

"And this new dress you need," Paula said. "What color do you have in mind?"

Fanny Lou giggled. "I was just tryin' to get a rise out of you. I'm not going out with Elijah. Lord, if he tried to kiss me good night, he'd kiss my boobs instead of my lips. Or I'd have to stoop, and with my old bones, I'd never be able to straighten back up."

Mitzi had dated a shorter man the semester she was in college. He always managed to stand on a higher step up to her garage apartment when he kissed her good night. If it hadn't been for that staircase, he would have probably kissed her on the boobs, too. But she and Graham had connected without a single problem.

Graham picked up his briefcase and gently closed the door behind him so he wouldn't wake the girls. Traffic was light that morning, so he arrived at work before eight. Vivien handed him a cup of coffee when he passed her desk.

"Good mornin'. You've got a meeting at eight thirty, so you can drink it slowly. After that, you're free for the day," she said.

"That's good. I want to shadow that new salesman for a couple of hours and see how he's doing." Graham went into his office but he left the door open.

He set his briefcase on the floor beside his chair, set his coffee on the desk, and sat down to relax for a few minutes before his meeting. He should have told the girls that he'd asked Mitzi on a date, but he wanted to savor the time he'd spent with her on Sunday and those couple of kisses a little longer. Besides, when he told them that he'd actually asked Mitzi out, even if it was an informal family affair, they'd immediately start thinking the *M*-word. Graham would need a lot of time to say that word out loud.

A shadow in his peripheral vision startled him and he sat straight up. He must've spent more time letting his mind wander than he'd thought. He leaned forward to pick up his briefcase and get the papers out for his meeting. When he straightened up, Rita was in front of his desk and Vivien was standing in the doorway with a disgusted look on her face.

She tapped her watch and mouthed, "Fifteen minutes." Vivien backed out and shut the door behind her.

Rita wore skintight jeans, an off-the-shoulder top, and high heels. Her long blonde hair framed her face and she'd applied bright-red lipstick.

"I've got less than ten minutes, Rita," he said. "What are you doing here?"

"I told you, my grandmother died. We're going through her house to get it ready to sell," she said. "Kayla said she'd seen you Saturday and she told you that we were thinking about getting back together."

"I'm not thinking any such thing." He couldn't believe that she was dressed like that when her grandmother had just died. Granted, times had changed, but she looked like she should be standing on a street corner, not mourning a relative.

"Well, darlin', I am, and you know I get what I want," she said. "I want to be a mother." She moved around the desk and started to massage his shoulders. "Remember when I used to do this after football games?"

He pushed away her hands and stood to his feet. "Rita, we're not in high school anymore, and we've been apart for more than a decade. I've moved on."

"With who?" She glared at him.

"Someone else, and I like her a lot. I don't want to ruin anything I've got with her. And she loves the girls." He went to the door and stood beside it.

"Honey, you never forget your first love. Whoever this woman is, she won't ever be able to make you forget me." She laid a hand on his chest. "I own this heart. I always have, since the first time I kissed you. You might as well go on home and break up with her, because I will have you back."

"Want to make a bet on that?" he asked.

"Don't need to. Like I said, I get what I want," she said.

"You wanted to be the wife of the owner of a Cadillac dealership," Graham said sarcastically. "You never did want me, Rita."

She tapped his chest again. "I want you now."

"It's too late."

"It's never too late for love." She blew him a kiss as she left.

He barely had time to get his papers out of his briefcase when Vivien said the CPA had arrived. Lauren was a tall, thin woman with short blonde hair and brown eyes. She had a no-nonsense, get-down-to-business attitude that he liked. He'd thought about asking her out a few times but never could find the right moment.

"Good morning, Graham. I've scanned everything and it looks good." She pulled a wingback chair around to his side of the desk and sat down. Then she removed her laptop from her briefcase. "I see you've got hard copies for me, just like your dad always did." She waved a hand toward the stacks of papers. "I've told you that all those aren't necessary."

"I like a hard copy when we go over the numbers. I see things clearer when I have real paper in my hands," he said, just like he did every three months at this meeting.

"Okay, then, let's get started so we can be done at noon." She nodded. "I bet you like a book in your hands better than a digital one, too, don't you?"

"You got me." He grinned.

He focused on everything Lauren said and even took a few notes to go over later, but in the back of his mind, all he could think about was Mitzi. He wanted to tell her about Rita coming to the office before the gossip spread through Celeste like wildfire. By the time he got home that evening, folks would have him and Rita making another trip to the courthouse.

The meeting lasted past noon, so Vivien brought in a light lunch for them, and they ate while they finished up. Lauren packed up her laptop and shook Graham's hand. "I hear that you and your ex-wife are talking. It's none of my business at all, but . . . well, just be careful."

"May I ask why you're saying that?"

"I knew her right after y'all's divorce. My advice, for what it's worth, is that if you do get back together that you make her sign a prenup, and that you get your company lawyer to draw it up."

"Thank you, but there's no way in hell I'm ever taking a chance with Rita again," he said.

"That's great news. See you in three months." Lauren waved as she left.

He removed his glasses and rubbed his eyes. Should things ever get really serious with Mitzi, would she be willing to sign a prenup?

Mitzi was walking across the parking lot to the party store when her phone pinged. The text was from Graham: Call me, please.

She sat down on a bench outside the store and made the call.

"Hello," Graham said. "I'm glad you called back. Do you have a few minutes?"

"Sure. I'm in town to pick up part of the supplies for the bridal fair. What's going on?" she asked.

"Could I meet you somewhere so we can talk in person?" he asked.

"I'm sitting on the bench outside the party store. It's not far from you. Want to join me?"

"I'll be there in five minutes. How do you take your coffee?"

"Black and strong, but I'd rather have a tall sweet tea," she told him.

"I'll stop by Starbucks on the way," he said.

Five minutes didn't give Mitzi enough time to get the supplies that they'd ordered for the bridal fair, check them to be sure everything was correct, and take them to her van. It did let her watch the people come and go, and that was something she'd always enjoyed, even as a child. When she'd go with her folks to the lake, she'd make up stories in her head about the people she saw, and she still did the same today.

An older couple, both gray haired, holding hands, and neither getting along with much speed, stopped for a moment and said hello to her before they entered the store. In her mind, they'd been married for more than sixty years. The lady had dark hair when she was young, and Mitzi imagined her wedding dress was white silk with a high neckline and butterfly sleeves.

A younger couple passed her next. They were arguing about the money the woman had spent on the decorations for their son's first birthday party. Neither of them even looked her way. From the huge diamond on the woman's finger, Mitzi would guess that the woman had worn a designer dress. The wedding had been huge, and then she found out that the man had spent all his money on the ring. The woman thought she was getting the lifestyle of the rich and famous, and then she realized that they were living on a shoestring and he still owed four years of payments on the ring.

The perfect dress, she thought. *We're in business to provide the perfect dress. Too bad it doesn't always mean that we can guarantee that dress will bring them a wonderful life full of rainbows and unicorns.*

She had no idea what Graham would be driving, but when she looked up and saw him getting out of an older-model pickup truck, she wasn't surprised. It fit him more than a fancy new Caddy. He waved with one hand and lifted a four-cup holder in her direction. She couldn't see anyone around him and wondered why he'd have four cups and not just two. Would someone else be joining them? If so, why?

"Good afternoon." Graham sat down on the other end of the bench and put the drinks between him and Mitzi. "I got two iced teas for you. One for now and one for you to have on the trip back to Celeste. It's good to see you, Mitzi."

"Good to see you, too, and thank you for the teas." She picked one up and took a long sip through the straw, relief washing over her because they would be alone. "You look tired. How's your day been going?"

"Good in some ways. Had a meeting with the CPA about quarterly taxes, and everything about the business is stable and growing. But not so wonderful in others." He took a coffee from the holder and sipped it. "Rita came to the office again. She's like a wart. Just when I think I'm finished with her, she shows up again. What do you suggest I do?"

"Go to the doctor and have it surgically removed." Mitzi wasn't sure at that moment whether she was his girlfriend, his friend, or his therapist.

"How do you do that?"

"Shoot her, I guess," Mitzi said. "I don't think wart remover comes in a big enough bottle."

His eyes widened and he set his coffee down, stood up, and extended a hand to her. She wasn't surprised at the vibes between them as he pulled her to her feet and hugged her tightly. "You are a genius."

"I didn't mean it," she gasped. "If you really try to kill Rita, then she'll get the girls and . . ."

"Honey, I'm not going to shoot her with a gun. I'm going to give her enough rope to hang herself. I'm going to make her sign a whole raft of documents laying out the plans if she wants to get back together with me." Graham kissed Mitzi on the forehead.

"You mean like a pre-prenup?" she asked.

"And in the documents, it's going to say that should we ever get serious, she agrees to the actual prenup," he said. "That'll surgically remove the wart forever."

But what if it doesn't?

"What if she's finally figured out that she wants to be a part of a family, and she wants to try to love the girls and you?" she asked.

"Trust me, darlin'," Graham said. "I know her, and she hasn't changed a bit. She's got dollar signs, not love, in her eyes."

"I hope you're right," Mitzi said.

"I don't have a single doubt in the world. Thank you so much for waiting for me and for being such a good friend. Can I help you carry anything out to the van before I get back to work?" Graham asked.

"There's nothing heavy." The way things were going, Mitzi thought they were more than friends. "Are we still on for Sunday?"

"Of course. Nothing has changed between us, and Mitzi, I appreciate being able to talk to you about all this more than you'll ever know," he said.

"That's what friends are for," she told him.

"I'm hoping for more than that." He kissed her on the cheek and whistled all the way back to his truck.

A roller coaster of emotions spun through her mind: Happiness that they could possibly be more than friends. Fear that her heart would break if it didn't work out. Worry that either or both of them were transferring the feelings they had for Dixie and Tabby into a relationship. With her mind still reeling, she took the cups of tea to her van and then went into the store to take care of business. Her thoughts were far from the bridal fair on Saturday right then. That word, *prenup*, kept running through her mind. If things did get serious between her and Graham, would he want her to sign one? Would that mean he didn't trust her?

"I don't care what he asks," she said as she got a cart and pushed it to the customer help station to pick up the things that had been ordered. "I'd be the one insisting on it—that way he'd know that I'd be marrying him because I'd fallen in love with him, not with his money."

Chapter Eighteen

Jody's shoulders ached that evening. Normally, she got up every hour and at least walked around the table a few times, but today she had wanted to get the veil that she'd spent days working on done. A bride from up near Sherman would be there on Friday for her final fitting, and the veil was literally the crowning glory. The dress was a simple off-the-shoulder satin, but the chapel-length train was set on a pearl tiara. Beads were not only scattered across the whole thing, but Jody had hand beaded the lace around the edges.

While she finished the last two feet of the train, her mind had wandered back to Quincy, and she worked for three hours without standing up. She locked up the shop and was about to go upstairs to stretch out when the phone rang. Mitzi was in the bathroom. It was Paula's turn to make supper, so Jody went back to the sewing room and picked up the receiver.

"The Perfect Dress," she said.

"Is this Jody?"

"Yes, it is. Who's this?" If it was someone calling about Lyle's motorcycle, she intended to give them an earful.

"It's Quincy. I thought I recognized your voice. I'm calling about the old trailer out on the property that I've bought from Lyle. He says he won't move it because it belongs to you. What do you want me to do with it?" he asked.

"Pour gasoline on it and throw a match at it." There were too many memories attached to the small trailer for her to want to keep the damn thing, and besides, the roof leaked. When it rained they'd had to set a bucket in the middle of the floor to catch the drip.

"You could sell it. The tires are good and—" Quincy said.

"Wait a minute," she butted in. "Don't do anything with it. I'll come out there right now and hook on to it."

"I'll meet you there," he said.

"I can do it all by myself," she told him.

"It's my property. Wouldn't want you to steal any of my dirt," Quincy chuckled.

"I'll be there in half an hour," she said.

"See you later." He ended the call.

Paula looked up from the stove when Jody arrived in the kitchen. Mitzi was at the counter, cutting up salad greens.

"So did we have a prospective bride on the phone?" Mitzi asked.

"No, it was Quincy," Jody said. "Y'all will have to save me some supper. I'm going out to get my travel trailer. He's officially bought the place from Lyle and wants the old trailer gone."

"I'm surprised you're bringing it back here." Paula eased fettuccine noodles down into the pot of boiling water.

"You sure you want that thing? Why don't you just tell him to take it to the salvage yard?" Mitzi said.

"At first I told him to pour gasoline on it and throw a match at it, but then I got a better idea. We could strip the interior out, take it to a body shop and get the roof repaired, and then have it custom painted and"—she clapped her hands once—"we'd have our trailer for future shows at a fraction of the cost of a new one."

"That's a great idea," Mitzi said. "You want us to go get this finished and set it aside? We could be out there in fifteen minutes to help out."

"No, I've hooked up to it in my old truck lots of times. I'll bring it back here and park it out back. After we get done with the bridal show, we can start work on it and then haul it over to Jason's Body Shop. He's really good with that kind of work." Jody headed for the back door. "And besides, Quincy will be there in case I need any help."

Her faded-blue vehicle looked more than a little bit like a poor country cousin when she arrived and parked beside his brand-new truck. He waved from the place where the garden had been and started toward her. Tonight he wore wrinkled jeans and a knit shirt that hugged his body. His scuffed-up boots said they'd seen lots of hard work, and his straw hat bore sweat marks.

"I was ready to invite you out to roast marshmallows and make s'mores while we burned this thing to the ground." He grinned.

For the first time, she noticed that he had a dimple on the right side of his cheek. "Why waste good marshmallows? We couldn't eat them. They'd be poisoned."

"But you're willing to keep the thing, knowing that whatever you do with it will bring back memories?" he asked.

"When I get done with it, there will be nothing left to remind me of my time with Lyle." She told him what she had in mind.

"That's crazy. You could buy one and not have to do all that work. You'll have to be careful not to do anything that will wind up knocking holes through the exterior walls."

"That's really none of your business. Maybe tearing it all out will bring me complete closure. It'll leave me with an empty shell to rebuild the inside however I want," she said.

"Women!" He threw up his hands.

"What about women?" She raised both eyebrows.

"You always overthink everything. Lyle's a bastard who had an affair and left you. Get over it."

She marched right up to him and poked her finger so close to his nose that it made his eyes cross. "You walk a mile in my shoes,

Mr. Roberts, and then you can stand here all self-righteous and tell me to get over it. I'll be hitching up to the trailer now and moving it off your precious property. If there's any dirt on the tires when I get it back to the shop, I'll be sure to put it in a box and mail it back to you. I wouldn't want you thinkin' I'm stealing it."

He took a step back. "Hey, I didn't mean to step on your toes."

"Well, you did." She stormed over to her truck, expertly backed it up to the trailer, got out, and hitched it without a problem. "Enjoy your land," she said as she slid behind the wheel, slammed the door, and started the engine.

He tipped his hat at her, got into his truck, and drove away.

The radio was blaring just like it had been when she turned the key earlier, but now it was playing the Pistol Annies' "I Feel a Sin Comin' On."

"Yeah, right," Jody said as she stomped the clutch and put the truck in gear. "The only sin I feel comin' on is maybe poisoning Lyle and slapping the shit out of Quincy . . . and maybe doing something evil to Clinton for Paula. But the sin I feel doesn't have anything to do with a tall, dark, and handsome guy."

Stop kiddin' yourself, that pesky voice in her head said.

Jody gripped the steering wheel so hard that her knuckles were white and her hands ached when she finally parked behind the shop. She turned off the engine and sat in the hot truck until salty sweat began to sting her eyes. Opening the door to get air didn't help since there wasn't any sign of a breeze blowing. Finally, she swung open the door and put her feet on the ground but didn't realize just how weak kneed she still was. She had to hang on to the door for a minute to get her balance.

Going back out there for the final time wasn't supposed to affect her like this. If anything, it should bring more closure, not open up even more anger. When did this business of acceptance arrive anyway?

She didn't bother unhitching the trailer but stomped into the house and went straight for a plate. "I'm mad and I'm hungry."

"Mitzi's upstairs. Do I need to call her and get out the ice cream?" Paula asked.

"No," Jody said. "I need food and maybe a good cold beer to settle me down. I just had a run-in with Quincy, and what should have been the end to the Jody-and-Lyle story wasn't." She told Paula the details of what had happened. "What is it about men? Just because they can settle something with three words, they can't understand that womenfolk need to figure out things."

"They're from Mars, remember?" Paula told her in a flat tone.

"I think they're from further out than that." Jody filled her plate and took it to the table.

Fanny Lou opened the back door and stuck her head inside. "Where's Mitzi?"

"Upstairs." Paula pointed.

Fanny Lou set a covered dish on the table. "That's seven-layer dip. I took it to my Sunday school committee meeting this evening. We had too much food, so it was barely touched." She pulled up a chair and shook out half the bag of chips into a bowl. "I'm glad we're here by ourselves. I'm worried about Mitzi."

"Graham?" Paula asked.

Fanny Lou got three spoons from the drawer. "It's better if you dip to the bottom and put it on the chip. And yes, about Graham. She's so damned happy that I'm afraid when they have an argument—well, you know her. Things are black or white in her world. There is no gray."

"It's either rainbows and unicorn farts, or nothing," Jody said. "She came from a pretty nice family, so she doesn't know how to argue and then make up."

"Exactly," Fanny Lou said. "I guess she's about to learn if this gets any more serious, because reality is being able to run the obstacle course that life throws at you and make it to the end without killing the person you're in the relationship with."

"I remember the first fight me and Lyle had after we moved in together. It was all over this old tomcat that came up to the back door. Lyle hated cats, but I couldn't bear to see it hungry, so I fed it without telling him. Of course it kept showing up and meowing every night. He threatened to shoot it, and I said I'd shoot him if he did. It took us a week to reach a compromise. I could feed the cat, but it couldn't come inside the house," Jody grumbled.

"And the makeup sex?" Fanny Lou winked.

"I'd like to say it was horrible but it wasn't. We were good together in the bedroom and I still get a stomachache when I think of him with the other woman," Jody fumed.

Fanny Lou sat down at the table with the girls. "I don't think my granddaughter has ever had makeup sex. She loves with her whole heart, but if someone breaks it, she's done with them. It's finished. There's no talking and she never looks back."

"I wish to hell I could do that." Jody's voice was still cold as ice.

Paula spooned a big mound of dip onto a chip. "We can hope this time will be different. She's perfect for those girls, and they love her."

Fanny Lou got up, went to the refrigerator, and brought out two beers and a root beer. "I need something to cool down my tongue." She popped the tab from a beer and handed the second one to Jody. "Root beer for you, darlin'. When I was pregnant with Mitzi's mama, it wasn't against the rules to drink a beer or even have a glass of wine, but times have changed. Mitzi may be perfect for the girls, but, honey, she needs to be perfect for Graham, and him for her, if this is going to work at all. He's the main dish. Those twins are just the dessert."

"Hey, hey, what's all this?" Mitzi said as she entered the kitchen. "Is that your seven-layer dip, Granny? Step back and let me roll up my sleeves, because I'm about to get all up in some of that."

"You don't have on long sleeves," Fanny Lou told her. "And where have you been?"

"I was doing a little inventory on the flowers left in the bins. I should make a run into Walmart and buy some more in case the girls want to do some last-minute stuff for the bridal fair." She got a beer from the refrigerator and sat down in the remaining chair. "Y'all decided whether you're going out on the pontoon boat on Sunday?"

"I'm going, but I won't be swimming. Y'all know how afraid of deep water I am," Jody said. "Not even Lyle—dammit to hell—why do I even mention his name? But what I was going to say is that even he couldn't talk me into learning to swim. If it's above my waist, I begin to panic."

"And I'm pregnant, so I won't be swimming, either," Paula reminded her.

"And I'm too damned old to jump in the lake," Fanny Lou said. "Have you and Graham been to bed yet?"

"Granny!" Mitzi dropped the chip before it reached her mouth.

"I was bein' nice. I could have asked outright if y'all had sex yet," Fanny Lou told her. "You come in here all aglow. Only thing that ever put that kind of look on my face was a trip to the bedroom with your grandpa." She giggled. "Sometimes I'd start a fight just so we could have makeup sex."

"Granny!" Mitzi exclaimed for the second time.

"That's what you do, darlin'. You argue. You go to the bedroom and make up. That don't mean you take jack crap from the man. No, sir. It just means that once the fight is resolved, then you reap the benefits. Come to think of it, maybe I should start an argument with Elijah and see if he's still able to do that."

Mitzi's cheeks went from cool to red hot in a flash. "Grandmothers aren't supposed to talk like that."

"It's the truth. Wait until you have a big argument with Graham, and you'll find out," Fanny Lou said.

Mitzi went to the refrigerator, opened the freezer, and stuck her head inside in an attempt to cool her cheeks. Paula nudged Fanny Lou and mouthed, "Thank you."

"Y'all are crazy," Mitzi said. "I'm going to Greenville to buy more flowers. Y'all can talk about makeup sex all night if you want to."

"I'd go with you but I'm so angry, I'm going to spend two hours cleaning out the trailer. There's pots and pans, and canned food we can use," Jody said.

"If there's going to be work, I'm out of here." Fanny Lou stood up.

"I'll get one of those old lawn chairs from the front porch and talk to you while you work off your anger," Paula said.

"See y'all later." Mitzi headed out the door with a wave.

⁓

"Hell and damnation!" Graham said when Rita caught him in the Walmart store that evening. This time she was dressed in shorts that barely covered her butt cheeks and sandals that showed off bright-red toenail polish that matched what was on her lips.

"I was in town to pick up cleaning supplies. Us runnin' into each other is pure karma. God is tellin' us that we need to be together." She ran a hand from his shoulder to his wrist. "Trust me."

"I lost the ability to trust you years ago, but I've given your idea some thought," he said. "I'm having the lawyers draw up what Mitzi calls a pre-prenup. When they get them done up, you can read over them and sign them. After that I might think you're serious."

"And what's this document going to say?" She glared at him.

"Simply that if our relationship doesn't work, you take out exactly what you brought into it. No settlements. No money of any kind. And that you relinquish all rights to the girls, like you did in the divorce. That if it works, you will be a stay-at-home mother and you will never have anything to do with the dealership," he said.

"You're bluffing," she said.

"No, I'm not. Right now I'm not interested in any kind of relationship with you, but if that's what you want, then I'm telling you up front that I won't even go out with you for coffee until you sign the papers," he told her.

"That's harsh. I've changed," she declared.

"You're married and yet you showed up asking me if I want to go to bed with you so you can get pregnant. Seems to me like you've changed, all right, but for the worse," he said.

She pushed her cart around his. "Don't judge me. You haven't lived in my skin all my life."

"I'm not judging. I'm stating facts. Now I've got somewhere I have to be this evening. And Rita, don't come back until you're ready to sign the papers. There's nothing here for you without that, and nothing for you even with it," he said.

Great advice, Mitzi. He paid out and had two bags of groceries in his hands when he saw Rita waiting outside the door. No sooner had he noticed her than he saw Mitzi coming straight toward them. She caught his eye and waved. He raised a hand with a bag still in it.

"So is this the new woman? Lord, Graham, she's huge." Rita's expression said even more than her words.

"Kind of like our daughters, right?"

"Don't put words in my mouth. Now I know I can get you back. No man in his right mind would ever take that lump of lard over me." She giggled as she took a few steps forward and got into an SUV with a guy who was probably her husband.

Still reeling from what his ex had said, he grimaced. "Hey, I didn't expect to see you tonight, Mitzi."

"Had to get more flowers in case we need them for the show on Saturday. Was that Rita?"

"It was," he said.

"She's like a bad penny, isn't she? Just keeps showing up," Mitzi said.

"Seems that way, but I told her about the prenup thing. She's not happy." He could never tell Mitzi what Rita had said about her. Hopefully that would be the only secret he'd ever keep from her.

"I wouldn't be happy, either," Mitzi said. "Looking at it from her standpoint, she thought she had this all wrapped up with a pretty bow on the front."

"Too bad." Graham set a bag on the ground and laid a hand on Mitzi's shoulder. "See you Sunday, if not before."

"Lookin' forward to it," she said.

Chapter Nineteen

Jody was the last one in the kitchen on Thursday morning. She poured a cup of coffee and sat down at the table. "I've been thinking about something. There's plenty of room in my trailer to put everything in it and take to the fair. It'll save us the cost of a rental, and I've laid awake half the night planning how we can put things in there." She took a sip of the coffee. "And people would think that we'd camped out in the parking lot so we could be first in the doors. They'd never know that we're going to get the title of queen bee of the whole show."

"I love the idea," Mitzi said. "We can hitch it up to my van after work and have it completely loaded before we go to bed tomorrow night. You're a genius, Jody."

"If I'd been really smart, I'd have seen the signs that Lyle was cheating, but my ego needs a boost, so I'll take the compliment," Jody said.

That evening they only meant to put the mannequins in the trailer, but after Jody had the idea of putting them on the bed and tying them down with bungee cords, they got excited. They hung the wedding and the bridesmaid dresses in the tiny closet. The small cabinet space in the kitchen area became a place for the bouquets and corsages, and the drawer held their business cards.

"I don't think we need to tear anything out," Mitzi said. "This is working perfectly. After Saturday, I vote that we take it to the shop and get it all prettied up for future shows, but let's leave the inside the same layout it is."

"And it would be a great place for me to retreat to after the baby comes when it's time to feed her," Paula said. "I'm glad you didn't burn it."

"I've always felt like I didn't do my part when we went into this business. Mitzi's dad bought us the house and Fanny Lou gave us some start-up money, and I know y'all put in your savings, but Lyle would only let me contribute five thousand. Y'all accepting this really helps me," Jody said.

"Hey, we couldn't make it without you and your skills," Mitzi reassured her as they made their way back into the house.

The business phone was ringing, and since Jody was the first one inside, she picked it up.

"Hello, Jody, this is Quincy. Are you over your snit?"

"I was stating facts. I was not in a snit," she answered.

"That's not what I'm hearing in your tone. I'll call back in a few days," he said. "You reckon you could give me your cell number?"

"If you need something, you can call this number," she said. "Good night, Quincy."

Both Paula and Mitzi were staring at her when she hung up the phone. "Don't start on me. I'm not ready to talk to him. Until I am, he doesn't need my digits."

❧

Ellie Mae showed up Friday morning with a hickey the size of a silver dollar on her neck. She'd covered it with a scarf, but when she undressed, there was no getting around what it was.

"Mama would have a fit if she saw it, so I wore a scarf," Ellie Mae laughed. "Has Graham marked you yet? I hear y'all are spendin' a lot of time together."

"No, he has not." Mitzi was tempted to pull her hair up to prove the point.

"Well, don't let Fanny Lou see it if he does. She's liable to shoot him dead." Ellie Mae held her arms up for Paula to drop the dress down over her body.

"And by the way, I heard that Rita is spending lots of time up in Whitewright taking care of her granny's things. She's been tellin' around that she and Graham are getting back together. I understand she's got to get a divorce first," Ellie Mae said as Jody pinned the back where the hidden zipper would go in later.

"I thought he was crazy for marrying her in the first place, and to do so a second time should be grounds for committing him," Jody said.

Mitzi could have hugged her, but instead she just turned Ellie Mae around to face the mirrors, hoping that she'd be so excited about the dress that she'd stop gossiping.

"It's beautiful! I love it so much, I'll hate to take it off for the honeymoon." She twisted and turned in front of the mirror to catch all the angles. "Darrin and I may do role playing. I'll be the blushing virgin bride, and he can be the dashing knight in shining armor that carries me away from an arranged marriage with some old lecher."

"You've been reading too many romance books," Jody said. "We'll probably have this finished by next Friday. Think we should leave a little extra material in the zipper-area seams in case you need it let out some at the last minute?"

"That would be great. I'm hoping I don't show any more than I do now until after the wedding, but it'd be better to be prepared. So when are you going to start your wedding dress, Mitzi?"

"I have to get a proposal first, then an engagement ring and time to design," she answered.

"Is it going to be white? Are you still a virgin?" Ellie Mae looked back over her shoulder at the backside of the black-lace dress.

"No to both," Mitzi said.

"The only thing I'd want other than this dress would involve me being a size ten. If I had been, I might have gotten one with feathers, but I didn't want to look like Big Bird. You know what I'm talkin' about," Ellie Mae said.

"Yes, I do, and the fact is that I've never wanted a big wedding. A trip to the courthouse would be just fine with me."

"But you own this lovely shop that specializes in dresses for women like us," Ellie Mae said. "And Harry and Fanny Lou would be disappointed."

Mitzi steered the conversation away from herself by asking, "So did you and Darrin have a round of makeup sex?"

"Oh, honey, we had several rounds." Ellie Mae winked. "As much as I hate to take this off, I guess you'd better unpin me so I can get back to work."

Mitzi removed the pins and helped her out of the dress, wondering the whole time if next year they should make a dress in black for the bridal fair. Women were always looking for something different, and black was certainly that, for sure.

⁓

Light shone from the windows like a beacon when Mitzi drove up to the Harrison house before daylight on Saturday morning. She hopped out of the van, leaving Jody in the front seat and Paula in one of the seats in back. One of the girls could sit beside Paula and the other one could have the whole bench seat behind them to herself.

"Good mornin'." Graham opened the door and motioned for her to come on in.

"Good mornin' to you, too," she said. "I wish you were going with us, but I promise to shoot pictures all day and send them to you."

"Will you do a video of Tabby on the runway?" he asked. "I'd love to be there, but it's impossible today."

"I sure will. Be prepared to be bombarded with pictures." The way he looked at her sent tingles down her spine.

They intensified when he traced her jawbone with his fingertip. "You are so beautiful, Mitzi."

The simple touch and words meant more to her than a million red roses or a long poem written for her.

"Hey, Mitzi, we're ready," Tabby yelled from the top of the stairs. "My hair is still in curlers but I'll take them all out before we get there."

"She means I'll take them out." Dixie pushed around her dad and tiptoed slightly to kiss him on the cheek.

"Have a good time." Graham hugged both girls before they went out the door.

Dixie bounced off the porch with Tabby right behind her, each of them carrying a tote bag in addition to their purses. "We'll send lots of pictures."

"See you about dark," Mitzi said.

"And then tomorrow we're going to the lake." Graham kissed his fingertips and then touched her lips. "That'll have to do until we get a little more privacy."

Sucking on a lemon couldn't keep the smile off her face all the way to Dallas that morning. When they arrived, the girls hurried out to the trailer hooked to the back of the van to help carry things inside.

Paula started to lift a folding table, but Tabby grabbed it first. "You don't need to pick up heavy stuff."

"We'll get the tables and chairs," Dixie said.

"I'm pregnant, not helpless," Paula argued.

"Yep, so that means you carry that little box with our business cards, and the one with the chocolate to give out to the customers.

Maybe we'll even let you take care of the crystal stand to display the candy and cards," Jody said.

"I'm not taking anything breakable," Dixie declared. "Clumsy as I am, I'd stumble over my own feet and break it."

"We must be related, because Grace is not my middle name, either," Mitzi chuckled.

"I wish we were kinfolk," Dixie said with a wistful tone.

"Not me. If we were kin, then Daddy couldn't date her," Tabby said.

"Well, I wish he'd married you when y'all were in high school."

Mitzi couldn't keep the blush from turning her cheeks scarlet. "That's sweet, honey, but it took both your mama and daddy to make you, and I wouldn't change having you in my life for anything."

"And there you have it," Jody whispered. "If you were worried about what they'll think of y'all dating, you've got your answer."

"I wish worries could be erased that easy," Mitzi said.

Seeing a bridal fair through the eyes of the girls was so much fun. Everything was new and exciting, just like it had been for Paula, Mitzi, and Jody the year before when they'd attended several in preparation for putting in the shop.

Covered in a lace tablecloth, their table was set up and ready. The archway stood off to the left with the bride mannequin in the center. Today she held a lovely pink bouquet to match the pale pink roses and greenery decorating the arch, and to the right of the bride stood her bridesmaid, dressed in mauve. A catalog with swatches of fabric rested on the table, along with a binder containing pictures of the dresses they'd already designed and made. From floral arrangements that excited the girls, to the cakes, to the fancy shops that specialized in beautiful premade dresses, and finally to The Perfect Dress display, there was something at the show to take the eye of a bride at every turn.

"This is unreal," Dixie said. "I didn't even know that places like this existed."

"I did but I had no idea they were this extreme. Look! They're opening the doors." Tabby pointed.

Mitzi had seen the cake display next to their table when they arrived, and she did her best to keep her eyes off it but just couldn't. One thing was for sure—the brides were sure to see it.

Future brides rushed into the room as if they were hitting a clearance sale at a department store. Once inside, they began to mill around, but no one even looked toward the end of the room where The Perfect Dress table was located.

"Sit tight, and don't worry," the lady at the cake table said. "We've got the best seats in the house."

Mitzi turned to see who was talking to her and wondered if anyone really bought or needed a cake that big. Each of the six tiers was decorated with life-size sugar roses. Who would want to cut into something so pretty? Or need a cake to feed a thousand people?

"I'm Glenda Smith." The lady handed her a card. "First time I've seen you at one of these. I try to make two a year, summer and the Christmas one. It's getting more and more popular to have a holiday wedding. Love the wedding dress and the fact that you brought the bridesmaid display, too. That's genius."

"Thank you." She stuck out her hand. "Mitzi Taylor."

Glenda shook hands with her. "I see you've got a lot of help."

"These are my partners, Jody and Paula, and our . . ." She hesitated, not knowing how to introduce Dixie and Tabby.

"We're the interns," Dixie said. "And Tabby will be modeling the wedding dress right there this evening. That's one big cake. Do you cut it to let people sample? How'd you get it in here?"

"In three vans, and no, we don't cut this one. It's not even real cake under all that icing. Just Styrofoam. My helpers will be here soon with the samples that we'll be offering for tasting. You'll have to try our new hummingbird cake," Glenda said.

A group of three ladies finally made their way to The Perfect Dress table. "I'm the bride and these are my bridesmaids. Do you really only make custom dresses for plus-sized women?"

"When are you getting married?" Mitzi asked.

"December, and I'm"—she lowered her voice—"a size sixteen. Is that considered plus-sized?"

"We make dresses for size fourteen and up," Paula answered. "So you're interested in a one-of-a-kind wedding dress? Let me show you the pictures of what we've already done. Then Jody can show you the sample fabrics we keep on hand in the store. If you like what you see, you can make an appointment with Mitzi to design the dress of your dreams." Paula pushed the photo album over to the edge of the table. "Y'all have a seat so you don't have to bend."

Mitzi kept an eye on the girls as they milled around from one table to another. It was like seeing everything for the first time through their eyes.

"We do bridesmaid dresses as well," Jody said.

"That's fantastic. You can see none of us are beanpoles," the girl said.

"Could I give you a card? It's got all our information on it in case you'd like to think about it and make an appointment," Mitzi said.

"I don't need to think about it." She picked up a card. "We all live in McKinney. Celeste isn't far. Can we get our name on the calendar now or do we have to call?"

Mitzi opened her appointment book. "What day is good for you? And will you all three be driving over?"

"Yes, ma'am, we will. I'm Kay Lynn Johnson. Next Friday would be wonderful," she said.

Mitzi ran her finger down the page until she reached the right date. "Morning or afternoon?"

"Afternoon," one of the bridesmaids answered. "Kay Lynn hates to get up early on her day off."

"Then let's say two o'clock," Mitzi said.

"That's great." Kay Lynn wrote the time down on the back of the card. "This is like awesome." She turned to leave and saw the wedding cake. "I have to have that thing, too. Only I want poinsettias instead of roses."

She and her friends moved over a few feet and started talking about cake. Glenda's samples arrived while they were still there, and Kay Lynn was busy tasting them when the next set of ladies came up to The Perfect Dress table.

"Looks like it's going to be a profitable day," Glenda leaned in to whisper from the next table.

"Yes, ma'am," Mitzi agreed, but she was looking at the text from Graham that had popped up on her phone: Missing you.

She hurriedly typed in: Me, too.

❦

Jody scanned the whole room and thought about all the brides-to-be there. If she ever trusted someone to get into another relationship, she intended to have a real wedding. Maybe not a big one, but a ceremony to seal the vows.

"Y'all ready to take a break for lunch?" Mitzi asked.

"It's noon? Man, the morning went fast." Jody pulled a cooler out from under the table. They'd packed sandwiches, apples, and chips but hadn't brought anything to drink. Dixie immediately volunteered to go outside to one of the many vendors and get drinks for everyone.

"I'll go with you," Mitzi said. "You can't carry in five drinks all by yourself and besides, I need to stretch my legs."

"While we're waiting on them, I'm taking a bathroom break," Paula said. "We've been so busy answering questions and booking appointments that I couldn't get away. But there seems to be a lull right now."

"They'll hit us hard at one o'clock. The latecomers arrive then." Glenda and her assistants moved back a few feet, circled their chairs, and dove into a bucket of fried chicken.

"I'm going with Paula," Tabby said. She leaned down to whisper in Jody's ear, "Next time we do one of these, let's make a stop by the fried chicken place. That stuff smells wonderful."

"It's something to think about, for sure," Jody said. "But we've got some amazing chicken salad sandwiches." A customer walked up to the table but didn't stick around long when she found out they only worked for size fourteen and up. Jody was putting out the food when she heard boots on the hardwood floor. When the footsteps stopped, Jody turned around to see who it was.

"Hello, may I help you?" she asked as she locked gazes with Lyle and her stomach sank.

"Hello, Jody." His tone dripped icicles.

"What are you doing here?" Her chest tightened. Pain shot through her temples, and her hands shook.

Kennedy looped her arm into Lyle's. "Honey, they don't sell cakes, and I don't need a wedding dress for our big ranch reception. What we need to look at is centerpieces for the tables and a cake. And I like this one right here."

Jody's hands knotted into fists. There was nothing she'd like better than grabbing a few of those sugar roses and hurling them at Kennedy. Or maybe just forgetting all about the girl and rocking Lyle's jaw with her fist.

"Isn't he just the sweetest husband ever to come to one of these affairs with me?" Kennedy crooned. "Now let's move over a table, darlin', and look at pretty cakes."

She tugged on his arm, and he followed without a backward glance. Jody thought she'd gotten past the anger stage, but the way her fingernails dug into her palms told a different story. She imagined smashing the whole container of chicken salad into Lyle's face, especially when he agreed Kennedy should order that huge cake.

Her parents were probably paying for the reception since all she'd gotten was a rushed courthouse wedding, but Jody hadn't even had that much. Forget the mushy chicken salad—she'd rather throw the fake cake at him, especially if the inside was something hard like concrete.

Paula and Tabby were giggling about something when they returned. At least, they were until Paula stopped in her tracks and her eyes shifted from Lyle to Jody. "Holy smokin' hell," she whispered. "What is he doin' here?"

"He's with his new bride, Kennedy. They're getting a wedding cake for the big reception the ranch is throwing for them," Jody explained in low tones.

"Your ex?" Tabby asked.

"That's right." Jody nodded.

Tabby shot a mean look toward his back and then promptly headed out across the floor, bypassing them on the way to where Mitzi and Dixie were bringing in cups of soda for everyone. Without saying anything, she took one of the three cups Dixie was trying to handle and started back to the display with it in her hand.

Jody watched Tabby from the corner of her eye as she wove through the crowd. Then Jody caught Mitzi's expression when she realized that Lyle was in the room. Her mouth set in a firm line and her jaws worked as if she were trying to swallow a green persimmon.

Tabby stumbled over her own two feet but quickly got control. Then she tripped over the toes of Kennedy's fancy boots and dumped the whole drink on Lyle's freshly starched and ironed jeans.

"Oh, my goodness, I'm so sorry. I'm usually not the clumsy one. But I was lookin' at that cake and wasn't watchin' where I was goin'. I hope I didn't hurt your daughter's toes," she gushed. "Please forgive me. It's not every father who's kind enough to come along with his child to these things. And now I've ruined your jeans. I hope folks don't think that you've peed on yourself. You really don't look old enough to do that, I promise. To have a kid as old as yours, you look pretty good."

"It's all right. I have a change of clothing in the truck," Lyle said through clenched teeth. "And this is my wife, not my daughter."

"Oh, sweet Lord." Tabby's hands went to her cheeks. "I'm so sorry. It's just that you l-look about like my father's age, and . . ." She stammered over the words. "Well, I'm glad you brought extra jeans. Forgive me for being so awkward. I hope I don't do something stupid when I'm modeling a dress for The Perfect Dress tonight. Did y'all stop by our table? We do custom wedding dresses for plus-sized women, like your wife. Why are you getting a wedding cake if she's already your wife?"

Kennedy tugged on his arm. "Let's go out to the truck and get you out of those wet things. And for your information, we're having a reception. That's why we need a cake and not a dress. One more thing: my size is none of your damned business. You're certainly not a skinny person, either."

Tears flowed down Tabby's cheeks. "Accidents happen. You don't have to get mean with me. I try to lose weight, but it's so hard."

"Let's get out of here." Lyle ushered Kennedy away from the table.

"I'll call you about when and where to deliver that cake," Kennedy called out to Glenda.

Mitzi draped an arm around Tabby's shoulders. "Are you all right?"

"Couldn't be better." Tabby wiped the tears away and grinned at her sister. "How's that for a performance?"

"That was standing-ovation material," Dixie giggled. "Who was that?"

"The sorry sucker who hurt our Jody," Tabby said.

"Then the reviews for your acting skills will be out of this world. I'll share my drink with you," Dixie said.

It started as a hardly audible giggle, but soon Jody was guffawing and wiping at her own tears with a paper napkin. "That was incredible," she finally said between hiccups.

"You are welcome." Tabby curtsied. "Now let's get into that chicken salad. Acting always makes me hungry."

Dixie set her two cups on the table. "She's not as pretty as you, Jody."

"Thank you for that." Jody set about making five sandwiches.

Mitzi unloaded two cups and opened a bag of chips. "Did you two take acting classes?"

"Nope, we've just put on shows for each other and for Daddy since we were little girls," Dixie answered. "Tabby can cry on demand. I can't, so I'm glad she was the one who knew who that sorry son of a gun was."

"Oh, honey, she did an amazing job. I just wish I'd have known what you were going to do. I'd have filmed it so I could watch it over and over," Jody said.

Paula held up her camera. "You are welcome."

"I've got the best friends in the whole world," Jody said past the lump in her throat.

⌇

Mitzi's stomach clenched as she and Tabby pushed through the double doors into the room where the models and their assistants would get ready for the show that evening. So this was the maternal instinct that people talked about. Anxiety and pride all rolled into one big ball.

A lady in a blue vest took a look at their lanyards and ushered them back to a table with a card that said "The Perfect Dress."

"You can set up right here. You'll be in the first fourth of the models in alphabetical order." She pointed toward the end of the room. "Your number is on the card on your table."

Mitzi's mother had used a camera to snap pictures of her at every school event and function, no matter what she was involved in. Now Mitzi was doing the same, only with a phone, as she took the first photograph of Tabby in her cute little white capris and shirt. "Before and after to send to your dad," she explained.

"Did Paula send that video to him, too?" Tabby opened her tote bag, set up a small, lighted three-way mirror, and laid out a whole array of makeup.

"Yep." Mitzi pulled up a chair and sat down beside her.

"Good." Tabby leaned forward and started with a few dots of liquid makeup on her face that she brushed outward. "He's going to tell me that it wasn't a nice thing to do but that I did it for a good reason."

"That's what I'd tell you." Mitzi propped her elbows on the table and rested her chin in her hands.

"I really do wish you'd been older or Daddy would've been younger so he would have noticed you in high school. He whistles a lot now. Why don't you ask him out on a real date? Not just a lake date." She applied eyeliner to her left eye.

"Men should ask women," Mitzi answered.

With one eye looking fabulous and the other not even touched, Tabby turned toward Mitzi. "This is the modern world. When I date, I'm going to ask a guy out. Daddy is kind of gun-shy when it comes to askin' women. And we haven't helped very much. We kind of sabotaged the first lady he got serious about because we were afraid he'd like her more than us. Then the next one was downright awful. But we like you. We promise to be nice if you'll ask him out. We'll even dress him up."

Mitzi snapped a picture of her, then sent it to Graham. "He'll get a kick out of seeing you getting ready."

Tabby went back to her makeup. "You're not going to talk about dating him, are you?"

"Don't think so," Mitzi answered as she sent the pictures to Graham. She got a text back immediately: I'm jealous. Wish I was there.

She sent back a smiley face and kept snapping pictures as the process went on. The lady in the vest came by and said, "Fifteen minutes and it will be your turn."

Tabby flipped her hair up in a messy bun on top of her head and put away all her things as methodically as she'd gotten them out. "Okay, I'm ready for the dress and the veil."

After Tabby took off her capris and shirt, Mitzi held the dress for her to step into. Tabby stood in front of a long bank of mirrors with a few other bride models as Mitzi fastened each little satin button on the arms of the dress. "I feel pretty in this. Do you think I'll like feel like this on my real wedding day?"

"Yes, I do," Mitzi assured her. "Now for the veil." She set the tiara on the top of Tabby's head. "I don't think I messed up your hairdo. If I'd tried to do that with mine, it would've looked more like a fresh cow pile than an elaborate style."

"It's all in the twist of the hand and the curls from those little pink sponge rollers you saw me in this morning."

Tabby inhaled deeply and then let it out slowly as Mitzi snapped another dozen or more pictures. "Oh, Mitzi, just look at me. When I get married, I want a veil like this. Nothing over my face to make me sneeze," Tabby said. "Okay, are we ready?"

"Depends." Mitzi snapped more pictures.

"On what?"

"If you're going barefoot or if you're going to wear the shoes in that box." Mitzi pointed.

Tabby giggled as she took out the shoes and slipped her feet into them. "I'm nervous."

"Not as much as I am," Mitzi admitted. "My mama used to give me a kiss on the forehead for good luck when I had something that made me nervous. Granny gave me one on the day we opened our shop since Mama wasn't here to do it. Now I'm giving one to you." She leaned forward and brushed a soft kiss on Tabby's forehead.

Tabby took a step forward and kissed Mitzi on the cheek.

"I wish my mother was here," one of the other models said.

"Not me," Tabby said. "I'd rather have Mitzi."

Mitzi got misty eyed and was so glad that she was there with Tabby.

"Five minutes." The coordinator pointed to Tabby.

"Maybe I need one more kiss to calm me down. I don't want to disappoint y'all, and I've got butterflies in my stomach," Tabby said.

"I don't believe it," Mitzi said. "Not after that performance with Lyle."

"That was pretend. This is real." Tabby pointed to her forehead.

"Three minutes. Come on over here and get ready to go through the curtains," the woman said.

Tabby started that way with Mitzi right behind her. "If I don't trip or freeze at the end of the runway, will you ask Daddy out?"

"No, I won't." Mitzi kissed her on the forehead one more time.

"If he asks you out, will you say yes?" Tabby pressed.

"We'll see," Mitzi answered.

The lady held up one finger.

"Go on so I can see you in the crowd. That'll calm me right down, and besides, you need to take pictures for Daddy." Tabby nodded toward the side door.

"And now, from The Perfect Dress, a custom plus-sized wedding shop in Celeste, Texas, we have Tabby Harrison modeling one of their creations," the man with the microphone said.

Mitzi had barely sat down in the chair beside Jody when Tabby stepped out with her bouquet in one hand and the other on her hip. As if she were born to be a model, Tabby slowly made her way to the end of the runway, flipped the train behind her as if she was doing the crowd a favor when she turned, and started back.

The applause was deafening, and a guy right behind them tapped Mitzi on the shoulder. When she turned around, he handed her a business card and asked, "I saw you hurry out just as they announced the model. Are you the owner of that place?"

"Yes, with my partners," she answered.

"Want to make up a few dresses in various sizes on consignment? I'd love to sell them in my shop in Houston. Finding dresses in anything more than an eighteen is tough, and I've had to turn away customers in sizes twenty up through thirty."

"No, thank you. We like to work directly with our customers."

"Well, if you change your mind, just give me a call. That's some gorgeous work and the fit is superb."

"Thank you. Now I've got to get back to help my model out of the dress." She stood up and offered her hand.

He shook hands with her. "I'm serious. If you get time to design a couple, I'll be glad to sell them."

"Well, how about that?" Jody said right behind Mitzi. "Next thing you know we'll be offered a reality show."

"Can't you just see that?" Paula and Dixie fell into place. "One pregnant owner. One jilted one, two teenagers, a grandmother named Fanny Lou who pops in any old time, and Mitzi, who—"

Mitzi whipped around and butted in before Paula could finish the sentence by saying that she was in love with a high school crush. "I will turn down a reality show without even thinking about it for a second."

"It's been a day," Jody said. "I'm ready to get a big cone of soft ice cream and go home. How about y'all?"

"Sounds good—I want rocky road," Dixie said.

"Me, too." Tabby had already removed the veil and the shoes. "I told Daddy that he has to ask you out since I didn't fall on my face."

Dixie pumped her fist in the air. "When's he goin' to do it?"

"I'm standing right here," Mitzi said.

"Yep, you are." Tabby grinned.

Chapter Twenty

They'd gotten home at a decent hour after the bridal fair, but all three of them were so wound up about all the appointments that had been made, there was no way they could sleep. They were still in the living room talking about how many dresses they could make in a month without losing quality when Mitzi realized it was three o'clock in the morning.

She yawned and stretched. "Girls, if we don't get to bed, we're going to fall asleep in church."

"I vote we miss tomorrow," Paula suggested.

Jody raised a hand. "I second that vote."

"No argument from me," Mitzi agreed as she headed off to her bedroom. She crawled beneath the sheets and shut her eyes, but sleep wouldn't come. Were Tabby and Dixie having trouble settling down, too? Were they still talking about the bridal fair and planning their next wedding bouquets? They'd spent a lot of time going through the photo albums at the floral vendors.

It was well past five o'clock when Mitzi finally fell into a deep sleep, and she didn't wake until almost noon. She crawled out of bed, made a stop in the bathroom, and then growled at her reflection in the hallway mirror. "I look like I've been run over by a Weed Eater and then thrown under a semi."

Jody pushed open the door to her bedroom. "You don't look that bad. Besides, you've got a couple of hours to get ready for your date. That's enough to nap and still transform you into Cinderella."

"Let's go get a cup of coffee. That'll make us feel better." Jody tugged at her arm.

Paula was already sitting at the table with a cup of hot tea in front of her. "Good morning. I hope that y'all feel better than I do this morning. I'm glad we don't do a bridal fair every weekend."

"It's kind of like the day after Christmas, isn't it?" Mitzi said as she got a Diet Coke from the refrigerator. "I don't want to go to the lake. Heat, bugs, and hot sun is not my idea of a great Sunday afternoon. I'd rather stay in my pajamas all afternoon and do nothing but lay up on the sofa and watch old movies. How about we call it all off and—"

"Are you sick? You all look like hookers after a tough Saturday night!" Fanny Lou burst in the back door before Mitzi could finish the sentence. She'd already changed from her Sunday dress into a pair of baggy jeans that had been rolled up to the knees, sandals, and one of the promotional T-shirts advertising The Perfect Dress across the back.

"Granny!" Mitzi gasped.

"I'm here to get y'all's tired asses in gear. Me and Harry decided that we're going to the lake with everyone. We're supposed to meet the Harrisons at the lake marina at twelve thirty. They're providin' a fried chicken dinner, and I'm starvin'. Graham and Alice both asked about you this mornin' at church, and the twins looked like they'd been drug through a knothole backwards. Y'all plumb wore them out yesterday. That video with Lyle and the spilled drink was so funny, I almost peed my underpants. Tabby showed it to me while we were passing the plate."

"We thought maybe we'd stay in this afternoon," Jody said.

"The hell you will," Fanny Lou said loudly. "After what them girls did for y'all yesterday and with no money changin' hands, you're goin' to all three get your asses up them stairs and come down here lookin' bright eyed and bushy tailed. It would disappoint them kids, and I ain't havin' it."

They all looked at each other, but no one moved.

Fanny Lou raised her voice another notch. "If I got to tell you again, it ain't goin' to be pleasant."

Mitzi grabbed her Diet Coke and carried it with her. "I'll be down in fifteen minutes. No need to put on makeup since I'll just sweat it off." She turned around at the door and asked, "Did you bring sunblock, Granny?"

"Plenty enough to go around." Fanny Lou nodded. "Don't any of us need to get skin cancer. Now get a rush on it. Harry is on the way, and we're all going in the van."

Mitzi hurried up the stairs with Paula and Jody right behind her. "Sorry I got y'all into this."

"Fanny Lou is right. It would be downright rude to beg off after the girls helped out so much," Paula said.

"And God knows I owe Tabby for what she did," Jody agreed. "I like to float around in a pontoon boat. Maybe I'll catch a nap while you flirt with Graham."

"Oh, hush!" Mitzi grumbled. "I'm not in the mood for jokes or flirting."

"Not even one little kiss?" Paula asked. "You can't tell me you'd turn that down."

Mitzi made it to her room before the other two, grabbed a pillow from her bed, and hurled it toward Paula. It landed just short of the door that Paula slammed shut. Paula peeked back out and stuck her tongue out at Mitzi.

Mitzi pulled her hair up into dog ears right above her own ears, put on a pair of denim shorts and a nice loose-fitting cotton shirt. She'd thought about stopping at the Galleria on the way home from Dallas, but she was too tired to even look at bathing suits, much less try them on. Besides, she wasn't ready for Graham to see that much of her skin.

She tossed her phone and wallet into a tote bag along with a rolled-up towel and more sunblock, even though her grandmother said she had brought plenty. It might be enough if she'd been a small woman, but Mitzi had a lot of lily-white skin to cover. Sun had never been her friend, not with the traditional pale skin that went with red hair. She stared at her reflection in the floor-length mirror on the back of her bedroom door. She was certainly not a petite little thing like Rita, so what did Graham see in her anyway?

$\sim$

"Have I got a bunch of sailors in this house ready to go to the lake for the afternoon?" Alice yelled as she entered her brother's house by the kitchen door.

"Not sailors," Tabby said. "We're pontooners. We got our bags packed with sunscreen and books. Daddy said we had to leave our phones at home."

"Smart man," Alice said. "Got your bathing suits on under those oversized shirts?"

Dixie pulled up her shirt to show off a bright-red suit. "How do you like it?"

"Looks fabulous. I'm wearing the same color under this caftan. We still on for a swimming race?" Alice asked.

"You bet we are," Tabby answered. "But we've got to give Daddy and Mitzi some privacy so he can ask her out on a real date."

"Hey now, I said I'd ask her. I didn't say when," Graham argued. Sometimes he had to set his heels or the girls would overrun him completely. He'd enjoyed the time and the kisses he'd shared with Mitzi, but something kept whispering to him that he should take it slow and not go too fast with her.

"It'll be your own fault if you let her get away from you. There's probably a dozen men just waiting in line at her back door to ask her out," Dixie declared with a toss of her hair. "Now let's get this show on the road. It wouldn't be good if our guests like had to wait on us to get there, would it?"

"'Guests,' nothing," Tabby argued. "Those people are family, not guests."

"Well, pardon me." Dixie did a head bobble that rivaled those crazy bigheaded dolls.

"You got everything you need, brother?" Alice asked.

"Yep, I do." He picked up a tackle box.

"Going to fish?" She held the door for him.

"Nope, just tucked everything in here. I'm really looking forward to being outside all afternoon." He crossed the porch and yard, got into the truck, and fastened his seat belt.

"Me, too. We haven't been out on the boat in weeks," Dixie said from the back seat.

"And we get Mitzi and Harry and Granny Fanny Lou today," Tabby said. "It's going to be wonderful."

Alice drove right to the marina and had just parked when Mitzi pulled in beside her. All five of them unloaded, and Graham looked over everyone's heads and winked at Mitzi.

Harry stuck out his hand. "Hey, Graham, looks like we're outnumbered today."

Graham shook it. "Looks that way. We might have to stick together to ward off all this femininity."

"That's what I figure," Harry chuckled. "Which one of these things belongs to you?"

"The one with *Just Cruisin'* on the back," Dixie answered.

"Me and Dixie named it when we got it. We used to go out every weekend." Tabby set her tote bag on a case of soft drinks and carried it down the boardwalk to the second slip.

"Hello." Graham took a couple of steps and stopped in front of Mitzi. "Nice hairstyle you got there."

She pulled her sunglasses down on her nose and looked up over them. "I'm glad you like my dog ears. I don't like to sweat."

"I do honestly like your hair, but your eyes mesmerize me." He immediately wondered if that was too bold, if maybe he was coming on too strong.

She bumped his arm with her elbow. "And you said you were shy around women."

"I usually am, but it's different with you." He winked.

It took two trips to get everything onto the boat. Then Alice rolled out the awning and started up the engine. When they'd gone out to the middle of the lake, she turned the steering over to Graham. "I'll be right back." She threw off her caftan, revealing a bright-red tankini underneath, and dove into the water.

Dixie and Tabby followed right behind her, tossing their cover-ups onto a side bench, and into the lake they went, headfirst.

"You swimming?" Graham asked Mitzi.

"Nope, not me. I don't have a bathing suit."

"Well, I do," Jody said as she peeled out of her shorts and shirt. "It's been years since I've gotten to be in the water, so here goes." She went in feet first and emerged a few seconds later with her long braids floating behind her. "I swear, next week, I'm cutting these things off. They're weighing me down."

"You wouldn't be the same without your braids," Mitzi told her.

"Paula?" Fanny Lou asked.

Paula shook her head. "I'll just sit right here in the shade and enjoy the scenery. How long do we leave them out there?"

"Fifteen minutes and then we're going to gather them in and have some lunch. I still make the girls wait half an hour after eating before they go back in the water," he answered.

"I bet that's why they wanted to get wet before we eat, right?" Fanny Lou said. "If we do this again, I'm dragging out my old yellow-and-black suit from the seventies. I'm just itchin' right now to get into that water."

"Not me. I'd sink like an anchor," Harry said. "Delores was half fish. She loved any kind of water—the ocean, the lake, even a backyard pool. She taught Mitzi to swim when she was only two years old."

"Really?" Graham raised an eyebrow. "I thought about putting a pool in for the girls, but they don't want it. They say that the lake is bigger, deeper, and lots more fun."

"I like a pool because it's private," Mitzi said.

Graham immediately reconsidered putting one in his backyard. There was plenty of room, and the yard already had an eight-foot privacy fence around it. He was imagining a cute little cabana-type atmosphere when the four ladies climbed back onto the boat.

"We're starving now for sure." Dixie grabbed a towel and dried her face before wrapping it around her wet hair.

Alice set about getting the food from the cooler—fried chicken, potato salad, coleslaw, and thick slices of dark rye bread. Then she opened another cooler and brought out icy cold cans of root beer. Tabby pulled paper plates from under the bench on one side. Dixie handed out plastic forks.

"I'm taking two chicken legs," Tabby said. "There's probably eight more, and I'll fight y'all for the last one."

"You can have 'em," Harry said. "I'm a thigh man."

"And you?" Graham nudged Mitzi on the arm.

"Wings all the way." She found four wings and claimed them all for herself. "This is really nice. I'm so glad that we came today."

"If you changed your mind about coming today, all you had to do was call me," Graham whispered to her. "I would have understood if you were tired from yesterday."

"I couldn't do that to the girls," she said.

"What about me? Could you have done that to me?"

"Are you trying to pick a fight?" she asked. "If so, then wait until we get home, because I'm not spoiling this day for the rest of our families."

"I'm not," he answered, but in the course of a few minutes, his day had changed from carefree and happy to gloomy. Then, as if the universe understood the way he felt, a strong southern wind whipped at the awning. Storm clouds gathered on the far horizon, and a few streaks of lightning zigzagged through the sky.

"Looks like we've got about another hour," Harry said. "Unless that storm circles around us, but it sure looks like it's making a beeline for us."

Dixie groaned. "I wanted to stay here until night and catch fireflies up on the bank."

"I even brought a quilt so y'all could sit on it while we caught them," Tabby said. "We can't even get back in the water to swim if it's lightning, can we, Daddy?"

"Rules are rules. I'll call up the weather on my phone." He held up his hand and crossed his fingers before he started scrolling through the icons for the weather. "Sorry, girls. According to this, we should start carrying things back to the truck soon as we eat. It says that it's going to hit in an hour. Strong winds, maybe even some hail. Y'all finish up your food, and I'll get the boat headed back to the slip."

The wind had picked up and thunder rolled by the time Alice and Graham got the boat tied off and things gathered up. A loud crack above their heads had him ducking as they all helped take coolers and food back to the truck. Dixie squealed and Tabby took off in a run with her load.

The temperature dropped at least fifteen degrees as Graham walked with Mitzi to her van. Everyone else was loaded up and ready to go when he bent slightly and asked, "Would you go out to dinner and a movie with me on Friday night?"

She shook her head. "No, I won't."

"Got other plans?" he asked.

Another shake of her head. "No, but we need to take a step back and figure out if we're starting something for us or for the girls. What happens if it all goes south and we hang on because we wouldn't want to disappoint them? Is this chemistry we feel between us real or is it a flash in the pan?"

"I like you a lot," he said.

"And I like you, too, but before we start breaking hearts, let's figure out why."

"Couldn't we just have a good time?" Crazy thing was that ever since he'd seen Rita in front of Walmart, he'd been wondering the same thing. It had nothing to do with what Rita said about Mitzi's size, and he didn't have any intentions of letting Rita back in his life. But he needed to be sure of his own heart before he offered it to Mitzi.

"I always have a good time when I'm with you," she answered.

"Well, then I'll leave it up to you, Mitzi. I feel something with you that I've never felt with another woman, not even Rita. I'm comfortable with you, and yet there's a spark of electricity that's brand new to me. But if you need time, then you've got it. When you get everything all analyzed out, you let me know. Call. Text. Come by the house. I hope you feel the same as I do, but if not, then you're probably right about not taking this to the next step. I won't bother you until you get things figured out." He took a step back without kissing her, even though he wanted to very badly.

"Did she say yes?" Dixie asked the minute he was in the truck.

In that moment Graham could understand why Mitzi said no, because he hated to tell them the truth, so he stretched it slightly. "She's got a lot going on for the next couple of weeks, as y'all well know. We're going to talk about it later."

"Then we'll help her out a lot this next week so that y'all can talk real soon," Tabby said.

Chapter Twenty-One

*Y*ou did what?" Jody almost dropped her glass of sweet tea when Mitzi told them about what had happened.

"I figured out that I was having more fun watching the girls play in the water than I was having watching him. And besides that, I like him too much to get into a relationship and then ruin things with everyone," Mitzi said.

"You look miserable," Paula said. "In my opinion, you're overthinking things."

"In mine, you're afraid to get hurt, and I hope my situation isn't causing you to back away from a good relationship," Jody said.

"I am second-guessing myself," Mitzi admitted. "Graham may be the best thing that ever happened to me. I know I'm making up excuses not to get into a relationship with him, because if I do and he breaks my heart, I might not ever get over it. And I am worrying so much about the future that I'm giving up the future. But I need to get this settled, so we need some time."

"We'll stand by you no matter what you decide," Jody said.

"Thank goodness we've got lots of business the next couple of weeks. I think best with a sketch pad and pencil in my hands," Mitzi said.

"Like I do with a needle," Jody said as she reached for the ringing phone. "The Perfect Dress."

"Hello, Jody, this is Quincy. Will you go to dinner with me? Any day this week would be good," he said.

"Are you going to stop calling me if I say no?" she asked.

"I am not," he answered.

"Well, then here's my cell number." She rattled off the numbers. "You have a nice evening, Quincy."

"You, too, Jody," he said.

"Was that Quincy?" Paula asked.

"Please, sweet Jesus, tell me that it was, so we can talk about something other than whether I made the biggest mistake of my life," Mitzi said.

"It was Quincy, and I've agreed to go out with him. Mainly to shut him up. One little date and he'll realize that I'm not all that interesting," Jody said.

"Don't underestimate yourself," Mitzi said.

"If he hadn't seen something he liked, he wouldn't keep asking," Paula told her.

"Maybe he's always gotten what he wants and he can't stand rejection." Jody started out of the room and then turned around. "I've got to admit, I'm terrified. I've never dated anyone other than Lyle. Never been with another man or even kissed another one."

"Then it's time." Mitzi followed her across the foyer, with Paula right behind them. "And I got to admit that I'm terrified, too."

"Add me to the list," Paula said. "Y'all are worried about relationships. I'm scared that I'll be terrible at this single-mother stuff."

"Thank goodness that we've got each other," Jody said and meant it from the depths of her heart.

Two weeks, a dozen appointments from the bridal fair, ten orders for flowers for weddings, and no calls or texts from Graham later, Mitzi still hadn't gotten things analyzed. No matter how many dresses she sketched, cookies she baked, or sleepless nights she endured, she was still in turmoil about Graham. She'd picked up and replaced the phone at least four times a day to call him, written a hundred texts but then deleted them before she sent them.

Then it was July Fourth, their first holiday to close the shop since they'd opened in December of the previous year. On Memorial Day they'd closed the doors, but they'd worked all day on a rush order for a dress. But after the past two weeks, they decided that they deserved a day off.

Fanny Lou came by that morning with a bag of doughnuts she'd purchased just before the pastry shop had closed the day before. She plopped it down on the table and took a gallon of milk from the refrigerator. "I've come to talk about this bullshit going on with you and Graham, Mitzi, and what's happening with you and Quincy, Jody. This has gone on long enough for both of you."

"Nothing to talk about. He asked me out when we went to the lake. I said no. He said to figure out what I want and then let him know," Mitzi explained in as few words as possible.

"And Quincy and I've been talking almost every day," Jody said. "When we know each other well enough, I'll go out with him. Maybe even this weekend."

"It's not fair to leave two good men hanging like this." Fanny Lou poured four glasses of milk and tore the doughnut bag down the side. "They ain't goin' to wait around forever. I heard this morning that Rita has been to see him three times this last week. All at the dealership. Do you want her back in those girls' life, or worse yet, back in his? Sounds like she wants another baby."

Mitzi knew all that already, but there was still a little niggling thought pestering her about why Graham was attracted to her. Every relationship she'd ever had came up short because she'd measured the guy by the kind of man she thought Graham was. There was no doubt about her love, but his was a different matter. Sure, he said he felt sparks, but that might be because he hadn't been with a woman in a while.

"Well, cat got your tongue, or are you going to comment?" Fanny Lou asked.

"I thought maybe Rita had given up." She picked out a jelly-filled doughnut and took a bite out of it.

"That woman is like them flesh-eatin' fish. Piranhas. She's made up her mind to have him and she just might get him if you don't decide what the hell you want. You're runnin' from your own heart."

Mitzi didn't argue, but why were so many people interested in her life? She was past thirty, had been working and making her own way for the most part for the past fourteen years. Sure, she'd screwed up a few times, but she'd learned from her mistakes.

"Why is it so important to all y'all that I date Graham? Is it because he's a big man, and I don't look so fat when I'm with him? Is it because he's got money, and y'all want to see me comfortable? Just what the hell has he got that keeps you pushing me toward him?" She could hear the chill in her own voice.

"Size and money ain't got nothing to do with it. You had a glow, a happiness and contentment, when you were spending time with him. The past two weeks you've been unhappy, even with this job that used to be your dream come true," Fanny Lou said. "I want you to be happy like you used to be."

"And Jody? She needs to be happy, too, right?" Paula asked.

"Absolutely," Fanny Lou agreed and turned to focus on Jody. "Quincy is a good, decent man. I know it hasn't been long since Lyle left you, but this might be the way for you to get all that shit finalized. Step outside your comfort zone and peel off that brand Lyle put on your heart all those years ago. There's good guys out there and Quincy is one of them. I'm not telling either of you to jump into what you call a relationship these days, but I am telling you to get things settled. I don't like the way you're acting."

"You're right, Granny."

"Do what you want with your lives," Fanny Lou said. "But please give us back our Mitzi and sassy Jody."

"We would pay good money or doughnuts or even chocolate ice cream if y'all would be happy again," Paula added. "If the girls hadn't spent so much time upstairs these past two weeks with their flowers, they would've noticed the difference, too."

"Whoa, wait a minute," Mitzi said. "Is this one of those interventions?"

"Hell, no," Fanny Lou said. "This is doughnuts and milk and friends havin' a conversation. Now I've got to go, but I'll be here to ride down to the fireworks show with y'all this evening. I hear Harry is making ice cream for afterwards, but he might want it to be a surprise so don't say anything. That sound good?" She grabbed another doughnut and waved as she left.

"We'll be waiting for you," Paula said. "I don't know what to do to get y'all out of the same emotional ditch, but if you'll tell me what will help, I'll move heaven and earth to make it happen."

"I feel like I owe y'all an apology," Mitzi said. "But I don't know what to say I'm sorry about."

"Me, too," Jody said.

"Mitzi, you're not happy. Go down there. Take him to bed. Or never call him or see him again. We don't care. What we want is our happy friend, the one who's the glue that holds all of us together, to be herself again," Paula said. "God, I would have gone crazy if I hadn't had y'all for support all these years. You know what kind of home life I had. Y'all were my escape and my hold on reality. And Jody, like Granny said, we miss your sass."

"Okay, then let's go upstairs, and have a *Friends* marathon today. Just mindless funny stuff to take my mind off everything. We'll turn off all our phones and ignore the business one if it rings. Think we could do that?" Mitzi asked.

"I'll get the chips and dip and a six-pack of root beer," Jody said.

"I'll bring up a package of pecan sandies and that bag of candy bars that I hid in the bottom cabinet drawer," Paula said.

"I'll have the first season started when you get there," Mitzi said.

∽

The big orange sun had turned the mesquite trees in the distance into silhouettes that evening when they reached the football field. By the time they'd started up into the already crowded bleachers, the pre-event had started. Someone down at the goal line picked up a microphone, asked everyone to stand for the flag salute, and to remain standing for the national anthem.

Everyone stood. Men placed their hats and caps over their hearts. Mitzi put her hand over hers and recited the salute, just like she'd done at every football game she'd attended at Celeste High School. After that, the high school band provided the music while some young guy with a singing voice as smooth as honey sang the anthem. As soon as it was over, the first burst of fireworks lit up the sky.

She was looking up as she sat back down, so she didn't notice the twins or Graham settling in behind her, but the prickle on the back of her neck clued her in. Then Dixie and Tabby each laid a hand on her shoulders.

"Did you save us these seats?" Dixie asked.

"Sure did." She turned around and caught Graham's eye. "What'd y'all do all day?" she asked them, but her gaze stayed on Graham's face.

"We cut out and sewed up these shirts for tonight," Tabby said proudly.

It was a simple pattern with an elasticized neck, raglan sleeves, and a cute little ruffle around the bottom, with white stars on a dark-blue background. The body of the shirt was red-and-white vertical stripes. Mitzi couldn't have been prouder of them if they'd made those shirts at the shop.

"They're beautiful," she said.

"Want to know what I did?" Graham asked.

"Surely you didn't baste or sew anything," Mitzi answered.

"No, I dried their tears when they kept breaking the gathering thread for those ruffles."

Harry sat down beside Fanny Lou and turned around to say, "Welcome to my world when it comes to girls and sewing. I've got a gallon of homemade ice cream aging up real good in the truck. I'm plannin' on takin' it to Mitzi's after this is over. Y'all should come join us."

"Yes!" Dixie did one of her fist pumps in the air.

"Mitzi?" Graham asked.

"No way we'll eat a whole gallon all by ourselves, so please say you'll come help us out," she answered.

"Then we'll surely take you up on the offer, Harry. I love your ice cream." Graham's knee brushed against Mitzi's back.

Short little bursts of electricity shot through her body at his touch. Two weeks away from him hadn't gotten him out of her mind any more than fourteen years of not seeing him had.

❧

Graham couldn't take his eyes off Mitzi that evening. All he could really see was her red hair and the way her neck curved to her shoulders, but even that much made him want to lean down and at least whisper a thank-you for inviting them for ice cream. He kept his distance because he was afraid if he got that close, he'd kiss that soft spot right under her ear.

Every day for the past two weeks, he'd picked up the phone to call her but never could make himself go through with it. And when Rita came by, supposedly to talk about the wedding and the time she'd spend with the girls, all he did was compare her to Mitzi. It didn't take a rocket scientist to figure out who came out first or who he wished would never come back into his life again. He'd been careful both times to step out of his office into the main lobby of the business to talk to her—and made sure that Vivien was right there at her desk. Rita had ruined his life once. She was devious and manipulative enough to do it again if he wasn't careful.

He watched the fireworks light up the sky and wondered what it would be like to live with Mitzi. Would they have fireworks of their own every night when they shut the bedroom door?

The show lasted the better part of an hour, and then the grand finale went up in a glittering American flag and it was over. Folks began to gather up their folding seats, blankets, and soft-drink cans and leave, but Graham sat still until Mitzi rose to her feet.

"Are you sure about this?" he asked.

"Absolutely," she said.

"Then we'll see you at the shop in a few minutes." What he wanted to say was that he'd missed her, but he held his tongue.

The girls were whispering in the back seat of the truck when he crawled in and fastened his seat belt. They stopped when he started the engine. He tapped the steering wheel while he waited for a chance to back out of the parking space.

"The ice cream is going to melt," Dixie moaned.

"I thought Celeste was a little bitty town. Where'd all these cars and trucks come from?" Tabby asked.

"Everyone for miles around comes to see the fireworks." He looked up into the rearview mirror.

"We don't care if the whole state of Texas came to Celeste tonight, though it kind of looks like that," Tabby said. "What we want to talk

243

about is Mitzi and when you're really going to ask her out. You've been an old bear since that day we went to the lake. And she's not been herself, either."

"I had a lot of summer work at the dealership," he said.

"That's your excuse. I imagine hers is that we've been real busy at the shop," Dixie said. "Y'all like each other. We figure the problem is me and Tabby. After that last woman who was mean to us, you don't want to take a chance on another one. And she don't want to make it like all weird between us and her if y'all had a lousy date."

"We ain't kids no more, Dad," Tabby said.

"Evidently not." Graham wondered how they'd grown up so fast over the course of a month. "So since you've figured out so much, what's your advice on the matter?"

"Ask her out to dinner and a movie, or a play in Dallas, or something fun for just the two of you," Tabby said.

"And if she says no?" Graham was finally able to get out of the parking lot and take his place behind a long line of vehicles going the same way.

"Then send her flowers tomorrow, and ask again. If at first you don't succeed . . ." Dixie said. "I can't remember the rest of it."

"Try, try again," Tabby finished the old adage for her.

"How many times do I try, try again?" He turned onto Main Street and found himself right behind Mitzi's van.

"The preacher at church last Sunday said something about seven times seventy. I wasn't listenin' good enough to know what that worked on, but it's a good start," Dixie said. "We're goin' to try not to fuss at you about this anymore. But we would like to see you happy again."

"That's my sister's decision. I'm going to nag you all I want," Tabby said.

Who would have ever thought that Tabby, the quiet twin, would have been the one to take a stand, and that Dixie, the mouthy one, would concede to let him make his own decisions? It was a complete role reversal, and it surprised him.

He parked behind the van and beside Harry's truck. The girls were out of the back seat and jogging toward the house before he even got his door open. The last one inside, Graham could see Tabby taking bowls down from the cabinet and Mitzi over at the table putting out strawberries and chocolate syrup. Harry came from the sewing room with a few folding chairs tucked under his arm. It was the perfect picture of a family all working together, and he loved it.

Everyone circled around the table. Mitzi scooped out bowls full for each one, and the room was filled with laughter and conversation about the fireworks show. Graham hung back until everyone else was served and then took a few steps forward.

"I guess what's left can be divided among the two of us," he said. "Unless you want to put it all in one big bowl and we'll share. Fewer dirty dishes that way."

"We need to talk," she said softly.

"About ice cream?" he asked.

"Something a little more serious. But not here." She scooped out a big portion for him and then pointed to the strawberries and chocolate. "Topping?"

"I like my ice cream plain." A chill ran down his back that was colder than the ice cream in the bowl. "When do we need to have this talk?"

"Soon, but in private. I'll text you," she whispered.

"I'll be waiting." Her hand brushed his when she handed off the bowl. He wasn't surprised at the electricity that passed between them—not one bit.

Chapter Twenty-Two

*D*ark clouds shifted back and forth over a skinny crescent moon doing its best to throw a little light into Mitzi's room that evening. A soft breeze brushed the limbs of the old pecan tree against the window. Like everything else, both of those made her think of the situation she had with Graham and the problems her friends were facing.

Jody had been like a dark sky with no visible moon until Quincy came into her life. Now there was a ray of light, however slim, in her eyes. For that, Mitzi would always appreciate Quincy. Paula, with her pregnancy by a total jerk, had lived with no light for months until she unburdened herself of the secret. After she'd confronted Clinton, it seemed like she was happier.

Mitzi couldn't sleep, so she sat up in bed and stared at that sliver of a moon hanging right outside her window. She fell back on her pillow, turned her back to the window, and shut her eyes tightly, trying to will herself to sleep, but it didn't work. Her mind wouldn't stop spinning in circles. Getting this thing settled once and for all with Graham had to be done, and soon.

She padded barefoot down to the kitchen, heated up a cup of milk, and added chocolate syrup to it. That usually worked wonders when it came to making her drowsy, but after half an hour, she was still wide awake. The clock on the microwave said it was twelve thirty—too late to text Graham.

Finishing off the last sip of milk as she carried the mug to the sink, she made a decision. It might be rash and quite possibly wouldn't produce a thing, but she had to try, or else she'd toss and turn all night. She couldn't just go marching down to his house and ring the doorbell at that time of night, she told herself. But if she didn't she wasn't going to sleep a wink. She made a deal with herself that if the house was totally dark, she'd come back home, but if there was a light on anywhere in the house, she'd ring the doorbell.

Before she lost her nerve, she took a deep breath and headed for the front door. She froze when it squeaked as she opened it. For a few seconds she couldn't move. The cool air from the house rushed out past her, while the hot night air almost seemed to push her back into the house. She started to close the door but couldn't make herself do it.

"Now or never," she whispered as she stepped out onto the porch. She didn't have keys, so she eased the door shut and didn't lock it. She'd be less than a block away, and most likely she'd be back in five minutes. The grass was cool and slightly wet on her bare feet as she crossed a couple of lawns on her way to Graham's house. Thank goodness no dogs set up a howl or folks appeared on their porches with loaded shotguns. That had to be a good sign, didn't it?

When she reached her destination, she found no lights pouring out from the downstairs windows. Looking up at the second floor, nothing shone there, either. But from the tour of the house the girls had given her, she remembered that his bedroom looked out over the back of the place. An unlocked gate would be her sign to continue this crazy venture. She pushed and it swung wide open, without even the tiniest squeak.

She was looking up at the dark windows when Graham's deep voice startled her. She jerked around to see where it came from, stepped in a gopher hole, and had to grab the porch post to keep from falling.

"I haven't been drinkin'," she said and wished she could grab the words and cram them back into her mouth. "That sounded kind of crazy, didn't it?"

"Not so much," Graham said. "I'm having a beer. Want one?"

"Yes," she answered, but she was glued to the post. She hadn't thought ahead to plan what she would say, and now no words were coming from her brain to her mouth.

"Guess you couldn't sleep, either," he said. "Come on up here and sit with me on the swing. You been thinking about this talk we're supposed to have, too?"

"Yes, I have, and here we are." Mitzi took a step toward his voice. The wood on the porch scraped her feet after the cool grass, but it was level and didn't have gopher holes. With a pounding heart she took a few more steps and then heard him pull the tab on a can of beer. Another step to the door leading into the screened porch, and a little flame from a match lit up the darkness. The glow of a jar candle flickered on the table in front of the swing where he sat. She stepped around a bistro set and almost turned around and ran back home when she realized that her hair was a mess, she didn't have a drop of makeup on—and she was wearing baggy pajama bottoms and no bra under her oversize T-shirt.

Graham handed the beer to her and patted the other end of the swing. She took it from him, sat down, and then noticed that the candle and a long lighter were sitting on the top of one of those tiny dorm-size refrigerators. "Like you said, here we are. According to the girls, I've been hard to live with since you turned me down for a date."

Mitzi took a long drink from the can and turned to face Graham. "I get the same thing from my family. But that's the problem, isn't it?"

"I like you, Mitzi, and I think you like me, too."

"You're right, I like you, Graham." There. She'd said it, and it felt good to get that much out. "Do I hear a *but* in your voice?"

"But you've probably been thinking the same thing. Do we feel this way as a by-product of the love we both have for Dixie and Tabby, or is it something real between us?" He sipped his beer and gazed out at the dark clouds covering the moon for so long that Mitzi figured he was about to say that, yes, he liked her but only as a friend. "I've given our relationship a lot of thought these past two weeks. Yes, you are good with the girls, but what I feel for you has nothing to do with my kids. There's chemistry between us that can't be denied."

Relationship.

He'd said that and not *friendship*. It's what she wanted, but doubts and fears clouded her still.

"But if we ignore it, it might die." She wiped the sweat from the can.

"Do you want it to go away?" He set his beer down on the floor and scooted over next to her. The touch of his shoulder to hers raised the temperature several degrees.

She shook her head slowly. "No, I don't. I've tried to analyze the way I feel when I'm around you, and you're right. I love Dixie and Tabby, but what we have is something that I can't put into words."

He stood up and pulled her close to his body in a tight hug. "I want us to be more than friends. I want to spend more time with you." He tipped up her chin. "Would you go out with me Saturday? A real date. A day just for us. That's the day the girls have to be in the wedding. I've reserved a hotel room so I'd have a place to stay while I wait for them. We could have the whole day to ourselves to do whatever we want."

"Yes," she said without a moment's hesitation.

"Good," he whispered as his lips met hers in what started out as a sweet kiss but soon developed into something much hotter as his tongue grazed her lips and begged entrance.

She opened up to him and turned to wrap her arms around his neck. With her breasts pressed against his chest, she could feel his heart thumping as fast as hers. When the string of scorching-hot kisses ended, she laid her head on his shoulder.

"And here we sit in pajama bottoms," she whispered.

"Darlin', I learned a long time ago that it's not what's on the outside that makes a woman beautiful but what's on the inside. That said, you'd be gorgeous in an old feed bag tied up in the middle with a piece of twine," he said.

"That may be the most romantic thing a guy has ever said to me."

He brought her hand to his lips and kissed each knuckle. "I'm not very good at romance, but this feels right."

"Yes, it does." No past relationship had ever felt so right.

"Anything else we need to talk about?" he asked.

"Right now I don't want to talk. I just want to sit here and enjoy the moment." She closed her eyes.

༄

When she awoke the next morning, the sun peeked over the edge of the far horizon, which meant it had to be at least six o'clock. Jody was probably already in the kitchen making coffee. Mitzi's head was still on Graham's shoulder. His cheek was nestled in her hair and his arm cuddled her. She eased out away from him and started to stand, but he tightened his grip on her.

"Don't go," he muttered.

"Have to. It's morning."

His eyes popped wide open and he adjusted his glasses. "Well, how 'bout that? We just spent the night together, and I slept like a baby."

"Me, too." She bent and kissed him on the forehead. "But now I've got to get home or gossip will have it that we did more than sleep. The girls don't need that when they're trying to get a new start."

He pulled her back onto his lap and kissed her on the lips. "I'll see you Saturday. Is eight too early to pick you up?"

"I'll be ready." She nodded as she straightened up.

"I'm free to text now, right?" he asked as she stepped off the porch.

"Oh, yeah," she said.

She jogged the whole way back to the house only to find the door locked. She rang the doorbell and no one answered, so she hurried to the back door. It was open, and just as she'd suspected, Jody was in the kitchen making coffee.

As Mitzi made her way inside, Paula came into the kitchen from the foyer. "Well, well! So that's why the front door was unlocked. I couldn't sleep, so I came down about two for a cookie. I figured we'd forgotten to lock up after the ice-cream party, but now we know better."

"Graham's place?" Jody asked.

Mitzi nodded.

"Great!" Paula and Jody said at the same time.

Jody pointed to a chair. "Sit down and tell us all about it."

"Not much to tell. We've got a date planned for Saturday. I get to spend the day with him while the girls do that wedding with Rita. We made out like teenagers. And now I'm going upstairs to take a shower and get dressed for the day." She crossed the kitchen in long strides.

"We want more details later," Paula called out as she left the room.

"You'll have them," Mitzi answered. She could give them a play-by-play of what she and Graham had said, but she'd never be able to describe the emotions she'd felt when they finally admitted that there was something between them—or the way his kisses made her go weak in the knees.

Chapter Twenty-Three

Shopping, or doing anything alone for that matter, was not something that Jody enjoyed. She'd had Paula and Mitzi to do stuff with her until they graduated. Then Jody had moved in with Lyle. Maybe in six months or a year, she'd be more comfortable with it, but today, when she pulled out a cart alone, she absolutely did not like it.

She made a beeline toward the greeting-card display to buy a birthday card for her mother. Wanda might be a cantankerous old gal, but a person only got one mother. Jody had always sent her a card and, when she could afford it, had the flower shop take a bouquet to her.

"Well, hello!" Quincy said as he rounded the end of the toy aisle.

"Hi." Jody glanced at a little dark-haired girl in the cart. "Who's ridin' shotgun with you today?"

"My daughter, Hazel. It's my weekend, and we're out buying food for the next two days," he said.

"You never mentioned a daughter," Jody whispered.

"I was waiting for our first date to tell you the story of my life," he said.

Jody went over to the cart. "How old are you?"

Hazel held up four fingers.

"Do you like to read?"

She nodded her head so fast that her dark hair fell into her cute little round face. "Nanny read to me, but not at Daddy's."

"That would be at her mother's—she has a full-time nanny," Quincy explained.

"Her mother?"

"Remarried," he said.

"Will you read to me?" Hazel asked.

Jody couldn't bear to tell the child no, but she couldn't say yes. She quickly looked at Quincy for an answer.

"Miz Jody has things to do today. Maybe another time," he said.

Hazel's lower lip shot out. Her chin quivered, and tears rolled down her cheeks.

"I can't stand to see her disappointed. It'd be easier if she threw fits, but she doesn't. That silent weeping tears my heart out," Quincy said. "I'll read to you soon as we get home. You can pick out the book."

Jody was not an impulsive person. She'd lain awake at night agonizing over moving in with Lyle for two solid weeks. When Mitzi invited her to be a partner in The Perfect Dress, that was the only spur-of-the-minute decision she could remember making. But seeing Hazel so sad turned her heart into a big blob of mush.

"I've got the whole day free. I'd love to read to Hazel if you don't mind. Where do you live?" Jody said.

"I won't turn that offer down," Quincy said. "The directions are complicated. Why not just follow me? That would be easier," he said. "And thank you, Jody."

She wiped away Hazel's tears with a tissue she pulled from her purse and said, "Don't cry, sweetheart. I'll go home with you and read as many books as you want me to, then your daddy can read to you after that."

Hazel ducked her head and grinned. "ABC?"

"Whichever ones you want." Jody hoped she wasn't making a huge mistake.

Quincy had been right about the directions to his place. She followed him all the way to the Celeste city limits sign. At the next section-line road, he made a sharp left. In less than a quarter of a mile, the pavement turned to gravel. She was glad that she had the windows rolled up, because she drove the rest of the way to a dead end in a cloud of dust.

He might be a big oil man, but the house was far from a mansion. A rather small, long, low ranch house with a wide porch around three sides, it was painted pale yellow. Lantana and petunias bloomed in the flower beds on either side of the walkway, and the lawn looked soft and green. That meant there was a sprinkling system, because in July the unrelenting heat had already turned most of the town's grass brown. Jody slung the door open and stepped out.

"Welcome to my home," Quincy said as he set Hazel on the ground.

A big yellow cat came out to greet them, rubbing around Hazel's legs and causing her to sit down with a thud on the grass. She wrapped both arms around the cat and kissed it on each ear.

"Meet Ophelia." He reached into the back seat of the truck and picked up two bags of groceries. "She likes the cat better than me or her mother."

Hazel shook her head. "Filly can't read."

"She can't say *Ophelia* so she calls her Filly. Crazy thing is that I've got to doing the same thing. And the cat doesn't mind. I've had her for ten years. Might be the only cat that's ever been in divorce court," he chuckled.

"I want to play outside," Hazel said.

"You mind?" Quincy asked Jody.

"Not a bit. We can read later." Jody sat down on the porch steps.

"It's almost dinnertime, sweetheart. Want to help me cook?"

Hazel shook her head and carried Filly to the porch, where she sat down beside Jody. "No. Can Jody eat with us?"

"Of course she can." Quincy bent to kiss her on the top of her head.

"She's really articulate for a four-year-old." Jody stroked Filly's fur.

Quincy set the bags beside the door, then sat down beside Jody and Hazel on the porch. "She's been like that from her first words. Sometimes she gets things a little mixed up but not often. And she's never met a stranger, which is why I never let her out of my sight."

Hazel smiled up at her dad. "Daddy, can we keep Jody?"

"For a little while today. How about we go make dinner and then Jody might read to you until you fall asleep for your nap?"

Hazel nodded and then held out her hand to Jody. "Mac and cheese and hot dogs?"

"Sounds great to me." Jody got to her feet and allowed Hazel to lead her into the house.

"Make yourself at home," Quincy said. "Hazel's room is the first door on the right down the hallway. I'm not much of a cook, but I do a fine job with what she always wants for dinner. But maybe for supper we can take you out for something a little better, like pizza."

"We'll see. I might need to get back to the shop," Jody said, just in case she decided to leave before too long. She kept going through the small foyer, the living room, and down the hall to where Hazel took her into a pretty room all done up in pink and lace. The child patted the cushion in a rocking chair, and Jody sat down, expecting Hazel to crawl up in her lap with a book. But instead, she showed Jody every toy in her room, including a dozen books.

What in the name of all the saints in heaven are you doing? Jody's mother's voice popped into her head. *Have you lost your mind? This man could be a serial killer who lures his victims in with that little girl.*

Hazel handed her a baby doll. Jody hugged it to her chest and set the rocker in motion with her foot. "Twinkle, twinkle little star," she began to sing to get her mother's voice out of her head.

"How I wonder what you are." Hazel picked up a doll and sat down in a child-size rocker beside Jody. "Up above the world so high," she sang and then started the song all over again as she cuddled her doll.

Jody felt a presence and looked up to see Quincy leaning on the doorframe. "Shhh," she said. "You'll wake our babies."

Hazel kept rocking and singing while Jody carried her doll to the miniature cradle and laid it down. As gently as if she were covering a real baby, she pulled a little blue blanket up over the sleeping doll. Following her lead, Hazel took her doll to the canopy bed and laid it on the pillow, then covered it with the edge of the bedspread.

"You're good at this. I'm surprised that you don't have kids of your own," Quincy whispered.

"How do you know I don't?" Jody asked.

"I asked Lyle when I bought the property," he answered. "He and his new wife both had a burr in their saddles the day we signed the papers. Something about a bridal fair?"

Hazel put one tiny hand in Jody's, quieting her urge to laugh, and the other in Quincy's and pulled them both toward the kitchen, where boxed macaroni and cheese and hot dogs awaited. "He and his new wife were at the event and . . ." She told him the story of what Tabby had done.

"After what he did to you, I'd say that doesn't begin to be enough humiliation," Quincy chuckled.

"Maybe not, but it sure was a step in the right direction," she said. "Well, Miz Hazel, this looks like a fine meal your daddy has made for us."

"The best." Hazel patted the chair beside hers. "You sit here. Daddy sits here." She pointed to the one on the other side. "Dinner is ready now."

"I ate a lot of this but not with hot dogs. Usually with pork 'n' beans right out of the can," Jody said as she waited for Quincy to prepare Hazel's plate.

"Oh?" Quincy raised an eyebrow.

"My mother isn't much of a cook."

Quincy raised a palm. "Enough said. I was raised in foster care from the time I was six years old. And we always had dinner and supper, not lunch and dinner."

"Us, too," Jody said. "I guess you're a self-made man, then?" she asked as she made herself a hot dog with mustard and relish.

"Started at the bottom when I was eighteen. Had a few lucky breaks and worked hard. It isn't an overnight success story, but here I am at forty, and I still like a dinner like this," he said.

"Thank you, Jesus, amen," Hazel said loudly and then picked up her hot dog with both hands and took a bite from the end.

"Her nanny is religious," Quincy chuckled.

"So's my mother." Jody laughed with him.

∽

Paula was only going to look around in the baby stores that Saturday morning and then get back to the store. Mitzi had gone to Dallas for the whole day with Graham, and they weren't on schedule at the shop, so Paula had planned to spend the afternoon doing some catch-up work.

The smell of baby powder wafted across the first store she walked into. She wondered how they'd done that until she saw a little boy dumping a whole container out on the floor. The manager, a tall lady with pink-and-blue streaked hair, and the child's mother found him at the same time. The mother started to apologize profusely, and the manager kept reassuring her the whole time she swept up the mess that it was all right.

"Clay, why did you do that?" the very pregnant mother asked.

Paula recognized Kayla immediately. Hoping that she hadn't seen her, she tried to sneak out of the store unnoticed. But she'd only gone a few steps when Kayla called out. "Well, hello, Jody—or is it Paula? I remember meeting you at the party store, but I'm rattled over this mischievous son of mine, and I never can remember names very well, anyway."

"It's Paula." She turned around and even managed to smile. "Kayla, isn't it? Wouldn't it be wonderful if they could come up with a scent that really smells like baby powder for these places? Customers would flock in and buy more than they planned."

It wasn't Kayla's fault that she was married to a philandering fool. But that didn't stop Paula's stomach from knotting into a pretzel at the sight of her enormous baby bump.

"Sounds like a great idea to me. If you come up with something that doesn't involve hot wax or spray, let me know," the manager said. "What can I help you with today?"

"I'm just looking around," Paula said.

"I'm ready to check out." Kayla pushed a cart full of little boy things to the counter. "And please add that baby powder that my son wasted to the bill." While the lady with the pink-and-blue hair ran her items across the scanner, Kayla turned around to Paula. "So is one of your friends pregnant? Clay, put down that baby oil and hold your hands behind you, or else get into the cart."

"I'm just looking for something to take to a baby shower at church." Paula didn't even feel guilty about the little white lie. She was tempted to tell the woman that she would be having Clay's half sister, but that would be opening a can of worms that should be left closed for all eternity. "I thought you'd be eager to get back to West Texas, as close to your due date as you are."

"I'm waiting on Clinton to finish up a job this weekend. He's up in Sherman, but he's going to pick me and Clay up tomorrow and we're all going home together. He's such a sweetheart. He wouldn't let me drive over here by myself to help Rita take care of Granny's things."

"It would be quite a drive from Amarillo," Paula said. "I used to live in Tulia, so I know."

"We actually live in Canyon," Kayla said. "And yes, I'm so ready to go home. Rita and I are finished now with our grandmother's stuff, and I'm so happy to get back home."

A voice inside Paula's head told her not to meddle, but she ignored it. "I thought your son was staying with his grandmother?"

"He was until last night. She had plans for the weekend, so Clinton brought him to Whitewright to me, then he went on back to Sherman for his job," she explained. "Looks like I'm ready to pay out. It's good to see you again."

Fanny Lou's old saying came to mind: *Might as well be hung for a hog as a piglet.* "Nice seeing you, too," Paula said. "You're staying in Whitewright, then?"

"Yes, Rita and I've been staying at Granny's place, but the only thing left now is a couple of old beds. No problem, though. It's only one more night."

"Sherman isn't that far away. You should go over and stay in the same hotel with Clinton. That way when he's off shift, you could spend time with him," Paula suggested, wondering how Kayla was so stupid that she didn't even think of why Clinton wouldn't want her and Clay to stay in the hotel with him. But then she shouldn't brand Kayla with that word when Paula had been dimwitted enough to believe his lies.

"That sounds like a great idea. Don't know why I didn't think of it. Clay loves to swim and Clinton mentioned the hotel having a pool, and like you say, when his shift is done we could at least be together," Kayla said.

"Two hundred forty-nine dollars and fifty-two cents." The lady set several bags on the counter.

Paula bought a baby rattle and a pretty little pink dress after Kayla left and then hit four more baby shops afterward. She stopped by a drive-through for takeout on the way back to Celeste. The gauges on her dash said that it was ninety-eight degrees and one o'clock when she got back to the shop. Hoping that Jody was home when she arrived, she hurried into the cool house by way of the back door, dropped two armloads of bags on the kitchen table, and yelled up the stairs.

"Jody, you here?"

The pink phone, sitting on a small end table right beside her, startled her when it rang loudly. She picked it up and answered, "The Perfect Dress."

"Paula?"

"Yes, who is this?" she asked.

"It's Clinton. You almost ruined my marriage," he said.

"Want to explain?" she asked coldly.

"Kayla just walked in on me in a hotel room with another woman."

"And that's my fault, how?" Paula giggled. "Maybe karma has finally bitten you on the butt. You are a horrible husband."

"She said that she saw you in a baby shop and that you suggested she could stay with me," Clinton said. "So thank you for trying to tear apart my family."

"Hey, that's not on me, big boy. You told me you were separated and you never mentioned that you already had a son. I didn't tell Kayla that to hurt your marriage, but to help it. Goodbye, Clinton, and don't call here again." She hung up the phone and slumped down on the nearest sofa. The baby kicked, and she laid her hand on her stomach.

"We can do this on our own, baby girl. We'll do just fine with your aunts Mitzi and Jody."

⌒⊙⌒

The drive from Celeste to Dallas had been so much fun that Mitzi completely forgot that Rita would be at the wedding. So it was a shock when she looked up and saw Rita coming across the parking lot toward the van. Wearing high-heeled shoes and a cute little strapless red sundress that barely reached her knees, she looked downright beautiful. Mitzi's blue-and-white checked shirt and white capris that had looked pretty cute that morning suddenly felt dowdy.

"Hello, Rita," Mitzi said cheerfully as she opened the passenger's door. "You probably don't remember me. I was just a freshman when you and Graham were seniors. I'm Mitzi Taylor." It wasn't easy to be nice to that witch, but she could do it for the girls' sake. After all, Rita was their mother, and if this new relationship between Mitzi and Graham was to go anywhere, Mitzi needed to be an adult, not the mudslinging hussy that she so wanted to be right then.

"I remember you well." Rita's eyes started at Mitzi's sandals and traveled slowly all the way to her red hair. "You've always been . . ." She paused a second before she said, "Tall."

"Never was accused of being petite." Mitzi grinned and turned her attention to the twins, who'd gotten out on the other side of the vehicle. "You girls need some help?"

"And now you're kind of like the girls' nanny, right?" Rita sneered.

"I'm their friend and they work for me." Mitzi turned her attention back to the girls. "Your dad and I'll help you get all this inside. Don't try to take care of it all on your own."

Rita followed Mitzi to the back of the van and barely glanced at the girls. "Those are nice dresses. I didn't know what you might choose, but they'll cover up . . ." She covered a fake cough with her hand before she said, "They will look good on you."

Mitzi moved over to stand closer to the girls. "They helped with the design. And they're teaching themselves to sew. They made the cutest little shirts for the Fourth of July fireworks. They've probably told you that they've been making all kinds of corsages and bouquets for us at the shop."

"I haven't talked to them in a while," Rita said.

Mitzi was glad she had both hands full so she couldn't slap the woman.

Tabby pulled out a tote bag and a small suitcase on wheels. "We love going to the shop every day. It sure beats sittin' at home all day, redoin' our makeup and fingernail polish."

Dixie was right behind her with her suitcase. "Daddy, if you'll get my makeup bag with all our makeup in it, that'll just leave the shoe boxes for Mother. Wait until you see the shoes that Mitzi dyed to match our dresses, Rita—I mean, Mother."

Neither girl had made an attempt to hug their mother, but then she didn't try to hug them, either, or even ask to help them. That left one reason she'd come out in the heat that morning—Graham.

"I'm sure they're lovely." Rita ignored the shoes and looped her arm into Graham's. "I was going to ask if you'd like to stay for the wedding."

"No, thank you." Graham picked up her arm and dropped it. Then he moved close enough to Mitzi to drape an arm around her shoulders. "Mitzi and I've got plans for today."

Oh, yes we do, Mitzi thought. *And they do not involve being anywhere near you.*

"I see. So that's the way it is?" Rita grabbed the two shoe boxes and stomped back toward the building, her heels sounding like short little blasts from a .22 rifle with every step.

"Yes, it is," Graham called out.

"Do we follow her, Daddy, or do we get to blow off this wedding and go with you and Mitzi today?" Dixie grinned.

"I'd like that a lot better than spending the day here," Tabby said.

"Guess we better follow her, since y'all agreed to be part of this affair," Graham said.

Rita disappeared inside a room and slammed the door behind her.

Tabby looked over her shoulder at her dad. "Maybe they wouldn't even miss us."

"A Harrison keeps her word. It's too late to back out at this point." Graham pushed his way inside the room, and the rest followed him.

Rita was uncorking a bottle of champagne over to their right. She poured a glass to the brim and drank down half of it before she turned around to her daughters. "We've set you up at the end of that table. If there's time, the professional makeup lady will take care of you."

"We do our own makeup, Mother," Dixie said. "The lady can use all her time on y'all."

"Could I have a word in private with you, Mitzi?" Rita asked. "In the ladies' room?"

"Of course," Mitzi said.

Graham laid a hand on Mitzi's shoulder. "You don't have to do this."

"Oh, yeah, I do." Mitzi kissed him on the cheek. "Don't worry. I can take care of myself." She would do her best to keep things civil, but she couldn't promise there wouldn't be a few drops of blood on the bathroom floor.

"Then I'll wait right here." Graham sat down in a chair by the door.

The girls were both busy setting out their makeup kits and didn't even notice when Mitzi followed Rita across the room and into a bathroom. Rita went straight to the mirror and, using her fingertips, fluffed up her long blonde hair. Mitzi leaned against the door and waited.

"Well?" Rita finally flipped around and glared at her.

"You called this meeting, remember? What do you need to say?" Mitzi prompted.

"Graham is mine. He always has been, since high school, and he always will be. A man never forgets his first love," Rita said.

"You're married, aren't you?" Mitzi asked.

"For now," Rita answered. "Seeing Graham again brought back all those old feelings, and I will have him again, right along with my daughters."

"I think seeing that Graham now owns the dealership put dollar signs in your eyes, not love in your heart. And, honey, everyone in high school knew that Graham wasn't your first love. I don't know which one of the football players was, but you made your way through several," Mitzi told her.

Rita's hands knotted into fists. "Are you calling me a slut?"

"If the shoe fits," Mitzi said. "Frankly, I don't care if you're a slut or a saint. What I don't like is the way you've treated your daughters. They think you're embarrassed of them because of their size, and that's why you left them and never even came back to see them for so many years. That scars a kid. You should be ashamed."

Rita's lip curled in a sneer. "You should know all about that fat business. Trust me, Graham likes small women, not b-big old . . ." She stammered when Mitzi pushed away from the wall and stepped closer.

"'Big old' what?" Mitzi asked.

"Tubs of lard," Rita shot out the answer.

Mitzi wanted to snatch the woman baldheaded, but that would make Rita the victim, and create more drama. "There's two sides to every person. The one that the world sees, and then that inward one. You might be little and cute on the outside, but the inside of you is black with rotting evil. If that's all you've got to say, then I'm walking out of here. But before I go, just remember that one woman's trash is another woman's treasure. I intend to cherish every precious moment I can spend with your beautiful daughters and with Graham. Y'all have a good day."

Mitzi left her standing at the vanity looking like she could kill someone with her bare hands. She slung open the bathroom door with such force that if Graham hadn't been there to catch it, the bang it made against the wall would have startled everyone in the room.

"You okay?" he asked.

"I'm fine," she bit out. "There's no blood and she still has all her hair, which is a miracle."

"Graham." Rita brushed past them both and went straight for the champagne table.

"Rita." He barely acknowledged her as he wrapped an arm around Mitzi's shoulders. "I guess we should be leaving, right?"

"I hate to leave the girls with that woman, even if she is their mother," Mitzi said through clenched teeth.

Graham hugged her closer to his side. "They'll be fine. Don't worry about them. They have my cell phone number and yours as well. I just hope they don't deck anyone, especially Rita, for making a wisecrack about their size."

Just thinking about that made Mitzi tense up. "If anyone does that, they can call me, and I'll come back here and do more than that. And I'll enjoy it, darlin'."

"Kind of protective there, are you?" Graham teased as they left the building. "Want to tell me what went on in the bathroom?"

"Ain't no 'kind of' to it. I fall in the whole serious business-of-protection category," Mitzi said. "I'll just say that Rita and I came to an understanding and leave it at that."

He stopped at the Escalade he'd brought home from the shop to use over the weekend. With a hand on each side of her body, he caged her against the door and kissed her—long and passionately.

Her knees wobbled when he stepped back, but her eyesight remained very good. There was no mistaking Rita with a cigarette in her hand, coming outside for a smoke. She propped a hip on the arm of a bench situated beside the door and glared at Mitzi.

"So where to first?" Graham asked.

"Do they have room service at that hotel?" she asked.

"Yes, ma'am." He opened the door for her and then leaned in to fasten her seat belt. On the way back out, he kissed her again.

"I've dreamed of spending a whole day with you since I was fifteen years old. A day when I don't have to share you with anyone, so let's make my dreams come true," she said.

"Yes, ma'am." His grin got wider. "Your wish and all that."

He was telling the truth when he said the hotel was nearby. Two blocks away, as a matter of fact. He tossed the keys to a valet and shoved the ticket into his shirt pocket. Then, with his hand on the small of her back, he guided her to the registration desk through the fanciest lobby she'd ever been in. Once he had a room card in his hand, he laced his fingers in hers and led her straight to the elevator.

"You've been here before," she said.

The elevator doors opened and he stepped inside. "This is where we hold the Cadillac conference every year. I've never brought a woman here. Just want you to know that." He slipped his arms around her waist and drew her close to his chest. "You should always wear pale blue. That shirt brings out your eyes."

"Thank you." She barely got the words out before his lips were on hers again. If she'd had any doubts about what she was about to do, they disappeared in that moment.

They were still kissing when the elevator doors opened. Feeling a little bit of a blush, she glanced over his shoulder, expecting to see people waiting to get on, but instead she was looking into an enormous living area. A glass wall at the end of the room showed off a spectacular view of the city of Dallas.

"Oh, my!" she gasped.

"I thought you deserved the penthouse," he said.

She crossed the room and took in the panoramic view in front of her. He slipped his arms around her waist and softly kissed her on the neck. "Like it?"

"Love it." She was suddenly nervous, unsure. "Graham, I've never undressed with the lights on."

"Then we won't turn them on, darlin'," he said as he backed her toward the bedroom. "And if you're uncomfortable undressing, then I'll do it for you." He tugged the shirt up over her head. "I've dreamed about this moment since I first walked into your shop."

"Really?" she asked.

"Oh, yeah, and that, darlin', is not a pick-up line."

In the mirror above the desk, she could see a king-size bed. That's when she kicked off a sandal and shoved the door shut with her foot.

Chapter Twenty-Four

*M*itzi awoke on Sunday morning and, without opening her eyes, scooted over in the bed to snuggle up to Graham, but a pillow met her body. For a single second, she thought he'd left her without saying goodbye. Then she realized that she was in her own bedroom above the shop and not in that fancy hotel with him.

Both Paula and Jody had been asleep when she'd gotten home the night before, but now she could hear pots and pans rattling downstairs and the buzz of their conversation. They'd want details of her day and night, and she wasn't sure she wanted to share them just yet, so she lay very still and tried to decide how much to tell and how much to selfishly keep to herself.

After a while, she slung her legs over the side of the bed, stood up, and padded downstairs in her bare feet. "Good mornin'. What's for breakfast?"

"I'm just finishing up the eggs," Jody answered. "Bacon is ready and biscuits came out of the oven a few minutes ago."

"What? No hash browns?" Mitzi joked.

"In the cast-iron skillet already on the table." Paula pointed. "You remember that sayin' about the north and south fairy tales?"

Mitzi shook her head. "No, but it's early. Maybe after a cup of coffee and a hot biscuit, I'll remember."

"Folks up north start off a fairy tale by sayin', 'Once upon a time'," Jody said.

"And us southerners start one off by sayin', 'You ain't goin' to believe this shit'," Paula said.

"So which fairy tale are y'all about to tell me?" Mitzi asked.

"I didn't say anything until now because I wanted all of us to be together." Jody flipped her long braids over her back. "I'm never cutting my hair because Hazel thinks my braids are like Rapunzel's and she likes the color because it reminds her of Filly."

Mitzi poured three cups of coffee and set them on the table. "Who is Hazel? And what filly?"

Paula helped carry the food to the table. "You've got my attention, too. Who are all these people?"

"Hazel is Quincy's four-year-old daughter. Filly is a big old yellow cat whose real name is Ophelia, but Hazel calls her Filly." Jody was the last one to sit down. "We should say grace. I'll do it." She bowed her head and said, "Thank you, Father, for this food, these good friends, and for knowing what's best for us even though we fight You every step of the way. Amen."

"Amen," Mitzi said as she took a sip of the coffee.

"Amen," Paula added. "Now go on."

Jody split open a biscuit and went on to tell them a detailed account of what had happened the day before, ending with, "She cried when I left, so I promised her that I'd see her again today. We're spending the day with her at the Dallas Zoo. I know we need to do some catch-up work with all the orders that the bridal fair brought in, but I promise to work until midnight all week to have this day off. Her mother picks her up at a McDonald's PlayPlace at five, so we'll have the whole day to play."

"Well," Paula said, her eyes twinkling. "You'll have about six hours after that to spend with Quincy before your curfew."

Jody held up both palms. "Okay, let me have it all right now, and get it over with. Pile on the jokes and the 'I told you sos' but there's nothing between me and Quincy but that little girl. They'll be here in an hour, and you're going to fall in love with her just like I did."

"And that's why you've got on your best jeans and drug out your good cowboy boots?" Mitzi asked.

"I'm not wearing flip-flops to the zoo," Jody said.

"I'm so excited for you that I'm not even going to tease you, but this brings me to *my* 'you ain't goin' to believe this shit' story," Paula said between bites.

"Fairy tale, not story," Mitzi reminded her.

Paula took a second helping of eggs. "I guess Madame Fate had something to do with my day, also. Who would you have thought I'd run into in a baby store?"

"Your sister?" Mitzi asked.

"Even worse. Clinton's wife, Kayla," Paula answered and then went on with her story. "I feel sorry for the woman, knowing what I do now, and he said that day he showed up here that he'd been faithful since our affair. It wasn't nice—matter of fact, it was downright mean of me—but I hoped she'd catch him if he was having another affair. She deserves to know, but I don't want to be in the middle of it. I never want him to know about the baby," she said, and then continued her story.

"Holy crap on a cracker!" Mitzi threw a hand over her mouth. "He had the balls to blame you? That man is crazy. I'm glad you're not tellin' him about the baby."

Paula opened her mouth to say something, but the doorbell rang.

"It's early for Fanny Lou to pick you up for church, Mitzi," Jody said with a glance toward the foyer.

"Granny comes through the back door, not the front." Mitzi got up and started in that direction. The bell kept ringing, time after time, until she unlocked the door and slung it open, half expecting to see the backside of a couple of kids doing a "ring and run" prank. She recognized Kayla immediately and blocked the entrance.

Kayla put her hands on Mitzi's chest and pushed, but it did as much good as a gnat trying to shove a horse out of its way. "I'm going to talk to Paula, so you might as well get out of my way."

"Let her through," Paula said behind Mitzi. "I'll hear what she has to say."

Mitzi stepped to the side, and Kayla stormed inside. "You are one hateful, unchristian, despicable woman. My poor Clinton told me that you've been comin' on to him for months. Ever since his daddy took sick. He told me all about meetin' you in the library over in Tulia and how you made advances. And since he wouldn't be untrue to me, that you've been trying to ruin his life. Callin' him at all hours and tryin' to get him to come over here and sleep with you."

"Oh, really?" Paula sat down on the sofa.

"You want to know the truth?" Jody's eyes flashed pure anger.

"I don't think she could handle it," Mitzi said.

"I'm not here to listen to any of y'all's lies. I came to tell Paula to stay away from my husband. No more calls. No more enticing him to cheat on me. We have an amazing marriage. No one will ever make me doubt Clinton again," Kayla said.

"What about that woman in his hotel room yesterday?" Paula asked.

"How did you know about that?"

"Clinton called me," Paula answered.

"She was a confidential informant who was there to talk to him about a case, and he told me that he only called you to tell you to stay away from him like he's done dozens of times," Kayla said.

"Was she fully clothed?" Jody asked.

"Yes, she was. When I arrived she was in the bathroom, and she came out with all her clothes on except her shoes." Kayla sank down on a sofa.

"And was the bed made or unmade?" Mitzi asked.

"It was mussed up, but Clinton never makes his bed." Kayla's voice didn't sound quite as defiant as it did before. "If he'd been doin' something he shouldn't, then he wouldn't have been so happy to see me and Clay."

"I promise"—Paula raised her hand as if she was being sworn to tell the truth, the whole truth, and nothing but the truth—"I will never call Clinton or have any dealings with him. I'll be glad that he's completely out of my life."

Mitzi wanted so badly to open her mouth and tell the woman exactly what kind of man she was married to, but she clamped it shut tightly and kept her peace. It wasn't her place, and if Paula chose to walk the high road, then Mitzi would respect that.

"Okay, then." Kayla pushed up off the sofa. "That's what I wanted to hear, and if I find out you've been callin' him or sending him any more lewd pictures of you, I'll figure out a way to sue you. I'm sure there's something that's illegal."

"Did you see ugly pictures?" Jody asked.

"No, I did not, and I don't want to, either. He's deleted them all to spare me the hurt." Kayla whipped around as fast as a pregnant woman possibly could and waddled out.

"You have a nice day, now." Mitzi followed her and locked up behind her.

"Bless her little ignorant heart," Jody said. "And I mean that in every sense of the word. But I would've probably been in the same frame of mind if Lyle's woman would have showed up at my trailer tellin' me she was pregnant. Lookin' back, it's probably best the way things happened, even if it did shock the crap out of me at the time."

"I just want her, him, and their drama out of my life. I want to raise my daughter with y'all's help and forget all about the man who got me pregnant," Paula said. "Let's go back to the kitchen and finish breakfast. I hope to hell that Mitzi's fairy tale is better than this."

"Oh, it is, trust me," Mitzi assured them. "But before I get into it, I got to tell you that you are one classy woman."

Paula raised an eyebrow. "Maybe I'm just protecting my future with my child."

Jody laid a hand on Paula's arm. "There's that, but you could have told her what a scumbag she's married to without even mentioning our baby girl."

"Thank you both. Now we'd better get breakfast done, and Mitzi and I need to get ready for church before your Quincy shows up with Hazel. By the way, I really like that name, but maybe I'd better not name my daughter that, since yours already has it," Paula said.

"*My* daughter? You're crazy," Jody said as she headed back to the kitchen.

"And time has run out for my fairy tale. Mind if we save it for tonight?" Mitzi asked.

"Not one bit. You can even add extra to it with whatever happens today," Paula said. "This has been one weird summer, hasn't it? I didn't believe in fate before, but I'm sure starting to believe in it now."

⌒૭

Three rows back from where she sat with Fanny Lou and Harry, Graham stared at Mitzi's gorgeous red hair lit up by the morning sun filtering through the church windows that morning. By shutting his eyes he could imagine the full, voluptuous body that went right along with it.

Tabby poked him in the ribs with her elbow. "If you start snoring, I'm going to kick you in the shins."

"I wasn't asleep," he said out of the corner of his mouth.

"Then don't even rest your eyes," Dixie said from his other side.

He took off his glasses and cleaned them with a handkerchief he took from his pocket. "You're not listening, either."

"No, but I'm not sleeping," Dixie said.

He managed to pick up a few words of the sermon after that, but if there had been a test after church, he certainly would've failed it. His mind kept going back to Mitzi in his arms after making love. Feeding her strawberries while they watched a movie that he couldn't even remember the name of. Brushing her hair and telling her how silky and soft it was.

Graham was jerked back to the present when the preacher asked Harry to deliver the benediction. As soon as everyone was on their feet, he made his way to Mitzi and whispered, "Want to go out on the boat again this afternoon? It's not supposed to rain today."

"I'd love to, but I still don't have a bathing suit," she said.

He leaned toward her and whispered, "Then we'll find a little cove and do some skinny-dippin'."

Mitzi's cheeks turned scarlet. "You better be watchin' for lightning bolts, talking like that in church."

Graham chuckled. "It does sound like fun, though, doesn't it? Maybe I'll put a pool in my backyard and then you won't ever need a swimming suit again."

"Swimming?" Dixie overheard the last part of the conversation and almost squealed. "I love going to the lake."

"I thought we might get a bucket of chicken and head that way soon as we change clothes," Graham said.

Tabby peeked out from around her sister. "Yes," she said as she raised a hand to high-five with Dixie.

"We'll pick you up in twenty minutes." Graham winked.

"I'll be ready," Mitzi said.

❧

Mitzi hit the back door in a run and then took the stairs two at a time on her way up to her bedroom.

"Whoa!" Paula called out from the living room. "What's the rush?"

"Graham invited me to go out on the boat again. I promise I'll work right along with Jody to catch up on the orders in the evenings next week. Y'all want to go along?" Mitzi pulled her dress up over her head and tossed it toward the bed.

"No, thank you. Fanny Lou is coming over. We're going to lunch in Greenville, and then we're going to look at cribs. I saw two I liked yesterday, but I thought it would be fun if she helped pick it out since she's volunteered to be the grandmother." Paula followed Mitzi into her bedroom and sat on the edge of her bed. "And then I do plan to put in a few hours in the sewing room this afternoon. Who would have ever thought one bridal fair would bring in a dozen orders, and that many more appointments?"

"I thought we might get a couple," Mitzi said. "I'm blown away by it. And we're already on the list for next year. We may have to hire more than one more seamstress if this keeps up."

She stopped in her tracks and her chest tightened. "Something just dawned on me. I stopped taking birth control a month after my last boyfriend, and we didn't use a bit of protection yesterday."

"So you did have sex?" Paula laughed. "Not that I'm surprised one little bit. You were glowing this morning at breakfast. Jody and I will expect the details on that when you tell us your fairy tale tonight."

"The fairy tale might turn into something very different if I'm pregnant," Mitzi said.

"I can tell you all about that." Paula handed her a bottle of perfume from the dresser. "At least you're not pregnant by a bastard like Clinton if you are, and, honey, I *was* on the pill. They're only like 99.7 percent effective. You could be a fertile Myrtle like me and wind up with a baby even when you're taking it."

"Remind me to make an appointment with the doctor tomorrow. My prescription has run out, I'm sure." When she finished jerking on a pair of khaki shorts and a cool cotton blouse, Mitzi sprayed a little perfume in the air and walked through it.

"You look great," Paula said.

They were on their way down the stairs when Fanny Lou yelled from the kitchen, "I'm here. Is Mitzi going with us?"

"No, she's got another date with Graham," Paula called out as she and Mitzi made their way across the foyer. "Mitzi's going to tell us everything this evening. Jody and I told her our stories from yesterday, but we ran out of time," Paula answered. "I'll tell you what happened to me over lunch. Jody can tell you about her new friend, Hazel, who happens to be Quincy Roberts's four-year-old daughter, this evening. And if we have to stay up until midnight, Mitzi is going to give us all the details of her weekend."

"Fair enough." Fanny Lou held up her fingers. "Three, two, one. Yep, I hear him on the porch and the knock on the door should be coming . . . now. He was loading up stuff when I drove past his house. I figured he'd be right along."

Mitzi opened the door and Graham stepped inside. "Hello, Fanny Lou and Paula. Y'all goin' to join us?"

"Nope," Fanny Lou said. "We've got plans. You kids just go on and have a good day with the girls. Be sure to keep this one lathered up with sunscreen. She can burn on a dark night. It's that red hair and white skin."

"I'll take good care of her," Graham promised.

"If I didn't believe that, I wouldn't let her go off with you," Fanny Lou told him.

"Well, thank you for that," he said.

He held Mitzi's hand all the way to the vehicle and opened the door for her. "Maybe I'd better just buy this thing. I'm outgrowing my truck for anything but going to work."

"Is that a bad thing?" Mitzi asked.

"Oh, darlin', it's a great thing," he assured her.

"Did you bring a bathing suit this time?" Tabby asked.

"No, sweetie," Mitzi answered. "But maybe one day next week, y'all can go with me to shop for one."

"That would be like really great," Dixie said.

Graham pulled the seat belt across her body and whispered, "I'd rather go skinny-dippin' with you."

"Shhh . . ." she shushed him and blushed at the same time.

"Drive fast, Daddy. We ain't even goin' to swim until we eat today. I'm hungry to death," Tabby giggled.

"Well, that brings back memories." Graham winked at Mitzi. "She used to say that when she was about three years old."

"Speaking of little girls, y'all have to meet Hazel," she said.

"Who's that?" Dixie asked.

Mitzi told them about the little dark-haired girl with blue eyes who had completely stolen Jody's heart. "I only got to see her for a minute this morning when Quincy came for Jody, but with her looks, she could be you girls' younger sister."

"We love little kids," Dixie said. "If Quincy and Jody ever need a sitter, just call us."

"I'll remember that," Mitzi said. "But I've got a feeling that Jody will cherish every minute she can spend with that child."

"So she likes kids?" Graham asked.

"I'm not sure that she likes all kids, but that one has taken her fancy," Mitzi said.

"Well, honey, you've taken my fancy," Graham said for her ears only.

⁓

There was no sneaking up the stairs to her room that evening, not with Paula, Fanny Lou, and Jody all sitting around the table with the leftovers from a large pizza in the middle of them.

"We bought a baby bed and Fanny Lou and I put it together. The nursery doesn't look so bare now," Paula said.

"And Quincy asked me out to dinner on Wednesday, and I said yes," Jody said.

Mitzi took the last chair and reached for a slice of pizza. "Graham and I are officially dating now."

"That's not enough detail," Jody said.

"Hey, all I get from you two is that there's a baby bed upstairs and you've been invited on a dinner date. I'll talk when y'all do," Mitzi said.

"We bought a white crib and the bumper pad is pink-and-white checks," Paula said. "That's all I've got except that Fanny Lou and I needed to go to church to pray for forgiveness for all the dirty words we said."

Jody raised her hand. "Fanny Lou, you were right to tell me to go out with him. I had a great time."

"And I like Graham a lot," Mitzi said.

"That's all?" Both of Fanny Lou's eyebrows shot up. "Just that you like him. We want a hell of a lot more from the both of you."

Paula focused on Jody. "We need to hear a little more about Jody's new feller first. How does he make you feel?"

"Free is the best way I can describe it," Jody admitted. "I'm at peace with everything when I'm with him. That sounds crazy, doesn't it?"

"Okay, now you." Paula turned back to Mitzi.

"Don't leave out a single thing," Fanny Lou said. "And you can start with yesterday and build up through today when you decided that y'all are dating."

Mitzi went to the refrigerator, got out a root beer, and sat back down. "Well, as us southern girls say when we start to tell a fairy tale, 'You ain't goin' to believe this shit.'"

Chapter Twenty-Five

The poor old air-conditioning system at the church could keep up with only so many bodies crammed into the pews like sardines. And now folks were being ushered into the fellowship hall, where a big-screen television had been set up for those who couldn't be in the sanctuary.

In the original plan, the wedding was supposed to be in a barn, but at the last minute Ellie Mae had changed her mind. Luckily, Ellie Mae had Paula, Jody, and Mitzi on the list for reserved seats, right along with Graham and his daughters. They were all shoulder to shoulder on the third pew, listening to a mixed CD of country music love songs.

Every song seemed to speak to Mitzi, but then the past week had been a whirlwind of romance that she still couldn't believe was real. In some ways, it seemed like it had been a month since she and Graham spent the day in the hotel room. In others, it was just yesterday. One thing was for sure: she loved him and was in love with him. When she'd told Paula and Jody that, they'd said it was the same thing, but it wasn't. A person could love someone else, but to be in love with them sat up there on a whole new plane. To have both was one of those miracles that only comes along once in a lifetime.

"Do you want a big affair like this when you get married?" Graham whispered to Mitzi.

"Yes, she does." Fanny Lou must've overheard, because she continued, "And I'm going to be the maid of honor. I'm already planning the bachelorette party. We're going to Las Vegas and we're going to paint the whole town red."

Mitzi shook her head. "A few close friends is all I want."

"Maybe a destination wedding with those friends?" he asked.

"Maybe." Mitzi nodded.

The music changed to something more traditional when the back door opened and an usher brought in Ellie Mae's mama, Iris. If there'd been a contest in the church to match up Ellie Mae with her mother, Iris would have been the last choice. She was a little wisp just over five feet tall and had a neat gray bun at the nape of her neck. The usher returned and brought in Darrin's mother. It wasn't difficult to see where the groom got his size. His mother was as tall as his father and had dark hair like Darrin.

"Bet he loves his mama a lot," Graham whispered.

"Why do you think that?" Mitzi asked.

"He likes bigger girls, like her."

Mitzi shut her eyes and tried to picture Graham's mother. As best she could remember, she'd looked a lot like Alice—not thin, but she probably shopped in the tall women's section.

"What do you like?" Mitzi asked.

"You," he answered without hesitation.

Darrin and his best man followed the preacher up the aisle to the pulpit and took their places. Ellie Mae's sister strolled down the aisle in her pretty red-satin dress with a portrait collar, pivoted, and stood in her place. The preacher raised his arms, and everyone stood and turned to watch the bride come down the aisle on her father's arm. She was a picture of beauty in her black dress and stylish hat, carrying the red-rose bouquet the girls had made. Several people gasped, but Ellie Mae was in her element, smiling and nodding to the folks as she passed by them. Instead of the traditional bridal music, "Marry Me" by

Martina McBride began to play as Darrin started down the aisle to meet her halfway. He shook her father's hand, tucked her arm into his, and escorted her the rest of the way to stand before the preacher.

"Wow!" Dixie muttered. "She's gorgeous. Daddy, can I wear black to my wedding?"

"Of course, darlin'. By the time you're forty, it'll be the most popular color," he whispered.

The song ended, and the preacher said, "You may be seated. Thank all y'all for joining us tonight to witness the union of Elvira Mavis Weston and Darrin Douglas Smith."

"What if I sang 'Marry Me' to you at our wedding?" Graham asked.

"Are you proposing to me?" Mitzi whispered.

"What would you say if I was?" Graham took her hand in his.

"I've been in love with you since I was fifteen, but this is too quick. Let's take it a step at a time," she said.

"Shhh . . ." Fanny Lou said.

Graham leaned over to whisper softly, "I haven't been in love with you that long, but I can guarantee you, I'll be in love until my dying day."

Mitzi squeezed his hand. "Me, too."

Basking in his words, Mitzi tuned out the rest of the ceremony and designed her own perfect dress for a wedding on a beach somewhere close to a lovely hotel.

Epilogue

One year later

*G*raham held Mitzi's hand as she pulled herself up the bleacher steps at the football field that evening for the Fourth of July ceremonies. Paula hadn't even looked pregnant until the last three weeks, but Mitzi looked like she'd swallowed a whole watermelon—one of those huge ones that fed at least twenty people.

"Just two more weeks," she groaned.

"And then you'll have to share the boy," Graham said. "Everyone will fight over who gets to take care of him."

"Over here." Fanny Lou waved from the fifty-yard line. "We've saved y'all a place."

"Thank goodness it's not all the way to the top," Mitzi said as she eased down on the seat.

Graham sat down beside her and wrapped his hand around hers. "Remember where we were last year at this time? I've got to tell you, darlin', this has been the best year of my life."

"I never get tired of hearing that. I love you, Graham, more today than when you kind of proposed to me at Ellie Mae's wedding. It's been my best year, too."

"If everyone will stand for the flag salute and remain standing for the national anthem, we'll get this fireworks show started," someone with a big booming voice said.

Graham stood and then extended a hand toward Mitzi. She took it, but the whole time she thought that even he, with all his strength and size, might not be able to pull her to her feet in another two weeks. They'd had a destination wedding in Florida the previous September. Her perfect dress had been a creation in blue lace. Tabby was her maid of honor. Dixie was the best man. They'd made their own matching dresses in off-white satin, styled a lot like the ones they'd worn to Lizzy's wedding. And all three of the ladies had gone barefoot. She and Graham had an amazing four-day honeymoon, but she'd felt a little guilty leaving Paula and Jody with so much work at the shop. They'd been such a hit at the Dallas Bridal Fair that they'd been invited to the Oklahoma City Bridal Fair in December. Between the first fair and the last, they now had a waiting list for custom-made dresses.

The first display lit up the sky within seconds after the music stopped, and everyone took their seats again. Just thinking of the heat made her very aware of the sweat puddle around the band of her bra. As if he could read her mind, Graham pulled a white cotton handkerchief from his pocket and dabbed the moisture from her face. Fanny Lou noticed and whipped out a cardboard church fan.

"Here, use this. Don't you dare go into labor or pass out in this heat," she said.

Graham took it from her and kept a breeze going across Mitzi's face. "Want to go on back home and sit under the air-conditioning? We don't have to stay for the whole thing."

She shook her head. "I'm not a delicate flower. I'm more like a big old wild sunflower growing out on a fencerow. And Daddy made ice cream for afterwards. That'll cool us all down."

"Ice cream?" Hazel squealed. "We get ice cream, too?"

"It's part of the July Fourth tradition. We watch the fireworks and then go back to the shop for ice cream," Jody explained.

Mitzi glanced over her shoulder. The diamond engagement ring on Jody's finger sparkled under the football lights. In another few weeks, after the baby was born, there would be another destination wedding.

Jody and Quincy were going to be married in West Virginia as soon as Mitzi could travel after giving birth. When Quincy had found out that Jody wanted a mountain wedding, he'd offered to take her to the Alps, but she'd refused. The hotel she'd found in Morgantown, West Virginia, had exactly the kind of place she wanted—a nice little veranda overlooking the mountains in the distance.

Mitzi visualized Jody in the dress that hung in the fitting room. A lovely cream- colored watered silk, it hugged her now curvy body and then belled out at knee level. When she'd tried it on the last time, she'd taken her braids down, and loose curls fell to her waist. Quincy was going to be speechless when he saw her on their wedding day.

The twins had offered to keep Hazel after the wedding. They'd made a spreadsheet of plans to keep her occupied and happy for a couple of days so that Quincy and Jody could get away for a short time in a nearby honeymoon cabin.

Paula would be the only one living above the shop after Jody moved out to the house with Quincy, and even that probably wouldn't be for long. She'd met a male nurse when she was in the hospital giving birth to Ivy Jane, and things were getting serious. He was sitting at the end of the row with the ten-month-old baby in his lap, smiling every time she clapped her hands over the fireworks show.

"If someone had told y'all last year at this time what would be happening in a year, would you have believed it?" Fanny Lou asked.

Mitzi shook her head. "Not in a million years."

"Looks to me like y'all need to be figuring out what Paula's perfect dress is going to look like," Fanny Lou said from behind her hand.

"That's her decision, and she'll tell us when the time is right," Mitzi said and then gasped during the last beautiful display in the sky.

"It is pretty, isn't it?" Graham leaned over and kissed her on the cheek.

"Yes, it is, but . . . this is a little embarrassing." She felt heat traveling into her cheeks.

"What?" he asked.

"My water just broke," she answered. "I guess what I've been having all day isn't false labor at all. Don't make a big deal out of it. I already look like I wet my jeans."

Graham helped her up with a hand and then pretended to stumble and, in the process of righting himself, spilled half a bottle of water in her lap.

"I'm so, so sorry, darlin'," he apologized. "Let's get you home. Alice, can the girls ride to the shop with you?"

"You are a genius," Mitzi whispered as they slowly made their way to the van. "I love you more right now than I did an hour ago."

He helped her inside and then raced around the back of the van to get into the driver's seat. "Keep those words in mind when you start to push." He grinned. "Just think, we get to meet our son in a few hours."

"Let's get me to the hospital and settled in before you call the rest of the family, okay?" she asked as a contraction took her breath.

"Anything you want, darlin'," he said. "But we'll have to let them know soon. If we don't show up at the shop for ice cream, they will panic."

"And there's another pain. That's only two minutes from the last one."

"We might get this baby before midnight yet." Graham put the van in reverse and pointed it toward Greenville. Fifteen minutes and seven contractions later, he parked near the emergency room and rushed around the vehicle to help Mitzi get out. A nurse hurried out with a wheelchair and took her away with Graham following right behind them.

Mitzi had been to the Lamaze classes, so she was as prepared as any expecting mother with a first child could be. And she hadn't worried about Graham because he'd been through all this before when the twins were born. Yet two hours into the labor, when they said it was time to push, she realized she should have been more concerned about Graham. He kept mopping sweat from her forehead with a cool rag and telling her how much he loved her. But not doing much else.

"I'm so sorry you're in this much pain," he said.

"You've been in the labor room before . . ." she panted like a puppy. "Oh, sweet Lord, I'll be glad to get this baby boy out into the world."

"Darlin', the twins were born by C-section. I wasn't in the room," he said.

"You could have told me that before," she moaned.

"It never came up."

The nurse came in and checked her. "Okay, you're at a ten and it's time to push."

"I'm ready." Mitzi remembered that Paula had to push for thirty minutes. She looked at the clock. If the baby could get there before midnight, he'd be born on the Fourth of July like she'd always wanted. She had twenty-eight minutes. She grabbed the bed rails and gave it all she had on the next contraction.

The doctor came into the room, guided Mitzi's legs into the stirrups, and pulled over a stool to sit on. "That's the way to get things done. Give me several more like that, and we'll get this job done in a hurry."

At two minutes until midnight, Graham cut his son's umbilical cord and put the screaming red-haired boy into Mitzi's arms. "He's beautiful."

"He's got my hair." Mitzi kissed the baby on the forehead. "But he's the image of you."

Midnight had come and gone by the time the medical team got the baby cleaned up and wrapped in a blue blanket. Mitzi wanted to stay in their little three-person cocoon for days, but the family—both those by DNA and those by love—were waiting, so she nodded to Graham to go get them. They filed into the room in awe at the baby lying in his mother's arms.

"Y'all come meet Taylor Graham Harrison. He weighs nine pounds, ten ounces and is twenty-two inches long. He's going to be a big boy like his daddy."

Dixie and Tabby didn't waste a bit of time getting from the door to the bed. "Oh, Mitzi Mama, he's beautiful," Tabby said. "We promise we'll spoil him rotten."

"So rotten that the garbageman won't even want him," Dixie giggled.

"But he's going to learn to play ball, not sew dresses," Alice declared.

"Maybe he'll be a ballet dancer. Whatever he wants is what he's going to be," Tabby said.

Alice and Fanny Lou both groaned.

"But today he's going to be a much-loved baby," Jody said. "I can't wait until Quincy and I have a sibling for Hazel. We've talked about it and we're going to start trying as soon as we're married, just like y'all did."

"Where's Ivy?" Mitzi asked.

"Quincy is watching her and Hazel at the shop." Paula touched the baby on his chubby cheeks.

"He has red hair." Tabby held her hand out toward Dixie. "Pay up, sister. You owe me five bucks."

"It's the light. His hair is going to be dark like ours. I get to hold him first," Dixie said. "Please, Mitzi Mama, let me be first."

"He's so beautiful." Harry wiped away a tear and kissed Mitzi on the forehead. "Your mama would be so happy to see our first grandbaby."

Mitzi patted her dad on the cheek. "She sees him, Daddy. Remember what you told me? There's holes in the floor of heaven and she sees all the wonderful things that happen to us."

Harry nodded. "That brings me peace. Now give that baby to his daddy. Graham should be the first one to hold him. After all, Taylor is his son."

Mitzi handed the baby to Graham. "Family, friends, a new baby, and the love of my life all in one place. I'm truly blessed."

"Life is good. No. Life is great," Graham said as Taylor wrapped his chubby finger around his pinkie.

Acknowledgments

Dear Readers,

Broken hearts come in all sizes and from all ages. The support of good friends and a quart of ice cream always help put the pieces back together. Such is the case with the ladies who own and operate The Perfect Dress, a custom wedding-dress shop that caters to plus-size women. Mitzi, Jody, and Paula grew up in the tiny town of Celeste—population less than a thousand—and coming home to set up a business there after living away had its very own set of challenges.

Mr. B and I have fifteen grandchildren, and twelve of those are girls. That means we get to do lots of shopping for prom, homecoming, wedding, and winter-formal dresses. Our granddaughters are all size ranges, some small and some plus size. This past year, when we began to plan for a wedding next fall for one of our plus-size girls, it got me to wishing there was a custom shop that catered solely to that size woman. Especially one that would make a black-lace wedding dress like she wants. So I invented one in my mind and called it The Perfect Dress. You're holding the story that came from my imaginary shop in your hands.

I owe a debt of gratitude to several folks for their hard work in taking my rough idea and helping me turn it into a book. First, all my thanks to my editor, Krista Stroever, for all she did to bring out every giggle, every tear, and even the anger in my characters. Without emotion, they wouldn't come to life, and she's a master at helping me accomplish that. And thanks to my editors at Amazon/Montlake Romance, Anh Schluep and Megan Mulder, who continue to believe in my stories. And a big thanks to my team at Amazon/Montlake Romance for everything from covers to promotion and all that happens behind the scenes to put a book on the shelf. And to my awesome agent, Erin Niumata. Without her, I could never accomplish what I do. Also my thanks to Mr. B, my best friend and soul mate. And last, though not least by any means, to all my fans for reading my books, for writing reviews, and for sending fan mail: I love you all!

As I write *The End*, I'm leaving behind good friends that I've made with these characters. I hope that when you finish reading it, these folks are your friends, also!

Sending all of you hugs until next time,
Carolyn Brown

About the Author

Carolyn Brown is a *New York Times*, *USA Today*, *Publishers Weekly*, and *Wall Street Journal* bestselling author and a RITA finalist. *The Perfect Dress* is her ninety-fifth published book. Her genres include women's fiction, romance, history, cowboys and country music, and contemporary mass-market paperbacks. She and her husband live in the small town of Davis, Oklahoma, where everyone knows everyone else, knows what they are doing and when . . . and reads the local newspaper every Wednesday to see who got caught. They have three grown children and enough grandchildren to keep them young. Visit Carolyn at www.carolynbrownbooks.com.